EXILE'S RETURN

ALISON STUART

The breathtaking conclusion to the GUARDIANS OF THE CROWN series, introduces a heroine with nothing left to lose and a hero with everything to gain...

England, 1659: Following the death of Cromwell, a new king is poised to ascend the throne of England. One by one, those once loyal to the crown begin to return ...

Agnes Fletcher's lover is dead, and when his two orphaned children are torn from her care by their scheming guardian, she finds herself alone and devastated by the loss. Unwilling to give up, Agnes desperately seeks anyone willing to accompany her on a perilous journey to save the children and return them to her care.

After enduring imprisonment, exile and torture, the fugitive Daniel Lovell has returned to England, determined to find his brother and kill the man who murdered his father. But the King has one last mission for him and there is the small matter of a desperate woman who needs his help.

Agnes finds her protector in Daniel Lovell and thrown together with separate quests – and competing obligations – Daniel and Agnes make their way from London to the English countryside, danger at every turn. When they are finally given the opportunity to seize everything they ever hoped for, will they find the peace they crave, or will their fledgling love be the final casualty of war?

EXILE's RETURN

GUARDIANS OF THE CROWN BOOK 3

ALISON STUART

Exile's Return

Copyright © 2016 by Alison Stuart

ISBN (epub): 9780645237887

2nd edition: Oportet Publishing 2022

Cover Design: Fiona Jayde Media

ABOUT THE AUTHOR

Alison Stuart writes historical romances and short stories set in England and Australia and across different periods of history. She is best known for her English Civil War stories and also THE POSTMISTRESS and THE GOLDMINER'S SISTER, stories set in the Victorian goldfields in the 1870s.

She also writes historical mysteries as A.M. Stuart and her popular Harriet Gordon mystery series is set in Singapore in 1910.

She lives in Melbourne, Australia with her husband and a geriatric cat. In a past life Alison worked as a lawyer across a variety of disciplines including the military and emergency services. She has lived in Africa and Singapore and, when circumstances permit, travels extensively - all for research of course!

To discover more about Alison Stuart visit her website or follow her on her social media accounts.

www.alisonstuart.com

BOOKS BY ALISON STUART

Australian Historical Romance

THE POSTMISTRESS (also in audio)

THE GOLDMINER'S SISTER (also in audio)

THE HOMECOMING (also in audio)

The Guardians of the Crown Series

BY THE SWORD

THE KING'S MAN

EXILE'S RETURN

GUARDIANS OF THE CROWN (BOX SET)

The Feathers in the Wind Collection

AND THEN MINE ENEMY

HER REBEL HEART

SECRETS IN TIME (also in audio)

FEATHERS IN THE WIND (BOX SET)

Regency/World War One

GATHER THE BONES (also in audio)

LORD SOMERTON'S HEIR

A CHRISTMAS LOVE REDEEMED (Novella)

(Writing as A.M. Stuart)

The Harriet Gordon Mysteries

SINGAPORE SAPPHIRE (Book 1)

REVENGE IN RUBIES (Book 2)

EVIL IN EMERALD (Book 3)

TERROR IN TOPAZ (Book 4)

DEDICATION

To my dear friend, Carol H, for having the faith that Daniel's story would one day be told and for being there through thick and thin over the years ...

EXILE'S RETURN

GUARDIANS OF THE CROWN
BOOK THREE

ALISON STUART

OPORTET PUBLISHING

CHAPTER 1

LONDON, 27 OCTOBER, 1659

*A*gnes Fletcher gripped the windowsill as a distant clock struck twelve, marking the fall of the executioner's axe.

James Ashby, the third earl of Elmhurst, was dead.

She closed her eyes and prayed that death had been swift.

Taking a deep breath, Agnes turned to face the room. The cold draught that rose between the ill-fitting floorboards of the inn lifted her skirts as she walked across to where the two children were playing a noisy game of knucklebones.

'You cheated!' seven-year-old Elizabeth, the eldest of the two, exclaimed.

Four-year-old Henry hurled himself at his sister, issuing a loud and high-pitched disclaimer that rang in Agnes's ears, jarring her nerves.

'Stop it!'

Something in her tone made the two children fall silent.

They looked up at her, their eyes wide and mouths open in surprise. Agnes rarely raised her voice.

'Why are you crying?' Henry asked.

Agnes dashed at her cheek, where the betraying tears streamed from her eyes. She dropped to her knees and gathered the two now-silent children into her arms.

Dear God, what is to become of us?

'Your father ... ' A sob caught in her throat.

Lizzie stood rigid in the circle of her arms.

'He's dead?' Lizzie's voice cracked.

All Agnes could do was nod in reply as the tears coursed unchecked down her cheeks. Henry began to wail and burrowed his golden head into Agnes's shoulder.

They had gone to visit James yesterday, the last visit permitted by the authorities. Perhaps, she had thought, as James went down on his knees to hold his children for the last time, it would have been easier on them all if they had stayed away. The memory of James's fair head bent over his children filled her eyes again.

He had risen to his feet and taken her hands in his. 'Agnes, dear Agnes,' he had said. 'Tomorrow I die, and you are all the children have left. You must fight for them. There is no one else.'

No one else except James's cousin, Tobias Ashby, but for once Tobias's malevolent shadow stayed away. Even he had the decency to allow father and children this last farewell.

There had been so much she wanted to say to James, but the words stuck in her throat. He smiled, a soft sad smile, and picked up a book from the table.

'Take this,' he said, pressing it into her hands. 'A memento of me, and our affection for each other.'

Our affection for each other.

He had kissed her, a soft kiss on her forehead, and she had gathered up the children and walked away from him. He would never know how she had longed for him to take her in his arms, and for the kiss to be that of the lover she had known, not a dear friend.

The tread of heavy boots on the gallery outside the room brought her back to the present. Agnes jumped to her feet, wiping the last of the tears from her face and straightening the children's collars as she waited for the knock on the door.

Three burly soldiers entered, followed by someone she had come to know well in the past few years; Captain Septimus Turner, Tobias Ashby's ever-present second in command. Turner scanned the room before bringing his gaze to rest on the woman and the two children who cowered behind her skirts.

'Madam, it is my unhappy duty to inform you that the traitor James Ashby is dead,' Turner said, without a flicker of emotion on his face.

Agnes tightened her grip on the children's hands. Henry shrank back and Lizzie buried her face in the bunched skirts of Agnes's gown, muffling her sobs.

Taking a deep breath, Agnes gathered her courage to ask the question that had kept her wakeful for too many nights.

'What is to become of the children?'

Turner glanced at Henry and Elizabeth with cold, dispassionate eyes.

'You will be summoned to Whitehall when your petition has been considered by the Committee. In the meantime, you are to remain here. You are not to leave London.'

'I can only pray that will not be too long,' Agnes said, thinking of her empty purse. 'The children should be returned to their home as soon as possible.'

Ignoring her, Turner turned to his men. 'We have the traitor's personal possessions. Where do you want us to put them?'

Agnes's resolve buckled at the sight of the familiar metal-bound box that James had taken with him into the Tower. Only her need to stay calm for the children steadied her.

'Well?' Turner demanded.

She waved vaguely at a dark corner of the inn room. 'Over there. Tell me ... was it ... quick?"

The man considered her for a moment. 'I was not present, but the Colonel assures me he died bravely and in the love of God, madam.'

Of course, Tobias would have been there.

Agnes straightened and replied in an icy tone, 'That is of no comfort.'

Turner's gaze met hers and for a brief moment some emotion, anger or amusement, she could not tell, flashed in his eyes.

He inclined his head and half turned for the door. 'I reiterate, you are not to leave London, Mistress Fletcher.'

'Am I under arrest?' Agnes raised her chin, cursing her lack of inches.

The man shook his head. 'No, but we will know if you try to leave and it will do your cause no favours.'

Agnes straightened. She could not imagine any other outcome other than safe return home to Charvaley. She took a deep, shuddering breath. 'And where would we go, Captain Turner? I have no money and no friends who would take us in.'

Not if they did not wish to incur the wrath of the children's only other living relative, Colonel Tobias Ashby. Tobias had been high in favour under Cromwell. Of course, since the Lord Protector's death, the world had shifted on its axis, and she considered the betrayal of his cousin may have been Tobias's attempt to keep in favour with the new regime.

'I will pray to God and put my trust in this Committee. I would remind you that I am the children's aunt and closer by blood than the Colonel,' she continued.

Turner regarded her without expression. He had no interest in hearing her plead her case; his loyalty lay entirely with Tobias.

He inclined his head. 'You will receive word when you are to appear before the Committee. Good day to you, madam.' He jerked his head at his soldiers. 'Come.'

The door slammed closed behind them and Agnes's resolve failed. She sank to her knees, burying her face in her hands as she wept. This time the arms of the two children circled her, as they added their tears to hers.

CHAPTER 2

BRUGES, 28 OCTOBER 1659

*D*aniel Lovell stood at a window in the makeshift audience room, looking down at the canal below, along which a barge laden with wool, probably from England, made its leisurely way. A steady drizzle of rain ran down the lead panes of the windows, adding a general bleakness to the morning.

No one paid him any heed. Behind him, the courtiers, dressed in their finery, jabbered like parrots. A parody of a king's court, Daniel thought. Up close the frayed cuffs and patched linen of those same courtiers bore testament to the reality of life lived in the shadow of an exiled king.

When his ship, the privateer *L'Archange,* had docked in Le Havre he could have taken ship for England, but he had come to Charles's court in Bruges for one reason only. The person he sought would not be found in England, not in the tumbled ruins of Eveleigh Priory. If his brother, Kit, were still alive, he would be here with the King. If not, at least here he could find someone who could tell him where Kit — or his grave — could be found.

Below him, the barge passed, and his thoughts were interrupted by the crash of a door opening. A sonorous voice announced the arrival of

His Majesty. Daniel turned to face his King, sweeping, like the others, into a deep bow.

At the age of eighteen Daniel Lovell had gone into battle beside this man; both carried with them dreams of honour and glory and the rightful avenging of the deaths — no, murders — of their fathers.

At the end of that bloody day at Worcester, the King had become a fugitive in his own land and Daniel, nursing a wound to his right arm, had huddled against the tomb of King John in the great Cathedral of Worcester, a prisoner like the hundreds of others who had survived the battle. With the cold stone pressed against his face, he had hoped that no one would notice the shaming tears of humiliation and fear.

His idea of vengeance at the age of eighteen had been ill-conceived and vague. The naive boy who had donned his father's armour and taken up his sword had died that day as surely as if a sword had pierced his heart. Eight years of exile had honed his bitterness like a blade and now he carried it on his shoulders like a carrion bird, picking at the shreds of his memory.

As he rose from his bow and looked into the dark, lined face of the King, it struck him that this man, only three years his senior, still had that indefinable aura that had inspired those who had answered his call all those years ago in the belief that they could vanquish Cromwell and regain the throne. But, like Daniel himself, the hopeful boy the King had been in 1651 had gone. Exile had aged Charles Stuart beyond his years.

Pausing only to acknowledge the presence of his most loyal subjects, the King strode the length of the room and slumped down on a high-backed chair, placed throne-like against the far wall. Charles scanned the room as if looking for someone.

A parody of a throne, in a parody of a court, Daniel thought.

'Where is the man my cousin sent?' The king demanded.

Daniel had presented himself to Sir Edward Hyde earlier that day, bearing letters from the King's cousin, Louis XIV of France. Now Hyde's gaze sought out Daniel standing at the window.

'Come forward, Lovell,' he said.

Daniel squared his shoulders and stepped forward, bowing again to the King.

The King looked him up and down.

'I thank you for your role as a courier, Master Lovell,' he said. 'I trust you found my cousin well?'

Daniel could afford to smile. His audience with Louis had been brief. On their return to France, the captain of *L'Archange*, Broussard had produced him as another trophy – the Englishman turned French privateer. It seemed to amuse Louis.

'An English privateer on a French vessel?' Louis had enquired with a cocked eyebrow. 'We have heard stories of the exploits of such an Englishman. What do they call you … ? Ah yes; *Le Loup Anglais*.'

'I assure you, a reputation undeserved,' Daniel had responded.

On a ship of escaped slaves and convicts, the anonymity of a nickname, deserved or ironic, became part of the legend of *L'Archange*. However, in his case the nickname, "the English Wolf", had been earned.

L'Archange needed to return to France for repairs, ending the career of the English Wolf. He had parted with the man who had saved his life, Broussard and his crew and had become once more plain Daniel Lovell, with letters bearing the royal seal of Louis XIV for his cousin Charles II of England.

'Your cousin is a most interesting man,' Daniel replied to Charles's question.

'Alas, I am something of an embarrassment to him.' Charles's hooded eyes seemed to recede further back in his skull at the thought of his cousin. 'You look familiar, Lovell. Have we met before?'

The question surprised Daniel, reminding him once again that this man had the greatness of kings about him. 'Once, briefly, a long time ago. At Worcester.'

The lines on Charles's face settled into deeper grooves. 'Ah … Worcester … '

Daniel nodded, and for a moment they were both transported back to that moment when two young men had thought they were invincible. Behind him, the atmosphere in the room shifted, an indefinable rustling like the dried leaves of an autumn tree. There would be many here who had stood shoulder to shoulder with the King on that day.

The King waved a forefinger at Daniel's face. 'A legacy of Worcester?'

Daniel touched the scar that scribed his right cheekbone, which served as a visible reminder to all who saw him of that terrible day. Beneath his severe clothes, no one would see the other scars, the twisted scar on his arm and the lines that crossed his back and circled his wrists. Those too were a legacy of Worcester.

'Hyde here tells me you have something of an interesting history. How did you come to be aboard a French privateer?'

Daniel hunched his shoulders, an almost unconscious habit he used to release the tautness of the scars that marred his back. He had been circumspect in how much he had revealed to Hyde and he repeated the story.

'After Worcester, I was sent to Barbados,' he began, conscious of a murmur rising in the room behind him. Barbados had been a death sentence and he had survived.

'I escaped the plantation to which I had been assigned and threw my lot in with the crew of *L'Archange*. I have sailed with them these five years past,' he said with a casual shrug.

A slow smile lightened the King's saturnine countenance. 'I assume you had little alternative, my friend.'

Daniel ducked his head in agreement.

'I'm not sure our friends in London have taken too kindly to the predation on English ships,' Hyde said.

Daniel fixed the courtier with a hard stare. 'We carried *lettres de marque* from Louis. We were not pirates.'

The King's moustache twitched. 'A fine distinction, my friend. Has it made you a wealthy man?'

Daniel hesitated. The five years of privateering had netted him a comfortable sum. Sufficient to restore a life in England he had not known since before the war, but hardly a fortune.

The King laughed and held up a hand. 'You do not need to tell me. Indeed, I do not wish to know.' He leaned an elbow on the arm of his chair and inclined his head. 'So why have you returned now?'

'I heard that Cromwell is dead,' Daniel responded.

'But you are still an escaped prisoner, are you not, and a privateer?

No doubt there is a price on your head.' The King leaned his elbow on his chair, stroking his moustache.

Daniel shrugged. 'Possibly, but that is not why I am here, Your Majesty. I am seeking news of my brother, Christopher Lovell. He –'

A hush fell on the room, and the back of Daniel's neck prickled.

'Do you mean Kit Lovell?' Hyde asked.

The breath caught in Daniel's throat as the King frowned. 'Lovell?'

'You recall the man, Your Majesty. That affair of Gerard?' Hyde leaned down to whisper in the King's ear, and Daniel's sense of foreboding trebled.

'Good God, I thought I knew your face.' An unfamiliar voice came from the courtiers behind him and, the tension broken, Daniel turned to see the speaker, a trim man of middle height with light brown hair curling to his shoulder.

He too looked familiar, but Daniel could not immediately place him. There had been many visitors to Eveleigh during the long years of the war. He could have been one of many.

'Sir, you have the advantage of me,' Daniel responded.

'Longley,' the man replied with a bow. 'Giles Longley. We played cards on the eve of Worcester — your brother, Jonathan Thornton, and I. Do you recall?'

Daniel stared at the man as small snatches of memory began to snap into place. A card game on the eve of Worcester. Kit and his friends playing their last hand before the battle that would decide their fates. They had tried to warn him but he had not heeded their words.

The arrogance of youth.

In the long years that had followed, he had often wondered what had become of them, the men that he had called the Guardians of the Crown. In his mind, they all lay dead on that field of battle.

If Longley still lived, then maybe there was hope for Kit?

Daniel swallowed. 'A lifetime ago, my Lord,' he replied.

Out of the corner of his eye, he saw the King glance at Hyde. Whatever private message passed between them, Hyde acknowledged it with a slight inclination of his head.

The King straightened in his chair. 'You are welcome, Lovell.

Welcome to my court and, God willing, soon to be welcome in a peaceful England.'

Daniel's lip curled. 'I am not so certain of the last sentiment, Your Majesty. As you pointed out, there will be some in London who would like to see me hanged for my alleged crimes.'

'They'll have to catch you first, my friend, and it seems you have your brother's aptitude for evasion. Longley,' the King indicated the dapper Viscount. 'Take our friend Lovell and introduce him to the joys of this town. They do good ale, but not much else I am afraid, Lovell.'

Dismissed, Daniel bowed and left the room, his question unanswered.

CHAPTER 3

'Tell me, Lovell, why have you come back now?' Longley asked as a greasy and ill-tempered pot boy slammed down their ales, slopping most of it onto the table.

Daniel looked around the crowded taproom. A haze of tobacco smoke hung in the air, tinged with smoke from the huge fire that burned at one end of the room. A fug of unwashed bodies and boiled cabbage completed the picture. He could not have been further from the dens of Fort Royal in Martinique, and it felt good.

He took a draught of the excellent ale and considered his reply.

'As I said, Cromwell's dead. His son has fled to the Continent. The time is right for the King to return.' Daniel paused. 'For us all to return. How many years has it been since you were last in England?'

Longley sighed. 'I've not been back since my own escape from Worcester. Is it really eight years?' He took a swig from his tankard, brushing foam from his well-groomed moustache. 'I long to return, but it is not quite so simple, my impetuous friend. We must see the King legally restored by the will of the people. Until such time we continue to bide here. Exile teaches you patience.'

Daniel smiled. 'Patience has never been one of my virtues, my lord. I have paid my dues and I am no longer a raw youth hungry for his first taste of battle.' He shrugged. 'The simple fact is, I want to go home.'

Giles studied him for a long moment. 'Longley will do ... and no, you're not a raw youth. I can only guess what you have endured over the last eight years. But why would you risk going back now? Why not wait?'

The questions surprised Daniel. It had not occurred to him to kick his heels within plain sight of England.

He considered his response. 'Let me just say I have some unfinished business.'

'Ah,' Longley's moustache twitched. 'And that is... ?'

Daniel studied the older man. 'I saw my father murdered in cold blood on the step of his own home, my lord. I cannot forget. I intend to find the man who gave that order.'

Longley's mouth tightened and he set his beer down on the sticky table. 'I counsel you now. The King does not want to see more blood spilled. If there is to be any reckoning, it will be at his hand. Who is the man you seek?'

Daniel shook his head. 'It is none of your concern, my lord. I came here seeking news of my brother, no other reason. No one has yet provided me with an answer.'

Longley's fingers beat a tattoo on the worn and stained tabletop. He sighed heavily. 'I am sorry it falls to me to break the news, but your brother is dead.'

Daniel had long since learned to school his face to betray nothing, but his jaw tightened and the word seemed to come through stiffened lips. 'Worcester?'

Longley shook his head. 'No. Kit Lovell survived Worcester. He may even have been a prisoner like yourself ... but he managed to get away. I came across him in Paris the year after Worcester, but he couldn't settle to an exile's life and went back to London. He kept company with others like himself. I believe they used to gather in a hostelry in the Old Bayly. What was it called ... oh, yes, the Ship Inn. How could I forget – they called it the Ship Inn Plot.'

'The Ship Inn plot?'

Longley waved a hand. 'That was one. Kit got himself involved in several plots to overthrow Cromwell and restore the King. None had the consent of the King, and mostly they were so foolish that even Cromwell laughed and set the plotters free.' He frowned. 'But even the Lord Protector's sense of humour failed when John Gerard brought over a French assassin. They may have succeeded had it not been for a traitor in their midst who betrayed them. Your brother was one of those caught and hanged.'

The breath left Daniel's body at the bald words *caught and hanged* and he looked away. His invincible brother, Kit, dead at the end of a hangman's rope – an ignoble end.

After all the years of believing Kit dead, it was as if he had died all over again. He realised now, that there had always been the kernel of hope that Kit had survived, but now a hundred thoughts crashed together. What had become of his grandfather ... his mother ... his sister?

'Hanged?' he managed to say with a voice that cracked with emotion. 'When?'

Longley frowned. 'It would have been the summer of '54.'

Daniel cleared his throat. 'Another wrong to right when the King is restored, my lord?'

'Indeed,' Longley replied. 'Those who died in the King's name will be pardoned and those, like me, who had everything stolen from them will have it returned, but what we remember so fondly may be sorely tested by reality,' Longley said. 'What of your home? Cheshire, I believe?'

'Eveleigh Priory, about five miles out of Chester, but as you say, the word "home" is an illusion, my lord. Parliament's men, led by a man by the name of Tobias Ashby, destroyed it in '48. My mother and sister were living in a few surviving rooms, reliant on Kit for whatever money he could spare.' He paused and shook his head. 'With my brother dead, I have no idea what has become of my family.'

Longley's moustache twitched. 'Have you had no contact with them?'

Daniel shook his head. 'No. While I was plying my dubious trade as a privateer, I considered it prudent to leave my mother and sister in the belief I was still in exile or probably dead. How many times can you ask your family to grieve for one person?'

Longley considered him for a long moment. 'Why would your family have believed you dead?'

Daniel switched his gaze to a far corner of the room. 'They sent me to Barbados,' he said. 'How many return from that hellhole?'

Longley frowned and probably would have continued his interrogation had it not been for the appearance of Sir Edward Hyde, pushing his way through the patrons to where they sat in their dark corner.

'You were not easy to find,' Hyde complained as he sat down, unbidden, and summoned the tap boy for another jar of ale.

'I wasn't aware you were looking for us?' Longley leaned back in his chair and picked up his ale.

'The King has a mission for you, Lovell,' Hyde said without preamble.

Daniel looked at the man. 'But the King knows nothing of me. Why would he entrust me with a mission?'

Hyde's moustache twitched. 'Whatever else the King may be, he is a shrewd judge of character. Your brother had certain talents and there is a hope that maybe you have inherited them.' He glanced at Longley. 'You've told him?'

Longley nodded.

Hyde's mouth tightened. 'You'll hear stories about your brother, so be prepared.'

Longley raised a hand. 'Not now, Ned ... '

Hyde glared at him. 'Why not now? It's better he is prepared, is it not?'

Daniel looked from one to the other. 'What stories?'

'There are those who believe he may have been in the employ of Cromwell,' Hyde said. 'In fact, he may have been the one to betray Gerard and the others to Thurloe.'

Daniel pushed his chair back from the table, a white spark of anger flaring in his breast. 'Kit? A traitor? Never! He was a king's man to the bone.'

Hyde waved him back to his seat. 'Calm yourself. I cannot say with certainty if there is truth to the stories; I merely repeat what some who were closer to the events believe.'

'If he were indeed a traitor, why would they hang him?' Daniel glanced at Longley.

'Unlike his fellow conspirators, his execution was private, conducted on the grounds of the Tower itself. No one can say with certainty that Kit Lovell died at the end of a rope,' Hyde replied.

Daniel shook his head as the enormity of what Hyde implied sunk in. It seemed impossible that his brother, the man he had known all his life would turn his coat, but if it were true, could Kit still be alive? Coming here had raised more questions than it had answers.

'Enough about your brother. I told you we have a commission for you.' Hyde dismissed the fate of Kit Lovell with a wave of his hand.

'You know nothing about me,' Daniel repeated.

Hyde glanced at Longley, who shrugged.

'What we know is that, like your brother, you are dead, are you not, Master Lovell? According to the official stories, you were sent to Barbados where you died of a fever.'

So that was the story Outhwaite had put out.

'Every second prisoner died of fever,' Daniel said.

'But you didn't. You escaped, and I am curious as to how a dead man is sitting here having an ale with us on a chilly night in the Low Countries.'

Daniel looked from one man to the other. 'I told you. I escaped … I was rescued by French privateers … that is all.'

Hyde shrugged. 'It makes no difference. Since Cromwell's death, the mood in England has changed. The time is right for the King to return but this, as you can understand, is no simple matter. There has been a group of men operating in secret with the King's commission. They call themselves the Sealed Knot but they have been relatively ineffective since Penruddock's uprising back in '55. Earlier this year the King issued a second commission. Part of that commission was to organise simulta- neous uprisings across the countryside, but the reach of the spy network set up by John Thurloe is long and we may as well have set up a town crier in the centre of London. The uprising in Cheshire was quickly defeated and unfortunately one of our key supporters, James Ashby –'

Daniel started and Hyde looked at him, his eyes narrowing. 'You know the man?'

Daniel shook his head. 'My pardon, I recognise the name Ashby, but the man I knew wore the uniform of Parliament.'

'Oh, you mean Colonel Tobias Ashby? A cousin, I believe. He has done well in the favour of Oliver Cromwell.' He shook his head, his mouth tightening. 'He commanded the martyred King's escort on the day of his murder.'

Tobias Ashby, that hard man of the Parliamentary forces who had issued the order to his men to shoot down Thomas Lovell in cold blood.

Murder and Tobias Ashby seemed to have much in common.

'Who is this other Ashby?' Daniel changed the subject.

'James Ashby. You may know him as the Earl of Elmhurst of Charvaley Castle in Lancashire.'

Daniel frowned. He had vague recollections of his father talking about Elmhurst but he could not remember meeting the man himself.

Hyde shrugged. 'He gave some nominal support to the King's cause during the wars, but rumour is he was equally as forthcoming to those who came on behalf of Parliament. Whatever his true feelings, his home at Charvaley survived intact and unmolested. Like many we will encounter in the next few months, who trim their cloth to the wind, after the death of Cromwell, James Ashby professed his loyalty to the King, and being in a position of some influence and power in the north, the King named him in his commission. A few months ago his men captured a consignment of coin bound for York. Charvaley was used as the hiding place. It was to have been passed on to our agents, but Ashby was taken before the handover could be affected and we believe the coin is still at Charvaley.'

'How much?' Daniel enquired.

'Four hundred new-minted Unites.'

Daniel let out a low whistle. A gold Unite was worth over twenty shillings.

'Such a sum could buy a deal of loyalty,' he said. 'Do those sitting in Whitehall know that Elmhurst has the coin?'

Hyde cleared his throat. 'We think Elmhurst may have tried to turn his cousin, Tobias Ashby, to the King's cause. As a result, it is likely that Tobias Ashby knows or suspects that the stolen coin may be at Charvaley.'

'If so, he misjudged his cousin. Tobias Ashby is certainly the man who denounced Elmhurst to the authorities,' Longley put in.

'And James Ashby did not protest his innocence and hand over the coin? Surely that would have earned him a reprieve from execution,' Daniel said.

'It would have availed him very little. During the taking of the coin, a personal friend of General Lambert's was killed. Lambert made it known that an example had to be set.' Hyde paused. 'I have been informed that Elmhurst died yesterday.'

Longley looked up. This was evidently news to him.

'We received the news only an hour ago,' Hyde replied in answer to Longley's unspoken question.

'Then what is it you think I can do?' Daniel enquired.

Hyde snorted. 'Elmhurst had few close friends but he has left behind a mistress, a woman by the name of Agnes Fletcher. She is currently lodging at the sign of the Blue Boar with Elmhurst's children. She is your key to Charvaley and the location of the King's gold. You have a pretty face, Lovell, use it.'

Daniel laughed. 'You put a lot of faith in me, Hyde. I am not possessed of a long history of charming the location of hidden treasure out of ladies. I am rather better at holding a knife to their throats.'

Hyde shrugged. 'If you think that might work.'

Longley spluttered into his ale. 'Hyde!'

Daniel drummed his fingers on the table. He cared not a jot for the fate of the late Earl or the missing gold, but were these men offering him a means to an end? It would be sufficient reward to look into the eyes of Tobias Ashby just before he killed him – as Ashby had killed his father – in cold blood and unarmed.

'And what do I get if I am successful?' Daniel enquired.

Hyde recoiled as if Daniel had made an importunate suggestion. 'You mean a reward?'

Daniel narrowed his eyes. 'I have seen my home destroyed, my father murdered, and in the last eight years, I have endured prison, torture, enslavement and worse in the King's name. I am done with all causes except my own. If I am to undertake this mission, it will not be for love of the King's cause alone.'

Hyde considered him for a long moment. 'Find the King's gold, my friend, and you will not find His Majesty ungrateful. He does not forget his friends.'

Daniel leaned forward. 'Curiously, I felt somewhat forgotten when I was lying in chains in Barbados.'

Hyde harrumphed and Longley interposed. 'Lovell, we understand that you may hold little love for the cause, but your assistance will hasten the process. If we can recover the gold left in Elmhurst's possession, we will see the King restored within months.'

Daniel looked from one to the other. 'Very well, but I would see full pardons for myself – and my late brother – and a restoration of lands and title, if they have been seized, as the price of my assistance.'

Hyde huffed out a breath as if he had been holding it in anticipation of Daniel's response. 'Of course, of course. Consider that done, my friend. There is a ship leaving Ostend on tomorrow night's tide. Be on it.'

Daniel flashed the man a hard, contemptuous look. 'I take no orders from you, Hyde. I am nobody's to command, not anymore.'

Hyde rose to his feet. 'Then don't waste time, Lovell. Major-General Lambert and his Committee of Safety are trying to hold on to power in London. Elmhurst's death was intended as a show of strength.' He glanced at Longley. 'Coming, Longley?'

Longley looked at his cup. 'I will finish my ale, Hyde.'

Longley waited until Hyde had pushed his way out of the crowded inn, before setting aside his empty cup.

'Don't make an enemy of that man, Lovell,' he said. 'He will control the throne when the King is restored.'

Daniel looked away. 'I do not seek to make an enemy of him, Longley, but I have no heart for the game of politics. I will do as I promised but that will be an end to it. My brother is dead and I have our family fortunes to rebuild.'

Longley nodded. 'I understand. Now, if I may request a personal favour of you?'

Daniel shrugged. 'If it is within my power.'

'I have letters for my family in Worcestershire. Would you undertake to deliver them safely into their hands?' When Daniel did not reply, he continued. 'They are just family letters,' Longley said with a hollow, humourless laugh. 'My wife has seen me but a very few times in the last ten years. You will find Lady Longley at the home of her brother, Sir Jonathan Thornton, a house called Seven Ways near Kidderminster.'

Daniel nodded. 'I remember Colonel Thornton from Worcester.'

Longley looked at him and shook his head. 'Worcester seems a lifetime ago. I see no trace of the boy I met that night.'

'He died in Barbados,' Daniel pushed back his chair and stood up. 'I lodge at the Laine Marchant.'

'I will deliver my missives to you there.' Longley rose to face him, holding out his hand. 'I wish you well, Lovell. Good evening to you.'

The men shook hands and Longley turned to leave. He took a few steps before turning around to face him. 'And Lovell, if you do see my wife, tell her … tell her that I will make amends for these past long years.'

CHAPTER 4

LONDON, 30 OCTOBER 1659

A stench of animal and human waste and decomposing vegetable matter rose from the Thames and exuded in waves from the dark, narrow streets that led down to the dock. Standing at the rail of the ship, his hands gripping the weathered wood so hard that the knuckles showed white, Daniel breathed in the fetid London air as if it were the finest perfume he had ever smelled.

He had come home.

The rickety plank that served as a gangway had been run out and now rested on the dock, a frail link between the present and the past. Daniel picked up the box containing all his worldly possessions, heaved it onto his shoulder, and took the plank in two strides. Oblivious to the curious glances from his fellow passengers and the men working on the docks, he set down his box and went down on one knee, placing the palm of his right hand on the mired cobblestones. If he still believed in God he would have given a prayer of thankfulness, but God had deserted him on a battlefield outside Worcester.

He straightened and stood on the dockside looking around. He had never visited London in his youth, and after years away from England the hustle and bustle felt more intimidating than a Spanish warship. He asked a passer-by for directions to the Blue Boar, shouldered his box, and set off in the vague direction in which the man had indicated.

Above him the old, crooked houses leaned out over the street, making the narrow cobbled ways more like tunnels than thoroughfares. Shopkeepers shouted their wares and under his feet, excrement Daniel suspected to be both human and animal covered the cobbles in a noxious slime.

He rounded a corner and was brought up short by a gaggle of men and women crowded around an angry man. The man screamed abuse and obscenities at someone on the ground. Every word was accompanied by a vicious downward blow from the walking stick he carried.

Daniel pushed his way through the crowd and gave an involuntary hiss of disgust when he saw the object of the man's fury was a child, a thin, ragged urchin huddled in a foetal position with his hands over his head to prevent the rain of blows, while the crowd around cheered the aggressor on.

Daniel set down the box and stepped forward. With one swift movement, he caught the man's arm as he raised it again.

'Enough,' Daniel said.

The man looked at him in surprise. He seemed well-dressed and respectable, but his flabby face was suffused with purple and spittle had formed at the corners of his mouth.

'Unhand me, sir,' he said.

'What has this child done that you should abuse him in this fashion?'

'He tried to steal my purse,' the man said. 'When I've finished with him, I will be handing him over to the constable to be put in the stocks. Little thief.' The man tried to wrench his arm free from Daniel's iron grip. 'You are hurting me, sir.'

'I didn't do it.' The boy raised his head, his voice muffled by his tears. 'I tried to stop him but he took to his 'eels and I was left standing 'ere.'

'Do you have his purse?' Daniel enquired.

The boy rose to his knees and held out trembling hands. 'Search me,' he said. 'I don't have no purse. Not a farthin'.'

Daniel released the man's arm and placed himself between the infuriated citizen and the child who cowered behind him. 'The boy has been punished enough. Go in peace and keep your purse more secure in future.'

The man rubbed the place where Daniel's fingers had dug into him. 'This is none of your business,' he said. 'Hand the boy over to me this instant.'

'Go on your way,' Daniel's hand dropped to the hilt of his sword.

Uncertainty flickered in the man's eyes and he took a step back. 'Would you draw your sword on me for the sake of a dirty piece of street refuse?' he demanded.

'I'll not see a child beaten in this fashion, whether he is guilty or not. I wouldn't treat a dog in such a manner. On your way.'

The man squared his shoulders. 'Very well. On your head be it, sir.' Retrieving his hat from a servant standing in the crowd, he stalked off his nose in the air, The gathered crowd dispersed, leaving Daniel with the child.

The boy scrambled over the filthy ground, wrapping his hands around Daniel's ankle. 'Fank you, sir. Fank you ... '

Daniel squatted down and disengaged the clinging hands. 'Are you much hurt?'

The boy looked up. He sported a black eye and a swollen lip. Tears had tracked through the dirt on his face and his clothes hung in tatters.

'I've 'ad worse.' The boy rose to his feet, brushing off his filthy rags as if they were the finest velvet.

'How old are you?' Daniel enquired.

The child shrugged. He was so ragged and undernourished he could have been any age from eight to fifteen. 'I was born before they cut the 'ead off the king,' he said helpfully.

That made him ten or older. Daniel considered him for a moment.

'Perhaps you can help me. Do you know the way to the Blue Boar?'

Beneath the grime, the child's eyes brightened. 'I do, sir.'

'Good, take me there and I will give you a coin.'

The urchin straightened, flinching as he flexed his shoulders. 'Carry yer box, sir?'

'No. I can manage that. What's your name, lad?'

'Matt, sir.'

'Do you have a last name?'

The boy shook his head. 'Not that I knows of. Me ma had too many gentlemen callers to say rightly who me father was. They just calls me Matt.'

'And your mother?'

'Dead sir, died of lung fever last winter. It's just me.'

Daniel smiled. 'And you earn your way with your quick fingers?'

Matt's smile faded. 'I earn my living best way I can, sir, but I ain't no thief.'

Daniel gave the boy a sceptical glance, and a wide grin split the boy's face.

'Not unless I can't 'elp it,' he said. 'But I didn't nick that cove's purse. It was me mate, Sam. He took off and left me to cop the blame.'

'Not much of a mate, then.'

'No,' Matt agreed with narrowed eyes and a tight mouth. 'Ere we are. This 'eres the Blue Boar, and a finer tavern you'll not find in London.'

He stood expectantly as Daniel fished out a coin, his eyes widening as Daniel flicked him a groat. Matt's grubby fingers closed over the coin and he looked up at Daniel with wide, bright eyes.

'Thank you, sir … is there anything else I can do for 'ee?'

'Yes, you can go and get yourself a decent meal,' Daniel said and turned to go into the inn, where the landlord waited for him.

'You don't want to be bothering yourself with the likes of him,' the innkeeper said as he gestured for one of his own boys to come forward and take Daniel's box from him.

Daniel glanced backwards. Matt stood where he had left him, looking down at the coin in the palm of his hand. Seeing Daniel look his way, the boy gave a cheeky grin, tugged his greasy forelock, and scampered off. Daniel shook his head and turned back to the innkeeper.

'A private room,' Daniel said.

'The best I have, sir. This way … '

They passed a masked woman and two young children in the gallery. The woman, cloaked and clad in unrelieved black, had both children firmly by the hand. The younger child, a boy, looked up and gave Daniel a curious stare.

'Good day to you, Mistress Fletcher,' the innkeeper greeted the woman.

The woman glanced at the two men and Daniel had an impression of brown curls framing a small, heart-shaped face, although the fashionable black velvet mask concealed her features. He stood to one side to let her pass. The boy looked back, staring at Daniel before the woman twitched at his hand and he hurried to keep pace with her.

'Nice lady,' the innkeeper said as he unlocked a door that led off the gallery, 'but those poor little mites lost their father a day or two ago.'

'Lost?' Daniel raised an eyebrow.

'Had his 'ead lopped off on Tower Green. He were an Earl or some such, so it's the axe for him, not the rope like us common folk.'

Daniel stopped. 'The name of the man?'

'Elmhurst. Lord Elmhurst. Always stayed 'ere when he came to London.'

'What did he do?'

'Traitor, they say. Traitor to what, I ask. These are strange times, my friend.'

Daniel glanced over the gallery in time to see the hem of the woman's dark cloak disappear under the gateway.

'Who is the woman?'

'Some kin of the earl. Mistress Fletcher's her name. Brought the children down a month ago and took the best room in the house. Every day she took 'em up to visit with their father.' The landlord's lips tightened. 'Now 'e's dead and I've not seen coin for bed and board this last week past. 'Ere's the room. Hope it suits.'

Daniel agreed to take the room and as the door shut on the landlord, he laid his hat and gloves on the table and walked over to the window. He had deliberately asked for a room facing the street and he looked down into the bustling thoroughfare below as he undid the knot on his cloak.

A small figure huddled in the doorway of the shop across the road from the inn, skinny arms wrapped around bare knees. Daniel shook his head. Show a beaten pup some kindness and it would follow you to the ends of the world.

'I'm not your saviour, lad,' he said aloud and straightened, craning his head to look down the street.

The woman and the two small children were walking back toward the inn. The elder child, a girl, dragged her feet as the woman pulled on her hand. The boy seemed content to bounce along beside his guardian, chattering away despite the lack of response from the woman. She walked with her slender shoulders bowed as if the very weight of the world rested on them.

The lure of treasure had been part of his life for the past five years and Daniel could not dismiss the thought that somewhere at Charvaley Castle there was such a hoard. What did Agnes Fletcher know of Elmhurst's recent involvement in royalist plots? Did the key lie with this woman?

Daniel considered her slight form, wondering what the velvet mask concealed. He imagined the Earl would not have chosen an ill-favoured wench to be his mistress. If indeed she had been his mistress. The thought intrigued him.

She stopped at a pie vendor and a few coins were exchanged for pies. Steam rose into the cold air from the warm offerings and the children looked up at her with wide, expectant eyes. They did not notice Matt, still crouched in the doorway, watching the transaction with a hungry look on his thin face.

Clutching their warm pastries, Agnes Fletcher and her two young charges hastened across the road and were swallowed up by the entrance to the inn.

Daniel walked back to the table, folding his black cloak neatly across the back of a chair. He yawned and glanced at the inviting bed. A few hours of rest were called for after the miserable crossing from the continent. Even after five years aboard the French privateer he still suffered seasickness.

He pulled off his boots and coat and lay down, letting the well-stuffed mattress envelop him in goose down. With his hands behind his head, he contemplated his next move.

A little further investigation into the subject of Mistress Agnes Fletcher may be called for, he decided as his eyelids closed.

CHAPTER 5

*A*s she watched the two children tossing a leather ball to each other, Agnes pulled the hood of her cloak up in an attempt to break the cold wind that blew off the river. She was running out of ideas to occupy two very bored children while they waited on the faceless men in Whitehall to decide their fate. Without the daily routine of visiting their father, they spent the morning in lessons and in the afternoon braved the cold, cheerless streets.

How long will they keep us waiting? The children need to be home among familiar faces and routines, not here in this dangerous, verminous city.

Yet it had been three days since James's execution, and still she waited for permission to leave the city. What was there to decide? She was the children's aunt, there could be no question that she would be a suitable guardian. The longer the decision took, the more her hope evaporated, along with the contents of her purse.

She had sold a ring James had given her to help ameliorate their condition, but that small cache of coins had all but run out. She barely had enough coins for a couple more meals, let alone the outstanding board owed to the innkeeper. Her fingers circled the chain around her neck. It would break her heart to part with the locket, but if needs must …

Lizzie's patience with her small brother proved to be finite and after he fumbled the ball in his pudgy fingers once again, she let out a squawk of indignation.

'You are too little! Aunt Agnes, please play with us.'

Summoning a bright smile, at odds with her sombre mood, Agnes picked up the ball and threw it to Lizzie.

'That's enough,' she said. 'Let's go back.'

Tossing the ball in the air as she walked, Lizzie chattered about her favourite games and how they should set up a swing in the garden at Charvaley. Agnes walked beside her, holding Henry's small hand.

'Would Father mind if we used the oak tree? Oh, I forgot.' Lizzie stopped, her mouth trembling and her blue eyes filling with tears.

The ball fell from her hand and ran unregarded down the filthy street.

A thin boy in ragged clothes stepped out of a doorway and retrieved the ball from where it had come to rest against a pile of horse excrement. He looked at it, wrinkling his nose before dunking it in a water trough.

Lizzie flew at him. 'How dare you touch my things, you horrible, dirty boy!'

'I never ... Here ... ' The boy took a step back, holding the ball in his hand.

'Aunt Agnes, he tried to steal our ball. Give it back at once!' Her blonde curls shaking with outrage, Lizzie put her hands on her hips and glared at the urchin.

The boy seemed to be rooted to the ground, apparently unable to speak or move in the face of Lizzie's anger.

'May I be of assistance?'

A dark shadow fell across them, and Agnes looked up to see the man she had passed on the stairs of the inn the previous day. An involuntary shiver ran down her spine as she took in his dark clothes, tanned face and the scar that ran across the right cheekbone, giving him a faintly sinister look. However, the smile that curved his lips and the twinkle in his light grey eyes alleviated his ferocious appearance.

'Thank you, but I think there has been a misunderstanding –' Agnes began.

The boy looked up at the stranger. 'I weren't stealing,' he said. 'It rolled away and I just gave it a clean. Honest, Cap'n!'

The man held out his hand and the boy dropped the object of dispute into it. With a courtly bow, the man presented it to Lizzie. 'Yours, I believe?'

Lizzie had the grace to colour. 'Thank you, sir,' she said.

Agnes prodded her charge in the back. 'I think you owe this boy an apology,' she said.

Lizzie's back straightened and the colour in her cheeks heightened. 'I will not apologise to this … this street urchin.'

The dark man frowned. 'But why ever not, mistress? He saved your ball and cleaned it for you. Didn't you, Matt?'

The boy, Matt, curled his lip in derision. 'I've no use for a stupid ball,' he said. 'Why'd I want to keep it?'

'Apologise, Elizabeth,' Agnes said, employing the tone that her young charge would recognise as an order.

Lizzie sniffed audibly and looked down at the filthy cobbles. 'Sorry,' she said.

Matt said nothing; he just stared at Lizzie with wide, fascinated eyes.

The man laid a hand on the boy's shoulder. 'Matt?'

"Pology accepted,' the boy responded, with the same amount of enthusiasm with which the apology had been tendered.

The man looked up and caught Agnes's eye with a half smile that seemed to say *Children!* and she wondered what this filthy bit of street refuse had to do with the dark, elegant stranger.

'Matt, I'm glad you are here. I have a task for you,' the man said.

The boy visibly brightened. 'Yes, Cap'n. Anyfing I can do for you!'

'Thank you for your assistance, sir,' Agnes said with a small curtsey.

He touched his fingers to the brim of his broad hat, around which a magnificent white feather curled.

'My pleasure, mistress. Good day to you, and to you, Mistress … ?' He bowed to Lizzie.

Lizzie straightened and dropped a well-rehearsed curtsey. 'Lady Elizabeth Ashby,' she said.

The man raised an eyebrow. 'It is a pleasure to make your acquaintance, my lady.'

Lizzie continued. 'And this is my brother, the Marquis of Chesterton, and my aunt, Mistress Fletcher.'

The man made suitable obeisance to all three distinguished personages.

'I am plain Master Lucas,' he responded, clapping a hand on the boy's shoulder, 'and this is Matt. If you will excuse us, Matt and I have errands to perform.'

Lizzie gave Matt a haughty glance and he responded with a rude gesture as he walked away.

Lizzie giggled and the three of them stood watching as the man, with his hand still on Matt's shoulder, marched the boy into the crowd and out of sight.

'Do you think he is a highwayman?' Lizzie asked.

'Good heavens, Lizzie. What makes you think that?' Agnes enquired.

'Or a pirate,' put in Henry.

'I am sure he is nothing more than a respectable merchant. It's starting to rain. Inside now!'

'Mistress Fletcher.' The innkeeper's wife waylaid her, handing over a folded and sealed letter. 'Message for ye.'

Agnes turned the letter over, her fingers tracing the seal of the Commonwealth in the heavy wax. Gathering up her skirts and her charges, she hurried back to her room before breaking the seal and scanning the contents. For a moment the words danced before her eyes as she tried to take in the meaning of what she was reading.

She let out her breath, unaware she had been holding it. Far from being the consent to the custody of the children she had expected, she had been summoned to attend a hearing of the Committee set up to determine the custody of the children of the late Lord Elmhurst and matters pertaining to his estate. The time stated was for two hours hence.

Her heart sank. This could only mean one thing – the news would not be good.

She took several deep breaths and turned to study her limited wardrobe. It would all be fine, she told herself. She was the children's aunt. There could be no question of the children remaining in her care. Tomorrow, they would be on the road back to Charvaley.

CHAPTER 6

'I didn't need no rescuing,' Matt protested as soon as they were out of earshot.

'No, of course not,' Daniel replied. 'You were about to be set upon by a girl and you would have just stood there and taken it.'

Matt looked down at his feet, roughly shod in a pair of cracked and broken shoes through which his filthy toes poked. 'Whatcha want me to do?'

Daniel considered the urchin. Someone who knew his way around the rabbit warren of streets could be useful.

'You can start by taking me to the Ship Inn.'

The boy's eyes widened. 'The Ship Inn over by Old Bayly?'

'I believe that's where it is.'

'Anywhere in London but there. That Nan Marsh has a tongue on her,' the boy said. 'Caught me stealing some pie one day. Told me never to show me face again.'

'Well, I'm not asking you to show your face. Just take me there. What you do after that is up to you.'

Matt stood poised for a fleeting moment between flight and compliance. When Daniel produced a coin from his purse, Matt needed no further persuasion.

'This way, Cap'n', the boy said, falling into step beside Daniel. 'So your name's Lucas?' he asked.

'It is,' Daniel replied. Lucas was just one of the many false names he had used in the last five years. It now almost seemed strange to use his own name.

'You a seafaring cove?' Matt inquired.

'Why do you ask?'

'Yer not all pasty and pale like the rest of us.'

Daniel considered his new young friend. 'If you are at all pasty and pale it is almost impossible to see under the dirt,' he said. 'You need a bath, Matt.'

The boy shuddered. 'Terrible bad for yer health, Cap'n.'

He stopped and gestured down a street that looked like any other street in this maze of a city. Halfway along an old inn sign creaked above the narrow, cobbled way. It had once been a galleon in full sail, but age and the fetid air had mellowed it to the point where it looked like a rowboat in a storm.

'Down there. I'll wait for you 'ere,' the boy said.

'This Nan Marsh has got the better of you, hasn't she?'

The boy squatted down and pretended an interest in a pile of refuse.

Daniel left him and, pulling his cloak around him, entered the establishment. It seemed respectable enough, the floor swept and mopped and the tables wiped. At this hour only a handful of patrons occupied the benches.

A thin woman with a hard face looked up from scrubbing a tabletop.

'What can I do for ye?' she enquired.

'An ale,' Daniel replied.

The woman straightened, wiping her hands on her apron as she studied him. She frowned and shook her head.

'Something the matter?' Daniel enquired, self-consciously touching the scar on his face. She did not seem the sort of woman to be discomposed by a mark on a man's face.

'Nah, just for a moment, I thought you was someone else.' She gestured at an empty table near the fire. 'Make yerself comfortable, I'll be right back.'

Daniel settled himself into the well-worn chair and looked into the freshly lit fire, watching as the green wood spat and caught, sending bright sparks and wreaths of smoke up the chimney.

'Here's yer ale.'

A man set the pot down in front of him and Daniel looked up. This time the spark of recognition was mutual. The man narrowed his one good eye, the other obscured by a silken patch.

'I know you,' the man said.

Daniel didn't know whether to curse or praise his luck. He should have realised that if this inn had been a habitual haunt of Kit's, there would probably be a reason.

'Eveleigh Priory, 1648?' he ventured.

The man sat down on the bench across from Daniel with a thump and swore. 'God's death. It can't be Dan'l ... nah ... he's dead ... '

Daniel studied the man, trying to recall the name of Kit's burly sergeant.

'Marsh, isn't it? You served with my brother.'

The man nodded. 'Aye, I did. Fought beside him for many a year.' He shook his head in continued disbelief. 'Well, well, Dan'l Lovell, as I live and breathe. You were a lad when I last saw you.'

The woman sauntered over. 'Jem, there's no time for sittin' here. There's wood to be cut.'

The man looked up and gestured to the woman. 'This is me sister, Nan.'

'And who's this?' Nan demanded, a scowl darkening her face.

'Would you believe it? This 'ere's Kit Lovell's brother, Dan'l, back from the dead,' Jem responded.

The colour drained from the woman's face and she stared at him as if he truly were a ghost. 'But you're dead and buried somewhere in the godforsaken Indies.' Nan sank on the bench beside her brother and stared at Daniel. 'Daniel bloody Lovell. Who'd have thought it? What's up with your family? Descended from Lazarus?'

'Now, Nan.' Jem elbowed his sister into silence. He leaned forward on the table, his hands clasped. 'So, Daniel, what brings you 'ere?'

'I am looking for news of my brother,' Daniel said. 'They told me that Kit used to come here.'

The woman's face closed like a door slamming. 'Didn't they tell you? He's dead. They 'anged him in '54.'

Jem shook his head and looked down at his big hands, clasped together on the tabletop. 'Dead,' he echoed.

Daniel cleared his throat. 'I know Kit's dead,' he said. 'I just thought maybe you could tell me a little more about the circumstances.'

Jem Marsh heaved a sigh. 'Got 'imself tangled up in some sort of plot to kill the Lord Protector.' He shook his head. 'He was 'ere when they took 'im.'

Nan glanced at her brother. 'You've said enough, Jem Marsh. Truth is there ain't much more to tell. We was right fond of 'im but he's dead. Don't know and don't care where you've bin all these years. Ye've got your own life to lead. Forget 'im.'

Daniel looked from one to the other. Neither appeared to be any more forthcoming, so he drained his ale and stood up.

Nan rose and faced him. She looked him up and down and her face softened as she shook her head. 'Ye've certainly got the look of your brother about you. Not as tall I wager but ye've the same eyes. Can't forget Kit Lovell's eyes; would make a woman wet 'erself if he looked at you the right way.'

Somewhat taken aback by the description, Daniel smiled. 'I've not heard him described in quite that way before.'

'Then you didn't know your brother,' Nan said, with what was probably intended as a saucy wink but looked rather more threatening on Nan's hard face.

No, I didn't.

Ten years his senior, Kit had been eighteen when he had ridden off to war, and they had seen precious little of each other during the weary years of fighting. It had only been in '48 that Kit had returned to Eveleigh and embroiled the family home in a futile action that had subjected the house to the bitter month-long siege that had ended in the death of their father and the destruction of the house. Kit had returned to England again in 1651, bringing with him the hopes of the young

King Charles II, and this time Daniel was not going to let his brother ride away. Despite Kit's every effort to dissuade him, Daniel had followed him to Worcester.

That had been a foolish and fatal decision.

He handed over some coins for the ale. Nan bobbed her head as her fingers closed over the coins.

'That'll do nicely.'

She looked up at him and her eyes narrowed. He gained the impression that she may have been about to add something, but a rowdy group of 'prentices fell through the door demanding ale. Nan gave Daniel a cursory nod and went to see to her customers.

CHAPTER 7

They kept Agnes waiting for more than an hour in a cold anteroom in the bowels of the old palace of Whitehall. Sour-faced clerks and red-coated soldiers passed in and out of the great oak doors, behind which a committee sat deciding the fate of two small children. With every moment that passed, her hopes faded.

The door opened and a clerk indicated for her to enter. Her heart fell as she saw not only the Committee of three men but Tobias Ashby. Ashby lounged against the fireplace, impeccably dressed in a scarlet coat trimmed with gold lace, which strained at the buttons across his stomach. The highly polished, metal gorget of an officer rested beneath his impeccable lace-trimmed collar. His brown, thinning hair curled to his shoulder and his moustache and beard were neatly trimmed. It had been a few months since she had seen him and it occurred to her that the peacetime army suited him a little too well.

While James gave every show of his loyalty to the new regime, his cousin had visited Charvaley many times in the last few years. James's general ambivalence to all matters political has been so fervent that even Agnes had not suspected his more recent involvement in the royalist plans to restore the King.

Tobias looked her up and down and inclined his head. She looked away from the supercilious smile he gave her.

A small, balding man sat between the two other commissioners. He neither looked up nor offered her a seat as she entered but continued to peruse the papers in front of him, which she hoped included her petition. She tried to read upside down but failed.

A clerk seated at the far end of the table sharpened his quill before dipping it in the inkpot.

'In the matter of the traitor the late Lord Elmhurst's children,' the chairman of the committee began, looking up at her at last. The clerk began to write. 'Are you Mistress Agnes Fletcher?'

Agnes clasped her shaking hands in front of her in an effort to control her nerves.

'I am,' she said, embarrassed by her high, tight voice.

'I have before me a petition by you for custody of the children of the traitor, one Henry James Ashby aged four, Marquess of Chesterton, and the Lady Elizabeth Ann Ashby, aged seven years. I am given to understand that you are the children's aunt?'

'I am sister to the Earl's late wife, Ann,' Agnes said.

'Your brother, George Fletcher, took up arms against the Commonwealth and died in the Lowlands in June 1652?' another of the Commissioners enquired. The man moved a few papers on the table, jabbing at one with his forefinger.

How do they know these things?

George had died in penury and drunken despair in Holland, leaving her quite alone in the world with his debts and no means to pay them.

'He ... ' she swallowed, biting back the words, 'he fought for the King, but my brother's decisions in life were not mine, sir.'

I just paid the price for them.

'As a consequence of his actions, and his failure to pay the fines levied against him, his property was sequestered?'

Agnes's hands tightened and she swallowed. 'He was unable to meet the fines and the property was sold, yes. As he resided on the Continent and I was homeless, Lord Elmhurst and his wife took me in. After my sister's death, on the birth of Henry, the care of the children fell to me.'

'And you feel this gives you the right to the legal custody of the children?'

She took a deep, steadying breath, the old, well-practised lie sticking in her throat. A small boy's whole future depended on The Great Secret.

'I am the children's aunt by blood and the closest to a mother that the children have ever known.'

'But where would you live? How would you care for them?' one of the other commissioners asked.

Agnes frowned, not understanding the question. 'Henry is the rightful heir to Lord Elmhurst's estate. We would return to Charvaley. Where else would we go?'

The three commissioners looked at each other and the president cleared his throat. 'Mistress Fletcher, the late Earl died without a will … '

'He had a will … I saw it … ' Agnes interrupted. 'He kept it in a wooden box in his room.'

The Commissioner shook his head. 'An extensive search of the property has been conducted and inquiries made, but no such will has been discovered.'

'He would never have gone to his death without making proper provision for the children. He told me that I was named their guardian … ' She glared at Tobias. 'You destroyed it!'

'Mistress Fletcher, control yourself!' The commissioner rose to his feet and brought the flat of his hand down on the table with a resounding thump that made his fellow commissioners start and the clerk reach for the inkpot.

Agnes fought to control her breath, her fingers clenched together so hard the knuckles showed white.

'In the absence of a will, it has been decided that your petition must be refused,' the president declared. 'A woman cannot take on the legal responsibilities you seek.'

'No!' Agnes took a step toward the table as the full enormity of their decision hit her. 'Dear God, no! What is to become of the children?'

The president held up a hand. 'Colonel Ashby,' he indicated Tobias with an ingratiating smile, 'is the direct heir to the estate of the Earl, after the boy, and it has been decided that he shall be appointed guardian and protector not only of the children but of the entire estate.'

She swung around to face Tobias. 'Not you. Anyone but you!'

Tobias's lip curled into an ingratiating smile. 'Mistress Fletcher, I know this is a shock to you ... '

She whirled back to face the commissioners. 'But what about me? I can stay with the children? Surely ... '

The president fixed her with an unblinking stare. 'You come from a family of known traitors. It is quite unthinkable that you should have continued access to such young, innocent minds. After discussing the matter with Colonel Ashby, we agree that you should not be allowed any further contact with the children.'

They couldn't possibly be separating her from the children! She must have misheard ... but she knew she hadn't.

'No! No ... the children are my life. They are all I have. Please don't take them away from me. Please ... '

The breath left Agnes's body and her knees threatened to fail her. She caught the edge of the table to steady herself.

'Mistress Fletcher, compose yourself,' the man's tone softened. 'I know this comes as a shock to you but believe me, we have the welfare of the children to consider. What you choose to do is your concern, and we believe it is in their best interest that you have no further contact with them.'

Agnes forced herself to straighten and she looked every man in the eye, including the hateful Tobias.

'They are only young. They won't understand. If you have a shred of human decency, at least let me prepare them and say farewell to them,' she said.

Tobias shuffled his feet. 'I would rather ... ' he began, but the president interrupted him.

'We are not entirely heartless, Mistress Fletcher. You may return to your lodgings with Colonel Ashby for the express purpose of packing the children's belongings and ensuring they are in a fit state to return to their home at Charvaley with the Colonel. That is all. You may leave now.'

In a trance, Agnes turned and walked toward the door. Dimly she was conscious of Tobias following her, but she took no notice until she felt his hand on her sleeve.

'Mistress Fletcher ... Agnes ... A word in private.'

She shook off his hand and turned and looked up at him, the anger rising like a gorge in her throat. 'Why you?'

He directed her into a dark, wood-panelled room and shut the door behind them.

His moustache twitched as he smiled. 'Why me? Why not?'

She studied him for a long moment. As James's closest male relative, Tobias would be the Earl of Elmhurst, had it not been for Henry's birth. Tobias, who had betrayed James without a flicker of conscience.

'James told me of your part in his downfall. Your promise to turn coat and then, the soldiers ... '

Tobias shook his head. 'It is regrettable that he involved himself in such foolishness. However, that is all in the past. We must now look to the future and ensure the children are kept safe, and that no blemish of their father's treachery will attach to them. On which subject, I have a question to ask of you, Agnes.'

She glared at him.

'You were close to my cousin; was he wont to confide in you?'

Agnes looked away. James did confide in her – when it suited him.

'What do you mean?'

Tobias's gaze slid past her. 'My cousin was directly responsible for the theft of some valuable property of the Commonwealth and the death of a good man. He went to his death without revealing the location of the property. Did he confide its location in you?'

Oh yes, she had held the shuttered lantern as James hurried the men and their heavy leather satchels into the house. But she had not asked, and he had not told her, what the satchels contained or indeed where he had secreted them.

'No,' she answered, truthfully. 'My concern was, and always will be, the children and the children alone. James's politics were of no interest to me.'

Tobias's eyes narrowed and she wondered if he disbelieved her. She had always been a bad liar.

'You are a gem among women, Agnes Fletcher if your sole concern was with hearth and home and not the business of men.'

The gall gathered in Agnes's stomach at the sarcasm that dripped from his words.

'The business of men saw the death of the children's father. You alone … ' she jabbed a finger in his direction '… have James's blood on your hands. Those children are orphans because of you and now you would take them from me. If you hurt one hair on their heads, Tobias … '

'My dear, Agnes, you quite terrify me.'

He looked down at her, his mouth curling in a sneer. Small and slight, she hardly presented a physical threat to a man who stood nearly a foot taller than her.

He held up a placating hand. 'Enough of these games. Please believe me, Agnes. I will take care of the children as if they were my own. They are my closest blood kin.'

She searched his face, looking for evidence of his veracity. It remained implacable. She had no choice in the matter but to trust him. She had to believe that he would act in the best interests of the children.

She sighed. 'I know what the commissioners said, but surely it's within your power to let me come with the children?'

Tobias's eyes hardened. 'Even I cannot go against an order of the Committee, Agnes.' He raised a hand as if to lay it on her shoulder in reassurance but thought better of it, making a pretence of straightening his collar. 'You have my word. The children will be safe in my care.'

A knock on the door made them both start. Ashby opened it to admit Septimus Turner. *Tobias's faithful hound,* James had called him. Turner was a slight man with ginger hair, moustache and beard, probably well into his forties. Not much above middle height, his figure was trim and he carried himself well. He had served at Tobias's side since the first engagement of the war.

He had with him a woman so pale as to be translucent – green-blue veins could be seen beneath the skin of her forehead and hands. Even her tightly compressed lips seemed bloodless.

'Captain Turner,' Agnes said with barely concealed distaste. 'I might have thought you would not be far away.'

Tobias gestured toward the woman. 'I do not believe you have met Septimus's sister, Leah?'

Agnes turned to face Leah Turner. She was dressed austerely in a dark grey gown with plain collar and cuffs, with her hair tucked beneath a matronly white cap. Only the ginger colouring of her eyebrows indicated that it might be a similar hue to her brother's.

By rights, the woman should have curtsied to another of superior rank, but she remained as still as a sentinel, her grey eyes fixed on Agnes's face. Agnes shivered and looked away from the unnerving stare.

'The coach awaits, sir,' Turner addressed his commander.

'Very good."

'They are only young,' Agnes made one last attempt to secure her position. 'Two men such as yourselves are not suitable for the care of such young children.'

Turner raised one ginger eyebrow and indicated his sister. 'The children will be in the care of my sister, Mistress Fletcher. You may rest in the assurance that they will be in capable and godly hands.'

The flesh on the back of Agnes's neck crawled. She didn't know Turner's sister, but her acquaintance with the mealy-mouthed Turner only increased her fear for the children.

She turned back to Tobias.

'What about me? Charvaley was my home … Where am I to go?'

'Charvaley was only your home by James's grace and favour. I am under no obligation to you.' Ashby's lip curled into a derisive smile. He placed a finger under her chin and tilted her face up. 'My dear Agnes, you've a pretty face. By all accounts, you have already bedded an Earl. It shouldn't be too hard to find yourself another protector.'

Anger flared and she raised a hand to slap him, but he caught her hand before it connected with his face.

'Now, now. That will never do. Of course, should you remember the details of the matter we just discussed, I may reconsider your position. In the meantime, I gave you my word. You may say your farewells to the children.' Squaring his shoulders, he turned to the Turners. 'I want to be away from London before dark. Let us go.'

~

AGNES HUNCHED into the furthest corner of Tobias's coach like a sparrow caught in a trap, wilting under the unrelenting gaze of Leah Turner. The woman seemed to be enjoying her misery. Beside her, Tobias had puffed up like a peacock, the buttons of his coat straining even more. He had gained control of the one thing he probably coveted more than anything, the earldom and estates. True, it was as a trustee only, but he had years before Henry reached twenty-one.

At the thought of Henry, a band tightened on her heart. It had never occurred to her that she could be separated from the children. Henry was only four, still in petticoats, still a baby. What could she say to them that would ease the parting – for all of them? How could she explain that she would not be returning with them to Charvaley?

At the sign of the Blue Boar, the coach turned into the courtyard, and Agnes dismounted even before the groom could put the footstool down. She took a deep, shuddering breath and, without looking back to see if Tobias and the Turners were following, she returned to the inn room where she had left the children in the care of one of the hostelry maids.

She stood in the doorway removing her gloves as the children ran toward her. She signed for the maid to leave, which she did with a quick dip of a curtsey.

'Aunt Agnes!' At their shrill cries of welcome, her heart broke just a little more.

In normal circumstances, she would have hugged them tight, but she could not bring herself to move. If she touched them, she could never let them go.

'That's enough,' she said, employing a hard tone that drove the nail deeper into her heart. 'Children, pack your belongings. You are leaving.'

'Where are we going?' Lizzie asked. 'Back to Charvaley?'

'Yes,' Agnes answered. She glanced behind her as a shadow darkened the doorway. 'Cousin Tobias has come to take you home.'

Henry shrank back against Agnes's skirts at the sight of Tobias. Behind him, the Turners hovered like dark birds of prey.

Instinctively Agnes's hand fell to Henry's shoulder, drawing his little body against her. He huddled behind her drawing her skirts around him.

'Are you coming too, Aunt Agnes?' Lizzie, older and more attuned to the complex undercurrents of adult life, glanced up at her.

Agnes swallowed and straightened her back, holding her head high. 'No, Elizabeth. Cousin Tobias is now your lawful guardian.'

'But I don't want to go with Cousin Tobias. I want to stay here with you!' Henry began to cry.

'Now, now, children,' Tobias said, in a tone that he probably thought of as soothing, but coming from a large man in a military uniform it caused both children to shrink back against Agnes. 'Charvaley is your home. You belong there.'

'But not with you!' Lizzie declared. 'Why isn't Aunt Agnes coming with us? I'm not leaving without Aunt Agnes!' She took a step forward, her hands on her hips, three feet of aristocratic outrage. 'I know what you did. You betrayed our father.'

Agnes thought she saw Tobias flinch at the harsh but truthful words, and wondered how much more Elizabeth knew about her father's betrayal and death. Adults always underestimated children.

'That is not the concern of children,' Tobias said. 'Mistress Fletcher, see that these children are packed and ready to leave in ten minutes. I will be waiting at the coach.' At the door, he turned and looked at her. 'And don't think of trying to escape with them. Say your farewells and bring the children to me.'

'Colonel ...' Leah Turner stepped forward. 'I can see to the children.'

Tobias held up his hand. 'Thank you, Mistress Turner, but I suggest you come with me. We will wait for them in the inn yard.'

'Thank you,' Agnes said, recognising that by leaving her alone with the children he was at least affording her an opportunity of a proper farewell. She supposed she should be grateful for that small kindness.

She waited until the door closed behind him and went down on her knees, her skirts billowing around her. The children fell into her arms.

'Please don't make us go with Cousin Tobias,' Lizzie said, her voice muffled against her shoulder.

'I have no choice, Lizzie. The colonel has promised he will take good care of you.'

'I hate Cousin Tobias,' Henry said with a vehemence that almost made Agnes laugh.

'You don't know him. He has your best interests at heart.'

Lizzie stood her ground, her eyes blazing. 'He did betray Father, didn't he? I heard Father telling you –'

Agnes straightened and fixed the child with a hard, uncompromising stare of disapproval. 'Eavesdroppers hear no good of themselves, Lizzie. Shame on you! I do not know what part if any, Cousin Tobias played in your father's arrest and it is not for you or me to judge him.'

Lizzie's mouth tightened and her eyes narrowed. 'Yes ... but ... '

Agnes held up her hand. 'It will not be spoken of again. What is past is done. You must be brave and strong. It would be what your father would expect of you. In a few days you will be back at Charvaley with the animals, and ... ' She named all the members of staff who had known and loved the children all their lives. 'Come on, let's pack your box.'

There was little to pack. Apart from their clothes, the children had few possessions — an odd assortment of wooden animals, the leather ball that Agnes had bought from a street vendor, and Lizzie's precious wooden doll. She tied the strings of their cloaks and settled hats on their heads. Handing the doll to Lizzie, she gave the children one last kiss and a hug.

'Come children, Cousin Tobias is waiting for you. Be very good for him and for Mistress Turner. It is a long journey home.'

She threw open the door and ordered the soldier waiting outside to bring the box.

As the children emerged onto the open gallery that encircled the courtyard, Henry pulled back at the sight of the large, black coach. Agnes tightened her grip on their hands.

'Remember your father. He was a very brave man and he would want you to be brave,' Agnes whispered to Lizzie, wondering if she was trying to convince herself.

'Good.' Tobias all but rubbed his hands together as they descended the rickety stairs into the inn courtyard. 'Come children, into the coach. I promise you a special treat if you are good for me.'

'What?' Henry demanded.

Tobias glanced at Agnes in mute appeal.

'If you are very good, Cousin Tobias will stop at the baker on the corner and buy you one of those sugar mice.'

Tobias's lips tightened. 'Sugar mice?' he muttered.

Agnes fixed him with a hard glare. 'They are Henry's favourite.'

Henry's fingers tightened on Agnes's and she recognized the jutting of his jaw, so like his father. Not even the promise of sugar mice would pry him away. Agnes went down on her knees, wrapping the small, sturdy body in her embrace, breathing in the scent of him, holding her to him. Captain Turner grabbed her arm, wrenching her away and thrusting her at one of the guards who held her tight as Henry was lifted by one of Tobias's soldiers and carried away, screaming Agnes's name. Another soldier had Lizzie firmly in his grip. Both children were unceremoniously dumped into the coach and the door slammed on them. Agnes had a brief impression of Lizzie taking her little brother in her arms as Tobias climbed in after them.

Lizzie's face, wet with tears, appeared at the window of the coach. She appeared to be wrestling Henry, who screamed uncontrollably and would have thrown himself out of the coach had not Tobias caught him by the collar and dragged him back. Released from the grip of the soldier, Agnes fell to her knees. She covered her ears with her hands and doubled over on the filthy cobbles of the inn yard, her body wracked with sobs.

'Agnes!'

She could not shut out the child's screams as the coach turned out of the inn yard into the street beyond.

CHAPTER 8

*R*eturning from his visit to the Ship Inn, Daniel arrived in time to witness the spectacle unfolding in the inn's courtyard. He recognized Agnes Fletcher kneeling on the muddy cobbles and his gaze moved from the sobbing woman to a large, portly man who stepped around the coach to harry the children inside.

The man glanced in his direction and Daniel drew back into the shadows, letting out a long exhalation of breath as he recognized the face of the man he had come to kill.

Tobias Ashby.

Ten years had not been kind to Ashby, but despite the portly belly and high colour, he was still recognisable as the man who had ordered the cold-blooded execution of Thomas Lovell on the steps of his own home. Daniel's hand dropped to the hilt of his sword, his breath quickening. If he had his pistol to hand …

He steadied his breath. Here and now was not the time to mete out his own vengeance, not if he wanted to avoid his brother's fate.

Besides, he had another purpose now, and he needed Colonel Tobias Ashby alive for the time being if the King's gold would be his.

A few onlookers had gathered to gawk at the woman's distress but no one moved to help her. Even as the coach rumbled out into the street, passing Daniel, Agnes Fletcher still knelt in the inn yard, her arms wrapped around herself, her body wracked with great gulping sobs. The innkeeper's wife touched her shoulder but she threw off the kindly hand and rose to her feet, glancing toward the street where the coach had turned.

'Henry!' she screamed, and seemingly oblivious to the stares and murmurs of the other patrons of the inn and the servants, she ran out into the street, passing Daniel, who hesitated only a fleeting moment before turning to follow her.

Passers-by stepped aside for the "mad" woman, and as the great black coach turned a corner Agnes ran after it, slipping on the mired street, screaming the children's names.

Daniel slowed his step as the coach trundled away, swallowed up by the press of people and vehicles. Agnes Fletcher stood in the middle of the road staring after it, tears pouring down her cheeks unchecked, oblivious to the angry shouts from a carter whose way she blocked.

Reaching her, Daniel touched her shoulder and put an arm around her to steady her, drawing her aside so the carter could pass. He drew her into the shelter of a doorway and she fell against him, her body wracked with heart-rending sobs.

'Calm yourself, madam,' he said, patting her ineffectually on the back.

The sobs slowed to gulps and she drooped in his arms as if all the fight had gone from her. Her voice muffled by his cloak, she said, 'They're gone. He's taken Henry and Lizzie. I'll never see them again.'

Her obvious pain twisted like a knife in Daniel's heart. God rot Tobias Ashby, he thought, glaring at the curious crowd who had gathered to gawk at the spectacle.

'Let's get you back to the inn,' he said, and even as he spoke her knees buckled and only his arm around her stopped her from falling.

He swung her into his arms, where she lay limp and unresponsive. As he hefted her against his chest, she seemed to weigh no more than a child herself, but looking down into her grief-ravaged, half-senseless face, he realised she was a woman well into her twenties.

He carried her back to the inn and laid her down on one of the large oak settles in the parlour. She lay quite still, like a broken doll, and he felt a qualm of concern. Hunkering down beside her, he chafed her hands, relieved when her eyelids flickered and she opened her eyes. For a moment she stared at him, uncomprehending, and then memory must have returned. Her face crumpled and large tears rolled unheeded down her cheeks as she sat up, wrapping her arms around her knees.

'Go away,' she said. 'I don't need your sympathy.'

Daniel cocked an eyebrow. 'There's gratitude for you,' he said.

The landlord's wife came over with a glass filled with a ruby liquid.

'For the poor lady,' she said, indicating the hunched, weeping woman.

Daniel drew the woman away out of earshot. 'What happened?'

The landlord's wife shrugged. 'A man came and took the children away.' She shook her head. 'Such a to-do!' She lowered her voice and jerked her head in Agnes's direction. 'I don't know what she'll do now. She is already a week behind in the rent. My 'usband's not going to stand for letting her spend another night under this roof unless she pays up. He's only let it go on this long for the sake of the children and their poor father.'

Daniel glanced at the broken woman and fumbled in his purse for the coins. The woman's face brightened as he handed over the coins that ensured Agnes Fletcher could spend at least one more night in the comfort of the Blue Boar.

As she counted the coins, she asked. 'Is she a friend of yours?'

'Never met her before,' Daniel said.

'Then you're a good man. God bless you, sir.'

He took the port and sat down on the settle beside Agnes Fletcher. She hunched away from him, her tangled curls of brown hair hiding her face from view.

He proffered her the glass. 'Drink this. Your room is paid for. Nothing more to worry about.'

Agnes hunched her shoulders and straightened, looking up at him. Life flickered back into her blotched and tear-stained face.

'Who are you? Why are you being so kind to me?' she said, wiping her face in a most un-genteel fashion on the sleeve of her gown.

Daniel set the glass down on the nearest table and swept his hat from his head. 'Daniel Lucas, madam. If you wish to be left alone, I will ... '

She laid a hand on his sleeve and her lips began to tremble again. 'You have been very kind and I am being ungrateful. Sit with me a while longer, sir, I beg you. I don't want to be alone, not just yet.' She frowned, recognition flashing in her swollen, red-rimmed eyes. 'But I know you, don't I?'

'A little altercation over a ball,' Daniel reminded her.

'Oh yes, Master Lucas. Henry thought you were a pirate.' Tears welled in her eyes again and she dashed them away. Taking a shuddering breath she glanced down at the glass on the table, picked it up, and downed the contents in one gulp.

She managed a wan smile. 'I'm sorry. I must look a fright.'

Daniel had to agree that she did not present a very attractive picture, with her swollen and blotched face and red-rimmed eyes and lank curls. So much for the comely wench. Agnes Fletcher was not one of those women who could cry prettily.

He kept his peace. 'A pirate? Really. What on earth made him think that?'

She touched her cheek in the approximate position of the scar on his face. 'That, probably.'

Daniel fingered the old injury, sustained in battle, not in any act of piracy. 'Ah. A childhood accident.' He assumed a solicitous expression and leaned toward her. 'I hope you don't think me impertinent, but your circumstances seem somewhat strained.'

She shook her head and looked around the room. 'I don't know what I'm going to do, Master Lucas. I've lost everything. And now he has taken the children.'

'And are they your children?' Daniel enquired.

Her throat visibly contracted and she shook her head. 'They are my sister's children. Their mother is dead and they have just lost their father. I am all they have left ... apart from that *man*.' She spat out the last word as if it left a vile taste in her mouth and tears spilled from her eyes again. The woman was a veritable water well. 'What are they going to do without me?'

Daniel's lips tightened. Even if their new guardian was anyone except

Tobias Ashby, it seemed a heartless act to separate the newly orphaned children from the one steady and loving person in their lives.

He signalled the innkeeper for another glass of port and Agnes consumed it as she had the first — in one gulp. She pushed the disordered curls back behind her ear. It did not improve her appearance.

He thought in normal circumstances she probably had very fine hazel eyes and an attractive smattering of freckles across a neat, pert nose. That nose was now scarlet and her eyes bloodshot and red-ringed.

She cleared her throat and said in a voice, thick with her recent grief. 'I crave your pardon, sir. You've been very kind, but I've troubled you long enough. Please return to your business and do not concern yourself for me anymore.'

Daniel shook his head. 'I'm not leaving 'til the morning. Can I at least buy you a meal?' Her lips parted for a moment, revealing neat, even teeth. She sighed deeply and lowered her gaze. 'You are very kind, sir, and I would welcome some company this evening, even though I may not be at my best.' She ran a hand through her disordered hair and looked up at him again, the ghost of a smile catching at the corners of her mouth. 'Perhaps allow me a moment or two to restore myself.'

Daniel smiled and inclined his head. 'It will be my pleasure. Take whatever time you need. I'll be waiting here.'

She stood up, running her hands down the stained and crumpled skirts of what had once been a gown of a fine quality green wool. He watched her weave between the tables and stools, the two glasses of port taking effect, and ordered a flagon of the landlord's finest red wine.

Perfect, Daniel thought. *This could not have worked out better if I had planned it.*

CHAPTER 9

*A*gnes sat on the edge of the bed in the empty room, her locket open in her hand. It contained nothing more than a curled lock of soft, blonde hair, taken from Henry's head the first time she had trimmed his baby curls.

She snapped the locket shut and replaced it around her neck while she considered her options. She could not just sit by and let the children be taken away from her without a fight. She had promised James and more than that she was bound in blood to the fate of Lizzie and Henry. Somehow, she had to find her way to Charvaley. Maybe, away from his masters in London, Tobias could be persuaded to let her stay.

She took a deep, steadying breath. She had to be realistic. She didn't know the way to Tobias's better nature, or even if he *had* a better nature. She could be of no assistance when it came to the location of the gold, but, what was it he had said? *You've a pretty face. By all accounts you have already bedded an Earl. It shouldn't be too hard to find yourself another protector.*

What if Tobias Ashby himself would be prepared to be her protector? What if she swallowed what little pride she had left and afforded him the opportunity? The very thought of him touching her made the gorge rise in her throat and she retched port into the slops bucket.

Wiping her face with a cold, wet cloth, she sat back on her heels and considered her current situation. Alone, penniless, and friendless, she stood little chance of making it out of London, let alone as far as Charvaley.

She glanced at the door to her room. She already had a protector waiting for her in the parlour downstairs. Could he be persuaded to provide her with the means to get there? When it came to feminine wiles, she had no tricks. She had always considered herself rather plain, and James had never once told her otherwise. Her mere presence at his table had been all the invitation he had ever needed.

Rising to her feet, she caught a glimpse of her reflection in the window and wondered how one threw oneself on the mercy of a total stranger looking like she did at this moment. She had been wearing her best gown to attend on the Committee and now it was covered in mud and worse.

She gave a bitter laugh. No man would want her looking as she did. Her fingers touched the locket and she wondered if Lucas would buy it from her. If not, she had no choice but to seek out a gold dealer in the morning and sell it for whatever she could raise.

She changed into clean petticoats and a respectable bodice with fresh collar and cuffs and arranged her disordered curls as best she could, washed her face again, pinched her cheeks to force some colour into her wan face, and forced herself to smile.

Drawing herself up straight she left the bedchamber, now so silent and empty without the children, and made her way back to the inn's parlour.

Lucas — she couldn't remember if he had told her his first name — waited for her as he said he would. He rose to his feet in a single, lithe movement and gestured at the chair across the table from him.

For a moment her nerve failed her. How could she even think about throwing herself on the mercy of a man she knew nothing about?

She supposed some women might find him handsome, with his brown hair, darkly tanned face and high cheekbones. James had been fair and, to be honest, softer. He had been starting to go to fat, not that she would have ever said anything to him. She found the hard planes of

Lucas's face and the strong mouth more than a little intimidating, and Henry was right, the scar did make him look piratical.

Outwardly though, his clothes were those of any respectable man of business. His jacket of good quality dark blue wool had been well cut in the latest fashion to set off his long, lean body. He wore the more fashionable falling bands in place of a collar and expensive lace trimmed the froth of cloth at his wrists. A man who took some pride in his appearance and had the means to purchase the best.

His grey eyes rested on her face. Something in those light depths, the colour of an icy stream, made her shiver.

Just as she considered making her apologies and fleeing to the safety of the bedchamber, he smiled, softening the cold eyes and curling those well-cut lips. Small lines creased the corners of his eyes and her moment of doubt vanished.

'Do I meet with your approval?'

She flushed, looked down at her mournful gown, and thought of her pale and wan face. As a seductress, she had a lot to learn. Staring at your quarry like a rabbit facing a fox was probably not a good way to begin.

She cleared her throat and forced herself to look up at him again, a smile fixed on her lips. 'I was thinking that you must have spent a great deal of time in warmer climes than ours, sir. I have never seen a man so dark.'

Lucas shrugged. 'I have travelled extensively, Mistress Fletcher.'

'Are you a merchant?'

Something flashed in the grey depths of his eyes. Amusement?

'A merchant? Perhaps,' he said with a shrug.

The more she looked at him, the more piratical he appeared for all his fine clothes. A sword hilt crowned with a jewel of deepest green winked at her, and she could have sworn from the line of his well-cut jacket that he carried a pistol tucked into his belt.

It would be madness to throw herself at the mercy of this man. What was she thinking?

She steeled herself. 'You have been very kind. Thank you for settling my account. There was no need ... I will repay you.'

His eyes creased at the corners as he smiled. 'Of course you will,

Mistress Fletcher, but for the moment you are my guest. Will you at least sit and eat with me?'

He gestured at the flagon of wine and a large pie that now took up most of the space on the tiny table. Agnes's stomach growled in appreciation.

'Please help yourself. The world's troubles will seem easier on a full stomach,' he said.

A man's response, that, she thought. Food — the panacea to all evil.

She seated herself with all the grace she would have used at James's table.

'I lied,' she said after several mouthfuls.

'Lied?'

'I do not have the means to repay you. I have nothing. Not a groat.'

'I know,' he said and leaned forward, his elbows on the table, his cold, grey eyes narrowed. 'I am not looking for you to repay me in coin, Mistress Fletcher.'

Agnes swallowed, taking his meaning. Men – they were all the same. What choice did she have?

She cleared her throat and met his gaze. 'I know I am indebted to you and whatever you want of me I will give you gladly, but I ask one more thing in return.'

'That is?' The man's mouth quirked at the corners and a seething resentment rose in Agnes. Here she was practically throwing herself at him and all he could do was smile?

'You assist me with the means to reach Charvaley, in ...'

'Lancashire?' he answered for her.

'You've heard of it?'

His mouth tightened and he sat back. 'Yes. What particular means do you have in mind?'

'Money to buy a passage on the Liverpool coach?' she suggested, having not considered how one travelled the countryside without the benefit of a private conveyance.

He nodded. 'I could do that, or ... ' he paused, his eyes narrowing.

'Or?' she prompted.

'I could take you myself.'

Agnes's heart skipped a beat. 'You would take me to Charvaley?'

'Yes. That is what you want, is it not?'

'Yes,' she whispered, her fingers circling the gold locket. 'More than anything but why would you wish to go such a distance ... for me.'

He studied her for a long moment, the tips of his fingers steepled, as if in deep consideration. He laid the palm of one hand down on the table. 'I think we should be honest with each other, Mistress Fletcher. We share one thing in common ... a mutual ... shall we say, *dislike* ... of Colonel Tobias Ashby. I have long-outstanding business with him and you wish to have the children restored to you. We have a common cause ... a common enemy.'

The grey eyes took on the sheen of polished steel, and despite herself she shivered. 'Can I ask what your business with Tobias is?'

'No,' he said.

It was on the tip of her tongue to ask if it involved the death of Tobias Ashby, but something in his hard face warned her not to ask such a question. If she agreed to go with him she was truly throwing in her lot with the devil.

He studied her face without blinking. 'Are we agreed?'

She opened her mouth intending to say 'No', but it was a soft 'Yes,' that fell into the tense space between them. Yes, she would go with this strange man. What alternative did she have? None. He sat back. 'Good, we are agreed. Now eat your supper. We will leave tomorrow morning.'

She stared at her plate, unable to comprehend what had just passed between them. Just like that, he had agreed to take her home, but he still had not named his price. She glanced up at him, but his face told her nothing, and she decided that if this man could reunite her with Henry and Lizzie, whatever he wanted would be a price worth paying.

With her dilemma resolved, she demolished the food put before her.

He watched her as she brushed the last crumbs from her lips.

'I like a woman with a good appetite,' he said.

'I was hungry,' Agnes said stiffly.

'Evidently. Now to business, Mistress Fletcher.'

'Business?'

'Yes, I need to know a little more about you. What, for example, is ...
was ... your relation to Lord Elmhurst?'

She frowned. Clearly, the man knew more about her than she did
of him.

'I was sister to the late Earl's wife. My sister Ann and her husband,
James, took me in when my brother died.' She cleared her throat. 'After
Ann died, the children came exclusively to my care and charge.'

'And now the Earl is dead you say you have lost everything?'

She looked down at the old, dark wood of the table, incised with
initials and dates of ancient inn patrons. She traced one such initial, a J
carved with almost intricate delicacy.

'Yes,' she said. 'I have nothing to my name. James died without a will.'

'And your brother ... he died in the King's service?' His voice had
dropped almost to a whisper.

She looked up. 'In a manner of speaking. He went into exile after
Worcester and died in The Hague a few years later.'

The man's mouth tightened and his hand rose to the scar on his face.
An unconscious gesture, she thought, but it told her everything she
needed to know.

'You were there?' she asked.

He flicked his gaze over her shoulder to an unseen object behind her
head, and for a moment she thought he would not answer.

'Yes,' he said in a clipped tone, 'I was there. One last question and you
will forgive my impertinence but it is important that we are honest with
each other ... were you mistress to the late Earl?'

Every fibre in her body screamed out in outrage at the audacity of
the question, but held by his cold, grey eyes all she could say was 'yes'.
She swallowed and lifted her chin in defiance. 'But if you think to bed
me, Master Lucas, I would have you know that I ... '

I... what...? I am not a whore?

'I believe I have the right to know a little bit more about you,' she
concluded.

He held his hand up and nodded. 'You have been honest with me,' he
said, 'and, as we are united in this venture, I should be honest with you.
My name is not Lucas, it is Lovell. Daniel Lovell. I was taken prisoner

after Worcester and sent to the West Indies.' He paused as if considering his next statement. 'Let us just say I have returned to England from several years in exile.'

He was still being less than honest with her, but that explanation would have to do for now.

'And you prefer not to use your own name because you are a little uncertain of your welcome in England?' she ventured.

That smile curved his lips again. 'Precisely. So to all intents and purposes, we shall travel together as Daniel Lucas and his sister, Agnes Fletcher.' His fingers beat a quick tattoo on the table. 'And you have my word as a gentleman that I shall view our relationship as just such.'

She hoped the palpable relief did not show on her face. Not that he was unattractive. In fact, after careful consideration, following their discussion she considered him most attractive.

'It might bear some veracity if you were to call me Daniel,' he suggested, adding with a half smile, 'which, I assure you, is my name.'

'Daniel.' She tried the name out and found she liked the way it sounded on her tongue. Daniel Lovell may be a man with a dubious past but she may have found her new protector.

Impulsively she reached across the table and laid her hand over his. 'Thank you. Our meeting was God-sent.'

A muscle twitched in Daniel's cheek and he looked down at her hand. It seemed so small against his. The muscles and sinews were strongly defined and there were pale scars on his knuckles and the backs of his hand. For all his gentlemanly accent and demeanour, he had known hard manual labour.

He slid his hand away from hers. 'I don't think God had much to do with it, but let us leave it at that. You must be tired, Mistress Fletcher.'

She nodded and ran a hand across her eyes. Now the crisis had passed, her body cried out for sleep.

'It has been a trying day,' she admitted and rose to her feet, every muscle in her body crying out in protest.

He pushed his chair back and stood. 'It has indeed. We will set out tomorrow as soon as I have procured horses. Do you ride?"

She nodded.

'I should warn you that I have an errand to perform on our way north. Letters to deliver to friends in Worcestershire.'

'As Lucas or Lovell?' she enquired, with a smile.

He shook his head. 'Lovell. The people we go to are friends of my brother's.'

'Your brother?' she enquired, hoping to elicit something of a personal nature from him.

'Like your brother, he's dead,' Daniel Lovell replied curtly. 'Now, I suggest you retire. We have a long ride ahead of us.'

She turned to leave, but stopped and looked back at him as he said, 'Good night, Agnes, and sleep well in the knowledge that whatever it takes, I will see you reunited with the children. You have my word.'

She frowned. 'That is a kind sentiment but why are you helping me?'

He met her gaze without blinking. 'I told you, we have a mutual interest.' Giving a half shrug, he added, 'And also because I abhor injustice of any kind, and to place the fate of two innocent children in the hands of Tobias Ashby, and, I have no doubt, Septimus Turner, is an injustice. Pack only what you can carry and be ready to leave by noon. Good night.'

As she reached her room, Agnes fell into a chair, physically drained. She stared at the empty fireplace, the autumn chill in the room winding around her like a cloak. She let out her breath, watching it steam in the light of the single candle.

Leaning on her hand, she thought about the man who had come to her rescue. *God sends his angels in strange guises*, she thought. But then, God has many different kinds of angels, and there was less of Gabriel and far more of Michael in the man who had offered her his assistance. Was Daniel Lovell or Lucas or whatever he called himself the slayer of dragons and avenger that would defeat Satan?

If she closed her eyes she could picture him, clad in black with his bright sword in his hand, facing a dragon. It would be fun to weave a tale for the children.

At the thought of the children, she jerked awake. She had to pack. For herself she had little but the respectable petticoats and bodice she was wearing, some clean linen, and ...

She looked at the box of James's possessions. Taking a deep breath, she knelt on the floor and opened it. If it had been tidily packed, someone had been through it, throwing everything in higgledy-piggledy.

She picked out a shirt, holding it to her face and breathing in James's scent, still so redolent in the fabric. For a moment her courage failed her. However flawed, her life had been happy and comfortable. Now she had no home, no money, and no prospects. Her single thread of hope was a man with a past who called himself Daniel Lovell.

CHAPTER 10

'What do you mean, you want to come with me?' Daniel put his hands on his hips and fixed Matt with a hard glare.

Did everybody in London want his company?

The urchin regarded him without blinking. 'You're a gentleman and I can learn to be your servant. I'd like that.'

'It doesn't suit me to have a servant, particularly one who looks and smells like you,' Daniel replied.

The boy's mouth turned down at the corners and he looked down at his feet, where a long, blackened toenail protruded from the broken shoe.

Daniel huffed out a sigh of exasperation and hunched down to look the boy in the eye. 'Look, lad. I don't know what's waiting for me where I'm going and frankly, you would be in the way. You can't come with me.'

'But I've got no other life, Cap'n.' The boy's voice broke on the verge of tears.

Daniel ran a hand over his eyes. Matt could be dead within a few years if he continued his hand-to-mouth existence on the streets, if not from illness or starvation, then the hangman's noose. He sighed and rose to his feet.

'If I can find a respectable job for you, will you promise me you'll stick to it and not go back to thieving?'

Matt frowned and shuffled his feet. 'Who'd want me?'

'I think I know just the person,' Daniel said.

He took the boy by the back of his filthy jerkin and propelled him toward the Old Bayly. Outside the Ship Inn, Matt struggled and squirmed in Daniel's unrelenting grip.

'You!' Nan Marsh greeted the sight of the struggling youngster with crossed arms and a look on her face that would freeze the fires of Hell.

'I believe you are acquainted with my young friend here,' Daniel said.

'What'd he do? Try to rob yer?'

'No, nothing of the sort. I have a favour to ask of you, Mistress Marsh, and I can think of no one better to accomplish it. I will pay you well to subject this verminous creature to a hot bath accompanied by a dose of soap. I think underneath all that dirt is a good-hearted lad who would make a good pot boy.'

The corner of Nan's mouth twitched and for a moment Daniel thought she might smile. She looked up at him with a definite twinkle in her eye as Matt protested, 'A pot boy, me? I don't fink so!'

Daniel lifted him off the ground and held him at arm's length until the boy stopped struggling.

Nan pushed her sleeves up and turned a gimlet eye on Matt. 'Leave him to me. I'll have 'im so clean you won't recognize him.'

'No!' Matt squirmed harder. 'Not a bath!'

'That's enough,' Nan said, closing her hand over Matt's wrist.

The boy gave Daniel a last despairing glance. He so resembled a pup that was being punished for some unknown transgression that Daniel had to choke back a laugh.

'I'm going to see to the purchase of some horses and when I return in a couple of hours I would like to see him clean and properly dressed.'

This time a slow smile spread across Nan's face. 'It will be my pleasure, sir,' she said. 'And I think we can rustle up some clothes that'll fit.'

'Excellent. And feed him too.'

Nan tugged at the boy's hand. 'Right, me lad, into the kitchen wiv you. And, sir, if you want good 'orses, try the farrier up by Aldgate.'

Daniel left the inn with Matt's outraged howls ringing in his ears.

Nan's recommendation proved to be a good one. Daniel purchased a black gelding with a white star, which looked to have the lines of good breeding in it, for himself, and a docile bay mare for Agnes Fletcher.

Back at the Ship Inn, he found an unrecognisable Matt sitting on a table in the taproom, eating an apple. He had been scrubbed to a raw pinkness, his hair cut short and standing up in spikes. From somewhere clothes had been found to fit him. Patched and second-hand, they were at least clean and warm and he had well-worn, but solid, shoes on his stockinged feet.

He looked up as Daniel entered the room. 'She tried to murder me,' he said, pointing an accusing finger at Nan Marsh who stood watching him, her hands on her hips.

Daniel winked at the woman and she rewarded him with a smile.

'You looked just like yer brother when you did that, sir,' she said. 'Do ye mind me asking where yer bound … just in case I needs to send word about the boy?'

Daniel's spine prickled. Something in the studied casualness of her tone made him think there was more to the question than first appeared.

'I have business with an old friend of my brother's, Sir Jonathan Thornton of Seven Ways in Worcestershire. You can send any word there. Sir Jonathan will know where to reach me from there.'

She nodded and he turned to the boy. 'It's time for me to go.'

The boy's face fell. 'But I want to come wiv you, Cap'n. Now I'm all clean and respectable like, I could be yer servant.'

'Do you know anything about horses?' Daniel enquired.

The momentary hesitation gave Daniel the answer as Matt said with great bravado, 'Of course I do. Brought up round 'orses I was.'

'Liar.' Nan lightly cuffed the boy's ears. 'Wouldn't know one end of an 'orse from t'other.'

'Thought so.' Daniel looked up at Nan. 'Can I leave him with you, Mistress Marsh?'

Nan regarded him for a moment. 'I could do wiv a good pot boy,' she said.

Matt let out a howl of outrage and Daniel gave the boy a conciliatory smile. 'I'll pay Mistress Marsh to teach you some manners and in return, you can help with work around the inn. When my business is settled, I'll come back. I give you my word.'

The boy cast Nan a baleful glance. She returned it in kind but she laid a gentle hand on the boy's shoulder. 'He ain't such a bad sort,' she said. 'Just needs a mother's touch.'

Matt looked up at Nan. 'You?'

She returned his glare. 'You just wait, me lad. I'll be the mother yer never knew.'

Daniel laughed and shook his head. 'I will return for the boy, Mistress Marsh. I just can't say when.'

He left Matt chewing on the apple core and Nan Marsh walked with him to the end of the street, where he'd left the horses, her arms wrapped around herself as a cold wind blew up from the river. She watched him swing into the saddle of the gelding and laid a hand on the bridle.

'You will come back, sir? It'd break the lad's heart if you didn't.'

Daniel nodded. 'I keep my promises, Mistress Marsh, and in turn, will you be kind to him? I don't want him running back to the streets.'

She smiled. 'Ask anyone, sir. Me bark's much worse than me bite and I've a soft spot for Lovells.' She raised a hand in farewell. 'I'll see you again, Daniel Lovell.'

DANIEL RETURNED to the inn to find Agnes Fletcher sitting in the parlour waiting for him. Well wrapped in a thick woollen cloak, she sat on a high-backed chair with a leather satchel on her lap. Her eyes, ringed with dark circles, looked huge in her pinched face, but the smile she gave him was warm and welcoming and more than a little relieved.

She stood up as he approached her, 'I thought ... '

'You thought I'd left without you?' he prompted, and a little colour stole into her pale face. 'I had some business to attend to. The horses are outside. Ready to go?'

She nodded and followed him out to the courtyard where the groom waited, holding the bridles of the two horses.

'The bay is yours. I'm assured she has a gentle nature,' Daniel said.

Agnes eyed the mare. 'I am to ride astride?'

Daniel shrugged. 'I could not procure a lady's saddle at such short notice. You did say you can ride?'

The woman bridled. 'Of course, it's just that … '

' … You are too used to a softer life, Agnes. If you are to travel with me you will ride astride.'

Agnes shook her head and smiled. The transformation to her haggard features took Daniel by surprise. Beneath the dowdy exterior of this little woman was a young woman, and a pretty one at that.

'I used to ride astride when I was a child. My mother called me a hoyden but never tried to stop me.'

Daniel took Agnes's satchel from her and strapped it to the saddle of her horse. 'You took me at your word when I said travel light,' he said.

She shrugged. 'I have very little of my own here in London,' she said. 'Everything else I brought here went with the children or I left with the landlord's wife to donate to the poor.'

Daniel bent and she placed a neat, booted foot in his cupped hands and lifted herself into the saddle with practiced ease. Quite the hoyden indeed, he thought. The groom adjusted her stirrups while she carefully and decorously arranged her skirts.

Daniel swung himself into the saddle of the gelding and glanced at Agnes. She looked the picture of a respectable sister in her dark cloak, with a high-crowned hat trimmed with a plain buckle atop a neat, matronly cap.

'I don't suppose you happen to know the way to Worcestershire?' he enquired of her.

Agnes's lips parted and she stared at him. 'What do you mean?'

'I've never travelled these roads before,' he admitted with a rueful smile.

The groom looked up at him. 'Ye need to take the Uxbridge Road,' he said. 'I reckon ye'll get as far as Uxbridge but watch out for footpads on Ealing Common. There's desperate men taken to the roads these days.'

Daniel nodded and glanced at Agnes. 'Thank you for the warning.'

CHAPTER 11

*A*gnes's mood lifted as they left the fetid streets of the city behind, with all its unhappy memories. Agnes straightened her hat and pulled her cloak tighter around her as a brisk autumnal breeze rose to meet them.

The large black horse ambled ahead of her at a gentle pace. Beneath Daniel's cloak the intricate basket hilt of an elegant sword at his hip, with its jewelled finial caught the light. The fine object seemed at odds with his plain dress and somewhat blunt manner.

'Where did you get that sword?' she asked.

He glanced over his shoulder at the sound of her voice. 'My sword? The generous gift of a Spaniard.'

'He gave it to you?'

'Not with any good grace,' Daniel said returning his gaze to the road ahead.

She kicked her horse forward to come abreast of him.

'So are you Lucas or Lovell today?' she enquired.

He glanced at her. 'Lucas, of course. Why do you ask?'

'If I am to be your travelling companion, it may be useful to know why you travel under a false name.'

His mouth tightened. 'I'm not sure if you want to know, but I promised you honesty. Call it prudence. I am quite possibly a wanted man in this country, Mistress Fletcher.'

Her heart sank. Her instincts had been right; she had thrown her lot in with a brigand of some sort. Admittedly a well-bred brigand.

'Perhaps I should ask what you did?' she enquired, trying to keep her voice level.

He sighed. 'A little bit of privateering.'

'So you are a pirate?'

He flinched. 'A privateer … there is a difference. However, I sailed aboard a French ship and we encountered the occasional English ship, so that may make me less than welcome if the authorities were to discover my true identity.' He glanced at her, a smile lifting the corners of his mouth, the grey eyes twinkling. 'You're safe enough with me, Mistress Fletcher. At heart, I am quite respectable, and as far as the English authorities are concerned, they know only of a man known as *Le Loup Anglais*. It is to be hoped they do not make any connections.'

She laughed. 'The English Wolf. A somewhat romantic name.'

'Not my invention, believe me.'

'So, how did you come to be a privateer aboard a French ship with such an exotic nom de guerre' she enquired.

His eyes narrowed and he turned his concentration back to the road ahead, a muscle twitching in his cheek. 'That is none of your concern.'

She had stepped over the unseen boundary in their burgeoning friendship. She let the silence pass between them before she tried a different tactic.

'Where is home for you?' she asked, urging her horse to come alongside him.

He gave her an infuriated glare. 'You ask a lot of questions, Agnes.'

'You asked me if I was James Ashby's mistress; I think that entitles me to ask you a few highly personal questions,' she responded.

His mouth quirked and that intriguing half smile lightened his countenance. 'Home, what's left of it, is Eveleigh Priory, near Chester.'

'And your family?'

He sighed. 'I am not deserving of this interrogation, Mistress Fletcher, but as you are so curious, I have a perfectly respectable mother and sister who, I sincerely hope, will be very pleased to see me.'

'Are they expecting you?'

He glanced at her, his face concealed by the brim of his low-crowned hat.

'I thought I might surprise them.'

'When did you last see them?'

'Eight years ago.' He paused, and added in a tight voice, 'They probably think I'm dead.'

Agnes studied his profile. Only the slightest twitching of a muscle near his mouth betrayed any emotion.

'Then I have no doubt you will surprise them,' she remarked bitterly. 'I don't understand why you would not go there now. If I were in your place ... '

He glanced at her, a flush of colour rising to his cheeks. 'You are not me, Mistress Fletcher. I have the King's business to contract first.'

She stared at him. 'The King's business? But I thought this was about Tobias Ashby.'

His mouth tightened. 'It is,' he said in a clipped tone. 'Ask me no more questions, or I swear I will leave you on the side of the road and continue alone.'

Chastened, Agnes dropped back. Now they had left the city behind, they were the lone travellers on this stretch of road. Ahead of them stands of trees loomed out of the autumnal mist, their leafless branches stark against the grey sky. Ealing Common. An eerie silence, unbroken even by birdsong, settled on the skeletal trees.

Daniel stopped his horse, loosening his sword in its scabbard. Agnes came back alongside him and he turned to look at her.

'I don't like this,' Daniel said. 'Can you handle a pistol?'

'Why do you ask?'

He unbuckled one of the two pistol holsters on his saddle, removed the guns and checked the priming. He held one of the weapons out to Agnes.

'I want you to take this.'

'No need,' Agnes said.

He narrowed his eyes. 'Agnes, this is not a moment for womanly sensibilities about weapons. I would prefer it if you took the pistol.'

Smug, self-satisfied, sod, she thought, fumbling in the specially designed pocket of her cloak.

She had the satisfaction of seeing a look of utter surprise cross Daniel Lovell's face as she held up her own pistol, a pretty object with a highly polished wooden stock inlaid with silver filigree.

'Good God,' Daniel blasphemed. 'Do you know how to use it?'

She gave him the look of contempt he deserved. 'Of course, I do. My brother had many faults, but he gave me this and taught me how to use it. He said a woman should know how to defend herself in time of war.'

Daniel raised an eyebrow. 'A sensible man and tell me, have you ever had cause to use it?'

She could hardly lie. 'No. Not in anger.'

He shrugged. 'Keep it hidden. We'll move a little faster to try and clear the common before the dusk sets in.'

He kicked his horse into a trot and Agnes followed suit, moving easily to the smooth gait of the horse. It had been a long time since she had ridden astride but there were some things you never forgot.

Despite their heightened vigilance, the attack, when it came, still took them by surprise.

An unearthly cry caused the sturdy black horse to break stride, going down on its haunches as a huge man leapt out of the cover of the bushes to seize its bridle. Daniel threw himself out of the saddle, landing with surprising agility on his feet, with his sword in hand.

Agnes's mare skittered sideways as a second man with a greasy hat pulled down low and a kerchief tied around the lower part of his face grabbed her reins with one hand. He reached out with the other and pulled Agnes from the saddle. She uttered a stifled scream as a knife pressed against her throat and an arm circled the upper part of her body, immobilising her with a hand that had only stubs of fingers. Bile rose in her throat.

Her right hand tightened on the butt of the pistol she held concealed in the folds of her skirt, but with the villain's arm pinioning her, she could not raise her arm to fire it.

'Your purse and your goods or I'll cut the lady's throat!' the man holding her called out.

The second man let go of the horse's reins and, brandishing a cudgel, lunged for Daniel. He dodged it easily.

'Put down your weapon,' the first man said. 'Or I will kill your pretty little friend.'

The knife pressed harder into her neck and Agnes uttered a small squeak as it pierced the skin and her blood, warm in the cold air, trickled down her throat.

'Be quiet!' The man's mouth came so close that she could smell the stench of onions and rotten teeth.

Daniel looked around and his eyes locked briefly with Agnes's. A fire burned in the grey depths and a shiver ran down her spine. He turned his attention on the man holding her and, without breaking eye contact with Agnes's captor, he laid the sword on the ground and straightened, raising his hands.

'Let her go,' he said in a low voice.

The man holding her relaxed a little, exhaling a breath of foul air in her ear. The questing stubs of his fingers ran around her neck, awkwardly extracting the chain of the locket.

'What's this then?'

'No! Not that.' Anger replaced fear and Agnes jerked her elbow backwards, straight into the man's soft underbelly. The breath left his body with a soft *Oof* and he staggered backward, the knife falling to the ground. Agnes whirled around and planted her knee in his crotch. He went down, whimpering.

Balancing her pistol in her hand, Agnes stood over the man, pressing the pistol to his temple. He stopped moaning, his eyes, wide and fearful, fixed on her face, his hands still clutching his abused private parts.

Out of the corner of her eye, she saw Daniel stoop to retrieve his sword and turn once more to face the big man. The man, whose gaze had been diverted by his companion's fate, remembered too late and flashed at Daniel with the cudgel but Daniel sidestepped, his sword catching the man's arm. The footpad looked at the blood that welled through his sleeve, gritted his teeth and came at Daniel snarling, with the cudgel above his head. Daniel neatly stepped under the upraised arm, the momentum of the man's charge skewering him on the slender blade of the Spanish sword.

The footpad stopped and looked down at the sword that pierced his chest, surprise registering in his eyes. The cudgel dropped to the ground, and as the man sank to his knees Daniel put a boot to his chest so he fell backwards, allowing Daniel to retrieve the sword. Agnes looked away, sickened by the sucking noise as the sword came free, followed by a bright spray of blood.

Daniel turned to the brigand who knelt cowering at Agnes's feet, his hands still pressed to his groin. He stooped to retrieve the locket that had fallen to the ground in the fracas.

'We didn't mean no 'arm,' the man whimpered. 'Let me go, guvnor. I served His Majesty in the wars. Lost everything, I did.'

Agnes glanced up at Daniel. The fire had gone from his eyes and he lowered his sword. 'Who did you serve with?'

The man licked his lips. 'Lord Hopton.' He held up his left hand, or what was left of it. 'That's all the thanks I got. Lost me fingers at Naseby. No good for workin' after that. Wife and kids died of starvation one winter and I took to the road.' A glimmer of hope gleamed in the man's eyes. 'You won't turn me in, captain?'

Daniel jerked his head at the man's companion. 'Your friend's dead.'

The man shrugged. 'Don't have friends in this game. If you hand me over, they'll 'ang me. Let me go.'

Daniel glanced at Agnes and gave a curt nod. She raised the pistol away from the man's head.

'Get on your way,' Daniel said.

The man scrambled to his feet. Clutching his greasy hat to his head, he took off into the woods as if the hounds of Hell were on his heels.

Daniel wiped the blade of his sword on a grassy tussock and restored it to his scabbard. He secured the placid bay mare and turned to Agnes.

'You're hurt.'

She raised shaking fingers to the cut on her neck. 'It's only a scratch.'

'Let me see.'

Lifting her chin, he narrowed his eyes as he scrutinised the cut.

'Let me just clean it a little. I'm afraid there is blood on your collar.'

From a pocket inside his jacket, he produced a square of neatly laundered cambric edged with lace and pressed it against the cut, wiping the trail of blood that led to her throat.

'Hold that there for a moment. It's almost stopped bleeding,' he said.

'What's this?' she enquired, holding out the pad of cambric, now stained with her blood.

'A kerchief. They're the height of fashion in Paris.'

Her eyes widened. 'You've been to Paris?'

He smiled. 'And met the King of France.' His fingers closed over hers, returning the pad to her neck.

'It's too dainty for your taste,' she said.

A smile twitched his lips. 'A lady gave it to me,' he said. 'A keepsake.'

She pressed the cloth against the wound, her gaze dropping from his. 'I see.'

His fingers circled the chain of the locket that the villain had pried from her neck. His touch sent a shiver down her spine.

'A pretty piece,' he said. 'Is it special?'

Agnes snatched it from his fingers and fastened it again, stowing it away out of sight beneath her collar.

Daniel stepped back and studied her for a moment. 'None of my business, apparently?'

'None!'

'So in addition to the use of a pistol, did your brother teach you that interesting manoeuvre, Mistress Fletcher?'

'He taught me a few useful things.'

And then left me.

'Remind me not to annoy you,' he remarked drily.

Agnes checked the kerchief. The cut seemed to have stopped bleeding.

'Enough of this chatter,' she said, indicating the dead man. 'What do we do with him?'

Daniel shrugged. 'He isn't going anywhere. We'll alert the next village we come to and they can deal with him, but I will save the sensibilities of the travelling public and move him out of sight. Can you take his feet?'

Agnes recoiled. 'Touch him?'

Daniel's eyes narrowed. 'He's not going to hurt you and I can't manage him alone. Have you never seen a dead man before?'

'Only those who have died peacefully in their beds,' she admitted.

Taking a deep breath, she hefted the man's feet as Daniel lifted him by the shoulders. As they moved him, the corpse let out a groan.

Agnes screamed and dropped the man's feet.

'It's only air escaping his lungs,' Daniel said. 'Pick up his feet again.'

'You have obviously had more experience with corpses than I,' Agnes said hotly, lifting the man's muddy and disgusting feet again.

'Too much,' Daniel agreed. 'This'll do. Behind this fallen log. I'll mark the place.'

Agnes removed her gloves and wiped the muddy objects on the damp verge as Daniel laid the dead footpad straight, covering the corpse's face with the man's own jacket. He carved a cross into the bark of a nearby fallen tree to mark the spot.

Returning to Agnes, he hefted her back onto her horse and led the animal along the road. They encountered the black horse munching peacefully on a sweet patch of grass a hundred yards away. At his touch the horse obediently raised its head, allowing Daniel to swing into the saddle. Sensing that it was not going to be made to go back the way it had come, the black horse turned with its ears pricked, pulling at the bit.

Daniel glanced around at Agnes. 'Do you suppose that beast of yours can move faster? This one wants to stretch its legs.'

'You mean a race?' Agnes felt the same thrill of the challenge she had felt when George had issued it. She had been the better rider and George knew it, but it never stopped him from trying to best her. It would be interesting to see if Daniel Lovell was made of sterner stuff. She pulled her hat from her head, securing it under her leg and with a whoop kicked the mare into action. Too surprised to resist, the mare took off at a hard canter. They passed the black gelding and she heard Daniel's answering *Huzzah!* and the thunder of hooves behind her.

She drew rein at the next crossroads with Daniel half a length behind her. He drew level with her, laughing.

'What did your mother call you?' he asked breathlessly.

'A hoyden,' she replied, fishing out her crushed hat and restoring it to her head.

They glanced at each other, and for a brief moment the look they exchanged said nothing else, except that they were both young and the hard ride had been fun and a chance to forget the cares that they carried with them.

They stopped at an inn for the night and Daniel reported the encounter with the footpads, although he failed to mention the man he had allowed to escape. In the inn parlour, the story of their adventure provoked much shaking of heads and comments about the state of the roads these days, with so many disaffected soldiers taken to brigandry.

Daniel's coin bought Agnes a bed for the night in a communal room and a meal. As she pushed the unspeakable mess that passed for some sort of stew around her trencher, she ruminated on the day's events.

'Do you suppose the story he told was true?' she wondered aloud.

Daniel shrugged. 'It rang true to me.'

Agnes sighed. 'I've led a sheltered life, it seems.'

He tipped his head to one side. 'Not so very sheltered. Few women of my acquaintance would know how to handle a pistol.'

Agnes felt a flush of pleasure rise to her cheeks at the unexpected praise if that's what it was.

'But what of your parents?' Daniel asked.

'My father was killed at Naseby and my mother died two years later,' Agnes said. 'It was just George and me... until Worcester.'

He paused in skewering a piece of unidentifiable meat. 'Why Worcester?'

'George had been restless for a long time,' she said. 'He was only seventeen when Father died. Too young for the responsibility of my mother and I and also too young for the war.'

'And your sister?'

'She married James before Father's death. After the King's murder, George sent me to live with Ann and James and sold off the estate to pay his debts.'

'And George went to Worcester,' Daniel said in a hard, flat voice.

'Yes, and never came back. He escaped to the continent.'

Daniel quirked an eyebrow in an unspoken *And?*

'He died there. Drank himself to death I was told, although the truth is that he passed out in a drunken stupor on the side of a road one winter's night, caught lung fever, and died within the week.' She sighed. 'He was long lost in drink before he went abroad.' She bit her lip, the grief at her brother's end long since resolved into a dull ache. 'No better than that poor wretch today. What about you, Daniel?'

'My father and my brother are dead. As to the rest of my family, our home was largely destroyed in '48. My mother, sister, grandfather and I were reduced to living in a few habitable rooms. I am hoping they are still there,' he added.

'But why do they believe you to be dead?' Agnes searched his face.

Daniel shrugged. 'I was taken prisoner after Worcester and sent to Barbados. They would have good reason to think me dead.'

'Why?'

His eyes flashed in her direction. 'Because no one returns from Hell.'

She lowered her gaze. 'They would have mourned you,' she said. 'I envy you, going home to a family who loves you.'

She thought of the only family she had left in the world, Henry and Lizzie, and felt the now-familiar tears prick the back of her eyes. She pushed back her chair and excused herself to take solace in the cold dark of the communal bedchamber. Mercifully, there were few travellers at this time of the year and she had the bug-infested bed to herself. She curled into a ball and, clasping the locket, she allowed the silent tears to fall.

CHAPTER 12

*A*lthough they encountered no further trouble, the weather closed in and rain and icy sleet turned the roads into a muddy bog. The inns they stayed in were verminous, the food often inedible, and sodden cloaks and boots did not dry overnight. Even the horses seemed fed up as they trudged along the lanes, cloying mud past their fetlocks, their heads lowered.

To Agnes's credit, she had not uttered one word of complaint, but after the encounter with the footpads she seemed lost in her thoughts and they travelled mostly in silence. Her silence suited Daniel. She had already proved herself too curious about his past and his reasons for being back in England.

The long days gave him ample opportunity to reflect on the lost years, and the stirring of the memories produced a miasma of depression that caused him to wake at night in a cold sweat. Cowardice, he decided. Fear of what he might find if he went in search of his mother and sister was all that stood between him and reconciling himself with what was left of his family.

As he lay awake in the long, dark hours, he thought of the two women alone and unprotected since Kit's death. Had they been left, like Agnes, prey to any man who purported to offer them protection? The resolution to avenge his father's death and his enslavement on Tobias Ashby began to waver.

'This is Bromsgrove.' Agnes's voice jerked him out of his reverie. 'Didn't the landlord of the last inn tell us that the house we seek is not far from Bromsgrove?'

Daniel nodded. A mistake; twin anvils pounded behind his eyes. He had been out of sorts for a couple of days, waking with a headache and sore joints that he attributed to the poor beds and being too long in the saddle after years of not riding. He wanted nothing more than to lie down and sleep.

'Who is this Sir Jonathan Thornton?' Agnes asked.

'I told you. A friend of my brother's.'

'Your dead brother?'

'I only had one brother.'

'And did he die in the war?'

'No.'

She studied him through narrowed eyes. 'So how did he die?'

Daniel huffed out a breath, watching it cloud in the cold, damp air. 'You ask a lot of questions, Agnes.'

She shrugged. 'I'm a curious woman, Daniel.'

No point in hiding the truth when it was public knowledge. 'If you must know, he was hanged five years ago for his part in a plot to kill Cromwell.' He turned to look at her. 'Agnes, do you mind another night in an inn? It's too late in the day to go on to Seven Ways.'

Agnes nodded and pointed to a neat half-timbered inn. 'The Black Cross. We can lodge there.'

Daniel saw the horses stabled and tramped into the inn. The landlady met him at the foot of the stairs.

'Your sister's already gone up. Leave yer boots, sir. I'll have 'em cleaned.'

Daniel sat down on the steps and pulled off the mud-encrusted boots. No doubt the good woman did not want mud tramped across her well-scrubbed floors.

'Where are you bound?' the woman asked.

'I'm seeking a house called Seven Ways, near here, I believe. Can you give me directions?'

A grin lit the woman's amiable, once-pretty face. 'Seven Ways? Yer after the Thorntons?'

At Daniel's affirmation, she nodded. 'Aye, I know the house well. An hour's ride, no more. Take the Kidderminster Road and ye'll not miss it. Red brick gates with round stones on the gatepost, and when you gets there tell Sir Jonathan that Sal at the Black Cross sends her love. Now, if you don't mind me sayin', you look dead on your feet, sir. I'll have hot water and supper sent up to your room if that suits you.'

Daniel ran a hand through his hair and nodded. Picking up the disreputable footwear, Sal bustled away in the direction of the kitchen. Daniel pulled himself to his feet. Turning he saw Agnes standing at the head of the stairs.

'She's right, you don't look at all well.'

'I'm fine. Just a little tired,' Daniel said curtly.

He wanted his bed, not a conversation, but Agnes seemed not to notice and followed him into the bedchamber. Daniel set his bag down on the floor and collapsed into a chair by the cheerful fire and pulled off his damp stockings, setting them to dry on the hearth.

'Please do me a favour and pass me my bag,' he said.

Agnes complied and, handing him the bag, said, 'Daniel. Is there anything ... '

'I'm fine!' he snapped. 'Just tired. Leave me, Agnes, and tell the land-lady I don't want any supper. I would rather be well rested to meet with Sir Jonathan tomorrow.'

She studied him, her head slightly cocked to one side. She knew he lied. He was not well. Daniel knew the symptoms, knew what they presaged, and just prayed he would make it to Seven Ways the next day.

'This Sir Jonathan, how well do you know him?' she asked.

'I met him once, a long time ago,' Daniel replied. 'Worcester ... ' he tailed off, remembering Colonel Thornton, a tall man with a lean, hand-some face, leaning forward in the candlelight, his mouth a grim line, his eyes glinting with the reflection of the flame as he said:

"Daniel, war has nothing to do with glory and honour. Have you ever smelt

the stench of death? Have you ever seen a man with his guts hanging out and still living, or a man with his face shot away? Have you watched a friend die of gangrene?"

Daniel had dreamed of glory and honour but Jonathan Thornton had been right. By the end of the following day, Daniel had seen all of those things and had cause to wish more than anything else that he had done as his brother had told him, and stayed at home.

CHAPTER 13

SEVEN WAYS, WORCESTERSHIRE, 12 NOVEMBER 1659

'This must be it,' Agnes said. 'Red brick gateposts and round things?'

The landlady of the Black Cross had been correct in her description, although the red brick gateposts had seen better days and one of the finely carved stone balls had fallen off its lopsided support and lay on the verge of the road with long strands of dying grass winding around it. Two iron gates hung drunkenly from the leaning supports, the coat of arms that had once been painted on a central oval long since faded and flaked away.

Agnes glanced at Daniel. He had turned breakfast away when it was offered and she knew he had not eaten the night before. His face had a sallow hue, his eyes sunken, the whites tinged with yellow. He shivered and hunched his shoulders, drawing his cloak tighter around him.

'Daniel, you are ... '

'I'm fine,' he interrupted her. 'Didn't sleep well. Let's get this over with. Just want to deliver these letters and we'll be on our way.' His words sounded slurred and she glanced at him in alarm.

They turned their horses onto a weed-infested, potholed driveway that curved around through trees concealing a long, low, red-bricked manor house surrounded by a moat from the road. Smoke curled from a couple of chimneys and as they approached, a groom came out from under the gatehouse, gesturing for them to cross the bridge. He took the reins of the horse and Daniel slid from the saddle, reaching up to assist Agnes down from her mare. His steadying hand on her elbow shook and she scrutinised his ashen face, her anxiety about his condition growing with every minute.

'How may I be of assistance?' The thin reedy voice of an elderly man came from the main door.

Daniel turned to face him. 'I have business with Sir Jonathan Thornton,' he said, his voice sounding oddly hoarse.

'May I say what the business concerns?'

Daniel ran a hand across his eyes and enunciated each word with almost deliberate care as if the act of speaking had become an effort. 'It is with Sir Jonathan alone.'

The steward stood his ground and Agnes took a step toward Daniel, as he swayed forward, catching himself with a shake of his head.

'At least give me your name, sir,' the steward persisted.

'Lovell … ' Daniel began. 'Oh, curse it.'

He slid to the ground in an ungainly heap.

Agnes and the steward stared at Daniel's crumpled body for the beat of several seconds before Agnes dropped to her knees, her hand going to his forehead.

'He's burning with fever,' she said and, looking up, addressed the elderly steward. 'Get help now.'

'I'll be fine in a moment. Just need a rest.' Daniel murmured without opening his eyes. She lifted his head onto her lap and stroked his forehead.

'You're not fine. How long have you been unwell?'

'It's been threatening for the last day. I hoped to be … ' A shudder convulsed his body.

A rustle of skirts announced the arrival of help; two women, one the lady of the house, to judge from her gown of fine blue wool and lace-edged collar and cuffs, and an older woman in plain russet.

Agnes's mind ran through all the possible ailments that matched Daniel's symptoms.

The steward said it for her, in a tone heavy with certainty. 'Plague, m'lady.'

Everyone around her recoiled and Agnes looked up into the anxious faces of the strangers on whose doorstep Daniel had just collapsed. 'We've just come from London but there's no plague there. At least I don't think so.'

Daniel opened one eye and another shudder shook him.

'Don't be ridiculous,' he managed. 'It's marsh fever. I've had it before.'

Everyone visibly relaxed. Able-bodied servants were summoned, and with an almost practised efficiency, Daniel was carried into the house and up two flights of stairs. The servants deposited him on a large feather bed in a guest bedchamber. The two women followed the strange procession, with Agnes bringing up the rear and another servant carrying their bags.

The older woman went straight to the bed and leaned over Daniel, untying his cloak strings.

'What's yer name, lad?' She spoke with a strong northern accent.

'Daniel Lovell,' he murmured in response.

'Aye well, ye've quite a fever on you. Marsh fever, you say.'

He gave a quick inclination of his head, grimacing.

'Ellen, I've some feverfew in the still room,' her mistress said. 'And sorrel ... '

The older woman looked up at her mistress. 'We can try, Mistress, but if it's marsh fever the only remedy is Jesuit Bark and we've naught any of that. A king's ransom won't buy us enough.'

Daniel clutched at the arm of the older woman. 'I have Jesuit Bark. Agnes ... ' He raised his head, looking around the room as if searching for something. 'It's in my bag.'

Standing at the end of the bed, feeling utterly useless, Agnes jumped at her name. Daniel's back arched as a spasm of fever went through him, and the two women turned to look at her.

'What does Jesuit Bark look like?' she asked.

The older woman gave her a withering glare. 'It looks like what it is, the bark of a tree. Hurry, lass.'

Agnes went through Daniel's leather satchel, scattering his few possessions around her until she found a parcel wrapped in oiled cloth at the bottom of the pack The other women gathered around her as she unwrapped it.

'I'm sorry, I have not introduced myself. I am Lady Katherine Thornton,' the woman in the blue dress said. 'And this is Ellen Howell.'

'Lady Thornton?' Agnes looked up and the woman nodded. 'I'm sorry we had to arrive in so dramatic a manner. It would not be how Daniel planned it.'

'And you are?' Lady Thornton prompted. Like the older woman, her voice bore traces of a northern origin.

Agnes felt the heat rise to her cheeks. 'Agnes Fletcher – Daniel's ... ' she was going to say "sister", as she had said at every inn for the past days. She shook her head. 'Daniel's friend ... travelling companion ... '

Lady Thornton smiled. 'There will be time enough for explanations later.' She held up what looked to Agnes to be sticks of dried bark. 'So this is Jesuit Bark.' She turned back to the bed. 'You are fortunate to be carrying it, young man.'

'Always have it ... never know when the fever will hit ... ' He squeezed his eyes tight shut as another tremor ran through his long body.

Lady Thornton handed the sticks to Ellen. 'You know what needs to be done?'

The woman nodded. 'I'll go and prepare an infusion,' she said.

'And we will make our patient more comfortable. Mistress Fletcher, will you help me strip him?'

Daniel's eyes shot open and he clutched at his jacket fastenings with shaking hands. 'Not Agnes.'

Agnes regarded him, with her hands on her hips. 'I've seen a naked man before.'

'But not me ... ' Daniel protested, with a clarity that belied his fevered state.

Lady Thornton looked across at Agnes, her lips tight with compressed laughter. 'If you're going to be coy, Master Lovell,' she said, 'Perhaps Mistress Fletcher had better leave the room.'

The man beneath her hands stilled. 'Please. I can see to myself ... '

'With these tremors?' Kate picked up one of his hands. 'We'll make do and mend. Mistress Fletcher, perhaps you can find Ellen and bring up water and cloths. She will be in the still room. Go down the stairs to the ground floor, and the still room is just before the kitchen.'

Agnes hurried down the stairs. As she reached the next level a door flew open, and a tall man in his late thirties stood in the doorway, his hands on his hips. His shirtsleeves were rolled up and a smudge of ink ran across the bridge of his long nose as if he had been scratching it with the wrong end of a pen.

'What is all this commotion?' he demanded and, seeing Agnes, he frowned. 'Who are you?'

Agnes dropped a curtsey. 'Agnes Fletcher – and you are Sir Jonathan Thornton?'

'Yes, but ... ' He ran a hand through his dark hair, the light catching silver strands. 'My apologies, Mistress Fletcher, I am working on the accounts and it makes me forget my manners.' He rolled the cuffs of his shirt down. 'I wasn't aware we were expecting guests. What brings you to Seven Ways?'

Agnes glanced at the stairs. 'My friend, Daniel Lovell ... '

He started at the name. 'Lovell? Daniel Lovell, did you say? Good God. Where is he?'

'Unfortunately, he has been taken ill – I was just going to find Mistress Howell.'

Thornton waved a hand in the direction of the lower floor while looking up in the direction from which Agnes had come.

'She'll be in the still room. Is Kate with him?'

Kate? Katherine ...

'Yes, she is,' Agnes replied.

Thornton relaxed, and for the first time, a smile lifted his lean face. 'Then he is in good hands. A poor welcome I am afraid, Mistress Fletcher. You continue on your errand, I'll not detain you.'

Despite the vague directions, Agnes found the still room. Dried hanks of herbs hung from nails in the ceiling and the walls were lined with shelves of jars and bottles. The room smelled of herbs and honey. It reminded her of her mother's still room from which had issued unguents and potions for all ailments and ills.

Ellen looked up from stirring a pot over a small fire. 'Come for the brew, have ye?' she said.

Agnes hovered uncertainly in the doorway while Ellen stirred the kettle. Anyone more like a witch would have been hard to imagine.

'I've come for water and cloths,' she said.

Ellen's sharp eyes appraised Agnes. 'Don't ye fret,' she said. 'I've seen worse.'

'I'm not fretting,' Agnes said, but her voice lacked conviction.

She couldn't imagine herself being cast adrift from Daniel Lovell, not that he had given her the slightest encouragement to form any sort of attachment. She had clung to him because he had shown her kindness when she needed a friend, and he was her means of getting to Charvaley. Nothing more but he was all she had.

'I've plenty of lasses come to me seeking the means to turn a young man's head,' Ellen said.

Agnes stared at her, aghast. 'I've no need of love potions and no wish to use one,' she said archly.

Ellen nodded and turned back to her work. 'As ye wish. We need to bring the fever down. There's cold water in that jug.' She indicated a large clay jug sitting beside a metal basin. 'Take those up, and ye'll find some clean cloths in that cupboard. Tell Mistress I'll be a while yet. It needs time to steep.'

The sound of voices drifted out of the half-open door as Agnes, balancing jug and basin and cloths, reached the guest bedchamber.

'Have you seen his back?' The voice was Jonathan Thornton's.

Agnes paused, her hand on the door, as Kate's soft voice responded, 'Dear God, who would do that to another human being?'

'Ah, Kate. These are cruel times we live in. Have you forgotten how ill they treated me?'

'No,' Kate's voice held a tremor. 'I'll never forget ... or forgive.'

Agnes knocked on the door and opened it slowly. She had thought to allow the couple sufficient time to collect themselves but found them in an embrace, Kate's head resting on her husband's chest, his arms around her.

The tenderness of the gesture touched her. James had never been outwardly demonstrative with her, or indeed his wife, in public or private. Whatever rumours may have been rife in Charvaley, their public behaviour had never been anything less than entirely proper.

The man on the bed moaned and flung himself onto his side, the sheets tangling around his hips, exposing his back to her. Agnes recoiled, the metal bowl slipping from her grasp. It hit the floor with a deafening clang. Jonathan retrieved it and set it on a table. Recovering her composure, Agnes set the jug down.

She understood now what Daniel had not wanted her to see. James had once had a miscreant whipped for stealing fruit from the orchard and had made the entire household watch as a deterrent. The man had twisted and screamed under the lash but the result had been nothing like this.

The interlaced pattern of heavy scars across the hard muscles of Daniel's back had been laid on with a vicious ferocity that should have killed him.

'They used a whip with a metal end,' Jonathan Thornton said, 'It would have torn the flesh from his bones.'

Agnes tore her gaze away from Daniel and looked up at him. 'How does anyone survive such a thing?'

Kate Thornton straightened. 'Luck and a strong will. Where did this happen?'

'It must have been Barbados,' Agnes said.

Jonathan raised an eyebrow and gave a low whistle. 'They sent him to Barbados? Good God, they may as well have given him a death sentence.'

As if aware of the audience gathered around him, Daniel rolled back onto his back and opened his eyes. He squinted up into Agnes's face.

'I thought I told you to go away,' he mumbled.

'You did, but I'm not going anywhere. It would be extremely inconvenient if you were to die on me,' Agnes responded.

He tried to laugh, but it turned into a cough.

Ellen entered the room with a flask and a beaker in her hands. With the practice of two people long used to working together, Kate raised Daniel's head and Ellen administered a decent dose of the tincture of Jesuit Bark.

Daniel swore and coughed, screwing up his face in disgust. 'Filthy stuff.'

'Aye, it may well be, but nothing that's good for you was ever made to taste pleasant. I think ye know that lad,' Ellen said, laying him back on the bolsters.

'He needs to rest,' Kate said. 'Mistress Fletcher, you must be exhausted from your travels. Let me show you to a room and I can arrange for a bath ... '

Agnes shook her head, her eyes only for the man on the bed.

'I will sit with him a while,' she said and looked up at Kate with an apologetic smile. 'This is not what Daniel would have wanted and I ... we ... would not wish to inconvenience you any more than we have. I can see to him.'

Kate Thornton's calm, grey eyes rested on her for a long moment.

'Very well. He is your friend; of course, you may sit with him. I advocate that you bathe his face and wrists to try and cool the fever. Ellen will come and relieve you later.'

Agnes waited until the others had left the room, although Ellen seemed somewhat reluctant to leave her patient in Agnes's inexperienced hands.

Taking a deep breath, she poured the cool water into the basin. Soaking one of the cloths, she perched on the side of the bed and sat there, holding the damp cloth in her hands, suddenly afraid to touch him with a degree of intimacy that their relationship had not permitted up until now.

In his austere dark clothes he gave an impression of being of slight build, but naked, at least from the waist up, his hard muscles confirmed the evidence of a life lived in physical labour.

He opened one eye. 'Still here?' he enquired.

'Yes, and I'm not going anywhere. You're stuck with me.'

He sighed and closed his eyes as a feverish tremor shook his body.

Agnes knew nothing of marsh fever, except that once a person contracted it, it returned again and again – and it could kill. After everything this man had endured, he could not die here, so close to home, and she would do whatever lay within her power to keep him alive. Even if that one thing was prayer.

His left hand lay outside the covers and she picked it up, turning it over. There were scars on his palm and calluses on the long fingers that curled with a curious vulnerability. She touched the cool cloth to the inside of his wrist, where the blood flowed closest to the skin. He turned his head away from her.

Using the cloth she began to stroke the long muscles of his arm, feeling the hardness beneath the fabric of the cloth. He gave a sharply indrawn breath and she looked up.

'Do you want me to stop?'

He shook his head. 'No, it feels … ' His eyelids flickered. ' … Nice.'

She ran the cloth across his chest, dampening the dark hair into soft whorls.

'Why didn't you tell me you were ill? We could have stopped … '

'I hoped it would pass. I didn't want to give into it … not in an inn. You wouldn't have known what to do,' he murmured, closing his eyes again.

'You must think very poorly of me,' she bridled.

He didn't reply and appeared to be asleep. She brushed a lock of hair away from his eyes. 'I can't let you die,' she whispered. 'You are my only hope of seeing my son … ' She broke off, her heart pounding at the disastrous slip, but if Daniel had heard her, he gave no sign.

CHAPTER 14

D aniel had been walking for miles, through a swamp wreathed
in mist. He could see the tree he sought but it never seemed
to grow any closer. The mud sucked at his boots and hands reached out
through the swirling miasma, clutching at his clothes, holding him back.
His breath churned in his chest in his efforts to reach the tree, and now
as the haze cleared he could see that it was not a tree but a gallows raised
high on a hillock, and a figure danced and twisted at the end of a badly
tied rope.

'Kit!' He screamed his brother's name as the figure stilled, turning a
mask of rotting flesh to look at him, the mouldering lips pulled back in a
macabre death's head grin.

'Hush.' A woman's voice pierced the fog and he jerked himself awake
the nightmare receding.

It took a moment for his breathing to still. A cool cloth brushed his
forehead and he forced his eyes open, blinking to allow the face above
him to come into focus. A woman ... a young woman with a heart-
shaped face and hazel eyes that gleamed gold in the light of the single
candle she held in her hand. She had taken off that awful linen cap and
soft, brown hair curled around her face.

'Agnes?"

She smiled and set the candle down. 'I'm here.'

'Where am I ... are we?'

He tried to sit up but she firmly pushed him back onto the bolsters.

'Seven Ways, the home of Sir Jonathan Thornton. You brought us here – remember?'

He had a brief, shaming memory of collapsing on the doorstep. Not quite the impression he would have wished to make on his brother's old friend.

He reached up and touched her cheek, soft as his mother's satin dress.

'Did I tell you that I like your freckles?' he said.

She frowned. 'My freckles?'

He traced the scatter across her nose. 'I'll count them. One ... two ... '

She should have batted his hand away and told him to stop being foolish; instead, she caught it and held it against her cheek for a long moment.

'I thought you were going to die,' she said, her voice uneven.

He extricated his hand from her grasp and pinched the bridge of his nose. 'After all the times in my life I could have died, it would be very annoying to die in a comfortable bed in England,' he said, adding, 'But unfortunately for me, the worst is yet to come.'

'But your fever is down,' she said.

'In an hour or so the ague will be back.' He took a deep, shuddering breath as he lay back on the bolsters. 'In the West Indies, at a certain time of the year, they have terrible storms that rage and destroy all in their wake, and suddenly it is calm and the sun comes out. That is the worst time of all because you know the storm will return, worse than before. The fever is like that.'

She swallowed. 'Ellen said to give you the infusion of Jesuit Bark when you woke.'

He nodded and she turned away. Liquid sloshed from a jug and she returned to the bed with a horn beaker. Sliding her arm beneath his shoulders, she lifted his head and he grimaced at the familiar taste of Jesuit Bark. Without it, he would have died years ago.

He swallowed the last of the bitter brew and asked for water. She refilled the beaker and he insisted on taking it from her, controlling his shaking hand with a supreme effort. It galled him to be physically weakened and reliant on this woman, of all women.

'I have some broth. It will take but a moment to warm it.'

He nodded and she turned away from him, busying herself beside the fireplace, where a cheerful glow lit the old, darkened timbers of the ceiling.

'So you've had this fever before?' She had her back to him as she stirred a pot on the fire.

'Several times. It is the legacy of my time in the West Indies.'

'But you've come through it?'

He shrugged. 'The attacks are further apart and not so severe,' he said. 'They get it in the Low Countries from where I have just come. That and the soaking of the last few days…'

She returned to stand by the bed, holding a wooden bowl in her hand. All trace of humour had gone from her face.

'It's not your only legacy of Barbados,' she said. 'I've seen your back, Daniel.'

The breath caught in his throat. No choice but to bluster his way out of it.

'Not pretty, is it?'

'Lady Thornton says you should have died.'

'I nearly did.'

'Why? What did you do?'

He pulled himself up in the bed. The distress in her voice betrayed the shock she must have felt – as any woman must feel. There had been a girl in Fort Royal who had recoiled from him and refused to touch him. That memory still stung like a raw nerve.

The spoon rattled in the bowl she held as she trembled – with cold, or emotion?

'Who did it?' she asked in a tight voice.

He shut his eyes and took a deep breath. How could he explain a man like Outhwaite, who delighted not only in the subjugation of his fellow man but the infliction of pain?

'It was a long time ago. I survived. I escaped. Are you going to give me that broth or let it go cold?'

She looked down at the bowl in her hand as if she had forgotten she held it. 'Do you need help?'

He glared at her. 'I can feed myself, thank you,' he said, and she handed him the bowl.

'Is Kit your brother?' she asked.

His hand jerked, spilling some of the soup on the bedclothes.

Agnes had cloths to hand and as she sponged the sheets, she said, 'You called his name in your sleep.'

He handed her the bowl and lay back, the memory of the dream still harsh and clear. 'Yes, Kit is … was … my brother. I dreamed I saw him on the gallows – a rotting corpse.'

She regarded him, her head slightly on one side, a gesture he had come to recognize in their short acquaintance.

'Were you close to your brother?' she asked.

Close? Had he been close to Kit? There had been a ten-year age difference and he had worshipped the ground Kit walked on, driving him mad when Kit graced Eveleigh with his presence. But Kit had always shown great patience with his young brother. Daniel smiled at the memory of his brother teaching him how to use a sword. He lacked Kit's natural grace and ability, but he had tried so hard.

'Yes, as close as we could be given he was ten years my senior,' he said. 'When the war broke out he and my father raised a regiment in support of the King. They fought side by side through the years of the war, returning home with stories of adventure and great victories. I yearned to join them and ride into battle under the banner of the Midhursts, side by side with my father and brother – all in the King's cause. Guardians of the Crown.' He could not hide the bitterness in his voice at the last words.

Agnes frowned. 'The Midhursts?'

He glanced at her. What harm in her knowing?

'My grandfather is – was, I can only assume he is dead now – Lord Midhurst.'

'So if your father and brother are now dead, does that make you Lord Midhurst?'

Daniel's tired mind grappled with that concept – grandfather, father, older brother, all dead.

'I suppose I am – whatever that means,' he said.

A smile caught at the corners of Agnes's mouth and she laid her hand over his, her mouth curving in amusement. 'Don't expect me to start calling you *my Lord* ... my Lord.'

He smiled in response, and his fingers closed around hers. *Such a little hand*, he thought.

'Go on with the story,' she said.

His eyes felt heavy. He needed to sleep and gather his strength for the next bout of the fever, but the dark and the candlelight and a desire to talk after all the years of silence had loosened his tongue. 'It all ended for us when the country rose again in '48. Kit and my father fought at the Battle of Preston and lost. They returned to Eveleigh with half the Parliamentary army on their tail. The house had never been built for a siege and my father surrendered, only to be shot in cold blood on the steps of his own home by ... '

Agnes's fingers tightened on his and she finished the sentence for him. 'Tobias Ashby?'

Daniel closed his eyes. 'Tobias Ashby. Before my father was even buried, he ordered the house destroyed. He took Kit prisoner, but some-where along the way Kit escaped and fled to France, leaving us all but destitute with only a few habitable rooms to live in.'

It was the next part that made the hard telling; Kit's return in 1651, full of braggartly tales of how the King would march into England and claim his throne. The angry confrontation with Daniel's mother, when Daniel had announced he would go with his brother. Anger ... so much anger. It seemed to be all he could remember now.

He swallowed. 'I followed Kit to Worcester with dreams of honour and glory ... and revenge for my father's death. The battle itself was anything except that.' The pressure on his fingers encouraged him to go on and his voice cracked as he said, 'I saw Kit fall just before the butt of musket took me down. When I came around I was a prisoner in Worcester Cathedral, and the nightmare had only just begun.' He turned his face away so she wouldn't see the pain that the illness would not let him disguise.

'You're tired. You should sleep while you can,' Agnes said. She pushed back a strand of hair from his damp forehead. Her touch sent a wave of fire through him and he shivered.

He nodded, his eyes heavy, sleep already beginning to steal up on him. 'I thought Kit had died but he didn't. He lived to die at the end of a hangman's rope.'

Agnes sighed and her hand softly brushed his face, probably as she would gentle the boy ... what was his name ... Henry?

Some recollection from his fever drifted into his consciousness. Something about the child. *My son* – she had said that, hadn't she?

The malaise washed through him and he could no longer retain his hold on the world; it dipped and slid, breaking into a multitude of colours and shapes.

CHAPTER 15

'Outhwaite! I'll see you hang for this.' Daniel sat bolt upright, his eyes wide and blazing with anger and fever.

Agnes caught his shoulders and tried to ease him back onto the bolsters but he fought her off, his flailing arm catching the side of her head. She staggered backwards, stars reeling before her eyes. The ague had returned, as he predicted, only worse than before.

'Outhwaite!' He screamed the name before falling back, his breath coming in laboured gasps.

Regaining her composure, Agnes returned to his side, with a wet cloth in her hand. 'Daniel, hush. He's not here. He's gone.'

She attempted to lay the cloth on his burning forehead, but he knocked her hand away. She stroked his temple and wondered if this man, Outhwaite, bore the responsibility for the scars that marred Daniel's back. *So many secrets for such a young man.*

The man beneath her hands quieted, and entwining her fingers with his, she laid her head on the bed. 'Live,' she whispered. 'Please don't die.'

She must have dozed. The creak of the door jerked her awake and the faint grey light of dawn illumined the room. The smell of fresh-baked bread preceded Ellen, who paused in the doorway studying the disordered bed, the restless man, and the exhausted woman.

She set the covered tray she carried on the table and straightened, fixing Agnes with a hard, unsympathetic eye.

'Ye've done enough,' she said. 'Got him through the worst of it. Now you need to rest. Can't have two of you ill.'

Agnes nodded and rose to her feet, too weary for conscious thought.

'You'll wake me if there's any change?'

'Only if it's for the worse. Ye'll find your bag and a bed made up for ye two doors down from this one,' the woman said and shooed her from the room.

Agnes followed the directions, suddenly so tired she could barely lift her feet. She opened the door to a pleasant, light-filled chamber. Hot water steamed in an ewer beside a basin and fresh towels had been laid out for her. A clean, soft, much-mended nightdress that did not belong to Agnes lay across the bed.

She studied her disreputable reflection in the mirror. Her hair badly needed a wash and her eyes were circled with dark rings. She sank onto a stool and buried her face in her hands. In the past month she had lost everything and everyone she held dear. It would be easy to curl up on the floor and surrender. *Too easy.*

Taking a deep breath, she stripped off her travel-stained clothes. Standing naked on a homespun rug that covered the floor, she inspected the innumerable bug bites that were the legacy of the inns they had stayed at. The itching drove her to distraction and she thought to ask Ellen Howell if she had some sort of lotion to ease the discomfort.

Pouring the hot water into the basin, she found a bar of sweetly-scented soap had been left for her and washed thoroughly from head to toe. Pulling the too-big nightdress over her head, she fell into the warm embrace of a soft down mattress and was asleep the moment her head touched the pillow.

CHAPTER 16

*A*gnes stretched her arms above her head and took a deep breath, revelling in the pleasure of lying between clean sheets redolent with the scent of lavender. From beyond the window, she could hear the sounds of the life of the manor house; a woman singing, her sweet voice rising into a tuneful soprano over the sounds of horses' hooves on cobbles.

Within the house, a young child cried and music – someone playing the virginals with a deft, sure touch – drifted around her. All these things that Agnes had lost and for which she longed with a yearning that was physical pain.

From the gloom, she surmised it must be evening. She had slept a deep and dreamless sleep and as she sat up her stomach growled, reminding her she hadn't eaten for twenty-four hours.

The door creaked open and a maid entered the room, carrying a pile of neatly folded clothes.

'Oh good, ye're awake,' the girl said. 'My name's Essie. I took the liberty of pressing your petticoats and washed your linens. They may be a little damp, so I'll hang 'em in front of the fire.'

The girl proceeded to hang Agnes's chemise and petticoat over the back of the chair. She turned to Agnes, a smile on her broad, cheerful face. 'If I help you dress, ye'll be in time to join the family for supper.'

Pushing her disordered hair from her face, Agnes glanced at the window. 'What time is it?'

'Four in the evening or thereabouts. It'll be dark soon.'

'I didn't mean to sleep so long.' Agnes swung her feet out of bed and stood up, stretching.

'Her Ladyship gave orders you were not to be disturbed,' the girl replied. 'And she said to tell you, your friend's fever is broken and he's sleeping soundly, so nothing to worry about. You want me to help you with your gown?'

Agnes let the girl help her on with her skirts and lace her firmly into the only clean gown Agnes possessed. With expert fingers, the maid twisted and pulled Agnes's hair into a neat coil in the nape of her neck, with curls framing her face. The effect was charming. It seemed a long time since Agnes had done anything more with her hair than force it under the hideous cap.

'Ye'll do,' Essie said, standing back to admire her handiwork.

Agnes attempted to smooth the worst of the creases from her skirts.

'Where will I find the family?'

'In the winter they eat in the parlour. I'll take ye down.'

As she passed Daniel's door, Agnes asked Essie to wait. She pushed open the door and entered. Daniel lay on his back in the disordered bedclothes, one arm outflung above his head and his face turned away from the door. Ellen dozed in a chair by the fireplace.

Agnes crossed the room, the floorboards creaking at her approach, but neither Ellen nor Daniel stirred. At the bedside, she looked down at the sleeping man. Beneath the tan his face was grey, his eyes deep sunken in coal-smudged pits. The scar across his cheekbone seemed to stand out more sharply in relief, but from the steady rise and fall of his chest, he seemed to be sleeping untroubled by fever.

She bent and brushed his forehead with her lips. He stirred and muttered, turning his head away, but did not wake. She closed her eyes and said a silent prayer of thanks before tiptoeing out of the room.

The Thornton family had gathered around a table in a pleasant parlour. A clattering of chairs greeted her entrance as the two men rose to greet her. Lady Thornton greeted her with a smile and indicated the place that had been set for her next to a young man who bore a strong resemblance to Sir Jonathan.

'I apologise for being late,' Agnes said as she took her seat.

'Not at all,' Lady Thornton said. 'You were beyond exhaustion. I hope you feel a little more rested now?'

Agnes nodded. 'I am indeed. Your bed is extremely comfortable.'

Lady Thornton smiled.

'Now, some introductions are in order,' Sir Jonathan said.

'To your right, Thomas Ashley ...' and so the introductions proceeded around the table. The shy girl with a heart-shaped face, who smiled at her shyly from under downcast eyes, was introduced as Tabitha Thornton, Jonathan's daughter. The fair-haired woman, a few years older than Agnes, was Lady Eleanor Longley, and the young girl of ten or twelve who sat beside her, Lady Eleanor's daughter, Anne.

'We didn't think we would inflict the small ones on you tonight,' Lady Thornton said with a smile.

Agnes returned the smile, thinking of the fretful child she had heard as she woke. 'I do hope to meet them. I miss my own ... well, not mine exactly, but they have been in my care since they were born.'

'Whose children are they?' Lady Thornton enquired.

Lady Thornton's calm gaze rested on her face and Agnes had the unnerving feeling the woman could see right into her soul and sense the lie, or at least the half-truth.

She gathered herself and managed a smile. 'My nephew and niece.'

Lady Thornton frowned. 'And what has become of them?'

Everyone at the table turned to her. Agnes looked from one curious face to the other. No point in lies, not here in this company, so Agnes told them her story, concluding, 'and Master Lovell very kindly offered to escort me at least part of the way to Charvaley.'

'But if they have been given into the legal guardianship of this man Ashby, what do you hope to accomplish once you reach there?' Lady Thornton enquired.

What indeed, Agnes thought.

She looked down at the soup in her bowl, her stomach rumbling its protest at her tardiness.

'I hope to satisfy myself that the children are well and happy,' she said without much conviction in her tone.

Agnes caught the quick glance that flicked between Sir Jonathan and his wife. The more she said it, the more foolish her journey seemed. Tobias Ashby could just turn her away at the gate and she had no legal standing, no right to demand entry. Her only right was to demand the return of her few possessions still at Charvaley. Nothing more.

She picked up the spoon and began to eat, but the talk of Henry and Lizzie had numbed the hunger pangs. Around her, the family chattered about the day-to-day matters of life at Seven Ways. Their obvious closeness and the apparent ordinariness of their lives only served to twist the knife in Agnes's heart.

CHAPTER 17

*D*aniel stared up at the red woollen bed hangings. As if being ill and helpless in the company of strangers was not bad enough, to be ill and helpless in front of Agnes Fletcher was humiliating.

Little snatches of memory came back to him. Had he really tried to count her freckles?

At that thought, he smiled. She had charming freckles. Perhaps one day she might let him finish counting them. And she had sat with him all that long night. She didn't have to do that. After all, they had known each other for such a short time. They were strangers … or had been strangers. His fingers tightened on the sheets. She had seen Outhwaite's legacy. After that, there could be few secrets between them.

The malaise that always settled on him after a bout of marsh fever cast him into dark places and rendered him incapable of thought, let alone action. He knew how this went. It could be days, if not weeks before he would be fit enough to continue the journey.

The door opened and the goodwife, Ellen Howell, bustled in, carrying a pile of folded linen. In their short acquaintance, he had learned that Mistress Howell was not a woman to be trifled with. She brooked no nonsense and neither did she cosset and fuss – although he had to admit that Agnes had not cosseted or fussed either. Agnes had sat beside him while the fever shook him, ready with a cool cloth and a comforting touch.

Since the fever had broken he had seen only Ellen, with her acerbic tongue, ready supply of noxious potions, and clean bed linen.

'I've found this for you,' she said and handed him an old, patched but clean nightshirt.

She crossed her arms and regarded him with an unblinking gaze as he pulled it on.

'Satisfy my curiosity, lad,' she said. 'That beating would have killed a lesser man. How did you survive it?'

'I nearly didn't,' he said, and when she remained silent, he added, 'I think it involved sea water and maggots.'

In truth, he had little memory of those first few days aboard *L'Archange*. The rough ministrations of a former slave who called himself Baptiste had been all that kept death away.

He preferred not to think about the maggots but Ellen continued, 'I'm a great believer in maggots,' she said, more to herself than him. 'Saved many a man with a suppurating wound.'

'You know a lot about suppurating wounds?'

'Aye, I do. More than a body should. They brought the wounded to us after Marston Moor, the mistress's husband among them.'

'Sir Jonathan?'

Ellen shook her head. 'No, her first husband.' Her lips tightened and she looked away. 'I couldn't save him.'

'I'm sorry,' Daniel said.

She sniffed and squared her shoulders. 'Aye, well. That's as may be. God blessed her with a good man and some fine, bonny bairns. And you my lad ... I've an unguent that would help soften the scars. Just get that pretty girl o' yours to do that once a day and ye'll be a new man.'

Daniel felt the colour rising to his cheeks. 'I think you mistake my relationship with Mistress Fletcher,' he mumbled.

The thought of Agnes bending over him and applying any sort of unguent to the scars on his back provoked mixed thoughts. On the one hand, a very physical part of him responded to the possibility of her soft hands. On the other hand, the mere thought that Agnes had seen his back and the hideous scars mortified him.

Something like a smile twitched Ellen's craggy features. 'Is that so?'

As if summoned, the door opened and Agnes herself entered, carrying a tray. She set it down across his knees.

'Soup,' she said. 'Lady Thornton insists you eat it all.'

Daniel glared at the invalid pap in the bowl. 'I would hate to disappoint Lady Thornton, but if she keeps feeding me this she will never be rid of me.'

Agnes cast him a sharp glance and Ellen put her hands on her hips and, addressing Agnes, said, 'When they start to get churlish and difficult, ye know they're on the mend.'

Daniel looked up, the spoon halfway to his mouth. 'I'm not being difficult. There are things I have to do. I just don't have time to … '

Ellen raised an eyebrow. 'Time to what, my lad? Ye're not going anywhere until I'm satisfied that ye're strong enough. Now eat that soup. Every last drop. Now I've better things to do than prattle with you.' She dropped a curtsey in Agnes's direction. 'Mistress Fletcher.'

Daniel waited until the door had closed and the sound of Ellen's firm footsteps had disappeared. 'She scares me more than the captain of the *Archangel*,' he said.

Agnes sat down on the edge of the bed. 'Me too, but she's right, Daniel. We are not going anywhere until you are quite well. I was … ' She looked away, her throat working. 'I was so scared I was going to lose you.'

'Why? As has just been pointed out, I've been nothing but rude and churlish and I've surely given you no reason to wish me well.'

She flashed him a sharp glance. 'You've given me every reason to wish you well. You have been a friend when I needed one, however base your motives.'

Daniel took another mouthful of the soup. Despite his protests about it being invalid pap, it was thick with vegetables and pieces of chicken and tasted wonderful.

'There are things in my past, Agnes … '

She raised her chin, a gesture he had come to recognize. For a tiny person, she had a strong will, and he suspected she brooked no nonsense, not from the children in her care ... or him.

'I've seen your back, Daniel Lovell. It tells its own story and I'll not ask you about it if you don't wish to tell me.'

He set the spoon back in the near-empty bowl. 'Thank you.' In truth, he had no idea how to even begin telling that particular story. He changed the subject. 'Is there a Lady Longley in this house?'

Agnes nodded. 'Lady Eleanor Longley is Sir Jonathan's sister.'

'I have some letters for her in my satchel, but I would like to see her.'

'Lady Longley?' Agnes frowned. 'I thought your business was with Sir Jonathan.'

'I met her husband, and he asked me to carry his letters for him. I thought maybe she would want some news of him too.'

'I'll fetch her.'

After Agnes left the room, Daniel set the tray aside, lay back on the bolsters and closed his eyes. He cursed the fever that always left him irritatingly tired. Ellen was right; it would be a week or more before he was fit enough to sit a horse for any distance.

The door creaked open and he opened his eyes. The woman in the blue dress with fair ringlets and startlingly blue eyes could only be Lady Longley. She crossed the floor and looked down at him, her cornflower blue eyes filled with concern as Agnes slipped into the room behind her.

Lady Longley may have been a few years older than him, but she was beautiful and he felt the heat of embarrassment rise to his face and wondered how her husband could bear to have been separated from her for so long. The preponderance of women in this household, after years of male companionship, took some getting used to, particularly as he only seemed to be meeting them at a significant physical disadvantage.

'I'm Lady Longley, Master Lovell. I do hope you are feeling recovered?' She smiled and laid her hand over his, soft golden curls falling around her face. 'I believe you have some word of my husband?'

He cleared his throat and extricated his hand. 'I am well on the road to recovery. Thank you for coming to see me, Lady Longley and yes, I met your husband recently and have some letters for you from him. Agnes ... can you find them?'

Agnes obliged, producing the crumpled and travel-stained packets from the bottom of his bag. She handed them to Daniel, who went through them quickly. He set the one addressed to Sir Jonathan aside and handed the others to Lady Longley. She carried them over to the window, where she stood with her back to the room, quickly scanning them without opening them.

'How kind of him to write to his daughter,' she said in an acerbic tone, waving the offending missive in the air before slamming it down on the windowsill. She leaned forward, resting her forehead against the glass.

Daniel glanced at Agnes. From her wide eyes, he took it that the reaction was not what she had expected either. Lady Longley straightened and turned around, looking from one to the other, colour staining her cheeks.

'I apologise. I am weary of this long separation. I have two children who do not know their father. Tell me, was Giles well when you saw him?'

'He seemed to be in good health,' Daniel replied. 'And if it's any consolation, he asked me to tell you that he will make amends.'

A bitter, humourless smile twisted Eleanor Longley's mouth and she tapped the letters in her hand. 'I will read these later. Is there anything I can do for you, Master Lovell?'

He shook his head. 'No, the kindness of everyone in this house has been quite overwhelming.' He cleared his throat and added, in the hope it might console her, 'Lord Longley seemed hopeful of returning to England with the King.'

'And then, of course, all will be well,' Lady Longley said with a noticeable crack in her voice. 'Excuse me, please. I will be better company in the morning.'

She turned and left the room.

Daniel glanced at Agnes. 'Was she crying?'

Agnes nodded as she bent to pick up the tray from where Daniel had pushed it. 'Yes. So many broken lives, Daniel. Is there anything else I can do for you?'

Daniel closed his eyes, covering them with his arm. 'Leave me. I'm poor company, Agnes.'

Her heels clicked on the wooden floor and the door creaked open.

'I will see you in the morning. Good night, Daniel,' she said.

As the door closed behind her, Daniel lay awake staring up at the panelled ceiling of the bed. *So many broken lives*, Agnes had said, and he was coming to see how much the affairs of men had impacted the lives of their women.

He thought of his mother and sister, forced to eke out an existence in a few rooms of a ruined house; of Agnes, who had nothing and no one; and Lady Longley, who had been forced to be mother and father to children, who would not recognise their father if he walked through the door.

And what had been the cause of all this misery? The stubborn pride of a little man who called himself King had brought England to civil war.

At that traitorous thought, he closed his eyes and turned his thoughts instead to that man's son, who had also suffered through his father's hubris. Charles reigned over a shadow court in a country that did not want him when his own throne waited for him here in England. There would never be peace until a king sat once more upon his throne in England and he, Daniel, still had a part to play in bringing the world back to rights.

CHAPTER 18

Leaving Daniel, Agnes found Eleanor Longley in the nursery, engrossed in a game of spillikins with a boy of about seven. A younger boy of Henry's age, still in skirts, seemed to be hell-bent on disturbing the game, while the nursery maid was singularly failing in the task of quieting a small girl of a similar age to the younger boy.

Agnes took the unhappy child in her arms.

'Now then, little maid, what ails you?'

'Teeth,' said the harassed nursery maid.

'Ah, teeth are nothing but a trial from the very beginning. Now, what is your name?'

The child stopped crying long enough to gulp out, 'Clare.'

'Clare, show me where it hurts.'

Clare opened wide and Agnes could see the red, swollen gum. She inserted her finger and rubbed the sore spot, swaying in the instinctive dance of all mothers. Clare's sobs reduced to gulps and she snuggled against Agnes, two pudgy fingers in her mouth.

'You have a good way with children.' Lady Longley rose to her feet.

'I love children.' Agnes looked down at the fair head against her shoulder and brushed the silken strands out of the child's eyes.

'This is my son, Charles,' Lady Longley put her hand on the shoulder of the older boy. 'Charles, this is Mistress Fletcher.'

The boy swept her a courtly bow.

'These two,' Lady Longley indicated the two younger children, 'are twins. Richard and Clare. They are Jon and Kate's children. You have met Tabitha, Jon's daughter, and Thomas, Kate's son by her first marriage, and my eldest child, Ann.'

Agnes smiled and shook her head. 'This is a very complicated family.'

Lady Longley nodded. 'Both Jonathan and Kate had other lives before they met. Kate's first husband, Tom's father, died at Marston Moor, and Jonathan only discovered Tabitha a few years ago. She is his natural child.'

A child of passion born out of wedlock? Agnes wondered and her gaze rested on Richard. 'My sister's child, Henry, is Richard's age. I cared for him since he was born.'

'You must miss him.'

Every moment of every day, with a pain that threatens to break my heart.

'Very much. And you, Lady Longley?'

Her companion pulled a face. 'Please, call me Nell. No one calls me Lady Longley. What about me? My home is in the possession of a poxy Roundhead. My husband, Giles, is with the King in the Low Country, where he has been for twelve years now with only occasional fleeting visits.' Lady Longley's face saddened. 'I have not seen him in eight years, but by all accounts, he does not want for company.'

Agnes caught her meaning in the sad twist of her mouth. She glanced down at Charles, who had turned to spin a top for his younger cousins.

'So he's not met his son?'

Nell shook her head. 'I had hoped Giles, like Jon, would make his peace and return before this, but I think he prefers his life on the Continent to that of domesticity with a wife and children.'

Agnes looked at Lord Longley's handsome wife and fine little boy and wondered how Longley could not want hearth and home.

'But enough of such gloomy domestic talk,' Nell said with a smile. 'Your friend Master Lovell is acquainted with Jonathan from the days of Worcester, I believe.'

'So he says. It is his brother, Kit Lovell, who was Sir Jonathan's friend.'

A smile lifted Nell's face. 'Oh, of course, Kit Lovell. I remember him. If I had not been so besotted with Giles, I could have fallen in love with Kit. He was half-French, I recall, with all the charm of Frenchman.' She frowned. 'He's dead, isn't he?'

'Daniel told me he was hanged a few years ago for some part in a plot to kill Cromwell.'

Nell nodded. 'Oh yes, I remember Jon reading about it in a London newssheet. But what about this brother, Daniel?'

The child Agnes held had grown heavy, her head lolling against her shoulder. 'I think someone is ready for bed,' she said, handing the drowsy child to the nursemaid.

'You too, Master Richard,' the nursemaid said.

The boy stuck out his lower lip. 'But I want to play wiv Charles,' he said.

'Charles is going to bed too. Kiss Mama,' Nell said, rising to her feet. She stooped and the boy threw his arms around his mother's neck, planting a large, sloppy kiss on her cheek.

Agnes's heart broke just a little more.

'They are such a joy for Kate and me,' Nell said, a fond smile on her lips as the door closed. 'Come, Agnes. I may call you Agnes? It is time for supper.'

As they left the room, Nell slipped her arm into Agnes' and leaned into her. 'Now tell me, Agnes. You and the handsome Daniel Lovell. Is it true, are you just friends?

'Hardly even that,' Agnes responded a little too quickly. 'Is he handsome?'

Nell's mouth quirked. 'Oh yes, he has some of the looks of his brother, but rather less ... French. I warrant that out of the sick bed, he is a fine-looking man.'

Agnes swallowed. 'I am no judge of these matters,' she mumbled. 'I know very little about him.'

Nell frowned. 'So, how do you come to be in his company?"

How strange it would sound to this woman if Agnes were to even try to explain that her relationship to Daniel came only from a mutual acquaintance with a man they both hated!

'As I told you last night, I was abandoned in London without the means to support myself and Daniel came to my aid.'

'A knight errant,' Nell held up her hand. 'But I won't ask anything more of you. I have learned that in this day and age it is best not to know too much.'

They had reached the door to the dining chamber and Nell pushed it open. The rest of the family was already seated. Agnes slipped into her now-familiar place at the Thornton table, and after answering Kate's question about how Daniel fared that evening, she let the family gossip wash around her.

CHAPTER 19

The following morning, Ellen Howell judged Daniel well enough to be allowed to dress and sit in a well-cushioned chair beside the fire in his room, a table beside him on which had been placed a jug of small ale and a plate with two late-season apples. A London news sheet lying unregarded on his lap, Daniel stared into the flames of the cheerful fire that crackled in the hearth.

It occurred to him that since meeting Agnes – since coming to this house – something in his universe had shifted and he could describe it in one single word: kindness.

The years of exile had been wasted years and had left him at the age of twenty-eight with only the prospect of a long and lonely life. There had been no room in his heart for sentiment or charity. His had been a hand-to-mouth existence, lived among hard men with a brutal job. When he had sought relief from life aboard a privateer it had been in the arms of the whores of Fort Royal. When he had been stricken with the fever it had been the rough tending of his shipmates that had nursed him back to health.

He looked around the pleasant room, redolent with the scents of beeswax polish and lavender. A fitful late autumn sun spilled in through the diamond panes of the window, bringing back memories of happier times at Eveleigh, a house of a similar age and history to this one.

He wondered now how real those memories were. It seemed he had lived his whole life in the shadow of conflict, but there must have been a time before the war when they had lived as a family at Eveleigh. He recalled games of hide and seek with Kit – on the occasions Kit had been at home. Being ten years older, there had been school and Oxford and other distractions for a young man, but when he had been at Eveleigh there had always been time for romping with his younger brother and sister.

But it was more than just the kindness of the strangers who had taken him in. There was Agnes – that perplexing little woman who had sat beside him as he tossed in fever. He remembered more than she probably realised, but most particularly the touch of her hands as she had cooled his body. No one had touched him like that, with such ... he struggled to find the word ... intimacy? Intimacy but not carnal desire. Her touch had come with – again, that word – kindness.

Or was there more than that?

He'd never been in love. Even with Jennet Pritchard, who had made no secret of her feelings for him. He had liked Jennet enough to have contemplated a life with her but love ... ? No, not love. If he had married Jennet it would have been for one reason only – an escape from servitude. She knew that, she understood. She had told him love could come later.

But it had been death that took her away and plunged him into Hell.

A rap on the door startled him out of his reverie and he straightened in his chair as Sir Jonathan entered the room, ducking his head to avoid one of the low beams of the ceiling. He had aged in the years since Worcester, the dark hair now streaked with silver and lines had been etched around his mouth and eyes.

'Good to see you up,' Thornton said. 'May I join you?'

'Of course,' Daniel waved a hand at a second chair.

Thornton sat down and stretched out his long legs, crossing his feet at the ankles. 'Mistress Fletcher says you have a letter for me, from Giles Longley.'

Daniel rose unsteadily to his feet and retrieved the letter from his bag. As he resumed his seat, Jonathan broke the seal and scanned the contents, his face grave. He crumpled it in one hand and tossed it on the fire where it sparked and glowed before bursting into a bright flame.

'England balances on a fine wire at the moment,' he said

'What do you mean?'

'The restoration of the King seems inevitable, yet there is still so much to do to accomplish it. Foolish ventures such as that which saw Agnes's brother in law lose his head do not help.' He glanced at the fire as the letter dissolved in ashes and fell into the hearth. 'The time for the sword is passed. Old soldiers like Giles and I can be of little use in the months to come. We must put our trust in politicians.'

Sir Jonathan lifted his right hand to smooth back the hair from his forehead, the cuff of his shirt falling away to reveal a circle of whitened scars around his wrist. Daniel caught his breath. The marks were unmistakable. He had seen them too many times before. He bore them on his own wrists.

'Manacles,' Daniel said aloud.

Jonathan rubbed his wrists as if he still felt the weight of the irons. 'You are quite right. I barely survived incarceration in the Tower of London in the months after Worcester.' He sighed. 'I've seen the scars you bear, Lovell. Do you wish to tell me about it?'

Daniel looked away. 'His name was Outhwaite. He was the overseer of the plantation to which I had been sent after Worcester.' He paused. 'He is dead.'

'Did you kill him?'

Daniel brought his gaze back to the fire. 'No. I would have done, without hesitation, but I heard that they hanged him in Holetown for his crimes. Justice was served.'

Thornton studied him with a knowing gaze.

'As you say,' Thornton said at length. 'Justice was served. Now, tell me about your time at the exiled court. What did they ask of you?'

Daniel looked up. 'What do you mean?'

'When you went to the court in Bruges, they would have asked something of you, I am sure.'

Daniel shook his head. 'I made it clear that I have no interest in their games. I have given eight years of my life for the decision to follow Kit into battle that day, Sir Jonathan. I have nothing more to give.' He paused. 'Did Lord Longley say something in his letter to you?'

Thornton stood up and walked across to the window. He stood for a long time in silence, his hands behind his back, before turning to face Daniel again.

'They want money.' Thornton huffed a humourless laugh. 'Giles knows full well they'll get nothing from me. It is as much as Kate and I can do to hold this estate together and provide for our family and our tenants from year to year.' He returned to his chair, leaning forward and gazing into the fire, his elbows on his knees and his hands clasped. 'The fines levied on us have been crippling but we have managed and now it begins again. I have nothing to spare for the King's coffers and nothing to give of myself.' He looked across at Daniel. 'Even if it were wanted, I gave my oath as a gentleman never to raise my sword against the Commonwealth. Much as that decision galled me, I gave it gladly. It ensured me home and hearth and contentment.'

Daniel frowned. 'And that is enough?'

Thornton returned his gaze to the fire and a rueful smile lifted his countenance. 'Between us, Lovell, there are days when the beat of the drums echoes in my blood, but the only thing of value I have left is my honour and I will not break my oath and take up arms again.' He straightened. 'And I can tell you, Lovell, because I know you understand. I have no desire to return to the Tower of London. In the meantime, I have plenty to occupy me in keeping this estate running and ensuring my tenants are fed, housed, and clothed, let alone my own family. My stepson, Thomas Ashley, will inherit the estate when he is twenty-one and I wish to ensure he has something worth inheriting; not the rundown, impoverished estate I found when I returned home.'

'Why would your stepson inherit it?' Daniel asked.

Jonathan shot him a quick sidelong glance. 'A decision of my grandfather, forced on him by my own recklessness. On his death, were I to have inherited, the estate would have been immediately forfeit. This way it stayed intact.'

'But if the King returns ... '

Thornton waved a hand. 'Thomas is nearly eighteen, and he has his own father's lands in Yorkshire. I would hope he will allow Kate and me to live out our lives here, but that is something we will discuss in the future. What about you?'

Daniel stared into the fire for a long moment.

'I went to Bruges seeking news of my brother,' he said at last. 'I had not thought he survived Worcester, but Lord Longley said he had lived but had been hanged for his involvement in a plot to kill Cromwell.' He looked up. 'Do you know anything about it?'

Thornton straightened slightly and shook his head. 'I know only what I read in the London news sheets. What I can tell you is that Kit was badly wounded at Worcester. I saw him fall. He had taken a pistol ball in his leg but you know how it was that day ... ' He trailed off and both men stared at the fire, reliving the horror of the third of September 1651. 'He wouldn't have escaped unaided and I can only assume he was taken prisoner. But it seems, unlike you, he did get away and lived long enough to get himself embroiled in the foolish plots of '54. By all accounts, they hanged him in the Tower of London.'

Daniel sensed an unspoken "but" in Thornton's words. He narrowed his eyes. 'You heard otherwise?'

Thornton shrugged. 'No ... yes ... foolish, unsubstantiated rumours that I give no credence to. But you knew your brother better than I.'

Daniel shook his head. 'I'm not sure I did. They intimated that Kit had turned coat. That he was a traitor, a spy set by the Commonwealth and that the plot was betrayed by him.' The knife twisted in Daniel's heart. 'If that is true I don't understand why he would have turned his cloak. The Kit I knew would never ... '

Thornton looked up sharply. 'Someone betrayed the plotters. Three good men died that day as well as your brother. The traitor in their midst may have been Kit or anyone else. Even the best of men can turn their cloak if the reason is just.'

Daniel swallowed. 'But Kit? Kit was a king's man to the bone.'

Thornton cleared his throat. 'There was a man, Cromwell's Secretary of State, John Thurloe. He organised a system of spies and agents that

Queen Bess' Walsingham could only have dreamed of. I would wager a bag of gold that half the men surrounding Charles are in the pay of the government. Nothing happens in the exiled court without Thurloe, or whoever it is who has replaced him, knowing about it. If Thurloe had an interest in your brother, he could be very persuasive.'

Something in the man's tone made Daniel look up. 'You met him?'

'Oh yes.' Thornton held up his hands, allowing the cuffs to fall away from his scarred wrists. 'I carry these as a permanent reminder of Master Thurloe. He thought to turn me to his employ.'

'But you didn't turn.'

Jonathan shook his head. 'No, but between us, it would have been very easy to have agreed to whatever he had to offer. Freedom for the price of court gossip? Don't think too poorly of your brother, if indeed he fell into Thurloe's hands. The choice, when it was offered to him, may not have been a choice.'

Daniel's fingers tightened on the arms of the chair. 'If he was responsible for the deaths of those three men, Sir Jonathan, I am not sure I could forgive him that, whatever the reasons.'

Jonathan's level gaze met his and held it for a long moment before he said, 'You are swift to judge, Daniel, but you may never know. Kit is dead, God rest him.' He gave a low chuckle. 'He was always trouble. What of the rest of your family?'

'I don't know. I left my mother and sister at Eveleigh. My grandfather was old and ailing when I left home, so I imagine he is long gone. With Kit dead, I am probably Lord Midhurst.'

Thornton smiled. 'Do I offer you my congratulations or my commiserations … my Lord?'

Daniel shook his head. 'Neither. I can make no claim on the estate while I remain outside the law.'

At this, the older man raised his eyebrows. 'And are you outside the law?'

Daniel laughed. 'Very much so. I escaped from my sentence in Barbados and I have had a profitable few years on a French privateer.'

Jonathan Thornton nodded, a smile touching his mouth. 'You are indeed an outlaw, my friend. But what of your plans? Why come back to

England now when you could have just sat quietly with the Court in Bruges and bided your time?'

Daniel hesitated for a long moment before he replied. 'I have unfinished business of my own.'

Thornton shook his head. 'We all have unfinished business, but there comes a time when we have to let the past lie.'

Daniel turned his gaze to the fire, watching the flames catch a twig with a leaf, sending it flying up the chimney. 'I witnessed my father murdered in cold blood. He had surrendered Eveleigh and yet Ashby ordered him shot on the steps of his own home. Ashby must pay with his blood.'

Thornton frowned. 'Ashby? Is that the same Ashby Agnes told us about?'

Daniel nodded and Thornton shook his head. 'So that is what binds you and Mistress Fletcher? Does she know you are seeking revenge on this man?'

Daniel swallowed. 'I've tried to be honest with Agnes. I've told her as much as she needs to know. Our interests align. If she wants the children returned to her keeping then only Ashby's death will accomplish that.'

Thornton's lips tightened and he frowned. 'Revenge is a dangerous master, Lovell. If there is to be a reckoning, for both of you, the time is coming with the return of the King. You must be patient.'

Daniel shook his head. 'No ... the King is preaching forgiveness and I can never forgive Tobias Ashby. It's all I have. It's all that has driven me for the last few years. It's what sent me to Worcester.'

'And Agnes is your entry into Charvaley?'

Daniel nodded. 'There is more to this than just my personal feelings, Sir Jonathan. You were right at the start, I do have a commission from the King – to find the gold James Ashby hid before he was taken.'

Thornton raised an eyebrow. 'Gold?'

Daniel met the man's eyes. 'Gold Unites. Elmhurst waylaid it on the way north and it was intended to be used to finance the uprisings of July that never happened. It's hidden somewhere in Charvaley and only Elmhurst knew where.'

'He told no one before he died?'

'I don't believe so. I am hazarding a guess that is why his cousin was so anxious to return the children to Charvaley. He too is looking for the gold.'

Thornton leaned forward, a frown puckering his forehead, but if he had been about to ask a question he got no further. They were interrupted by a hurried knock and Ellen Howell bearing a lunch tray.

Rising to his feet, Thornton said, 'Whatever your plans, Lovell, you are welcome to rest here and regain your strength. We will talk later.'

With that he turned and strode from the room, leaving Daniel to the mercy of Ellen.

CHAPTER 20

SEVEN WAYS, 20 NOVEMBER 1659

The horse fidgeted, shaking its head with a jingle of the bridle. Its rider sighed. He had been watching the red brick house for too long. He was cold and his horse sensed that a warm stable and food lay within its reach.

He had never been a coward, had always faced whatever life threw at him — even death — but now he felt fear clutching at his heart as it had never done before.

A hundred questions crowded his mind, deafening him from one big question. *What if the note had been wrong?*

The horse shifted its feet, its ears swivelling.

'You're right,' the man said aloud. 'If nothing else I get to see an old friend, although what in God's name am I to say to him …'

He straightened in the saddle and kicked the beast forward.

As he rode into the courtyard and looked up at the red walls and mullioned windows, he tried to recall if he had been here before. It seemed familiar, but those harum-scarum days of the war had begun to merge and blend.

Leaving the horse with a groom, he asked to see Sir Jonathan Thornton but refused to give his name. The elderly steward seemed to take this lack of courtesy in his stride and showed him into a room that may have once been a parlour, but the chill in the air indicated that it was now only be used for suspicious visitors.

He removed his hat and gloves and set them on the table, and was in the act of untying the strings of his cloak when the door opened. The two men stood staring at each other for a long, long moment.

'Christ!' Sir Jonathan Thornton blasphemed.

'I have been called many things but never, ever compared to the Good Lord,' Kit Lovell replied.

Jonathan closed the door behind him and leaned against it for a moment.

'Like our Good Lord, it appears you have the ability to rise from the dead,' he observed.

Kit held up his hand to stay the inevitable questions. 'A long ... very long story, Thornton.'

Thornton continued to stare at him as if he were indeed a ghost. 'What brings you here? ... Of course, your brother ... But how?'

Kit's heart skipped a beat. 'So it's true? He's here?'

Jonathan nodded. 'Been here just over a week. He's recovering from a bout of marsh fever. How the hell did you know?'

Kit afforded himself the luxury of a small smile. 'I have friends in London who sent me a message.'

It had been a cursory note, written in Nan Marsh's poor hand. *Daniel. Seven Ways.*

Just three words, but it had been enough. No one ever forgot a name like Seven Ways.

'He's in the library,' Jonathan said at last. 'He ... thinks ... knows ... you are dead. Do you want me to speak to him?'

Kit shook his head. 'No. This is between the two of us.'

Jonathan nodded. 'This way, then.'

Picking up his hat, gloves and cloak, Kit followed his old friend through the winding maze of corridors of the old house. Jonathan stopped outside a carved oak door and looked across at Kit with a question in his eyes. Kit shook his head. He would face this meeting alone.

He opened the door, revealing a long, low, pleasant room overlooking the front entrance to Seven Ways and the ancient moat that surrounded the manor house.

In the scene he had rehearsed a hundred times on the long ride from Hampshire, Kit had seen Daniel as a nineteen-year-old ... still, to his way of thinking, a boy. But the man by the fire, who looked up with enquiry in his eyes, was not a boy but a man, lean and hard, with lines around his eyes and mouth that spoke of hardship and suffering.

Daniel let the book he held slide unregarded to the floor as he rose to his feet.

'You ...' The word came out as a hoarse whisper.

'Good morning,' Kit said, affecting a bravado he did not feel. 'I believe you have been looking for me?'

'Daniel, I found that ...' A woman's voice jolted him and he turned to see a young woman standing by a bookshelf, a slim volume in her hand.

She looked from one man to the other, her brow creasing in puzzlement.

'Daniel, are you all right?' she enquired.

When Daniel didn't move or speak, Kit recovered himself sufficiently to sweep her a courtly bow.

'Please excuse my brother,' he said. 'He seems to have lost his tongue and his manners. Christopher Lovell, sometimes known as the Comte D'Anvers, but to my family just Kit.' He forced himself to smile. 'You, *mademoiselle?*'

'Kit?' She swung her gaze to Daniel. 'But you're ...'

'Dead?' Kit suggested. 'One evening, when we are better acquainted, I shall tell you a most interesting story, Mistress ...?'

The girl coloured and sank into a curtsey. 'Agnes Fletcher, sir.'

Kit turned his attention back to Daniel, seeing now the pallor of recent illness beneath the tan and the dark smudges that shadowed his brother's eyes.

'You've been ill. Are you recovered?' he enquired.

Daniel found his voice. 'A bout of marsh fever.' He glanced at the woman. 'Agnes, can you leave us?'

She set the book down and hurried toward the door. 'Of course,' she said. 'Can I fetch refreshments ... ?' When neither man answered she ducked her head and slipped out of the room, closing the door behind her, leaving the two men alone.

'How did you find me?' Daniel asked with a noticeable crack in his voice.

Kit shrugged. 'I received word that you were in England.'

Daniel narrowed his eyes in thought. 'It could only be from the Ship Inn.'

No point in lying. 'Jem and Nan Marsh have been loyal friends. They know the whole sordid story. Of course, they told me of your unexpected reappearance in civilization.' Kit searched his brother's face, at once so familiar and yet the face of a stranger. So many questions to ask, so much to say, but all he could manage was a strangled, 'When I received Jem's message, I thought it best to see for myself before I break the happy news to the rest of the family. We've been ... disappointed before.'

'The family?' Daniel asked in a tight voice.

'Your mother, your sister, my wife, our children ... our adopted children,' Kit said, realizing as he said it how much had happened in the intervening years. He didn't even know where to start. He took a deep, steadying breath, struggling to keep his emotions under control.

Daniel turned away and paced the room for a long moment. He stopped in front of Kit and cleared his throat.

'Everyone told me that you died ... executed for your part in a plot. How ... '

'When it comes to Lazarene resurrections, Daniel,' Kit interrupted, 'I could ask you the same question. We went to Barbados to bring you home, Thamsine and I.'

Daniel frowned. 'Who's Thamsine?'

'My wife.'

Daniel let out a long breath. 'You went all the way to Barbados? Why? Did you think you could spirit me away?'

Kit flinched at the bitterness in Daniel's tone.

'Yes,' he replied, reaching into his jacket, and tossing a paper down on the table between them. Daniel picked it up. Yellowed and brittle with age, it crinkled as he unfolded it. He scanned the contents and let it fall back.

'It's a Pardon ... my Pardon.' He ran his hands down his face and stared down at the seemingly innocuous paper. 'All the time I was a free man and I never knew?'

'They told us you were dead,' Kit said. 'Dead of a fever.'

Daniel looked up. 'Outhwaite,' he said, and this time Kit heard the hatred in his brother's voice.

He laid a hand on Daniel's shoulder.

'I know the truth, Dan. I know what that man, Outhwaite, did to you. I made sure he went to the gallows.'

His brother's throat worked, his lips compressed so tightly they looked bloodless. He shook off Kit's hand, turned away and walked over to the window where he leaned on the windowsill, taking deep breaths before he turned back to face Kit.

'And what of you? They told me you died at the end of a rope.'

All humour went from Kit's face. 'I did.'

'Then how are you standing there?'

Kit subsided into a chair and ran the fingers of his crooked hand through his hair. 'It is such a long story ... '

A spark of anger flared in Daniel's face and he held up a hand. 'Only one thing matters. Is it true? Are you a turncoat?'

Kit felt the breath leave his body as surely as if Daniel had hit him. 'Who ... where did you hear?' His bluster died away. He wanted to deny the truth but he knew from the look of growing revulsion on Daniel's face that his face betrayed him.

Daniel took a step back. 'It is true? You betrayed your friends, everything you believed in?'

Kit rose to his feet. 'You don't understand. I have to explain ... '

'No, you don't!' The spark flashed into a blaze of anger. 'While I suffered in Barbados, you betrayed the cause we believed in. Damn it, Kit. Good, loyal men died because of you.'

Kit closed his eyes. It was easier to allow Daniel to rage and rail at him than deal with the unspoken lies between them.

Daniel continued, his voice tight with rage. 'So you live in obscurity, under an assumed name ... Do you jump at shadows, Kit Lovell? Because the King will return and what will be your reckoning then?'

Kit held up a placatory hand. 'Daniel, please— '

Daniel stood aside and opened the door. 'I don't want to hear excuses. You're a filthy turncoat. It would have been better for both of us if I had never set foot in the Ship Inn. Go back to whatever hole the Comte D'Anvers occupies. I never want to see you again.'

For a long, long moment Kit couldn't move. He understood Daniel's anger, probably better than Daniel himself. Perhaps in time they could meet again and he could tell his brother that everything he had done was for his sake, but not now ... not here.

With deliberate care, he turned and collected his belongings.

'You will always be welcome at my home – Hartley Court in Hampshire.'

Daniel glared at him. 'I will never set foot in any place where I will find you,' he said. 'Does mother and Frances know you are alive?'

'Yes. Do they know about you?'

Daniel shook his head. 'No.'

'Then it would be a kindness to advise them. I have no doubt they will be anxious to be reunited with you, but they deserve better than a surprise on their doorstep.'

He swept past Daniel, nearly colliding with the woman ... Agnes? Was that her name?

She set down the tray she carried. 'I was just bringing you some refreshment,' she said. 'Are you leaving so soon?'

Kit glanced back seeing Daniel standing by the window, looking out at the grey, autumnal day.

'Please present my apologies to Sir Jonathan, *ma'm'selle*, but I cannot stay. I have done what I came to do.'

He inclined his head and walked out of the house. Gathering up the reins of his horse from the waiting groom, he swung into the saddle.

'Wait.'

He turned to see Agnes running from the house, her skirts caught up in her hand. She laid a hand on the horse's bridle.

'Please don't give up on him,' she said.

He looked down into her face, *rather a pretty face*, he thought, with her upturned nose and smattering of freckles, but there were lines of anxiety creasing her brow and he wondered for a moment what part this woman played in his brother's life.

'Mistress Fletcher, whatever he might think, I have never given up on my brother,' Kit replied stiffly, 'but he needs time, maybe we both need time.' Kit managed a smile. 'Daniel is fortunate to have a friend in you, Mistress Fletcher.'

A sprinkle of colour stained her cheekbones. 'Just an acquaintance, Master Lovell. Nothing more.'

She turned and walked back into the house, passing Jonathan Thornton at the doorway.

Kit watched her go. 'Just an acquaintance?' he mused aloud.

Jonathan laid a hand on the bridle. 'You're right. You both need time. Christ, Lovell, you have to expect your arrival to have come as a shock. I advise you to go to Bromsgrove and take a room at the Black Cross.'

Kit looked down at his old friend. 'Thornton, it is not my appearance that is the shock, it is the realisation that his brother has feet of clay.'

Jonathan Thornton looked up at him, holding his gaze. 'I think you owe me at least the courtesy of the whole story, Lovell. Dismount and walk with me to the gate. Dead men should not be appearing at my front door unless there is a very good reason, and you are the second one this month.'

CHAPTER 21

The rage had begun to die even as Daniel crossed to the window in time to see his brother, leading his horse, walking away from the house with Jonathan Thornton beside him. They walked in step with an easy camaraderie that spoke of their shared past.

Kit moved with a noticeable limp and Daniel lowered his head, remembering Worcester and, in the confusion of the battle, hearing his brother call his name. As Daniel had turned to respond, he had seen Kit fall, but he'd been unable to reach him before he too had been felled and his world changed forever. In some ways, he realized, it had been easier to think of Kit as dead on that battlefield. The truth was too hard.

A pain, every bit as physical as a blow to his stomach, doubled him over.

It couldn't be true. Everything he had ever believed about his brother had evaporated. Kit, the hero of his childhood, had betrayed him as surely as the men he sent to their deaths. Why? What possible reason could Kit have given for his change of allegiance? Did he really want to know?

Taking a deep breath he straightened. He had to get out of the house. He did not want company or sympathy – he wanted alcohol and oblivion.

He turned for the door as Agnes opened it. She stood framed in the doorway, her hand on the catch.

'What do you want?' he snapped.

'I came to see ... if there is anything ... ' she faltered and he could see the hurt in her eyes.

'I need nothing, particularly not a woman's sympathy,' he said.

'Daniel, as your friend ... '

'Friend? I don't have friends, Agnes. I have known you for what ... ? A month? Friendship takes time and we don't have that time. Now leave me. I'm going to find an inn and have a quiet drink – by myself.'

She stood aside to let him pass without a word.

Daniel retrieved his cloak and hat from his room, before plunging out into the cold, grey afternoon. Heavy rain clouds rolled in over the trees but he didn't care. There would be an inn close by and he set out with a firm stride, turning his face gratefully to the cold rain.

He returned to Seven Ways in the small hours of the morning after a long evening tucked into the corner of the parlour of the village inn. His plans for oblivion had been thwarted by his recent illness. It only took one small jar of wine before the overwhelming urge to sleep overcame him and the landlord had to wake him and throw him out into the cold, damp night.

The old house slumbered in darkness, except for a tiny flickering light high up in the guest bedchamber– his chamber. He took the stairs two at a time, conscious of every creak and groan from the ancient risers. The door to his chamber stood slightly ajar and he took the precaution of inching it open.

Agnes sat beside the dying embers of the fire, curled up in the chair, wrapped in a blanket. Conflicting emotions churned through him. His anger at Kit still simmered below the surface, mingled with guilt at his harsh words to Agnes.

She hadn't deserved his wrath or hard, hurtful words. In truth, she had been a good friend to him, and he wondered where an arrangement of mutual convenience had turned to friendship. He huffed out a breath – an inconvenient bout of marsh fever had changed the nature of their relationship forever.

She looked so innocent and peaceful, lit only by the light of the fire, and another emotion altogether stirred and tightened in the pit of his stomach. How easy it would be to take her in his arms and take the solace he needed. He yearned to bury his face in her soft hair and drink in the scent of her, but like a half-healed scratch he also needed to pick at the scab of hurt and betrayal, cause the blood to flow, feel the pain ... feel something ... anything.

He threw the door open loudly enough to wake her with a start.

A smile lit her face. 'Daniel. Thank heavens. I was worried.'

'Why? I'm not one of your children,' he snarled.

The smile died on Agnes's lips.

He took a few steps into the room, throwing his hat onto the chest and fumbling with the strings of his cloak.

'Concerned that poor, ailing Daniel may take cold in the horrible rain?' The heavy sarcasm in his tone should have been enough to warn her.

'Concerned for you, yes,' she said, a slight tremor creeping into her voice.

'I'm fine, Agnes. Nothing a copious quantity of appalling wine at the nearest hostelry couldn't cure,' he lied.

His sodden cloak joined the hat and they stood staring at each other.

'There is some supper on the tray,' she said, waving her hand at the table, where a jug and covered tray had been placed.

'I'm not hungry.'

'You should eat —'

He rounded on her, all his anger for Kit directed at this one person. 'I do not need you to mother me, Agnes. If you want to help me then lie down on the bed and spread your legs, just like you did for Elmhurst ... God knows you owe me for your board and lodging.'

All the colour leeched from her face and he immediately regretted his words.

'Agnes ... ' He put out his hand but she hit it away and ran from the room.

He heard the door to her room open and close and sank onto the bed, burying his head in his hands.

CHAPTER 22

*W*ith her back braced against the door to her bedchamber as if she expected Daniel to come rampaging down the corridor, Agnes fought to control her breathing and push away the hurt intended by his words.

Her brother had once taken her into the woods on a tour of some rabbit traps he had set up. They had come across a young fox, clearly terrified and in pain, caught in the teeth of a larger trap set by the gamekeeper. She had begun to cry as the animal attacked George with bared teeth and claws, resisting all his efforts to help.

'Hurt animals will lash out,' George had said, as he loosed the teeth of the trap and the animal made a bid for freedom.

She had told Kit not to give up on him. She could not disregard her own words.

Her breathing stilled and she opened the door onto the silent corridor. Faint light spilled from the half-open door to Daniel's bedchamber. For a long moment, she hesitated, torn between slamming her door on him forever or returning to face his anger once more.

Hesitantly, she pushed open the door, prepared to flee if he rounded on her again, but somehow she didn't think he would. Like that hurt fox, he had lashed out at her because she was there, for no other reason.

Daniel stood at the window, looking out over the peaceful country-side, painted a silvery white by the full moon that had broken through the rain clouds. He didn't look around or move as she came to stand beside him, although he must have heard the creak of the floorboards. His hands rested on the windowsill, the fingers of his right hand curled around a crumpled sheet of paper.

They stood side by side for a long, long minute in total silence.

'Why? Why did he turn his coat? Why did men have to die?' Daniel's words were slurred, but with emotion, not drink.

That was not a question she could answer. Instead, she touched the paper he held. 'What's that?'

He glanced down at his hand as if seeing the paper for the first time, and with a heavy sigh slid it across the sill toward her. As she picked it up, he gave a hollow, humourless laugh. 'It's an official Pardon for all my sins. All this time I have been a free man, Agnes. I could have come back to England years ago – I could have just walked away from the planta-tion. Instead … ' He broke off. 'He told me that he came looking for me in Barbados, to give me this. He was too late. Outhwaite had already done his worst.'

She swallowed. 'Who is this Outhwaite?'

He looked sideways at her. 'He was the overseer of the plantation to which they sent me with the Scottish prisoners after Worcester.'

She held her breath, hoping her silence would be invitation enough for him to confide in her.

'I don't know if it was because I was English or I was the son of a viscount, but my case was quite different to those of my fellow captives. I was given a cabin and allowed to walk the deck, and when we arrived in Barbados I was assigned to a sugar plantation. I could read and write and I became the clerk of the estate. The owner of the plantation treated me as he would a respected paid employee. I had a room in the house and the freedom to come and go. It was – endurable.'

He balled and unballed his hands, stretching his fingers as if trying to steady himself.

'Despite being a prisoner, I had no complaint about my life. Pritchard's daughter Jennet and I formed an attachment of sorts.'

A flutter of disquiet stirred in Agnes's heart.

'You were in love?' she asked through tight lips.

Daniel gave her a sharp glance and shook his head. 'She loved me,' he said in a flat tone, 'but my motives were not prompted by anything more than a liking for her. Pritchard dropped hints that were we to marry, my release could be secured, my future guaranteed as his son-in-law, so I agreed.'

The flutter grew to the full-scale beating of a bird's wing and she acknowledged with a shock that what she felt were pangs of jealousy. She hadn't realised how much this man had come to mean to her in the past few weeks.

'You married her?'

'No. She died of yellow fever a week before our wedding.'

Agnes bit her lip as the jealousy died away as quickly as it had arisen. The death of Jennet Pritchard had been merely a marker on the journey that had brought him here.

'Pritchard's grief was so great he had a seizure and became paralysed and unable to speak. Management of the plantation fell to me. Of course, if I had married Jennet it would have been quite different. But with Pritchard ill, to all intents and purposes I was still a prisoner with no right to claim management, and the overseer of the prisoners, a man called Outhwaite, did not hesitate to remind me of my station.'

At the mention of the name, every muscle in his face contracted, stretching the skin tightly across the high cheekbones. His eyes became dark smudges, filled with an unimagined pain.

Agnes reached out and put her hand over his. A secret for a secret? Could she, would she dare, confide in him as she was asking him to confide in her? Maybe ... but not yet.

'He ... ?' She swallowed. 'Your back?'

He flexed his shoulders as if he still felt the fall of the metal-tipped scourge. 'Among other atrocities he committed, and not just on me.'

'Sometimes,' she said, her fingers tightening on his. 'It helps to speak of what troubles you.'

He pulled his hand away and gave a harsh, humourless laugh. 'You are always ready with advice, Agnes. Outhwaite is dead. Dead these four years past but he still haunts my nightmares. I came across a newssheet that reported that he and three of his men had been hanged in Holetown for murder – my murder and another's. When I read the news it filled me with anger that he had not died at my hands. Hanging was a merciful death.'

His mouth clamped shut, a hard, thin line, and Agnes knew that she would hear no more. Whatever had lain between Outhwaite and this man still ran too deep for the whole truth.

Wherever Outhwaite was, Agnes hoped he was rotting in Hell. She smoothed the paper against the sill of the window and lifted it, squinting as she tried to make out the words, but they were illegible in the poor light of the moon. Only the heavy scrawled signature and the seal proved its authenticity.

She looked up at Daniel. 'Was this the price demanded of Kit for turning coat?'

He drew a sharp audible breath. 'What do you mean?'

'He could surely not have obtained a Pardon for you unless ... '

Daniel looked down at her. 'Are you saying that he bought my freedom with his life and his conscience?'

'Only he can tell you that, Daniel.'

He looked away. 'I let him go without giving him the chance to explain.'

She folded the paper and handed it back to him. He took it, turning it over in his fingers.

'Agnes, I owe you an apology for what I said.'

'Yes, you do,' she replied. 'I'm not a whore, Daniel. My reasons for becoming James Ashby's mistress are ... my own.'

'Is he the father of your child? Henry is your son, not your sister's, isn't he?'

She drew a deep breath. He knew. 'We called it The Great Secret, Daniel. I am sworn to keep it.'

His gaze didn't move from her face. 'Secrets are always dangerous, Agnes. Ashby's dead, what difference can it make now?'

She shook her head. 'There is too much at stake.'

He could make whatever suppositions he liked. They both had their secrets.

They stood in silence once more, their hands on the windowsill. Daniel covered her left hand with his right, running his calloused thumb in a circle across the back of her hand.

'You have such a tiny hand, Agnes,' he said in a low voice. 'I fear I might crush it.' He lifted it, pressing her fingers to his lips. 'If I could only take back those terrible things I said to you.'

Agnes swallowed. The touch of his lips on the tips of her finger was sending her stomach into a roiling mess, stealing the very breath from her lungs. 'They were spoken in haste and anger,' she said, finding her voice. 'I know they were not meant for me.'

His hand strayed to her hair, smoothing the disordered curls away from her face.

'Don't go. Stay with me, Agnes,' he said, in a voice hoarse with emotion.

Her heart skipped a beat but she forced herself to step back and he dropped his hand.

'Is this another pleasant invitation to lie on your bed and spread my legs?' she asked.

He flinched and caught her hand again, drawing her toward him, his gaze, even in the thin light of the moon, steady.

'I'm not asking for anything more than companionship, Agnes. I just don't want to be alone ... not tonight.'

Every nerve in her body tensed, her need for companionship, for human touch, every bit as great as his. She choked back the sob but it escaped unbidden and her body convulsed as he drew her into his arms, kissing her hair.

'Please don't cry.' He raised his hand, smoothing the hair away from her face, wiping away her tears with his thumb. 'Forget what I said and go back to your bed.'

She shook her head. 'I don't want to go back to bed.' She cupped his face in her hands, forcing his gaze to meet hers. 'I'm crying because it is the first time in a very long time ... ' she struggled to find the words ' ... that I feel wanted for who I am.'

His fingers meshed in her hair as he pressed her to his hard, lean body. 'Is that all we are to each other, Agnes? Two lonely people finding solace in the dark?'

'Is that such a terrible thing?' she ventured.

'I would like to think that maybe it is more than that,' he said.

She found her voice. 'I would truly like to think we were friends, Daniel Lovell, despite what you might have said.'

The moon appeared from behind a cloud, lighting the ghostly smile that caught Daniel's mouth. 'I would like to think of you as a friend, Agnes, however short our acquaintance. Probably my only friend.'

He slid his arms around her, drawing her in against him. She closed her eyes, breathing in the scent of him. He was not James Ashby. He was something quite different from James. Younger, leaner, harder. Tempered by suffering, scarred by war and worse.

Her pulse quickened and as their lips met she closed her eyes, succumbing to a hunger she had never known before, her body melting against his until it seemed they were just one being. Still entwined they fell onto the bed, fingers grappling at laces and buckles.

Agnes pushed away from him, searching his face, losing herself in those grey eyes, now hazy with desire.

'I ... I am not a virgin.' She pushed the hair from her face with a self-deprecating laugh. 'Stupid of me, you know that.'

A chuckle rumbled in his chest. 'Neither am I, but I've never tumbled a girl who wasn't willing. Agnes ...?'

All she had to do was say "no" and he would let her go. She would go back to her own bed and life, such as it was, would go on as it had before. But what sort of life did she have? Did either of them have?

They were both waiting for something to happen. Perhaps this would be part of it?

CHAPTER 23

*D*aniel woke with a start from a nightmare in which he stood in a crowd watching as his brother was led to the gallows. He tried to call out but his words were lost in the noise of the crowd. At the last minute Kit turned and looked out over the baying mass, which grew silent as Kit raised a finger and pointed directly at Daniel.

He sat up, the sweat on his naked chest and forehead turning clammy in the cold pre-dawn. Beside him, someone stirred and a small hand came up to rest on his arm.

'Daniel?'

He looked down at the woman beside him, seeing only her shadow in the dark.

Agnes.

A wave of remorse flooded him as he remembered how she had given herself to him completely and apparently unconditionally. He had used her to assuage his misery and his guilt with little thought or consideration for this woman.

He lay down on his side, propping himself on one elbow as he ran a finger down the line of her jaw, imagining her small earnest face with its smattering of freckles, aware that her gaze was fixed on his face.

'Agnes, I'm sorry,' he said.

'For what?'

For taking you, for using you, for giving you nothing in return when you have given me so much.

'I should never … ' he began, but she laid a finger on his lips.

'Hush, it was my choice.'

He gripped her hand, holding the fingers against his lips, kissing each tip before releasing her and trailing his fingers along the line of her jaw and the hollow of her throat. She had a woman's body, curved, soft and warm to the touch.

He stilled. 'Agnes … ' He struggled to find the words. 'Have you ever taken pleasure from laying with a man?'

'I've only lain with one man. My mother and sister told me it was a woman's lot to bring comfort to a man, not to expect anything in return. I never asked or expected it to be different.'

'Did James love you?' he asked.

She didn't answer at first. Her chest rose and fell in a silent sigh. 'Love was not a consideration. James was kind to me, that was all I asked.'

'He wouldn't marry you?'

She gave a huff of laughter. 'Marry me? He couldn't. The Church forbids marriage between a man and his wife's sister, and James would never have gone against the teachings of the Church.'

Even when that woman was the mother of his son?

The reason for the Great Secret suddenly became so much clearer. With the taint of illegitimacy, Henry could never inherit his father's estate, but if no one knew or suspected that the child's mother was not the Earl's wife …?

He wondered about the circumstances that surrounded Henry's birth and why Agnes had willingly borne the child. Maybe she would confide in him but not now … not here.

He turned the question. 'Did you love James?'

This time she answered without hesitation. 'Yes.'

God rot James Ashby, Daniel thought. Had James realised what a treasure he had in this woman, or had she just been a convenience to be used like any one of his possessions?

But Ashby was dead and he, Daniel Lovell, who should have been dead, was alive and Agnes lay in his arms as if she had always belonged there.

'What about you, Daniel? Apart from Jennet, have you ever loved?'

He curled a tendril of soft, brown hair around his finger. Love was not something he had had much time for since his first calf love, the head groom's daughter. Jennet had loved him to the point of embarrassment but he had not reciprocated the emotion, only the intention. A marriage to Jennet had suited him. In his hopeless situation, it had spelled not only freedom but a future. He had kissed her but there had never been anything more physical than that. He had certainly never told her that he loved her. Whatever else he may be, he was not a liar. When she died his grief had not been at her loss, but at what her loss had meant to him personally. The thought shamed him now. Jennet had deserved better.

But this conversation was not about him. He wanted to know about the woman in his arms, the woman who stirred something within himself that he did not recognise. He took a deep shuddering breath, knowing that in taking Agnes to bed he had stepped out onto treacherous, unfamiliar ground.

But even as he had that thought, she jerked out of his embrace and lay beside him, staring up at the ceiling of the bed, her hands folded across the covers. The few inches between them now yawned like a gaping chasm.

'Daniel, you need to understand. Love is a luxury a woman in my position cannot afford. I have to look to a man for my protection and the simple comfort of a roof over my head. All I have to give you in return is my gratitude and my friendship – don't ask for my love,' she said.

In a swift movement, Daniel swung himself over her, pinioning her between his knees and holding her forearms down against the mattress. In the greying light of dawn, her eyes widened but she did not struggle.

'Gratitude is not enough, Agnes. If nothing else, let me show you that a woman has a right to be pleasured.'

The last few years had not been without female companionship, and the willing girls of Fort Royal had taught him something about how to please a woman. He pulled back the covers exposing her to the grey light of the early dawn. She shivered in the cold air but did not protest as he let his fingers stray over the soft, silky smoothness of her inner thigh.

She braced beneath his touch, her breath exhaling in a gasp. 'I … I've never been touched like that before.'

He silenced her with his lips and let his fingers coax and gentle the woman in his arms until her breath came in short gasps and she cried out, arching her back before falling back spent and shuddering. He slid his hand across the flat plane of her stomach, the skin beneath his touch contracting.

She lay supine in his arms, her chest rising and falling as if she had run a hard race.

He allowed her only a fleeting moment or two of spent passion before gathering her in his arms and rolling onto his back, bringing her with him. She took him inside her without resistance, moving in rhythm with him until he too came to climax and they both cried out from the sheer joy of the moment and she collapsed, spent, on his chest, her soft curls spread across his body.

He lay awake, his fingers playing in her hair. While her surrender to him had seemed to be complete and unconditional, there had been something she had held back, and a lump rose in his throat. He recalled the girl in Fort Royal who had recoiled in horror, calling him "*un lépreux*" – a leper.

Like that girl, Agnes had not touched his back.

CHAPTER 24

Slipping from Daniel's bed before the servants came to light the fires, Agnes skipped barefooted along the cold floorboards to her own bed-chamber. Shivering, her breath frosting in the cold morning air, she pulled on her clothes and sat down heavily on the edge of her bed, staring, without seeing, at the world outside her window.

She touched her lips, warm and swollen from Daniel's kisses, and smiled. Wrapping her arms around herself she hugged herself tightly, reliving the memories of the previous night. Every nerve in her body seemed to crackle as if her skin still responded to the touch of Daniel's fingers.

At the thought of his hard, strong body, her own heart melted and a warm glow spread up from her toes. It was all she could do not to run back to his room and into the warmth of his arms and do it all over again.

Was it possible that this was love, she wondered? Was it love to want to be with someone every moment of the day?

He had given her more in one short night than her years with James Ashby. James had only ever taken his pleasure but Daniel had cared for her, her pleasure as important to him as his own.

She just hoped that in the passion of the moment he had not noticed that as they had made love, she could not bring herself to touch his back, the wheals and grooves that marked his torture at the hands of Outhwaite, foreign to her touch, inviting a degree of intimacy she could not give.

She hunched her shoulders and huffed out a long, shuddering sigh. Surely that reticence on her part could only mean one thing – that whatever had driven her to his bed last night had not been love. If you loved someone then it shouldn't matter. A cold, grey reality as chill as the dawn light encircled her.

'What have you done?' she said aloud.

What if there was a child? A child born of lust? A child born to a penniless and homeless mother?

James had always been so careful. After Henry there could be no more children, no suspicion to cast the faintest doubt on Henry's parentage. Now, in one night of passion, Agnes had thrown all that caution to the wind.

She rose to her feet, pacing the room. 'You fool!' she castigated herself.

At the window she stopped, looking down into the courtyard where a milkmaid, her pails swinging from the wooden brace across her shoulders, hurried toward the house.

There could be no repeat of last night, however much she … or he … may desire it. They would meet as friends, nothing more.

But her resolve weakened when they met at the door to the parlour. A smile lightened his face and his arm circled her waist, drawing her into his embrace. At the touch of his lips on hers, the last of her resolution slipped away. Only the sound of footsteps on the stairs behind them caused them to jump apart.

Kate Thornton rounded the corner, her gaze going from one guilty face to the other.

'Are you going to stand there all day?' she enquired. 'Or shall we break our fast?'

Agnes slid into her now-familiar seat at the table. Jonathan Thornton, intent on reading a letter, did not glance up. The only other person at the breakfast table was Tom Ashley.

'Father's had a letter from the Freemans,' Tom said, addressing his mother.

Kate's face lit and she glanced at Agnes and Daniel. 'Our uncle and aunt in London,' she said. 'Jon, what news?'

Jonathan set the letter down. 'They are intending to visit in the spring,' he said.

'That is something to look forward to,' Kate said. 'What other news?'

Jonathan tapped the table with his forefinger. 'I'm not sure what to make of it, but Nathaniel writes that the Committee of Safety is in disorder. Rumours are flying around that General Monck may raise the Army against them.'

Thomas Ashley's eyes widened. 'But Monck's in Edinburgh. Lambert holds sway in England.'

Jonathan's mouth quirked. 'It would not take Monck long to march on London, Tom, and if the Army does defect to him then Lambert may find himself with no troops. Interesting times.'

Kate sighed. 'I am weary of interesting times. I long for peaceful times.'

'They are coming, Kate,' Jonathan said, laying his hand on hers. A look of silent understanding passed between them.

Agnes glanced at Daniel, whose attention was devoted to buttering a large slab of bread, and wondered what it would be like to have a man who could look at you in such a way.

Daniel turned his attention from the bread to Jonathan. 'But it is not such a simple matter of the King returning. There is a whole system of government to be restored.' He cast a quick glance around the table. 'And past wrongs to be righted.'

Jonathan nodded. 'You are right. There are still many obstacles to the King's return.' He glanced at his stepson. 'Tom, if you have finished eating, I need to speak with Daniel.'

Tom cast Daniel a questioning glance and rose from the table, excusing himself.

Daniel cleared his throat. 'Before you begin, I owe you an apology for my high-handed behaviour yesterday.'

Jonathan shook his head. 'You owe no apology, Daniel. I blame Kit. It is typical of your brother to make an entrance and a quite understand-able shock ... for me as well, believe me.' He held up his hand. 'But that was yesterday, and I had a long talk with Kit about the circumstances of his return from the dead.'

Agnes glanced at Daniel. His face had drained of colour. 'What did he say?'

Jonathan shook his head. 'That is his story to tell, not mine. He tells me you were pardoned.'

Daniel traced a pattern on his platter with the point of his knife. "I owe him the right to an explanation. I suppose he is halfway to Hampshire. If I leave immediately I may stand a chance of catching him up.'

A smile creased the corners of Jonathan Thornton's eyes. 'It is a long way to Hampshire, but I don't think you need to travel that far. You should find him at the Black Cross in Bromsgrove.'

Kate Thornton leaned forward. 'Go and seek him out, Daniel.' She glanced at the window. 'It's perishing cold outside, so dress warmly – we don't want a relapse of the fever. Your horse will be saddled and ready in half an hour.'

Daniel pushed back his chair and stood up. 'Thank you for persuading him that I was not a completely lost cause.'

Jonathan shook his head. 'He knows that, Daniel, and besides, it is Agnes who went after him.'

Daniel shot Agnes a glance, indecision and annoyance flashing behind his eyes.

Agnes met his gaze. 'I have no family, Daniel. Mother, father, brother ... all dead and buried, and now even my sister's children have been taken from me. If Kit were my brother I would not want to lose him. Not again.'

Daniel looked away, a muscle working in his jaw. 'So you would go after him, would you?'

'Without hesitation.'

Half an hour later they gathered in the courtyard where the black gelding stamped impatiently, its breath frosting in the crisp air.

Kate stepped forward and straightened the linen around Daniel's neck. 'Make peace with your brother, Daniel, and he is welcome to return with you. The beds at the Black Cross can be a little lumpy.'

Daniel glanced at Agnes. 'What do I say to him?'

She looked up at him and shook her head. 'I don't know that, Daniel.'

They stood looking at each other for a long moment, and it seemed as if Agnes saw him for the first time with startling clarity; the lock of dark brown hair that fell across his forehead, the arch of his eyebrows, the tell-tale white creases at the corners of his eyes, the scar that crossed his right cheekbone, the long nose and the curve of his well-cut lips. Now so familiar and so beloved.

The "pirate" that she and the children had met on that first day in London suddenly seemed a long way removed from this man. The walls Daniel had built up around himself, which had enabled him to survive what surely would have killed a lesser man, had begun to crumble, and at last, she was seeing glimpses of the man Daniel Lovell should have been –could still be.

Alone and friendless, they had found each other, but she knew that whatever passed between the brothers in Bromsgrove would change the fragile balance of her relationship with him. Like a flash of powder in the pan of a musket it had burned brightly and momentarily but now it was gone.

Even as this thought crossed her mind, he drew her into his arms and brought his lips down on hers with bruising intensity.

'Agnes … ' His voice sounded ragged.

She pushed him away. 'Go,' she said.

A muscle twitched in his cheek, and as if remembering the presence of his hosts, he turned and swung himself into the saddle.

'I will return by evening,' he said, leaving the *with or without my brother* unsaid.

IN THE PARLOUR, Kate stacked an extra log on the fire and the flames leapt higher. Agnes drew closer to the warmth, holding out her hands.

'We haven't had much opportunity to talk, you and I,' Kate said.

That was true. Since her arrival at Seven Ways, Agnes had been drawn to Nell's company. They were, after all, closer in age and shared a love of children and matters domestic. Agnes gained the impression from Nell and her own observation that Kate Thornton wore her responsibilities as a heavy mantle, with little time to spare for her two children or just the simple pleasures of life.

As Kate sat down in one of the chairs beside the fire, it struck Agnes that she had never seen Kate without some item of mending or a list in her hand. Now the woman closed her eyes, leaning her head back, letting her hands rest loosely on the arms of the chair.

'I am so tired, Agnes,' Kate said, closing her eyes. 'I yearn for peace as if it were the sun. It is always we women who pay the price for war,' she continued. 'While Jonathan and Daniel and his brother have seen their share of suffering, they had choices. You and I, and Nell, we were not given those choices but we have to live with the consequences.'

Agnes nodded. 'I think you are right.'

Kate opened her eyes, her gaze resting on Agnes's face. 'I can see in your face that there is more to your story than you are willing to share, Agnes. Secrets are dangerous. They can devour you from inside.'

Agnes swallowed. 'Some secrets can,' she agreed and changed the subject, 'Has it been so very hard for you here?'

A bitter smile twisted Kate's lips and she drew a deep, shuddering breath. 'These have been very lean years, my dear. The fines on this estate alone ... but then I don't need to tell you how hard they can be. You lost your home.' Recollecting herself, she said, 'We are more fortunate than many, such as your family, and I have been blessed by having the man I love by my side. It has made it easier to ride out the hard winters when we wondered how we could feed ourselves, let alone our tenants.'

Agnes studied the woman. Kate could not have been older than her mid-thirties, but she carried the years of hardship in the lines of her face.

'It will change when the King returns,' Agnes said.

Kate's mouth twitched. 'When the King returns? That is a refrain I have heard before. I see no point in letting my hopes get the better of me. In the meantime, we face another long, cold winter. But enough of our troubles. Kit Lovell's return will probably change your plans. What will you do?'

Agnes shook her head 'I will continue to Charvaley,' she said.

Kate frowned. 'And what exactly is it you intend to do when you reach Charvaley?'

Agnes shifted uncomfortably under the woman's clear-eyed gaze.

'To be honest, Lady Thornton, I don't know. I have some possessions there which surely give me a right to return. But in truth, I must see the children again. I couldn't bear it if they were unhappy or ill-treated.'

'Do you have reason to suppose they would be?'

Agnes thought of Leah Turner's thin, mean lips and shook her head. 'I don't think they will be ill-treated, but they won't be loved and they are so little … ' She bit her lip to stop the tears.

Kate sighed. 'I don't know what advice to offer you, my dear.'

Agnes shook her head. 'I am not seeking advice.'

'Then what is it you want?'

Agnes rose to her feet and paced the floor, before returning to the fire. 'I want a home, like this one. A home with a husband and children, and a laundry maid singing in the yard … ' She broke off and looked away. 'Perhaps, once the King is restored to the throne, the children can be returned to my care and the injustices will be redressed.'

Kate smiled. 'Once again, that refrain, Agnes – when the King returns. *If* the King returns …'

'No!' Agnes cut in. 'I have to believe it, Lady Thornton. I have to hope.'

Kate nodded. 'I have been blessed in my life by good people who have helped me when I needed it and I want you to know if ever you need help or assistance, Agnes, do not hesitate to come to us. God knows Jonathan and I have seen our share of trouble. We would never turn away anyone who needed us. Go to Charvaley, satisfy yourself that the children are in good hands, but come back here. There will always be room for you.'

Agnes blinked. She had never met such generosity of spirit. 'That would be a debt I could never repay, Lady Thornton. Surely I would just be another mouth to feed?'

'Oh, I'm sure you will find a way to make yourself useful, Agnes. You are a resourceful young woman and there is always Daniel Lovell … ' Kate trailed off with a knowing smile.

'No.' Agnes shook her head. 'Daniel is on his own journey.'

Kate's calm, grey eyes studied Agnes for a long moment. 'I saw the way he looked at you just now, and you at him. Whatever drove you both together has now become a partnership. But you are right, you and he need to decide whether you continue on your current path together or take different paths and wait to see what transpires in the next few months.' She rose to her feet, once more the brisk, efficient mistress of the house. 'Doors will open for you, my dear. You just have to be ready to walk through them.'

CHAPTER 25

The landlady of the Black Cross hailed Daniel like an old friend and directed him to the same private chamber he had occupied on his recent stay. Daniel stood looking at the door for a long moment before rapping firmly on the dark oak.

'Enter.'

Taking a deep breath, he opened the door and stepped inside. Kit had been sitting at the table, a half-eaten meal set before him. Seeing Daniel, he rose slowly to his feet, apprehension momentarily clouding his face. His eyebrow quirked in a manner so familiar that Daniel felt transported back to his childhood. This really was his brother, the idolised Kit. All the anger and resentment that had suffused him on the previous day began to slough away.

'You came,' Kit said.

'There seems to be a consensus at Seven Ways that I should hear your side of the story before I pass judgment on your actions. I want to know why you turned coat.'

Kit nodded. He walked over to a table and poured two cups of wine from a jug. Although Kit tried to disguise a shaking hand, the wine slopped in the cup as he handed it to his brother. Daniel took the cup but didn't drink.

'It is probably a little early for wine,' Kit said, taking a draught and setting the cup down on the table.

He turned and paced the floor to the window and stood looking down into the street below. His shoulders rose and fell in a silent sigh before he turned to face his brother, casting his face into shadow.

'The answer is simple. I was offered a choice,' he said. 'My life for yours.'

My life for yours?

Daniel sank onto the nearest chair, bereft of words.

'On condition I became an agent of the Commonwealth, I would win your freedom. Please understand, I had been very badly wounded and maybe was not thinking as clearly as I should have done but it seemed quite a simple decision at the time. It was no choice ... not for me. Passing on scraps and snippets of gossip seemed harmless enough, but as time went on they – should I say John Thurloe – wanted more and more and I got drawn further and further into the plots, but still I justified it. What were the lives of a few old comrades for that of my brother?'

'Jonathan Thornton was offered the same choice,' Daniel said.

'No, he wasn't. Thurloe was not holding his brother hostage,' Kit replied.

'But he would have died rather than turn his coat ... ' Daniel persisted.

'No!' Kit's voice cracked. 'You're not listening to me. This is not about Jonathan Thornton. This is about you and me, Daniel. You were a boy who had followed me to war because of my foolish tales. You should never have been at Worcester, but the blame that you were there rests entirely on me. Thurloe offered me a chance to make it right. I took it.'

Daniel stared at this man he hardly knew. Had Kit really been prepared to sacrifice other lives for his, or had there been a baser motive?

'But men died because of you,' he said, between tight lips.

Kit turned back to the window. 'Yes ... good men who didn't deserve to die. Don't think for a moment that I don't live with their ghosts on my conscience. I would have saved them if I could but I ... ' He broke off.

Daniel saw his brother's reflection in the mottled glass, his face contorted with pain. 'I was too late.' Kit concluded.

'And you? Is it true that you were tried and what of the stories you were hanged?'

Kit took a shuddering breath. 'I found myself caught on my own petard, which suited the authorities. My death was staged to convince the world that I was not the turncoat. But make no mistake, they hanged me, Dan.'

'That was the story I hear. But did they actually hang you?'

'They were very convincing. I went to the scaffold, truly believing I was going to my death.'

He turned back to face Daniel and undid his carefully tied neckcloth to reveal a faint white mark circling his neck. Daniel stared at the scar the rope had left. When Outhwaite had tortured him there had been a time when he had prayed for death, but he could not imagine going to the gallows, feeling the rope around his neck tighten.

For a long moment, the two brothers stood staring at each other.

'And this bought my pardon?' Daniel said at last, hardly able to voice the words.

Kit nodded. 'Only to be given the news that you were dead.'

Daniel looked down at the cup of wine in his hand and drained it in one swallow, setting the empty cup down on the table.

He crossed the floor to face his brother, surprised that he now looked Kit in the eye. The Kit of his memory had always been taller ... and stronger. But the Kit of his memory had died on the battlefield of Worcester, just as the boy who had been Daniel had perished. Now he faced his brother as a man, an equal.

'They know,' Daniel said, 'or at least they suspect that you may have been the traitor.'

'They?'

'The Court.'

A muscle at the corner of Kit's lip twitched. 'Ah. Hardly surprising. I was not the only agent among the King's men. Some were double agents who knew I was in the pay of the Commonwealth.'

'The King will return,' Daniel said.

'It seems so,' Kit gave a careless shrug as if the return of men who knew his sordid past was of no concern to him.

'What will you do?'

Kit heaved a sigh and looked away. 'Kit Lovell died at the end of a hangman's noose. To the world, I am the Comte D'Anvers, who lives a quiet domestic existence in the Hampshire countryside in a house of women.'

Daniel smiled. 'A house of women?'

'Thamsine ... did I tell you I am married? My wife tells me that it is a kind of poetic justice. I'm not sure I quite understand what she means. But between my wife, my sister, my stepmother, Thamsine's two nieces, and my own daughters, I am completely outnumbered and defeated.'

Daniel caught his breath. 'Mother and Frances are with you?'

He nodded. 'Your mother took some persuasion, but Eveleigh is completely uninhabitable.' He paused. 'They are both well.'

Daniel tried to order his thoughts. He put the questions about his mother and sister to one side.

'And Grandfather?'

'Dead these six years.'

Daniel reached for the jug of wine and poured them both another cup. 'If the King returns will you go on being the Comte D'Anvers?' he asked as he handed the cup to Kit.

Kit shrugged. 'I have no choice. Kit Lovell is dead.'

'Where does that leave me?'

'You, brother, are the rightful heir to the title and the estates. You are now Lord Midhurst. I have a clever lawyer in London who can sort through the mess.'

Kit gestured for Daniel to sit and resumed his chair, taking a draught of the wine.

Daniel swirled the wine in his cup, watching the blood-red eddy he created. 'One thing I don't understand. If I was being used as a hostage for your loyalty, why did they send me to Barbados?'

He looked up to see a smile lighten his brother's face. 'Because if they'd left you in England, Thurloe knew damn well I would have moved heaven and earth to help you to escape, and we'd have both been safely on the Continent before he had time to react. I was too valuable to Thurloe to let that happen.'

'That explains my relatively civilised treatment,' Daniel said. 'That is until ... '

'Until Pritchard's health failed?' Kit leaned forward. 'I told you yesterday. I know the story, Dan. I know what Outhwaite did.'

Daniel sighed, flexing the muscles in his back and feeling the scars contract.

The gesture did not escape Kit. All humour drained from his brother's face. 'Show me.'

Slowly Daniel rose to his feet, removed his jacket and lifted his shirt, revealing his back to his brother. He heard Kit's sharp, indrawn breath and hastily restored his clothing.

'It was all I could do not to kill the charmer there and then,' Kit said.

'You met him?' Daniel resumed his seat and reached for the wine, his hand shaking.

Kit nodded. Thamsine and I went to Barbados. We had to see for ourselves that you were truly dead. We saw to it that Outhwaite met his just end but we left with more questions that no one could answer.' He narrowed his eyes. 'Are you ready to tell me how you got away from Outhwaite?'

Daniel sucked in his breath. He had never once spoken in detail of those dark months between Jennet's death and Outhwaite's attempt to kill him. Not even to the man who had rescued him. He refilled his cup and took another deep draught of the wine. At this rate, he would be soused before lunch.

'Outhwaite – you met him. Black, white, male or female — to him we were no more than chattels to be used and dealt with at his whim. If he had been hanged six times over it would be no compensation for the crimes he committed.' Daniel licked his lips, his mouth suddenly dry. 'He fancied himself a suitor to Jennet Pritchard's hand. Neither Jennet nor her father ever countenanced that match. Jennet fancied herself in love with me, and ... ' he looked away, 'I'm not proud of the fact I encouraged her. If I had married Jennet I would have gained my freedom and become heir to Pritchard's estates in Barbados. It didn't seem such a bad lot in life. Unfortunately, Outhwaite saw me as the rival to Jennet's hand, and in his cups one night promised, rather melodramatically I thought at the time, vengeance.'

'Ah, why else do people kill?' Kit said. 'Love, money ... power.'

'He wanted all three, but most particularly money and power,' Daniel agreed. 'My pleasant future came to an end when Jennet contracted a fever and died. Pritchard succumbed to the palsy that left him bedridden and I was left alone in a power struggle with Outhwaite. He had the law on his side and I was quickly disabused of any thought I might have had of continuing to run the plantation on behalf of the sick man. After all, what was I? Just another prisoner, who had enjoyed some privileges denied to most.'

Daniel rose to his feet and paced the room, struggling to find the words for the events that had followed. 'I interrupted him sporting with one of the girls, and while he had his breeches around his feet, gave him a beating. I hardly need to add that she was not a willing party to the transaction.'

Kit let out a harsh breath. 'I had him down as a bastard the moment I met him.'

A wry smile twisted Daniel's lips at the memory of Outhwaite rolling on the ground, his eyes bulging in pain as he clutched his privates, into which Daniel had sunk his boot.

'He made me pay for that moment of triumph. He had me whipped and thrown into the Pit ... ' Kit's head jerked up at recognition of the word and Daniel shook his head. 'You've seen it? A space not large enough to stand in or to lie down – exposed to the elements.' He shuddered at the memory, unable to even begin to describe what it meant to endure the Pit for a day, let alone many days. 'After a week, he hauled me out and sent me out into the fields with the other slaves.' He looked away. 'I should have just bided my time, kept my peace, turned a blind eye ... '

'To the murder of an innocent man?' Kit put in.

Daniel shot his brother a sharp glance. 'You know?'

Kit nodded. 'You had friends willing to tell the story. According to their account, you witnessed Outhwaite beat one of the other prisoners to death.'

'Outhwaite and two of his overseers killed one of the Scottish prisoners. The man had tried to escape, and it was supposed to be a lesson to us all. Unfortunately not one I took to heart. I attempted to get away, to raise help in Holetown, but Outhwaite set the dogs after me. They hunted me down like an animal.'

Kit rose to his feet and laid his hand on Daniel's shoulder. 'You don't have to tell me anymore.'

But the veil of his silence kept so closely for all the intervening years, had been breached, and the words tumbled out. Shaking off his brother's hand, Daniel continued. 'This time he beat me with a scourge, left me in the Pit, and when he thought I was dead, threw me into the jungle like a piece of refuse to rot into oblivion.'

Wine slopped on his hand and he put the cup down, clutching at the table to stop himself from shaking. 'I don't remember much, except that the base instinct to survive must have prevailed. I dragged myself through the jungle to the beach. That's where Broussard and the crew of the *Archangel* found me, barely alive. They took me back to the boat, nursed me back to health ... ' He took a deep, shuddering sigh. 'I owed those Frenchmen my life, and I repaid it as a faithful member of Broussard's crew for the last four years.' He looked up, aware that tears were streaming down his face and he was helpless to stop them. 'And now I find I have been a free man all that time. I could have returned to England ... I could ... ' He broke off, unable to continue.

So many could-have-beens.

Kit's voice cut through, harsh with emotion. 'God knows we tried to find you,' he said. 'We left Barbados with the faintest of hope that you may have survived, but as the years passed and we heard nothing more, that hope died.'

He drew Daniel toward him and into his embrace. Daniel surrendered to the gesture.

'Forgive me?' Kit's voice cracked.

Daniel broke the embrace and held his brother by the forearms. 'Forgive you for what? You have nothing to blame yourself for. It was my decision to follow you to Worcester. Mine alone. I never once blamed you for what befell me. It's you who must forgive me.'

Kit sucked in a shuddering breath and laid his hands on his brother's shoulders. No more words were needed.

'It's almost over,' Kit said at last, breaking the moment and turning away. 'Do you suppose we can start again in a peaceful world?'

Daniel forced a smile. 'It is something of a shock to find myself a free man and, apparently, Lord Midhurst. But you … ?'

Kit shook his head and turned back, spreading his hands in a gesture of defeat. 'My life has always been a tangle. To the world I am a dead man, but I married a wealthy woman and we live a comfortable life, so I have little to complain about, alive or dead.' He smiled. 'I look forward to you meeting Thamsine. You'll like her. She has had her share of trouble in the past, but we are content now.'

'You mentioned daughters?'

A fond parent's smile softened his brother's sharp features. 'Two. The youngest, Maria, is but a baby and then there is Jane, named for Tham's sister. She is my heart's delight, but unlike her namesake, I fear she takes after me. I worry for any man who would take her on.' Kit stretched his arms and folded himself into the nearest chair as if finally allowing himself to relax in his brother's presence. 'We also have two wards — Tham's nieces — as well your mother and Frances … '

The breath tightened in Daniel's throat. 'Did you tell Mother that I have returned in one piece?'

Kit shook his head. 'She didn't take the news of your death well the second time. I dared not risk a third resurrection unless I was certain.'

There were hundreds of questions battling in Daniel's mind, but there would be time enough to fill in those missing years. He studied his brother for a long moment, his gaze moving from the crooked fingers of his right hand – another gap in the story that needed to be told – to the deep lines etched on Kit's face.

Daniel considered that the decisions he had made in his life had never simple choices between life and death. Yet Kit had thrown away everything he believed in, and his actions had led directly to the judicial deaths of three innocent men. Small wonder he lived with their ghosts.

'Come back to Seven Ways with me,' Daniel said, adding. 'Lady Thornton insists the beds here are lumpy.'

A slow smile lit his brother's lean face. 'They are indeed, but there's no hurry. Pass that wine jug..'

CHAPTER 26

*E*ssie had lit a fire and Agnes hunkered down beside it, poking it into life. She could hear the distant sound of laughter drifting through the house. Daniel had returned with Kit, late in the afternoon. Both were in high spirits. Their return had been greeted with warmth by the Thorntons and dinner in the Great Hall had been ordered.

Agnes had sent Essie with her regrets and the message that she was indisposed, and she didn't think she would be missed. Kit Lovell's arrival, his reconciliation with Daniel, and the reunion with his old comrade in arms belonged to the Lovells and the Thorntons, not to her.

She rose to her feet and paced the room, her arms wrapped around her body to still the tears of self-pity that rolled down her face. She knew she should be pleased that the lonely, anguished man she had taken to bed only the previous night had been reunited with his brother but his happiness only served to drive home her own loneliness. Kit had given Daniel back something she could never match – his family — and that left a hollow emptiness in her heart.

She had convinced herself that Daniel was no different from James Ashby. He had taken what she had offered, wrapped up in soft words and a consideration that James had never demonstrated, but as she had with James, she had been in danger of mistaking lust for love.

Agnes sank onto the edge of the bed and lowered her head, twisting the chain around her neck. Her fingers closed around the worn, familiar shape with the lock of Henry's baby hair, unable to explain the feeling of dread that circled her chest like a band as she thought of the child. She seemed to hear him calling for her. She clenched the locket tighter. She had a son who needed her, and she couldn't tarry any longer.

She didn't need Daniel. Back in London, she had been grateful to find a man, any man, willing to help her, but as the days had gone by she had gained confidence. She could, she would go on without him.

The small matter of money could be overcome, somehow. Perhaps she could prevail on Daniel to lend her some coins, and if she got desperate, sell the locket. After all, it was only a thing, a means to an end.

Filled with this new resolve, she rose to her feet and began to pack her few belongings into the worn leather satchel. She hesitated over the delicate square of cambric Daniel had given her when they were attacked by footpads. By rights, she should have returned it, but in a gloomy inn room, she had washed it clean and folded it carefully, stowing it away with her few precious belongings. She pressed it to her lips. He wouldn't miss it, and she wanted some small thing to remember him by.

At the bottom of the satchel, she found James's book of poetry, forgotten and unread. Pulling it out she pressed it to her face, breathing in the scent of leather and glue, but all trace of James himself had long since evaporated.

Idly, she riffled through the pages of *The Faerie Queen*, nearly dropping the book as a piece of paper worked itself loose from where it had been concealed and fluttered to the floor. She set the book down and picked up the paper, her eye drawn to her name scrawled across the top of the page. Holding it close to the candle, she read:

To my darling Agnes.

James had never called her *his* or *darling* in all the years of their acquaintanceship.

I have not been the best a man can be to a woman who has loved him as you most assuredly have done but know this, I have, in my own rough fashion loved you and regret that I must now leave you mourning once again. I have charged you with the care of my children and I fear for them should they be taken from your charge. Agnes as I once shewed you one of my schoolroom pranks, look again at this work of Spenser and remember me, Your James.'

Agnes dashed the fresh tears from her eyes and looked at the paper in her hand. *As I once shewed you ... ?* She frowned as a small fragment of memory came back to her.

It had been one of their rare moments of intimacy, a sharing of childhood stories. He had told her of a secret code he and a friend had devised in the schoolroom. Her hand shook as she raised the paper to the wavering candlelight, and her heart skipped a beat as tiny motes of light trickled through holes in the paper.

'No.' She breathed the word aloud, recognising the holes for what they were – evidence of the code James had told her about.

Setting the paper down on the table, she took a deep breath. The answer was in the pages of *The Faerie Queen*. If she could match the holes to a page of verse, the hidden message would be revealed.

'Which page?' she asked aloud. Like most of Spenser's work, it was a long, rambling poem.

She sat down at the table and, opening the book, laid the paper over the first page. The paper fitted the page size exactly but none of the holes aligned with the text. On the second page, the holes aligned but the resulting letters were nonsensical.

On the fifteenth page of the poem, she ran her fingers over the page, feeling the slight indentations he had used to mark the letters. Holding her breath she laid the paper over it and, painstakingly extricating each letter, read the message James had left.

The children guard that which they seek.

Just to be certain she checked all the other pages of the poem, but this was the only one that made sense and the only page with the indentations.

'What does that mean?' she asked the dead James.

But he deigned not to answer.

The children were the clue. Her mind ranged through the well-remembered corridors and rooms of Charvaley. The nursery? She took a steadying breath. Who would think to search for gold in a children's nursery?

She jumped at the gentle rap on the door, but before she could answer, the door opened and Daniel sauntered in, his jacket unlaced and the cloth loose around his neck. She set the book and paper on the table and rose to meet him.

'Lady Thornton said you were unwell,' he said.

'I was ... I am,' she replied.

'But I would like you to meet Kit.'

'I have met him,' she responded, conscious of the hard edge to her words.

'I wanted you to know that you were right, Agnes ... Kit paid a heavy price for my Pardon.'

'And all is resolved between you?'

He nodded. 'Much lost time to catch up on but I think we have reached an understanding and for that, I have you to thank.'

She shook her head. 'Please don't thank me.'

I couldn't bear it.

'Agnes ... ' He reached out, cupping the back of her head in his hand and drawing her toward him. She recognised the look in his eyes, a wolfish, hungry look, for what it was – lust.

She knocked his hand aside and took a step back.

'No,' she said before he could speak.

A flash of anger creased his brow but was gone as quickly as it came. He dropped his hand and stared at her, a frown creasing his forehead.

'I don't understand ... ' he began.

Fuelled by her resolution not to allow a repeat of the night before, Agnes brought her chin up and glared at him. 'You presumed because I came willingly to your bed once that I would do so again? You were wrong. I will not be used or presumed upon again.'

As I was by James.

He reached out and stroked her cheek, a frown creasing his fore-head. 'Is it something I said ... something I did? I thought ... that you and I ... '

At his touch, Agnes's resolve began to waver. His gentle caress sent shivers of desire running down her spine.

It took an effort, but she batted away his hand.

How could she explain that it was precisely because the nature of their relationship had changed that she had to turn him away? For both their sakes she had to make the cut and make it deep.

'I came to you last night for one reason only. Because you needed me. But not tonight. I am not a whore to be used at your convenience.'

He flinched and she knew her barb had struck home. 'That is harsh, Agnes. I will never think of you that way.' He touched the tip of her nose and when she turned her face away, he withdrew his hand, the wolfish gleam dying in his eyes.

'I will be leaving in the morning,' she said.

He frowned at her. 'Leaving?'

'You are recovered and no doubt you will be returning with Kit to Hampshire to see your family. I will continue to Charvaley ... alone.' Even as she said the word, her resolve wavered. What genteel woman travelled the roads of England alone?

His eyes narrowed. 'How? I made you a promise, Agnes.'

'And I'm not holding you to it. Your circumstances have changed in a way you could not have foreseen. Mine have not. I still have two children who need me and I have to find my way to Charvaley.'

That cold dread, the fear for Henry, clutched at her once more. She would leave this minute if she could.

He considered her for a long moment. 'But you're wrong, Agnes. Nothing's changed,' he said at last. 'Not while Tobias Ashby is at Charvaley.'

She laughed. 'Surely you don't really plan to kill him?'

His high cheekbones coloured at her derision. 'That has been all I have thought of for the last ten years, Agnes.'

'That is a boy's dream, Daniel. Put the past away. You have a future now.'

He stiffened. 'I don't understand what has changed between us, Agnes.'

Nothing, she thought. It felt like every nerve in her body had been strung tight. If he touched her again, she would fall apart.

Mercifully, when she did not reply he straightened, setting his jaw. She had hurt him and her heart yearned to take him in her arms again, murmuring apologies.

'We will talk in the morning, Agnes. If nothing else, I cannot in good conscience permit you to travel alone. If you do not want my company then suitable arrangements will need to be made.'

He gave her a perfunctory bow and turned on his heel, the movement catching the paper on the table. It fluttered to the floor and he stooped to pick it up. Before she could snatch it from his hands, he had scanned the contents.

'James Ashby's idea of a love letter?' He turned back to her, handing her the paper.

'His last letter to me.' She took the paper, glancing down at the familiar handwriting. 'He said more in those few short sentences than he said to me living. I found it in a book he gave me on that last day. I hadn't thought to open it until tonight.'

Daniel shook his head. 'I'm sorry. It was wrong of me to read it.'

She shrugged. 'It's of no matter.'

He turned again for the door. 'Good night, Agnes. Stay your plans another day and we will contrive to work something out.'

She shook her head. 'No. I must go, Daniel. I ... I can't explain.'

He turned back, his eyes wary. 'Agnes?'

'I have a terrible ... feeling about Henry. He's in danger.' The words sounded so foolish said aloud.

In two strides he had returned to her, placing his hands on her shoulders and turning her to face him.

'Is that what all this is about, Agnes? Henry?'

She nodded.

Daniel reached out and touched her hair, his hand once more cupping the back of her head and drawing her toward him, but not as it had been before, with lust in his eyes. This time she saw only understanding.

161

He folded her in his arms, kissing the top of her head. 'You are right, Agnes. It's no longer about Tobias Ashby. That was a boy's anger.'

She pushed away from him. 'Leave me, Daniel. I meant what I said. I will not share your bed again.'

He turned, and with a strangled 'I shall bid you good night,' left the room, leaving her alone in the cold.

CHAPTER 27

aniel returned to his bed-chamber and found Kit standing by the fireplace, poking a recalcitrant log with the toe of his shoe. He looked around as Daniel entered.

'I came to say good night,' he said.

Daniel shut the door behind him. 'I went to see if Agnes … ' He felt the heat rising to his face, like an anxious schoolboy wilting under his brother's cynical gaze.

'No joy there?' Kit said.

Daniel cleared his throat. 'I may have been mistaken about her feelings for me … ' Advancing into the room, he ran his hand through his hair. 'Damn it, Kit, you're the expert on women. Is it possible to understand them?'

Kit shrugged. 'Not in my experience, and trust me, I have plenty of opportunities to observe the female of the species. Let me just say, don't abandon hope, if that is where your heart is leading you. However, if it is not your heart that is leading you, then I advocate finding an obliging serving wench.'

'Wonderful brotherly advice,' Daniel remarked, throwing himself into a chair by the fire.

Kit remained standing. 'I came to see if you were up to the ride back to Hampshire. We can leave tomorrow.'

Daniel looked up and shook his head. 'No. Hampshire will have to wait. I made a promise to Agnes to escort her to Charvaley.'

Kit's eyes brightened. 'Charvaley?'

'The Earl of Elmhurst's seat in Lancashire.'

'Oh yes, wasn't he executed recently?' Kit said, adding. 'I do see the London news sheets.'

'Agnes was … ' Daniel hesitated, ' … sister to Elmhurst's late wife. She was guardian to his children, but Whitehall in its wisdom granted custody to Elmhurst's cousin, Tobias Ashby.'

The name provoked the reaction he expected. Kit straightened, all humour draining from his face. 'That's a name I never thought to hear again,' he said in a low, controlled voice. 'Why in God's name is she tangling with him?'

'She is frightened for the children,' Daniel said and went on to explain Agnes's situation, leaving aside any mention of Agnes's true relationship to the boy.

'What does she hope to achieve by turning up on the doorstep? He is under no obligation to admit her,' Kit said.

'I don't know what she intends, but I owe it to her to keep my promise to her.'

A muscle twitched in Kit's cheek. 'I understand. It's been a long day and we can talk again in the morning. Good night, Dan.'

Although his body ached with weariness and the strain of the day, Daniel lay awake for a long time in his lonely bed, his arms behind his head, staring into the darkness as the day's events turned over in his mind. The anger he had carried with him, that had sustained him for the last eight years, had been snuffed out by knowledge of the sacrifice his brother had made. He wondered if he would have had the courage to make the same decision.

But what he had gained on one hand he had lost on the other. For the span of a breath his life had been complete; he thought he had found not only his family but also that elusive emotion, love. But Agnes had cut that ground away from beneath his feet, and he tried to remember what had passed between them the previous night that should have given him the clue that she had come to his bed for one reason only – pity.

But he had made her a promise, and even if it meant delaying a journey to Hampshire with Kit, he would see her to Charvaley. If Tobias Ashby had not already found it, the King could wait on his gold and Tobias Ashby on the King's justice.

His mind settled, and sleep claimed him.

CHAPTER 28

*A*gnes set the *Faerie Queen* down on the breakfast table. Jonathan Thornton leaned over and picked it up.

'Spenser,' he said. 'Not my taste in poetry, I'm afraid.'

'Nor mine,' Agnes said. 'But James – Lord Elmhurst – gave it to me.' She looked at Daniel, steeling herself. 'Daniel, I need to talk to you.'

Daniel looked up from buttering a slab of bread. 'What about?'

'James.' She tapped the book. 'I should have told you something last night – it is about something James did.'

Daniel glanced around the table at his brother and Jonathan and his wife. The younger members of the Thornton family had already eaten, to judge by the scattered platters. 'You are among friends here, Agnes.'

'There is something hidden at Charvaley. Something that Tobias Ashby wants.'

'You mean the King's gold?' Jonathan inquired.

She stared at him. 'How did you know about that?'

Jonathan looked at Daniel, who glared back at him. 'Oh dear, I appear to have spoken out of turn,' he said.

Agnes rose to her feet, her eyes only for Daniel. He had known all along about the gold. Everything – their meeting, his concern for her, his willingness to take her to Charvaley – became clear. It had been about the gold, not any concern for her well-being – or the children. For a brief heartbeat, she considered hitting him, or at least taking the book and leaving the room.

'That was what it was always about, wasn't it? All that talk about revenge on Tobias Ashby was nothing but a ruse,' she said at last, forcing the words between tight, angry lips.

Daniel coloured and shook his head. 'No, you're wrong. It was always about Ashby. The gold was just a convenience.'

'And I was just a convenience?'

Daniel cleared his throat and made a pretence of smearing honey on his bread. She forced her anger down. James had trusted her with his secret; now she had to trust this man.

She looked around the table. 'So you all know?'

Kit leaned forward. 'I have no idea what you are talking about, Mistress Fletcher, but it sounds most intriguing.' He glanced at Daniel. 'You can deal with my brother later. Evidently, his conduct may have been less than gentlemanly. In the meantime, you can confide in us.'

Kate Thornton looked at Daniel. 'I think you owe Agnes an explanation.'

Daniel toyed with the buttered bread, as honey dripped down the sides onto his hand. 'I hold a commission from the King to recover a consignment of gold Unites stolen by the Earl in July. Elmhurst went to his grave without disclosing where he had hidden the coin. They told me in Bruges that Agnes may know something about its location.' He set the bread down and looked at Agnes. 'Agnes, I confess to seeking you out for that reason, but everything that happened since then ... '

Hot, stinging tears of humiliation sprang to her eyes. 'I don't think I can ever trust you again.'

Daniel winced as if she had hit him. Agnes held him in her hot angry gaze, glad that she had turned him away last night, whatever it had cost her.

'Trust is a valuable commodity and easily betrayed.' Kate Thornton's tone was icy. She glanced from Agnes to Daniel. 'But from what I have come to know of the two of you in the past two weeks, whatever perfidious motives Daniel may have had in seeking you out in London, Agnes,

I think what lies between you now is a true friendship. Don't throw it away.'

'I want to know more about this gold,' Kit interrupted the awkward silence that followed Kate's speech.

Agnes hesitated, tapping her fingers on the cover of the book. She had come this far; she may as well throw in her lot with these men.

She held up the leather-bound book. 'Last night I discovered James's last letter to me. It's a coded message.'

Jonathan leaned forward, his elbow on the table. Kit sat back, his arms crossed, a frown creasing his brow. Daniel tilted his head to one side, a mannerism she had noted from their time together. All three of them had lived in the shadows, and what she needed now were men capable of facing Tobias Ashby.

'Tobias asked me about the gold in London, which means he hadn't found it before James's death. I denied all knowledge of it, but I will tell you what I do know. In July some men came late one night with four leather satchels and deposited them in the library. James said I was the only one he trusted, and I held the lantern as they brought the satchels inside.'

Jonathan narrowed his eyes. 'Did you see what was in the satchels?'

'No, and neither did I see what James did with them. They were gone from the library the next morning. I could tell they were heavy from the way the men carried the satchels but I didn't see the contents.'

Daniel nodded. 'Four hundred gold Unites, freshly minted in the Tower and sent north to support the quelling of the uprising.'

Kit gave a low whistle, his sharp gaze catching Jonathan Thornton's eyes.

Agnes set the book down, laying her palm flat on its cover. 'I couldn't bring myself to look at this book – until last night, and that's when I found James's letter. If I've read the code correctly I think he has hidden the gold somewhere in the children's nursery at Charvaley. I have lain awake half the night trying to think where it could be hidden. I can only think that there must be a secret chamber I don't know about.'

Jonathan sat back in his chair and for a long moment, the only sounds in the room were the gentle hiss as a log settled on the fire and the patter of the rain on the windows. 'James Ashby's gold could be the difference of months if not years to the King's return,' he said at last. 'Why do you think the hiding place is in the children's nursery?'

Agnes opened the book and demonstrated the code.

'The children guard that which they seek.' Jonathan frowned. 'The children's nursery? Why there?'

'It's an old house, older even than this one,' Agnes said. 'There would be hiding places that were long forgotten. What if James had stumbled on this one when he was a child in that same nursery? He had no brothers or sisters who survived infancy. No one to know except him.'

'If we could retrieve the gold ... ' Jonathan Thornton mused aloud. 'Kit, what say you?'

Kit nodded. 'It's not a task for one man.'

'No!' Kate pushed her chair away and rose to her feet, colour high on her cheekbones. 'Don't even think it. You made me a promise, Jonathan Thornton.'

Jonathan rose to meet her, taking her hands in his. 'I made you a promise never to take up arms again,' he said, 'and I have honoured that promise, Kate, but if the recovery of this gold can facilitate the restoration of the King, would you have me walk away? This is a different case, it's not the same as openly taking up arms and riding into battle.'

'A fine distinction, Jonathan!' Kate shook off his hands and strode over to the window, where she stood with her arms wrapped around herself. She turned back to look at her husband, her face once more composed.

'I know I cannot stop you, Jon,' she said after a long moment, 'and God knows we have suffered long enough under the rule of Parliament. Go, if you must, but come back to me.'

Daniel looked at his brother. 'Kit? Your wife is not here, what would she say?'

Kit's mouth quirked and he glanced at Kate. 'Probably much the same as Kate, but I am weary of jumping at shadows and skulking behind hedgerows in Hampshire. I want ... I need the King's forgiveness.'

Agnes saw no humour in Kit's face, just a terrible sadness, and she realised what Daniel's freedom had cost his brother.

Kate gestured at Agnes. 'You do realise that the only way to this gold is through this woman. Would you endanger her life for a few gold coins?'

Kit shook his head. 'Kate's right, Jon. It is not just about us. Daniel and I know better than anyone what Tobias Ashby is capable of.'

Agnes looked from one to the other.

'Thank you for your concern, Lady Thornton, but the choice is mine,' she said. 'Not only does he have the lives of two innocent children in his hands, but Tobias Ashby betrayed James.'

'How?' Kit asked.

'He came to James with stories of unrest in the Army. He persuaded him that in the event of an uprising, he could bring all his troops and more besides. James believed him and committed to joining Booth's uprising in Chester. He was taken on his way to join Booth – by his cousin.'

Kit scowled. 'He was a fool and now he is a dead fool.'

'I tried to warn him,' Agnes said, 'but he believed his cousin's blandishments. Tobias Ashby wants only the Elmhurst title and estates,' she paused, 'and the gold.' She picked up the book. 'Now I have what he wants and the power to knock on his door and demand admittance.'

'What are you proposing, Agnes?' Jonathan asked.

She swallowed. 'If you are willing to help me, I can gain entry into the castle. With one of you posing as my manservant, I could buy some time to find the hiding place. You could take the gold and I ... ' she tailed off. In the dead hours of the night, the plan had seemed so simple, now it seemed childish.

'You want the children,' Kate said.

Agnes nodded.

Kate looked at her husband. 'Well?'

'With one of us inside Charvaley, it could be done in a single night,' Jonathan said.

'Ashby knows me,' Kit said.

'And you would not pass as a manservant,' Agnes said, looking at Jonathan.

Jonathan straightened. 'I would have you know that I once enjoyed a formidable reputation as a master of disguise.'

'She's right,' Kate said. 'Not you, Jon.'

'It's my commission,' Daniel said. 'I was only a boy when Ashby last saw me, I doubt he would remember me.' He glanced at Agnes, 'And I owe it to Agnes to keep her safe.'

'Very well,' Kate said. 'Agnes, with Daniel inside Charvaley and these two outside, I entrust these men with your life.'

Agnes drew a sharp breath. 'The truth is I fear for the children more than my own life.'

Kate crossed to her and took her in her arms. 'Agnes, if there is any danger, please promise me you won't throw your life away for gold.'

Agnes stepped back and met Kate's clear, grey eyes. 'Never for gold, but I would for the children.'

Kate nodded. 'I understand.' She looked around at the three men. 'I presume you will wish to leave as soon as possible? I think these two need to talk.' She ushered her husband and Kit out of the room, leaving Agnes alone with Daniel.

Agnes crossed her arms and glared at him. 'Well? Was it always about the gold?'

He returned her gaze. 'I said what I had to say, Agnes. When I left the Lowlands, it seemed a simple proposition to endear myself to you, get into Charvaley, and make good my escape – with the gold. Then I met you.'

She narrowed her eyes. 'How can I believe anything you told me is true?'

He shook his head. 'Everything I have told you about myself is the truth, Agnes.'

'It's what you didn't tell me,' she said. 'You didn't trust me.'

'I didn't know you,' he protested, 'but I do know you now, Agnes and I –' He swallowed. 'I owe you my life.'

Agnes stared at him. 'Your life?'

'Yes, my life. Marsh fever can kill but because of you, I didn't die. If I were indeed a knight of old, I would kneel at your feet and pledge my life in your service, but as you well know I am a former slave and a privateer and any such gentlemanly notions were long since beaten out of me, so you will just have to learn to trust me.'

He swept her a lowly bow and turned away. At the door, he glanced back to look at her. 'You are wrong about one thing, Agnes. This is no longer about the gold or Tobias Ashby Whatever your feelings for me, you have my word that I will do whatever is within my power to give you back your son,' he said. 'Whatever it takes.'

CHAPTER 29

EVELEIGH PRIORY, CHESHIRE 25 NOVEMBER 1659

'This is it?' Agnes spoke first, breaking the heavy silence.

The four of them stood on a weed-infested forecourt, looking up at the ruined façade of a once-grand house. Scorch marks still blackened the walls and ivy, dead leaves clinging to the stems, curled through and around the empty windows like worms through a skeleton.

Daniel's breath clouded in the cold air. 'I don't remember it being this bad,' he said, his voice taut with emotion.

The decision to take a detour to Eveleigh had been Jonathan's. Although they might have thought it, neither of the Lovell brother had raised the subject. Surprisingly, although it meant a delay of several days before reaching Preston, Agnes had agreed.

Kit cleared his throat. 'It has deteriorated badly since I last saw it,' he said. 'The east wing was, as you know, still habitable.' He indicated a wing of the house that still retained its roof, although it sagged in places and several windows had been boarded up. Others still retained glass.

'I had a difficult time persuading your mother to leave,' Kit continued. 'It was only much later that she admitted that she had not wanted to go because of the hope you may one day knock on the door. She feared you would find no one here.'

Daniel swallowed. 'And yet here I am.'

Something brushed his hand, and instinctively his fingers curled around Agnes's gloved hand. He returned the slight, reassuring pressure before she slipped her hand away.

With heavy steps, he walked across to the front of the house, where a fine set of stairs still rose to the portico and the gaping hole that had once been the front door. He sat down on the top step, his elbows on his knees.

'Ashby shot him here,' he said. 'On these steps. He died in Kit's arms.'

He looked down as if he still expected to see his father's blood running down toward the gravel of the forecourt. A wave of emotion swept through him and he covered his face with his hand. Not since that first night after the battle, with his aching head pressed to King John's tomb, had he felt such helplessness.

A hand rested on his shoulder and he looked up to see Kit, offering what he could in wordless comfort and understanding. He took Kit's proffered hand and rose to his feet.

'Where is he buried?' Agnes asked.

Daniel pointed through the now-leafless trees to the little chapel that had served the Midhurst family for the centuries that they had owned Eveleigh. Kit flung his arm across Daniel's shoulders and they tramped through the woods followed by Jonathan and Agnes, their footsteps silenced by the heavy fall of leaves.

Like the house, the chapel lay in a ruinous state, its roof was mostly gone and only the splintered remains of the once-beautiful old stained glass still adhering to the window frames. Ashby's soldiers had delighted in destroying the idolatrous images.

The ancient oak door still hung drunkenly on its hinges, and despite its parlous state, it groaned as Kit pushed it open. Birds and animals had made their homes in the corners and among the rafters and the flagged floor lay thick with dust and leaves. The monumental tombs of Midhurst ancestors had felt the full fury of the Parliament soldiers, the faces destroyed beyond recognition.

Daniel crossed the floor to the stone altar that still stood in its place. Hunkering down, he swept the dried leaves from the flags.

'We laid him here,' he said. 'There is no memorial stone, but if there was it would read *Here lies Thomas Lovell, foully murdered on the steps of his home by one Tobias Ashby, of the Army of Parliament.*'

'We will ensure his place is marked, Dan,' Kit said.

Her too-long skirt brushing the dried leaves away in a soft sigh, Agnes knelt beside him, laying a bunch of yarrow flowers on the unmarked grave. Her gloved hand rested for a moment on the cold stone and she closed her eyes, her lips moving in silent prayer.

When she was done she looked up at him, laying her hand on his sleeve. Daniel laid his hand over hers for a fleeting moment. Their gaze met in a moment of quiet understanding.

'I'm sorry about the yarrow, it was all I could find, apart from gorse,' she said, rising to her feet.

At the far end of the chapel, Kit shivered and rubbed his hands together. 'We have tarried long enough in this mournful place,' he said.

They walked back to the horses, and as he swung into the saddle, Daniel gave the ruins of his home one last look. 'I will rebuild it,' he said.

Kit cast him a sideways glance. 'It will take a fortune.'

Daniel smiled. 'I have, if not quite a fortune, enough.'

Kit nodded. 'I would like to see it a home once more.'

Jonathan's nondescript mare capered with impatience. 'Time we were gone. We are clear on the plan? Daniel, you and Agnes go ahead to Preston and send Ashby a note to say you have recalled something of interest and you would meet with him.'

'Make him come to you,' Kit had suggested. 'He needs to dance to your tune.'

Agnes nodded and glanced at Daniel. 'Well, Lucas, are you ready?'

Daniel touched his fingers to the battered brown felt hat he had purchased off one of the Thornton grooms. They had taken care to ensure that their roles were convincing. Agnes, wearing a once-elegant but outmoded riding habit borrowed from Nell Longley, rode the black gelding.

He had to admit that she managed the animal with considerable skill. He had the bay mare and carried no sword, only two pistols, necessary for the defence of his mistress from the predations of the road.

'We will see you at Charvaley,' Jonathan said.

'You know where to go?' Agnes enquired of Jonathan.

'Your directions should be adequate. Just make sure the good lady is expecting us. I do not like surprising old ladies unnecessarily,' Jonathan remarked.

According to Agnes, Margaret Truscott, or Old Peg, as the family called her, had been nursemaid to James and then to Henry and Lizzie. Agnes had told them that when Old Peg had broken an ankle falling downstairs, James had judged her too old to continue actively in his service and had settled a grace and favour cottage on her, a little way out of the village.

'Can this woman be trusted?' Kit enquired.

Agnes nodded. 'With my life. As soon as we reach the castle, I will send Daniel with a note to Peg to tell her to expect you.'

Jonathan nodded. 'Until we meet again, Mistress Fletcher. 'He doffed his hat in farewell as Daniel and Agnes put their heels to the skittish horses. Agnes glanced at Daniel, her eyes bright. 'I'll race you to the crossroads,' she said.

'That's hardly fair –' Daniel began but she was gone, crouched low over the horse's neck, her wide-brimmed hat, secured only by a string, flying out behind her.

'Damn you,' Daniel muttered, startling the placid bay into action with a hefty kick. She sprang forward but stood no chance of catching her stablemate.

～

THEY STOPPED FOR LUNCH, turning aside from the road to find a quiet dell where boulders covered with a patchwork of bright green moss and orange lichen tumbled down to a stream, swollen now with the autumn rains. In summer it would be a pretty place, with old, gnarled trees for shelter and soft grass.

Daniel spread his cloak on a large, flat boulder and Agnes set out the simple repast of bread, cheese and ale she had purchased in the last village they had passed through. She perched on the boulder, swinging her feet like a small girl.

'Tell me about Henry,' Daniel said.

She jerked, looking around at him in surprise. He did not seem like the sort of man with the remotest interest in small children.

'What do you mean?'

His gaze met hers, his eyes the colour of the cold stream. 'I am guessing that you have never spoken of Henry as you should … as his mother, not his guardian. So, tell me about him.'

She blinked. She had never allowed herself to think of the child in that way. 'What do you want to know?'

'All those little things mothers talk about,' he said.

She smiled. 'He cut his first tooth at four months, and started walking before he was one.'

He laughed. 'And who does he look like?'

'You've seen him. He has James's fair colouring but he has my eyes, I think.' She smiled fondly, remembering the soft downy hair and the baby smell of her son. 'He is a typical boy who loves his wooden sword and his toy soldiers. I hope he grows up in a peaceful world where he never has to take up real arms.'

'Unlike us?'

She nodded. 'It's all we know, isn't it Daniel?'

He sighed. 'Nearly twenty years of strife, Agnes.' Daniel bit into the bread and chewed thoughtfully, staring at the water that broke over the boulders.

'How have you stood it all these years?' he asked at last.

The old, familiar ache cloyed her heart.

'I loved my sister,' she said, 'but in truth, I have wanted more than anything to hear him call me Mother.'

'Whose idea was the deception?'

'Ann's. I wonder now if she knew her days were numbered and wanted to give James the heir he craved. When she put the proposition it all seemed so very sensible.'

Daniel said nothing, his silence inviting the confidence she had never shared before.

'Elizabeth's birth nearly killed Ann. The doctors advised against any more children, but James wanted a son – he needed a son. He told me the last thing he wanted was for Tobias to inherit on his death, so the three of us decided that I would carry James's child and we would pretend it was Ann's.'

Daniel cleared his throat. 'You agreed to this arrangement? Willingly?'

Agnes lowered her head and nodded.

'I fancied myself in love with James. It was a foolish notion and not …' She paused, remembering the awful fumbling and James's grunts and groans. He had been nothing like Daniel. 'Not what I had expected. Henry was conceived quickly enough, and as soon as I was sure, James let it be known that Ann was once more with child but the doctors had advised her to remain confined to her bed-chamber until the child's birth. So Ann and I passed the next few months closeted away, attended only by Peg. When Henry was born …' She took a deep, steadying breath. 'Ann took to her bed, lauded as the mother of James's son. I …'

'You?' Daniel prompted as she hesitated.

'I had to watch my son in my sister's arms, a wet nurse brought in to suckle him, while … while my breasts were bound.'

She couldn't bring herself to look at him. The pain, both physical and emotional still raw even after all the years.

'James bought me presents.' Her fingers closed on the locket around her neck, James's gift to her. 'I told myself that their happiness was reward enough, but we lost Ann within a year to consumption and the children fell to my charge.' She looked up. 'I didn't wish my sister's death and I mourned her. I still do, but there was a part of me that rejoiced. I had Henry for my own, at last.'

'What if the child had been a girl?'

It was a question she had asked herself many times during her pregnancy. Agnes shook her head. 'I don't know. I assume James and Ann would have acknowledged the child in the same way, but …'

'What about James?' Daniel prompted, a harsh edge to his tone. 'He had his son – was he done with you?'

She let out a deep sigh. 'James still came to my bed, when it suited him, but God, in his wisdom, did not curse me with another pregnancy. Every month I gave thanks that I had been spared the shame and humiliation, but … ' she bit her lip, ' … there was a part of me that yearned to hold a child of my own in my arms.'

Daniel rose to his feet, brushing crumbs from his breeches. He stood in front of her and took her hand in his, curling his fingers around hers.

'You are too hard on yourself, Agnes. What more selfless act could you have performed for your sister, or your child?'

Agnes lowered her head. 'If James hadn't died—'

He tightened his grip. 'But James is dead. He chose his path. You are now all those children have.' He raised her hand to his lips and kissed her fingers. 'I wish I had an ounce of your selfless spirit, Agnes.'

She laughed and pulled her hand away. 'Selfless? I think not. The day is wasting, Daniel, and if we want to be at Preston by nightfall, we should be on our way.'

CHAPTER 30

CHARVALEY CASTLE, LANCASHIRE 27 NOVEMBER 1659

*D*aniel had not known what to expect from Charvaley Castle. The village of Charvaley lay hard up against the castle walls, where it had nestled for centuries in the protection of the lords of the castle. It boasted a collection of well-kept cottages, a church with a solid square tower, a small inn, and a market square before the old gatehouse of the castle.

The village lay quiet, blanketed in an autumnal mist through which the bulk of the castle loomed above the little houses. It was one of those castles that had long since ceased to be defensible, its crumbling walls transformed into a fine residence by successive generations of Ashbys. Only the gatehouse and a couple of towers remained of the original castle, the walls no doubt softened by wallflowers and ivy in summer. Now only dried stalks clung to the old stones, giving it a bleak and forbidding aspect.

The picture of benign innocence ended at the gate, where he was stopped by two red-coated soldiers. Turner's men, he supposed. He told them his business was with Colonel Ashby and of a personal nature.

'Colonel's not here,' one said. 'Gone to London.'

Daniel considered this information. It could be a blessing in disguise if Ashby were away from home. 'Then I will speak with Captain Turner,' he said.

One of the guards scratched his ear as he considered. He gave a curt nod and stood aside to let Daniel pass.

The residence, built, Daniel guessed, in the early years of James's reign, fronted the courtyard. He was shown through the large, elegant front door into a spacious, tiled entrance hall.

'What is your business with Colonel Ashby?'

Turner stood at a door with one hand on the handle, as if he meant to deal swiftly with this visitor. For a brief moment Turner frowned, and Daniel wondered if he had been recognized. He had deliberately not shaved since leaving Seven Ways and hoped the dark stubble concealed his identity from those who remembered a fresh-faced boy.

Daniel fumbled in his pocket and produced Agnes's note. 'I bring a note from my lady,' he said, affecting the inflections of his native Cheshire.

'And who is your mistress?' Turner's lips curved in a sneer.

'Mistress Fletcher.'

Turner relinquished his hold on the door handle and approached him, snatching the note from him.

'It's meant for Colonel Ashby,' Daniel protested. 'My lady was most insistent.'

'In the Colonel's absence I have his complete authority,' Turner said, breaking the seal.

He read the contents and looked up. 'Where is your mistress now?'

'Waiting in Preston, sir. She said to say how she knows she's not welcome here but would speak with the Colonel.'

Turner compressed his lips and glanced at the note again. 'Very well, I will return to Preston with you.'

AGNES HAD BEEN WATCHING for Daniel's return from the window of her chamber, the most expensive the inn could supply. Seeing Septimus Turner riding beside him, she took a step back, her stomach churning.

She had been prepared to face Ashby, had all her arguments in place, but Turner was an unknown quantity. How much did he know of his master's business?

At the peremptory knock on the door, she turned to greet her visitor.

Turner swept his hat from his head and gave her a cursory bow. She returned his half-hearted gesture with a mere inclination of her head. His gaze flicked to Daniel, who had opened the door to admit Turner and now stood deferentially to one side as if awaiting further orders.

'I was expecting Colonel Ashby,' she said, ignoring the implication in Turner's gesture. Daniel would not be leaving the room.

Turner's lips compressed. 'The Colonel has been in London, although we expect his return in a day or so. There is nothing you need to say to the Colonel that cannot be said to me.'

Agnes narrowed her eyes and allowed a thin, humourless smile to play on her lips. 'Oh, but there is, Captain Turner. When I spoke with the Colonel in London I was in shock, but since I have had time to reflect, I find my memory about certain events of the last year has become a little clearer.'

Turner's face betrayed nothing, but his body stiffened and she knew she had hit the mark. Turner knew about the gold.

'What do you want?' he enquired.

'Of you, nothing. I will return with you to the castle and await the Colonel,' she said.

'But ... ' Turner began, but she raised a hand.

'I will see the children,' she said. 'If you deny me that, I leave Preston today and that will be an end of it. Ashby will never know what it was I came to tell him.'

Turner's jaw worked. She could almost hear his brain churning through the conflicting orders. He was a man who only responded to orders and his were plain. Agnes Fletcher was not to be admitted at Charvaley.

He looked down at the hat in his hand and cleared his throat. 'Very well. Do you have a horse? I brought no coach.'

She nodded and he gave a curt inclination of his head. 'I will be waiting downstairs.'

She heard Turner's boots on the stairs and let out a heartfelt sigh as Daniel closed the door.

'You did well,' he said, turning to her.

Agnes shivered. 'He scares me more than Ashby.'

He crossed the floor to her and for a long moment, they stood facing each other. The weeks in an autumnal England, and his illness, had faded his tan, but the dark stubble on his chin and the scar on his cheek only served to make him look more exotic, more piratical, as Henry would have said.

She longed for him to touch her, to fold her in his arms and tell her all would be well, but she had set the barriers between them and there they would remain.

'I'm not a conspirator,' she said. 'I just want my children and my home. Should we leave a message for Jonathan and Kit?'

Daniel shook his head. 'They know where to go. I think we can trust them to find their way. Now, I'd better be a good manservant and go and organise the horses. I shall see you downstairs ... madam.' He gave her a low bow, and picking up Agnes's travelling satchel, Daniel left the room.

Gathering up her cloak and hat, Agnes took a deep breath and stepped into the unknown.

CHAPTER 31

*W*as it possible for Charvaley to remain so completely unchanged?

It had only been three months since she had left, hurrying to reach London, as James had sent news that his captors had indicated that he would die. She remembered every moment of that hellish journey with two miserable, fretful children. She had left with no thought except for James and no expectation that she would not be returning.

Then it had been late summer; now the chill winds of autumn lifted the edges of her cloak as they rode under the gatehouse into the well-maintained courtyard, surrounded on three sides by the residence and on the fourth by a high wall that led out into the gardens that had been James's pride and joy.

Agnes did not recognise the servant who helped her dismount from the black gelding and she looked at him curiously. The Charvaley steward had been a cheerful, round-faced man, not this dour, unsmiling minion.

'Where's Gibbs?' she asked Turner.

Turner shrugged. 'The Colonel preferred to have people he knew around him and brought his own people from Broughton.'

Agnes stared at him, thinking of the elderly but loyal Charvaley staff who had served the family. A small, nagging doubt insinuated itself into her mind. She had imagined returning to joyful acclaim from the staff and servants. Not this cold reception from people she did not know.

What had become of them? Had Tobias cast them out to make their own way in advance of winter?

'He has replaced them all?' she asked.

'Not all,' Turner replied.

Leah Turner waited at the massive oak door, dressed in a gown of a sombre russet colour with plain collar and cuffs unrelieved by lace or embroidery, her hands clasped in front of her, the keys of the house hanging from a heavy ring at her waist. At the sight of Agnes, the woman's lips compressed with disapproval to be nothing more than a slit in her face.

'What is she doing here?' she demanded of her brother. 'The Colonel gave orders ... '

Turner held up his hand. 'Peace, Leah. She is here to await the return of the Colonel.'

'You could have sent me word to expect a visitor,' Leah complained.

'I do not intend to inconvenience you, Mistress Turner. I have come to see Colonel Ashby – and the children,' Agnes said, collecting up the too-long skirts of Nell Longley's riding gown.

'You are not welcome here,' Leah Turner said.

'Sister,' Septimus Turner spoke. 'Mistress Fletcher has good reason to see the Colonel and we must accommodate her until he returns. Please extend her the courtesy of a guest.'

Inwardly Agnes seethed. *A guest? In her own home?*

She picked up her skirts and mounted the steps but Leah Turner did not move, remaining an immovable obstacle to the entrance.

'It will not be possible to see the children,' Leah Turner said. 'Not while the Colonel is in London. Our orders are quite explicit on that subject.'

Agnes studied the woman through narrowed eyes. She had to be careful which battles she picked, and however much it grieved her to be so close to the children, for the time being, this might be one she would have to concede.

'It has been a long, tiring journey,' she said. 'Be so good as to conduct me to my room, Mistress Turner.'

Leah's mouth twitched. 'As we were not expecting guests, there is no bed made up, but if you care to follow me. You … ' she addressed Daniel, 'see to the horses.'

The woman turned and proceeded into the house.

'I know the way to my bedchamber,' Agnes said.

She received no response, and her heart sank as the woman turned right instead of left at the top of the stairs, leading her toward the old part of the castle, to a badly lit, cold room with heavy stone walls, only partly relieved by a couple of heavy tapestries and a small half tester bed.

No fire burned in the fireplace and the room smelled musty and damp. Protest would be pointless. It was not unreasonable to have expected her not to be returning to Charvaley. No doubt the pleasant, airy chamber that had been hers for the past eight years had been reassigned.

Leah Turner pointed at the wooden chest at the end of the bed.

'That is yours, I believe. Your belongings were set aside should you send for them,' she said. 'I will have the bed made up and a fire lit.'

Agnes removed her hat and gloves, setting them on the chest.

'Mistress Turner — Leah — I would like to see the children.' She repeated the request in a soft, placatory tone. A woman appealing to a woman.

Leah's face betrayed no emotion. 'I will send food and drink for you and water to refresh yourself. Good day, Mistress Fletcher.'

Agnes pulled at the strings of her cloak as she looked around the austere room. What had she expected? To be welcomed back with open arms?

She stared at the heavy iron-studded door. Leah Turner could rot in hell – she would see the children.

She tried the latch and to her surprise, it opened but leaning against the wall outside was one of Turner's soldiers. He straightened on seeing her.

'Who are you?' she demanded.

The man whipped off his hat and shuffled his feet. 'Trooper Brown, ma'am.'

'Am I under armed guard?' she enquired.

The man frowned and scratched his chin. 'My orders are to see you get a good rest,' he said, 'And to take you to Mistress Turner or the Captain when they send for you.'

'Am I not permitted the opportunity to stretch my legs?'

'Not in my orders, ma'am,' the man said.

Her heart sank. She'd not come home, she had walked into virtual, if not actual, imprisonment, subject to the whims of the Colonel or Captain Turner, and stood little chance of either seeing the children or investigating the hiding place for the gold while she remained trapped in this room. She wondered how on Earth she would even get a message to Daniel.

Agnes retired back into the chamber and stood for a long moment looking at the heavy chest, the only item of furniture she had brought from her childhood home. She knelt beside it, running her hands over the smooth wood, now black with age. With her finger, she traced the familiar figures of David and Goliath on the lid. No need to look in her belongings for the key. The old lock had been prised open.

With a heavy sigh, she opened the lid and found her possessions had been thrown in with no order or respect. The only thing she treasured, a Bible box that had belonged to her father, sat at the top of the pile. She lifted it out, noting with distress that, like the chest, the lock had been prised open. Had they been looking for something that may have given them the clue to the gold, she wondered?

Mercifully, it looked as if everything within the box remained intact, albeit bearing the evidence of having been disturbed. Letters from her father and brother, her father's Bible, and the sorts of trinkets and mementos a young girl collects in her lifetime, ribbons and broken bits of jewellery of no value. She lifted them out one by one, a sense of violation washing over her. These were her special, private things, and the thought of Ashby or Turner or one of his rough soldiers handling them made her feel quite ill. She carefully repacked the box, adding *The Faerie*

Queen to the contents, and set it on the small table, one of the few pieces of furniture in the room.

She sank onto the chair beside the table and looked around the grim room. Perhaps it had been a terrible mistake coming here. Even knowing Daniel was also within the castle walls, and Kit and Jonathan not far away, she felt very alone and very afraid, not so much for herself but the children. She laid her head on her arms, sinking into a miasma of misery.

A tentative knock at the door brought her back to the present, and hastily wiping any tell-tale tears from her eyes, she rose to her feet. At her bidding, a maid entered the room carrying a tray. The scent of still warm, freshly baked bread rose from beneath the cloth and Agnes's stomach growled, reminding her that she hadn't eaten in a very long time.

'Welcome home, Mistress Fletcher.'

'Sarah!' The sight of Sarah Truscott's broad, smiling face cheered her. It was all she could do not to throw her arms around the girl.

'It's so good to see a familiar face. I thought the Colonel had replaced all the staff,' she said, watching as Sarah set the tray down on the table.

Sarah scowled. 'Most of 'em. Leastways those that had any position. The likes of me he don't care about.'

'I'm pleased to see you. How is Old Peg?'

'Auntie is not as strong as she should be,' Sarah frowned. The girl was Peg's great-niece, her only living relative. 'But she'll be cheered to know you are back where you belong.'

'I am only visiting, Sarah,'

Sarah glanced at the door. 'Why've they set a man on t' door?'

'To make sure I don't go wandering off in search of the children.' Agnes laid a hand on the girl's arm and said in a lowered voice, 'Tell me, Sarah, are they well?'

A shadow crossed the girl's face and her mouth turned down at the corners. 'By all reports, but no one sees 'em outside of Mistress Turner and Hannah the nursery maid.'

Agnes frowned. 'They never leave the nursery?'

'Not since they've been back from London, but the weather's been foul and there's always the chance of a small one catching a chill. Don't fret yourself, Mistress Fletcher. They'll be fine, just you see.'

Agnes regarded the girl's open, friendly face. Just because she was the great-niece of the woman she had sent Daniel and the others to did not mean she was an ally.

'I'm sure you'll get to see 'em in time, Mistress Fletcher. Now you eat up, while I make up the bed,' Sarah said. 'If you don't mind me sayin', you look a mite peaky. I'll get that lazy sod outside to see to the fire.'

A grumbling Trooper Brown soon had a fire burning on the hearth while the girl briskly dressed the bed. Agnes ate the more-than-adequate repast of bread, jam, and cheese washed down with a familiar small ale. At least some things hadn't changed.

Sarah regarded the empty platters. 'You must've been hungry.'

'Where's my manservant, Lucas?' Agnes enquired, conscious that Brown could probably hear every word.

A slight colour stained Sarah's cheeks. 'He's your manservant, is he? Last I saw he was in the kitchen being fed up by the kitchen hand. She seemed to think he needed feeding up, to judge by the food on his plate. I must say, he's got all the girls atwitter and he's barely had time to take off his boots.'

Agnes forced a smile. 'He's trouble, that one,' she said. 'But I could hardly ride through England alone and he seemed a good, strong lad.'

'Aye, he's that, right enough,' Sarah agreed, rather too readily, Agnes thought. 'I'll leave ye now. If ye need anything, get 'im out there to earn his bed and board,' Sarah jerked her head at the door behind which Trooper Brown had retired.

'Can you tell Lucas to come and fetch my boots? They need cleaning.'

Sarah held out her hand. 'I'll take 'em for ye.'

Agnes shook her head. 'Thank you, but I need to speak sternly with Lucas. I can't have him flirting with every maidservant in the castle.'

Sarah closed the door behind her, and Agnes caught a glimpse of Trooper Brown picking his teeth. She could do nothing while he stood by the door with his orders. Subject to the whims of Leah Turner and her brother, Agnes lay down on the bed. Whatever restrictions she had to endure, she would do so for the children. She would be good and biddable to whatever Tobias and the hateful Leah wanted. Her fingers tightened on the chain of her locket. She would do whatever it took just to be with the children again.

CHAPTER 32

'*A*re you Lucas? Your mistress summons you.'

Daniel looked up from the bowl of excellent stew that the pretty kitchen maid had set before him. The same girl leaned on the table, watching him as he ate. It took some effort to keep his eyes on the stew and not on the creamy white breasts that spilled from the girl's tightly laced bodice. In another time and place, he would not have hesitated to follow the path down that the girl wished to lead him.

The interruption came as a relief and he rose to his feet, knocking the stool over in his haste.

'My mistress?'

The maid frowned. 'Aye, Mistress Fletcher. Says you are to come and collect her boots for cleaning.'

'Thank you for the food … err … Ellie,' he addressed the kitchen maid, who rose languidly to her feet, with ill-disguised disappointment written in her downturned mouth.

He turned back to Sarah. 'Where will I find my mistress?'

She frowned. 'They've put her in the old part o' the house,' she said.

'You'd best take me up to her,' he said. 'I'd get myself lost in these corridors.'

Sarah smiled, the gesture lifting her plain features. 'Aye, it has its secrets, this house. Come with me. I'll show you.'

'Thank you … ' Daniel cocked an enquiring eyebrow.

'Sarah Truscott,' the girl said, a slight flush colouring her cheeks.

Truscott? He wondered if she was kin to the woman Agnes placed so much trust in.

'She used to be mistress here, you know,' Sarah continued as they climbed the servants' stairs.

'Is that so?' Daniel said. 'You were here in the days of the late Earl?'

She nodded. 'When the Colonel came they kept me because I've skills in the still room.'

The stairs wound up through the ancient walls of the original castle. As they wended their way upward, Sarah pointed to the doors they passed. 'Through there is the Great Hall,' she said. 'That's part of the old house and this door,' she stopped and opened the snug-fitting door, 'puts you on the gallery. We go this way.'

They crossed the wide gallery, from which an elegant staircase descended into the entrance hall. Leah Turner waited for them at the head of the stairs.

As Sarah curtsied, Daniel bowed obsequiously.

'Aren't you Mistress Fletcher's man?' Leah addressed Daniel.

'Dan'l Lucas, ma'am. I do serve Mistress Fletcher.'

'What are you doing up here?'

'My mistress summoned me, ma'am.'

'There is no need for you to attend upon her. Sarah can see to her needs.'

Daniel regarded the woman. Was she deliberately keeping him apart from Agnes?

'Mistress Sarah has her own responsibilities, ma'am. Mistress Fletcher would think it strange if I abandoned my duties. She's not a prisoner here.' The slight note of enquiry in his voice caused Leah Turner to stiffen.

'And where did Mistress Fletcher find you, Lucas?'

'London, ma'am.'

Leah opened her mouth to say something but thought better of it. She swept past them, her stiff skirts crackling her unspoken disapproval.

Sarah grabbed his arm and hustled him away through a maze of corridors to another set of ancient stairs leading to a gloomy passage, lit only by thin, high windows. A soldier lounged on a stool outside a door. He looked up at their approach, hauling himself to his feet.

Outrage surged through Daniel.

'Why is my mistress under guard?' he whispered to Sarah.

She shook her head. 'I don't think the Turners want her going anywhere that doesn't suit 'em,' she replied.

'Who are these Turners?'

'He's captain of the Colonel's Lifeguard and she's his sister. The Colonel brought her in to take charge of the poor wee mites. If you ask me,' Sarah lowered her voice, 'she's sweet on the Colonel. I'll leave you here, Lucas.'

A wave of revulsion rode over Daniel at the thought of Leah Turner and Tobias Ashby together.

'Who's this?' The soldier lurched off his stool to bar Daniel's way. He stood nearly half a head taller than Daniel, with shoulders that filled the breadth of the narrow space.

Daniel looked up into the man's face. 'I'm the lady's man. Who are you?'

He could almost see the information being processed behind the man's dull eyes. *All brawn*, he thought. He knew the sort.

'Trooper Brown,' the man replied. 'Cap'n Turner set me to look after 'er.'

'Look after her? Then you're welcome to clean her boots,' Daniel replied.

Brown grinned, revealing a mouth of yellowed, rotting stumps. 'You're welcome to her boots. She's a nice lady. Came out to chat to me, she did, asked me if I'd wife and bairns.' He shook his head. 'Twenty years in t'army, I told her. Ain't no time for hearth and home.'

'Indeed,' Daniel replied. 'Then you better let me in.'

'Door ain't locked,' Brown replied and sank back onto his stool.

Daniel knocked and Agnes opened it, standing aside as he entered the room. She closed the door behind them and looked up at him. Her lips parted, and he saw the fear in her eyes. Her surroundings, more prison than bed chamber served only to emphasise her vulnerability. She didn't deserve this treatment.

It would have been so easy to draw her into his arms, but Daniel made no move. He hadn't touched her since that night in Seven Ways when she had told him that she had taken him to her bed for one reason only – pity. It didn't matter how often he revisited their night together in his memory – he was certain that what might have begun with pity ended in something far deeper and more meaningful to both of them. Now the only way he could deal with her was to keep his distance.

'You sent for me, ma'am,' he said, conscious of the guard beyond the door.

Her lips twitched into a smile. 'My boots are filthy.'

He took a step toward her and lowering his voice said, 'Do you think I'm your servant to order about?'

She smiled. 'We have to make it convincing, isn't that what Jonathan said?'

'Jonathan Thornton did not know what a demanding wench you are. Now, where are these boots?'

She produced her mud-caked riding boots. 'And get the mud out of my skirts, too,' she announced imperiously, thrusting the muddy garment into his arms as well.

'Very good, ma'am.' He frowned. 'How do I get mud out of skirts?'

She cuffed his arm. 'Wait for the mud to dry and then brush it off. Have you seen Old Peg yet?'

He shook his head. 'Not yet. I've been ... '

'A little distracted?' Agnes raised an eyebrow. 'Pretty kitchen maids, I hear.'

He cleared his throat and changed the subject. 'The girl, Sarah. Is she a relative of this Peg?'

'Her great-niece.'

'Can she be trusted?'

Agnes shrugged. 'Six months ago I would have said: "with my life".

Now, I don't think we can afford to trust anyone. She is fortunate to still have her place and she knows it.'

A beam of sunlight forced its way through the dusty panes of the small window, illuminating Agnes's face. Daniel resisted the urge to kiss the tip of her nose, with its dusting of freckles.

He took a step toward the door. 'I'll leave you now. That Turner woman does not wish me paying court on you, so I may find my way barred next time.'

'But I am not a prisoner, at least, so they tell me,' Agnes said.

Daniel glanced at the door. 'I'm not sure I am prepared to argue with Trooper Brown on that point. He's twice my size.'

The smile faded from Agnes's face. 'They are keeping me from the children. To be so close … '

This time he broke his self-imposed rule, cupping her face in his left hand and stroking her cheek with his thumb. He expected her to push him away but she leaned into him, resting her forehead on his chest. With a supreme effort, he dropped his hand and stepped back.

'This will take a little patience,' he said. 'I'd better go and find Old Peg before Jon and Kit arrive on her doorstep.'

'Daniel,' she said as he turned to go. 'No dallying with the kitchen maids.'

He smiled at the guilty memory of the buxom girl and turned back to look at her. 'Got to look convincing, Agnes.'

'Just not too convincing,' she said with a smile.

DANIEL STOWED Agnes's boots and petticoats with his few possessions in the corner of the kitchen to which he had been directed. He had no fears of his bag being searched. It contained nothing but clean linen and a battered Bible he had bought from a stall in Preston. They would also find a small pistol, but that should excite no comment. These were dangerous times and he would be a fool to travel without a weapon to defend himself and his mistress. He carried only a knife strapped in a sheath against his chest. He fiddled with his belt, missing his sword's comforting presence.

Conscious of the urgent need to seek out Peg Truscott, he returned to the stables, where a sullen stable boy indicated the horses. Daniel saddled the gelding and led it out into the cold, late afternoon. Glancing up at the lowering clouds, he shivered. It would be dark within the hour.

'Goin' back out?' the stable boy inquired.

'This 'un showed signs of lameness on the ride here,' Daniel replied. 'Thought I'd just put 'im through his paces again before dark.'

He led the horse out through the gate, waiting until he was out of sight of the castle before mounting up and turning north, following Agnes's directions. One mile out of the village, in a heavily wooded valley, he found the narrow path by the fallen oak. It wound among the trees, crossed a brook, and led to a low, single-room cottage in a glade. The cleared ground had been turned over to different plants, most of which were no more than twigs in the late autumn chill.

A wreath of smoke rose from the chimney, and as he dismounted the door opened and an elderly woman leaning on a stick came out to meet him.

She looked up at him with faded blue eyes that held more curiosity than fear.

'Are you Peg Truscott?'

Her eyes narrowed. 'What's your business?' she demanded.

'I bring a message from Agnes Fletcher,' he said.

The woman's eyes widened. 'Agnes? Is she back?'

'She's at the castle,' Daniel began warily.

The woman nodded. 'If ye're a friend of Agnes's, you'd best come in, young man.'

He ducked his head to enter the cottage, blinking to allow his eyes to adjust to the gloom. The little room smelled of herbs and baked bread. He looked around, taking in the simple cot, the table with four stools arranged around it and an old, battered wooden chest that stood against one wall. The only other furniture was two solid chairs furnished with cushions, standing on the rush mat before the hearth.

A low peat fire burned in the hearth before which laid an old dog of indeterminate breed. It raised its head and looked in Daniel's direction with milky eyes, emitting a low growl.

Daniel hunched down beside the animal, scratching its ears. The dog closed its eyes, its tail beating a crescendo of delight at the unexpected attention.

'What's his name?' he asked.

'*Her* name is Bonny because she were such a bonny pup when I found her.'

'Not a pup anymore,' Daniel said.

The woman sat down in one of the chairs, laying her stick down beside her. She reminded Daniel of his own nursemaid – pink-cheeked and round. The sort of motherly arms that would wrap around a small child and instantly make them feel safe and loved. She should have been up at the castle, not here in this lonely cottage.

'My name is Daniel ... ' He hesitated, wondering if he should reveal his identity.

'Daniel'll do,' the woman said. She frowned. 'You bring trouble on your heels.'

The back of his neck prickled. 'What do you mean?'

'I don't need any gift of sight to know that Agnes' return means trouble for Ashby.' She waved at a chair. 'Take a seat, my lad. Ye've been ill. I can see it in yer eyes.' She smiled, revealing toothless gums. 'It's not every day handsome young men come a-calling, so humour an old woman. Give me your hands.'

A shiver ran down Daniel's back and he hesitated. He had seen a woman in Martinique, an old African woman who was rumoured to be able to tell a man's fortune in his hands. He had laughed it off and refused to be drawn into her circle. Now he could not resist.

She took his hands in hers. Although gnarled with age, their touch was soft. She caressed the back of his left hand, turning it over in her palm. 'I can see a person's past, and ... ' She did the same with the right hand, '... and his future. You choose.'

'My past,' Daniel said. If she were a fraud then he would tell soon enough by what she purported to see there.

With her thumb she caressed the back of his hand again, turning it over and running her fingers along the lines of his palm. Her face grew serious and she shook her head.

'I see pain and loneliness. Too much suffering for one so young.' She looked up and he returned her gaze with a sceptical lift of his eyebrow. *Easy enough in such troubled times to say such things.* 'You carry the scars of a great wrong.' This time she closed her eyes, holding his hand between both of hers, rocking back and forth as she spoke. 'There is a long journey across the sea. Heat and sickness and terrible crimes. Darkness, thirst, pain ... and death.' Her eyes opened, looking at him but not seeing him. 'Ye've looked death in the face – more than once.'

Daniel pulled his hand away, a trickle of sweat running down his face. 'How can you know ... ?'

The woman slumped back in the chair with her eyes closed and didn't appear to hear him. Daniel jerked to his feet and strode out into the cold, crisp air, where he leaned against the stone wall of the house, his breath coming in short gasps as he fought back the wave of conflicting memories and emotions her words had conjured.

'Ye've faced yer demons boy.' The woman stood at the door. 'And ye beat 'em down but they'll keep trying. All your life they'll come a-knocking at the door.'

Daniel turned to look at her. 'You can tell me my future?'

She met his eyes. 'Aye, but not now, not today. There are still words to be written on that page. Go back to the castle. Back to Agnes. She'll need you sorely in the days to come.'

'I have two friends. Agnes has told them to come here. She told them they would be safe here.'

She nodded. 'Aye, as safe as anywhere around here. Tobias Ashby's coming was a bad day for us all. When will they be here?'

'Tomorrow,' Daniel replied as he swung himself into the saddle.

She shook he head. ''Tis a bad business up at the castle. I'll be glad to see that man gone. Is that why ye've come?'

The memory of their recent conversation still fresh, he said with some asperity, 'You are the seer of all – you tell me.'

She laughed. 'Ye've a tongue to you, young man. Go in peace.'

He turned his horse back toward the road, glad to be away from the cottage and its strange inhabitant. He turned his mind to all that had to be done in the next twenty-four hours.

Ashby's absence was a blessing. God willing, they could accomplish what they came to do and be gone before he returned. However, he acknowledged, the whole plan relied on Agnes finding her way into the children's room, and it didn't appear that the Turners were going to allow that to happen.

'Out of the way!'

He had been so lost in his thoughts that he'd not heard the sound of a coach coming up behind him. He managed to move his horse to the side of the lane as the coach, drawn by four perfectly matched chestnut horses, rushed past him, the horses labouring under the coachman's whip. The blinds were drawn but he recognised the arms on the door as those of Elmhurst and his heart sank. It could be none other than Ashby, returned early from London.

Mud churned up by the hooves and wheels spattered both him and the horse. He cursed aloud but the coach had moved on.

Dusk had closed in as he led his filthy horse into the stable.

The stablehand snickered. 'Bin for a swim in the mud?'

Daniel jerked his head at the coach, which stood in the stableyard; two other stablehands were busying themselves with the exhausted, mud-spattered horses.

'Whose is the coach?' Daniel enquired. 'Nearly ran me down.'

'The Colonel returned from London,' the boy replied. He frowned in disapproval. 'Looks like he drove the team hard to get here. No respect for 'orses. He could've killed 'em. His late Lordship would never ... ' He broke off, conscious he'd spoken out of turn to a stranger. 'Want me to see to your 'orse?'

Daniel shook his head. 'No, you've got your hands full. I'll see to my horse.'

Cleaning and settling his horse took a good hour and it was gone dark when Daniel returned to the kitchens.

He had to warn Agnes of Ashby's return if she did not know already. He sought out the cook and asked for a light meal to carry up to his mistress. A grumbling kitchen hand obliged and Daniel slipped up the kitchen stairs, trying to remember the route through the rabbit warren of an old house to Agnes's quarters.

He had to stop a footman to ask for directions. The man glanced at the tray.

'I'll take it,' he said.

'No,' Daniel said. 'She has orders for me no doubt.' He rolled his eyes to indicate that Agnes was one to issue orders and the footman smiled.

'Like that, is she?' he said and gave Daniel the directions he needed.

Brown did not bother getting to his feet as he approached.

'Cold as a witch's heart out here,' he grumbled, knocking on the door and opening it to admit Daniel.

Agnes had been sitting by the fire reading a book and she jumped to her feet. A lock of hair curled down across her forehead and his fingers twitched. He longed to push it up behind her ear.

The guard remained in the doorway, watching as Daniel set the tray down on the table.

'Yer supper, Mistress,' he said.

'Thank you, Lucas.'

She looked him up and down. 'What do you mean by presenting yourself to me in this state?'

Daniel, who had thought he had done a fair effort of cleaning off the worst of the mud, looked down at himself. 'I took the gelding out for a ride,' he said. 'I was worried that it was going lame.'

'I see, and … ?'

'We got caught in a narrow lane by the Colonel's coach,' he said. 'Seemed in a hurry to get home.'

Agnes's mouth formed an O of surprise. She swallowed, and with a quick glance at the soldier, said, 'Have they found you a bed for the night?'

'I'm to sleep in the kitchen, as is my place,' Daniel replied.

'Thank you, Lucas.'

'Any orders for me, Mistress?' Daniel enquired obsequiously. He could almost feel himself tugging his forelock.

The light of amusement flashed in her eyes and she bit her lip.

'No, nothing for now,' she said. 'Good night.'

Daniel closed the door behind him and lingered as Brown sank onto his stool again.

'You here for the night?' he enquired.

'Unless they send someone to relieve me,' Brown grumbled. 'Punishment for not cleanin' me kit properly. That Turner is a stickler.'

'If she,' Daniel jerked his head at the door, 'needs anything, ask for me. The name's Lucas.'

'Lucas,' the man repeated. 'Better get back and clean those boots she gave you. They'll keep you busy tonight.'

Daniel pulled a face. 'Got me own to do too,' he said.

Nothing for it, he considered as he returned to the kitchen. He would be spending the evening in the kitchen, cleaning boots with an ear on the downstairs gossip.

CHAPTER 33

*A*gnes passed a restless night, tormented by the thought of Henry and Lizzie being so close and not even knowing she was in the castle. What if Ashby sent her away without seeing them?

Sarah brought her breakfast, and when she enquired after Lucas, Sarah said only that he had been busy in the stable with one of the horses. The maid also brought the summons Agnes had been waiting for. Colonel Ashby requested her presence.

A fire had only just been lit in the parlour, and Agnes's breath misted in the air as she stood with her eyes demurely downcast and her hands clasped in front of the serviceable green woollen gown she had retrieved from her chest. She closed her eyes, breathing in the familiar scent of beeswax that arose from the well-polished furniture, before dropping a deep and respectful curtsey in the presence of her nemesis.

This is for the children, she told herself, as she brought her gaze up to meet Tobias Ashby's self-satisfied smirk.

Ashby, clad for once in a plain blue woollen suit of clothes, not his more familiar military uniform, stood with his back to the fireplace, his arms folded and his eyes narrowed as if he was inspecting her for signs of rebellion. Septimus Turner stood by the window, looking out across the damp gardens as rain speckled the diamond panes. Leah Turner was notable for her absence.

Tobias rubbed his hands together. 'It's going to be a cold winter,' he said conversationally, with what looked like a smile lifting the corners of his straggly moustache. 'I trust your journey here was not too fraught. Did you come far?'

Agnes ignored the question, clearly aimed at establishing where she had been for the last weeks since she had been abandoned in London.

Tobias picked up her note from the table. 'You sent this. What is it you have to tell me?'

'You will hear nothing until you let me see the children,' she said.

Tobias narrowed his eyes. 'If that is how it is to be.' He nodded at Turner. 'Go and fetch them.'

Alone with Tobias, Agnes squared her shoulders. 'Did you know that I have been kept a virtual prisoner since my arrival?'

Tobias's moustache twitched again. 'My dear, Agnes, you may recall that you were forbidden this house. We could hardly have you wandering around without some form of protection.'

'Mistress Fletcher to you,' she responded. 'I have been mistress in this house since the death of my sister. I'm not sure what I needed protection from.'

Tobias opened his mouth to respond, but a shrill cry from the doorway interrupted him.

'Aunt Agnes!'

Agnes turned on her heel and held out her arms to the two small people who came hurtling toward her. She went down on her knees, burying her face in their warm, sweet embraces, breathing in the scent of her child.

Her child. As much as she loved Lizzie, Henry was her very blood and being.

Still on her knees, she drew back.

'Let me look at you,' she said. 'Henry, I swear you have grown two inches at least and Lizzie, darling Lizzie, you must have grown at least four.'

Inwardly her stomach quirked at the sight of their pale, drawn faces.

Dark circles shadowed their eyes and their movements seemed slower, more inhibited.

'Children!' The frosty command came from Leah Turner, and at the sound of her voice, both children stiffened in Agnes's embrace. Agnes rose to her feet, drawing the children in against her skirts.

'Thank you for the care of the children, Mistress Turner. It is pleasing to see them looking so well,' Agnes said in a civil tone.

Much as she wanted to fly at Leah and demand to know how the children were being treated, she didn't need or want to make an enemy of this woman.

Leah fixed her gaze on Agnes. 'You spoiled these children for too long. They are wilful and disobedient and I have been forced to chastise them for their wayward behaviour. I am pleased to report they are beginning to see the Word of the Lord and to learn meekness and humility.'

Lizzie whimpered and pressed her face into Agnes's skirt. A cold hand tightened around Agnes's heart. *Chastise* in Leah Turner's lexicon could have just one meaning.

'I assure you, Mistress Turner,' Agnes said, her voice tight with emotion. 'I was diligent with their study of the Bible. Perhaps it is the manner in which you present it that is the difficulty. I have always found them biddable children.'

'Enough!' Ashby's harsh tone cut across the tension. 'Now, you have satisfied yourself that the children are in good health. Leah, return them to the nursery. Ag … Mistress Fletcher and I must talk.'

The children clung tighter to Agnes. Their very silence concerned her and she turned to Tobias. 'You will get nothing from me unless you allow me free access to the children while I am here.'

'Colonel —' Leah protested.

Tobias fixed his gaze on Agnes and she returned it without blinking, grateful he could not see how her stomach churned.

'Very well. I don't anticipate your visit here will be protracted. Leah —' he held up his hand, forestalling any further protest.

Agnes bent and kissed the children. 'I just have to talk with Cousin Tobias. I will be up presently,' she said. 'Go now with Mistress Turner.'

Lizzie took Henry by the hand, and with dragging footsteps, the two children crossed to Leah. The door slammed shut behind them and Agnes turned once again to face Tobias.

He gestured at a chair. Agnes glanced at Septimus Turner, who had not moved from his position by the window. Ashby followed her gaze and said, 'You may leave us too, Turner.'

Turner looked from one to the other, his brow furrowed. Meeting the impassive face of his superior, he inclined his head. 'Of course.'

Tobias waited until they were alone before he took a seat in the chair by the fire. He ran a hand down his face as he said, 'Forgive me, I am a little weary. It was a long journey from London in this atrocious weather. These are uncertain times and I do not wish us to be enemies, Agnes. You must understand, I am bound to obey the letter of the Committee's order.'

'No one can accuse you of failure to exercise diligence in your duty, Tobias, but may I remind you the directive of that Committee may not outlive the King's return?'

He gave her a sharp glance. In his younger days he had been quite a good-looking man, she recalled. They had met at James's wedding to Anne in the early years of the war. James's avowed neutrality, and the fact Tobias was his heir until a son was born to James, ensured regular invitations to Charvaley in the following years.

He had even, and she shuddered at the thought, made overtures through James for her hand in marriage. Her obvious revulsion at the suggestion, and the fact that beyond her connection to James's wife she brought nothing to the marriage, had quickly dissuaded him.

'You may be right, Agnes,' he said. 'But until the order changes, the children are in my care and custody. I shall do all in my power to ensure their health and happiness, but children take ill and sometimes there is nothing to be done except pray.'

Something in his tone made her skin crawl.

He straightened in his chair and tapped the note again. 'Enough of this. What is it that you have to tell me?'

She took a steadying breath. 'I have been thinking much on our conversation in London,' she said, 'and I may have recalled something of use to you about the valuable property you mentioned.'

'*May* have recalled something?' Tobias's lip curled back in derision, showing yellowing teeth beneath the straggly hairs of his moustache.

Agnes ploughed on. 'This is an old house, Tobias, riddled with hiding places. What exactly is it you seek? If I knew then I may have a better recollection of hints James may have dropped.'

Pulling at the ends of his moustache, Tobias narrowed his eyes. 'Your paramour,' he said with a snarl, 'was responsible for the theft of a shipment of gold. We believe the gold may be hidden here.'

Agnes made a pretence of surprise. 'Gold? What makes you think it is still here and not already with the K … Charles Stuart?'

'Because our agents at the court of Charles Stuart report that someone has been dispatched to recover it.'

This genuinely surprised Agnes. Did he mean Daniel?

'You have spies at the exiled court?'

He waved a hand. 'Of course, we do. Charles Stuart does not sneeze without us knowing.'

'Who is this man who has been sent?'

Tobias shook his head. 'Unfortunately, our informant did not have that information. A stranger at court was all he could tell us.'

So Daniel's identity was safe for the moment.

'You had James in custody for months; why did you not ask him directly?'

'Oh, we did – even showed him how he could be persuaded if we had a mind.'

A sick knot of fear and revulsion gathered in Agnes's stomach. 'James said nothing of being tortured.'

Tobias gave a huff of humourless laughter. 'It is not politic to torture Earls,' he replied. 'Now, let us stop this prevaricating, Agnes. You have my word that you can spend time with the children. Just tell me where the gold is hidden.'

Agnes cast a glance at the door and took a few steps toward Tobias, lowering her voice. 'There is a hiding place in the room James used as a study,' she began.

Tobias threw up his hands. 'I know of that one. It was empty. Do not forget, Agnes, I knew this house as a child and James and I spent many a long hour looking for its secret places. I'm not the fool you take me for.' He leaned forward, so close their foreheads almost touched. 'This is not about the gold. You want the children.'

Agnes raised her chin, looking the man in the eye. 'I tell you truthfully that I well recall the night that the gold arrived. At the time, James secured it in his study. If it is not there then he must have moved it alone.'

Ashby turned away from her, pacing the room several times. 'That is not enough, Agnes.'

She shook her head. 'It is everything I know, Tobias. But in my time here, James showed me many of the hiding places in this house. Grant me time to search my memory and we will see if my knowledge is the same as yours. I care nothing for gold but I am motivated by the greater desire to see the children are safe and well. I will look for it and if I find it, then it is yours to do with what you will on condition the children are restored to my care.'

Tobias tugged at his beard and rose to his feet. 'You have until dusk tomorrow night. If the gold has not been located you will leave this place and never return.'

Agnes nodded.

Taking a few steps toward the door, she said, 'May I go to the children now?'

Tobias waved a dismissive hand. 'Go. I am not the monster you think me, Agnes. The children have missed you and it may cheer them to see something of you.'

Relief flooded Agnes, and she found herself feeling genuinely grateful to this man.

He continued, 'I will see you at supper. In the meantime, think hard about your situation, Agnes. You have until tomorrow.'

'You wish me to dine with you?'

He turned to face her, his face a hard mask. 'Of course. You are my guest, are you not? Or do you prefer to eat alone in your chamber, with my man at your door?'

~

"The children guard the secret," James had written.

Just one secret? The bitter thought twisted like a knife in Agnes's heart. James had harboured many secrets and hidden them well.

She walked slowly along the corridor that led to the children's nursery, counting off the doors to the unused bed chambers. The children occupied a large room at the end of the corridor. She opened the door of the chamber adjacent to it and peered in. The only furniture was a dusty bed without a mattress or hangings, a table, and a chest. She paused, squinting at the wall abutting the nursery. Just to be certain she walked back into the corridor and into the bedroom again several times.

Her heart skipped a beat. She had never noticed that the internal dimensions of this room did not match the external. At least four feet abutting the nursery were unaccounted for. She had been right. All she had to do now was to locate the entrance within the nursery.

An unfamiliar thrill of anticipation ran down her spine.

Taking a deep breath, she opened the door and walked into the all-too-familiar room. which served as both bedchamber and nursery. As the children were still considered little, they shared the massive oak bed with its heavy red woollen hangings.

The children were alone with a sour-faced nursery maid, who sat by the fire darning stockings. What had Sarah called her? Hannah? Lizzie sat beside her, apparently engaged in needlework.

Hannah glanced up, a frown creasing her disagreeable face. 'Who are you?' she demanded without rising to her feet.

Agnes drew herself up. It was hard to be imperious when you barely touched five feet but she did her best.

'I am Mistress Fletcher,' she said. 'I am aunt to these children and sister-in-law to the late Earl. I expect better manners of you, young woman.'

Hannah flushed, set down her sewing, rose to her feet, and bobbed a curtsey.

'Sorry ma'am,' she stuttered, a sulky caste to her mouth.

'What is your name?' Agnes demanded while she held the upper hand.

'Hannah, ma'am.'

'Leave us, Hannah,' Agnes ordered.

Hannah shuffled her feet and looked at the toes of her shoes. 'Mistress Turner —' she began.

Agnes fixed the girl with a hard stare. 'I will answer to Mistress Turner. I have the consent of the children's guardian to spend some time alone with them. Go.'

Mumbling to herself, the nursery maid left the room, no doubt in search of Leah Turner.

At once the atmosphere lightened. Henry ran to Agnes, almost tripping over his skirts in his haste. She took him in her arms and held him tight, pressing her face into his soft, downy head until he began to squirm. Lizzie set her needlework down and, with more dignity than Henry, crossed the floor to Agnes's embrace.

'Are you staying, Aunt Agnes?' Lizzie asked.

'I'm just here on a very short visit,' she said.

'You're not coming back to live here?' Henry's lower lip began to tremble.

'Not for a little while,' Agnes replied, conscious that her smile lacked conviction.

'But you will come back?' Lizzie insisted.

Agnes looked into the girl's knowing eyes. 'I can't make promises, Lizzie,' she said. 'Believe me when I say this is not my doing.'

Lizzie pouted. 'No, it's Cousin Tobias. He wants Father's title.'

'Lizzie! You will not speak ill of Cousin Tobias. He is your legal guardian.' She smiled. 'I'm here now. Shall we play a game?'

'A game? But Mistress Turner has forbidden —' Lizzie began.

'Mistress Turner is not here and she does not need to know.'

'Spillikins?' suggested Henry.

'How about hide and go seek?' Agnes said. 'I will count to fifty and you two must hide somewhere in this room.'

The children grinned at her.

Agnes covered her eyes and began to count. She smiled at the sound of giggling and the children's feet pattering on the floorboards.

'No, Henry, you can't hide with me,' she heard Lizzie whisper.

'Forty-eight, forty-nine, fifty ... coming, ready or not!' Agnes said.

The entrance to the hidden cavity had to be concealed somewhere in the wall adjoining the room next door, a wall lined with heavy oak panelling of some age and covered in a large, moth-eaten tapestry of Noah's Ark. She wondered if Tobias in his searching had even thought of looking in the children's nursery. As she contemplated the length of the wall, she hoped it would not take her too long to find.

'Are you hiding?' she called out and was rewarded by Henry's squeak from behind the bed hangings.

She made a show of searching out the two children, finding Lizzie hiding under the bed. They both pretended to be stumped about Henry's whereabouts, despite the shoes peeping out from beneath the hangings and the barely stifled chuckles.

The children begged her to play again, which she was happy to do. After the third round, Lizzie looked up at her with a frown.

'Why do you keep looking at the tapestry?' she said. 'I won't hide there. That's where the ghost lives.'

Agnes blinked. The ghost? It was the first she'd heard of a ghost – at least in this part of the house.

'When did you see the ghost?' she asked, trying to keep her voice neutral.

Lizzie frowned in concentration. 'A long time ago ... before Father went to London. It was summer and I was hot in the bed, so I had pulled back the curtain a little way.'

'What did you see?'

'A man all in black. He walked straight through that wall.' Lizzie pointed melodramatically at the tapestry.

'Were you scared?' Agnes asked.

Lizzie shook her head. 'No. He looked a bit like Father.'

Probably because he was the child's father, Agnes thought.

She gathered the child into her arms. Henry, feeling left out, jumped at them, knocking them to the ground. They subsided into a giggling, happy pile on the floor.

'What is this?' The outraged voice from the doorway froze them.

Lizzie and Henry found their feet and cowered behind her skirts as Agnes rose to face Leah Turner. The maid, Hannah, lurked behind her mistress, a tight-lipped smile on her face. Leah's already pale face seemed drained of all colour, her lips an invisible line of outrage.

She pointed a finger at the children. 'You ... and you ... there will be no supper for either of you.'

'Mistress Turner. The children are not to blame. We were playing ... ' Agnes protested.

It seemed impossible that Leah's eyebrows could rise any higher. 'Playing?'

'Hide and go seek,' Agnes said.

The colour rose in Leah's face. 'We do not play games in this house. As I feared, you are a vile influence, Mistress Fletcher. Leave this room at once.'

Two pairs of small hands clutched Agnes's skirts.

'Don't leave us,' Lizzie sobbed, terror rising in her voice. 'She'll beat us. I know she will. She beats us all the time. She has a birch stick –'

Agnes straightened. 'I will not be dismissed like a common servant. I am aunt by blood to these children and I am here with the consent of their guardian. I am not leaving them until I am ready to do so and if I choose to lighten their lives by playing games, I will.'

Leah turned to Hannah. 'Fetch Brown and Simpson.'

Hannah turned and scurried away and Leah took a step into the room.

'You have cosseted these children to the point where they are ungovernable. They need discipline. They need to have the word of the Lord beaten into their spoiled little minds.'

'Beat them? I will not permit you to touch them. I was mistress here before ever you were and their father entrusted these children to me before his death.'

Leah's lip curled. 'But he failed to confirm his instructions in a will, or so I am told. Tobias ... Colonel Ashby is their legal guardian. We will see how much influence you hold in this house.'

Two burly soldiers appeared at the door, one of them Trooper Brown. Leah turned to face them. 'Take her,' she pointed at Agnes. 'And secure her in her chamber.'

As the men entered the room, Agnes backed away with her arms around the two children. 'How dare you,' she said. 'I am not to be treated this way.'

'Don't make trouble.' The soldier who must be Simpson reached out to grab her arm.

Agnes batted his hand away. 'Don't touch me.'

'You,' Leah indicated Brown. 'Take the children.'

Brown lunged at Henry, who screamed, trying to get further behind Agnes's skirts, but the man got a purchase on him, lifting him away from her and holding him at arm's length to protect himself from Henry's kicking feet. Agnes swung around to defend the child and in that instant Simpson grabbed her around the waist, knocking her feet from underneath her and pulling her away from the two children.

With the hysterical cries of the children resounding in her ears, Agnes was borne away in the iron grip of the soldier. Kicking and struggling availed her nothing and as they reached the top of the stairs she stopped resisting.

'Put me down,' she said, employing her most glacial tone. 'I demand to be taken to Colonel Ashby on my own two feet, not carried like a sack of potatoes.'

The man glanced at Leah who nodded. He set her down but kept a tight grip on her arm as they descended the stairs.

Not since she was nine years old and had been caught stealing apples from the orchard had Agnes felt so humiliated. She stood before Tobias, her hands clasped penitentially before her and her gaze lowered as Leah recited her crimes.

'Tobias ... ' Agnes began.

'Address the Colonel properly,' Leah cut in. Standing beside Tobias, Leah bristled with self-righteous indignation.

'Colonel Ashby,' Agnes shot Leah a sharp glance. 'I know we all have the children's best interests at heart.'

'And their best interests are not served by unseemly romping in the nursery,' Leah cut in. 'The children are wild and undisciplined, Colonel.'

Tobias stroked the end of his moustache, his gaze on Agnes.

'Leah, my dear,' he said at last. 'I appreciate your zeal, but Mistress Fletcher and I have an understanding. I am allowing her to spend time with the children while she is in this house. I do not believe this will be an extended visit.'

Leah cast Agnes a look that came close to firing blue sparks of pure malevolence.

'This woman is a whore,' Leah raged. 'Bedding men for her convenience. The carnal act is for one reason alone, the begetting of children.' She pointed a finger at Agnes. 'It is God's judgment on you that you have not been cursed with a bastard child.'

Agnes stared at the woman in stunned disbelief.

'You bewitch men,' Leah continued. 'You are no better than the Whore of Babylon. Colonel, you must see that her presence here can do nothing but harm to the children.'

Tobias had turned puce and his jaw worked as he tried to formulate a response. 'Enough of this unseemly spatting,' he said at last. 'I appreciate your concern, Leah, but Mistress Fletcher has my word. She is the children's aunt and entitled to the respect that entails.'

Agnes glared at Leah. 'I believe I am owed an apology for my rough treatment.'

Tobias sighed. 'Yes, I think perhaps you are right. Leah?'

Leah turned hot, angry eyes on Tobias. 'Apologise to a whore?'

'Apologise to the aunt of my wards,' Tobias replied in a glacial tone.

A shudder ran through Leah as she straightened. 'Very well. Mistress Fletcher, you have my apology for the misunderstanding.'

Agnes raised her chin. 'I need fresh air,' she said. 'With your consent, Cousin Tobias, I wish to go for a ride.'

'Colonel ... ' Leah made one last bid to re-establish her position.

Tobias looked almost relieved. 'Leah, let me be quite clear. For the next twenty-four hours, Mistress Fletcher is my guest with all that

213

implies, and she has unfettered access to the children. After that, she will be leaving.'

Leah, her face still white with anger, inclined her head. 'As you wish, Colonel.'

He waved a hand. 'I do wish. Now go, both of you!'

CHAPTER 34

*N*ews of the commotion upstairs had reached the kitchen and set the tongues of the servants wagging. Both the old and the newer members of the household staff had been quietly appalled at the treatment meted out to a woman who wanted nothing more than to spend time with two children who were her blood kin. Daniel found himself the centre of attention from the curious servants and was glad when he received Agnes's order to have her horse saddle coupled with an imperious demand for her boots and riding skirts.

He had both horses saddled and ready as she swept out of the house.

'Do you wish me to accompany you, ma'am?' he enquired for the benefit of any servants or soldiers in the vicinity.

'Thank you, Lucas. Just keep your distance,' Agnes replied, waiting for him to assist her to mount. She placed one booted foot in his cupped hands and he hoisted her into the saddle. After the long weeks of travel, this was now a well-practised manoeuvre, but she managed to exude an extra degree of haughtiness and disdain as she arranged her skirts across her saddle.

As she adjusted her stirrups, he recalled the heartbroken waif he had met in London. She bore little resemblance to this outwardly confident woman. He had to remember she had been quasi-mistress of this house for many years. More than that, she had been the mistress of an Earl. Only he knew that beneath that proud demeanour, her heart was breaking.

Keeping a respectful distance he followed her out of the castle. Out of sight of the village, he kicked his horse forward to draw level with her. Agnes drew in a deep breath of cold air, letting it out in a cloud, and gave him a rueful smile.

'I can breathe again,' she said, turning her face to the sky. 'I feel like I've been holding my breath ever since Turner came to fetch me.'

'Are you going to tell me what the rumpus is about? It set every tongue in the house wagging,' Daniel said.

A flush of colour rose to her cheeks and she recounted the events that had led to what she described as a humiliating interview with Tobias Ashley. The barely contained outrage exuded from her as she concluded, 'Those poor children, Daniel. Leah Turner has them completely cowed.' She looked up at him and a single tear rolled unbidden down her face. 'I have decided that whatever else I do, I have to get them away from here.'

Daniel reached across and wiped the tear away, his gloved hand lingering on her cheek.

'Agnes, you know that's not possible,' he said gently. 'We are here for the gold. We can't carry away two children. Be patient.'

She dashed his hand away and he straightened in his saddle. Her tears could avail her nothing. He would have moved heaven and earth to rescue the children, but he just couldn't see how that could be accomplished without compromising everything else.

'Let us get the gold away,' he said, 'then we can look at what best to do for the children.'

She sniffed and returned her gaze to the road.

'Did you find the hiding place?' he asked.

She glanced at him and her lips twitched in a rueful smile. 'Unfortunately, Leah interrupted me before I could find the entrance, but I know where it is. There is a cavity between the nursery and the bedchamber adjoining. The entrance has to be in the nursery. Lizzie told me she saw a ghost, her father I presume, disappearing into the wall.'

A small spark of excitement flared in Daniel's heart. The years of privateering had given him the scent for treasure of whatever kind, and he could almost feel the gold in his hands.

They turned down the narrow path that led to Peg Truscott's cottage. At first sight, all seemed as it had the previous day, a curl of smoke rising from the little building. No horses or signs of anyone other than the good woman who lived there.

'Are you sure they are here?' Agnes asked as Daniel lifted her down from the horse, his hands lingering on her waist for a fraction too long.

The old lady appeared at the door and held out her arms. Agnes stumbled up the path, tripping on her skirts, to fall into Peg's embrace.

'Oh, my girl, my girl,' Peg crooned, her eyes closed and joy radiating from her.

Agnes's shoulders heaved with silent sobs.

Conscious that Agnes needed a moment or two to compose herself, Daniel secured the horses at the back of the cottage, where he found two horses already in residence in a ramshackle shed abutting the cottage. Entering by the low back door, he blinked, allowing his eyes to adjust to the gloom. A haze of wood smoke mingled with tobacco suffused the cottage.

'What took you so long?' Kit's familiar drawl came from the direction of the fireplace where he and Jonathan sat in the two chairs. Jonathan had stretched out his legs, propping his feet on a log of wood as he puffed on a long-stemmed clay pipe. The dog had laid her head on Kit's lap and he was scratching her ears while her tail thumped the floor.

'What if we were Ashby's men?' Daniel demanded.

'You weren't,' Kit remarked mildly. 'We've been watching for you. Ah, Agnes.'

Kit gently disengaged the dog, who returned to her familiar place on the hearthrug. He rose to his feet and bowed as Agnes entered the cottage, followed by Peg, who shut the door firmly behind her, plunging the cottage into gloom.

Jonathan removed the pipe from his mouth and stood up, offering his chair to Agnes.

'Mistress Fletcher, I can only begin to imagine what a trial this is for you. Take a seat and tell us what you have managed to discover,' he said.

Daniel cast his brother a glance as Agnes settled herself on the chair. Jonathan Thornton had a charm singularly lacking in either Lovell. He wished he had Jonathan's ability to put Agnes at her ease and instil an air of confidence in the situation.

Behind them, Peg resumed her seat at the table and began shelling peas. Daniel glanced at her, but the old woman was humming to herself and did not appear to be listening. Jonathan leaned against the chimney breast, tapping his pipe out on the stonework.

Agnes looked around the gathered group. 'We only have tonight,' she said in a low voice. 'Ashby gave me until sundown tomorrow to find the hiding place.'

'And it's where you thought?' Kit asked.

'I know where the hiding place is,' Agnes replied, 'but I didn't have time to locate the actual entrance.'

Kit paced the tiny room. He failed to duck to avoid a beam and banged his head. As he stood rubbing it, Peg Truscott looked up. 'Mind your head, young man,' she said, 'This cottage weren't built for the likes of 'ee.' Her hands stilled and her gaze scanned the group by the fireplace. 'What is it you are seeking?'

Agnes spoke first. 'We are looking for the entrance to a hiding place in the children's nursery, a priest hole, probably.'

Peg returned to her peas, her fingers working without breaking rhythm. 'Are ye now. I thought that place long forgotten.'

'James knew it,' Agnes said. 'Do you know where it is?'

The old woman chuckled. 'I've worked in that nursery since I were a girl myself,' she said. 'Ye'll find the catch in the third panel from the door.'

Agnes laughed. 'Why didn't I think of asking you? Thank you, Peg. That's saved us the search.'

'What's the garrison strength?' Jonathan addressed Daniel.

'I've counted twenty-four troopers. They have a token guard on the main entrance but the kitchen entrance is unguarded.'

'What's the best way to get inside?'

'Leave the horses in the trees beside the gate to the kitchen garden,' Agnes said. 'Daniel can let you in through the kitchens and I can meet you at the top of the servant stairs and guide you from there.'

'What about your guard?' Daniel asked.

'Guard? He's got you under guard?' Kit stopped his pacing.

'If you call a large, burly soldier who appears to be in residence outside my bedchamber a guard, then yes, I am,' Agnes said. 'I think he is intended more to prevent me accessing the children than to prevent any other kind of mischief on my part.'

'That's a problem,' Jonathan said. 'We need you. Any chance of slipping past him?'

Agnes shook her head. 'Only if he's asleep ... but he's not the only difficulty. There are the children and their maid. They all sleep in the nursery.'

'I've an answer to that.' Peg Truscott rose to her feet and crossed to a cupboard beside the fireplace. Inside, the shelves were packed with clay pots and mysterious packages. She pulled one out, shook her head, and put it back again.

'Ah, here it is. Tincture of poppy.' She held up a flask. ''Tis a sleeping draught of my own recipe. Will knock out a horse.'

Kit put his arm around the woman's shoulders and kissed the top of her head. 'You are a marvel, Mistress Truscott. So all you have to do, Agnes, is get two children and two adults to drink some of this. Any ideas?'

Agnes caught the scepticism in his tone. 'If I take supper with the children ... I am loath to drug them though.'

Jonathan looked at her, his eyes narrowed in thought. 'Do what you think is right, Agnes. Will there be much to carry?'

Agnes shook her head. 'I saw four satchels. I don't imagine James upended the contents into one great chest. He would have wanted it portable.'

'How heavy are they?' Kit asked.

'Four hundred coins means one hundred coins per bag.' Jonathan looked around. 'Does anyone have a Unite?'

Kit undid his purse and tossed the gold coin to him. Jonathan picked it up, weighing it in his hand.

'Four satchels is manageable. Excuse us, Mistress Truscott, I need your table.'

With a heavy sigh, Peg moved the peas and took her seat by the fire as Jonathan cleared a space on the table and gestured for them all to sit down. He produced a crumpled sheet of paper and a stick of charcoal from his travelling bag.

'Draw us a plan of the castle, Agnes, and the best route to get there and away undetected.'

Agnes complied and the men leaned in closer, asking questions, confirming plans.

Setting the charcoal down, Agnes looked around the table at the grim faces of the men.

'It's not just the gold. I am bringing the children.'

Kit glanced at Daniel. 'The children? When did they become part of the plan?'

Jonathan straightened, running his hand through his hair. 'Agnes, I ... we understand your concern, but we have limited resources. I just don't see how we can carry out two children as well as the gold.'

Agnes stiffened. 'The children come or this is the end of my cooperation.'

'This is madness,' Kit said. 'The children are not your responsibility, Agnes. They are safe enough where they are.'

'No, they're not,' Agnes said, her voice rising in distress. 'Leah Turner beats them and I fear for Henry's life. Tobias covets the title. They are only little ... children die ... ' She broke off, fighting back tears.

Peg rose to her feet and put her arms around Agnes. 'They're right, dearest, you can't just make off with 'em. You know that. You'd have the whole wrath of Ashby and his soldiers on your heels.'

Jonathan swept the plan off the table and consigned it to the flames, where it flared brightly before dying into the peat. With his hands on his hips, his gaze rested on Agnes.

'Our mission is the gold, Agnes.'

She opened her mouth to protest but he held up his hand. 'I do not mean to be heartless but think of it. Peg's right, if you take the children now, you will be pursued from one end of England to the other as a kidnapper.' He laid a hand on her shoulder. 'Agnes, I know what it is to risk your life for a child, and I know the trouble it brought me. The days of men like Tobias Ashby are numbered. The King will return within months and then I will be in a position to assist you in petitioning him for custody of the children. I have, or at least I had, some little influence with Charles. Please, I counsel patience.'

Agnes looked away, her fingers balled in a fist. She knew he was right but every instinct in her cried out to liberate her child.

'Patience is not one of my virtues,' she said between stiff lips.

'Evidently,' said Kit. 'You and my brother have that at least in common. So we are agreed?'

Everyone nodded, although Agnes's acquiescence lacked enthusiasm. If Kit and Jonathan were successful in liberating the gold without alerting the castle garrison, then Agnes and Daniel would remain within the castle. Agnes could show Tobias the empty hiding place, hoping he would assume that James had divested himself of the gold and Agnes and Daniel could leave Charvaley as they had come, through the front door.

'Until tonight,' Jonathan said.

CHAPTER 35

*T*he clock on the church tower struck two. Glancing back to ensure the bolsters she had stuffed in the bed resembled, at first glance, a slumbering body, Agnes closed the door behind her and crept on stockinged feet past the slumbering guard.

At supper in the nursery, Agnes had kindly insisted Hannah share in the evening repast with the children and, dispatching the maid to fetch the children's night clothes from where they warmed in front of the fire, she slipped the sleeping draught into the jug of small ale while the girl's back was turned. Agnes had allowed the children a few small sips before removing it from them. Enough, she hoped, to render them sleepy without being drugged. She left the jug and cup with the assumption that once she was alone and the children in bed, Hannah would finish it.

Trooper Brown sprawled on his stool, snoring loudly, his legs akimbo and drool running from his open mouth. While she had taken supper with the children, Daniel had conspired to provide the man with a full jug of drugged wine. The empty jug lay on its side, the last of its contents shining wetly on the floor.

Her fellow conspirators waited for her in the shadows of the servant's stairs. She had never seen a more villainous band. The three men wore cloths wound around the lower parts of their faces, hats pulled low down on their brows: Jonathan, the tallest, Kit identifiable by his swagger, which she had discovered disguised a limp, and Daniel by his slighter build and lithe movements. Like her they were in stockinged feet, their boots carried in bags over their shoulders.

They followed her down the silent corridors and up the stairs that led to the nursery.

The door opened with the slightest click and Agnes slipped in first. The only light in the room came from the window, a waning moon, casting cold shadows across the floorboards. The curtains of the children's bed were pulled tight against the cold night. Hannah slumbered in a pallet at the foot of the bed, and like Brown, she snored stentoriously. As Jonathan lit the candle on the table, Agnes flicked back the curtains on the big bed and smiled down at the two children curled up together like dormice in the enormous bed, their slight forms making little impression in the vast space. Both were sound asleep. Reaching out a finger, she stroked Henry's soft cheek.

Soon, little boy, she promised.

The tapestry rattled on the rod as Daniel drew it aside and Agnes glanced at the slumbering Hannah. The girl snorted and turned onto her side. No sound came from the children and she restored the curtains.

The four conspirators stood looking at the old, worm-ridden panelling. Jonathan held up the candle. Counting from the door, Agnes located the third panel, gratified that its location accorded with the point where Lizzie had indicated the ghost had passed through the wall. Running her fingertips along the seams of the oak panel, she found an unnatural indentation. She pushed on it, heard a slight click, and a section of panel eased away, revealing the stone wall.

She glanced at the men and Kit stepped forward, pushing on a corner of stonework. A whole section of the wall swung inward with hardly a creak, leaving a gap about four feet square. Kit stepped back and let out his breath in an audible sigh and Jonathan gave a curt nod to his companions as he advanced on the opening, crouching down to look into the space beyond.

Illuminated by the candle, as Agnes had anticipated, it was a long narrow space, no more than four feet wide, running between the walls.

Given the juxtaposition of the two rooms, it was not an anomaly that would be easily detected unless you were looking for it.

Just inside the entrance, piled in a tidy heap, were the four leather satchels she had seen on the night James's men had brought them to Charvaley.

Daniel bent toward Agnes, and placing his mouth close to her ear, he whispered, 'Stay by the door and keep watch.'

She nodded and took up a position beside the door, leaving it open a little way to get a view of the corridor. The house slumbered in peace.

Daniel, with his slighter build, disappeared into the opening and handed out the four heavy, leather satchels.

Kit pushed the hiding place shut. Well-oiled, it slid back into place with barely a click, and he had his hand on the tapestry preparatory to pulling it back into place when a sharp cry of anguish came from the children's bed.

They all froze in place, the three men turning to Agnes.

Henry. One of his nightmares.

As Hannah stirred on her bed, Agnes cast a frantic glance at Daniel.

'See to the child,' he whispered and jerked his head at the others. 'We must away.'

Agnes pulled the tapestry across the wall and hurried across to the children's bed. She slipped behind the curtains, and taking the whimpering child in her arms, she rocked and hushed him, her heart hammering beneath her bodice.

'Please, be quiet,' she whispered to the little boy.

'Agnes!' Although Henry was still half asleep, her name seemed to echo around the quiet room. Every nerve in Agnes's body jangled.

'Don't go away again,' the boy murmured, sleep beginning to claim him once more.

She held him closer, her heart breaking as he stilled, and once more he slept. Just a few more minutes, she told herself, before she needed to return to her room. Just a few more minutes to hold her son. She closed her eyes and laid her cheek against his soft curls.

CHAPTER 36

*I*n the corridor outside the nursery, the moonlight streamed in through the windows casting fractured lights across the bare boards, which creaked ominously as the men hurried across them. They had almost reached the turn that led into the main gallery when they heard the unmistakable sound of heavy feet coming toward them.

Beside Daniel, Kit swore under his breath. '*Merde.*'

With a sharp gesture of his hand, Jonathan indicated for them to scatter and melt as much as possible into the shadowed recesses of doorways and corners.

As the interloper rounded the corridor his footsteps became stealthier, the floorboards protesting as if someone were trying unsuccessfully to tiptoe along the corridor.

Daniel tried the handle of the nearest door but found it locked. Squeezed into the shadowed doorway, Daniel held his breath as he recognised the man as one of Turner's men – Simpson. What would Simpson be doing here at this hour, and acting in such a furtive manner?

The answer came when the man rapped softly, his ear to the nursery door. 'Hannah? Remember your promise ... '

When no one within the room stirred, Simpson knocked again. Daniel thought about Agnes, trapped in that room, and bit back a groan.

He carried no weapon except his knife and he cast about the gloomy gallery for something – anything – he could use to incapacitate the man.

'Hannah! I'm coming in … ' Simpson said in a syrupy tone.

To Daniel's dismay the door opened and the nursery maid, barefoot in her chemise, her hair sticking out wildly, lurched into view.

'What are you doing here?' she demanded, her voice slurred with sleep and the drug.

The man chucked her under her chin. 'We had an arrangement, remember?'

The girl softened, her arms circling the man's neck. 'Oh yes … the brats are asleep, come inside.'

Concealed behind a tapestry, Kit must have shifted his weight. A floorboard creaked, sounding like a musket shot in the silent corridor.

'Wha's that?' Hannah said, removing her arms from around her paramour's neck.

Simpson whirled around. 'Who's there?' he demanded in a voice that would have woken the dead. 'Someone's there – come out and face me.'

Daniel's mind whirled. How could something so simple go so wrong? Now was not the time for sentiment. The priority was getting the gold away. His life, and Agnes's, had to be something he worried about later.

Daniel broke cover, his knife concealed in the palm of his hand, and stood between Simpson and the others. Behind him, he heard Kit and Jonathan's footsteps breaking into a run as they disappeared into the gloom of the gallery.

'Help here!' Simpson yelled. 'Intruders!'

Daniel held his ground and Simpson lunged toward him, taking him to be unarmed. Like Trooper Brown, Simpson seemed to have been recruited for his size. Daniel could never hope to best him in any form of unarmed combat – all he could do was hope to slow the man down.

Simpson uttered a bellow and rushed at him. Daniel neatly side-stepped, plunging the knife low into the man's leg. Simpson stopped in his tracks, looked down at the hilt of the knife as Daniel wrested it free, and dropped to his knees with a gurgle.

Daniel hesitated, torn between getting past the screaming maid and extricating Agnes and making good his own escape. If he stopped to rescue Agnes, they would both be taken. He would be more useful to her as a free man.

'*Sorry, Agnes,*' he said in his thoughts and pausing only to collect the satchels he had set down, he turned and ran.

CHAPTER 37

*a*t the first knock on the door, Agnes froze. She laid Henry back in his place and peered through the curtains at the end of the bed where she could see the maid.

Hannah muttered and groaned and turned restlessly on her pallet. Agnes willed her back into slumber but when the second knock came, more insistent than the first, Hannah awoke, pushing her hair from her eyes and stumbling from her bed toward the door.

Agnes's breath caught in her throat. She was safe enough for the moment but if the noise woke the children or... God forbid, the alarm was raised ... Without a second thought she slipped off the bed on the far side, out of sight of the door, and slid under the bed, just as Lizzie had done when she had played hide and seek.

She inched her way toward the head of the bed where it stood against the wall and flattened herself to the floor. Closing her eyes, she struggled to control her breathing, both from fear and the dust that rose from the unswept boards. From beyond the doorway, she heard Simpson's upraised voice and the clatter of his boots on the floorboards. A moment of silence followed and Hannah began to scream.

Agnes inched her way to the edge of the bed, from where she had a good view along the corridor. Simpson lay sprawled on his back, his head in Hannah's lap. The maid's screams alternated with choking sobs.

They've killed him, Agnes thought.

Any one of the three men would be capable of such an act without thought or compunction. They had all killed before. Simpson's booted foot twitched and Agnes let out a sigh of relief. She did not want murder added to their list of crimes.

She could see no sign of Daniel, Kit, or Jonathan and she prayed they had got away.

The corridor filled with servants and soldiers, including Septimus Turner, hurriedly pulling on his jacket and his sister, in her nightgown with a loose coat pulled over it. Turner pulled the sobbing maid to her feet and, holding her by her forearms, appeared to be cross-examining her. All he succeeded in doing was increasing her distress. She pointed down the corridor, away from the nursery.

Turner whirled on his heel, gathering those soldiers who had answered the maid's cries. They set off at a run along the gallery and out of sight. Agnes balled her fist against her mouth. All she could do was pray that they had got away.

In the corridor all the attention turned to the wounded man who writhed on the floor, clutching his leg. No one was looking at the nursery door. Agnes wriggled out from under the bed and sidled out of the room, keeping to the shadows. As she reached the gaggle of servants clustered around Simpson, she elbowed her way into the group as if she too had been forced from her bed by the uproar.

'What's happened here?' she demanded in an imperious tone.

Everyone turned to look at her. 'Intruders, ma'am,' one of the servants answered.

'Take this man to a bedchamber and tend to his wounds,' Agnes said and turned on Leah. 'Has anyone checked the children?'

Leah stared at her. 'The children?'

'Your responsibility, as you are so quick to remind me.' Agnes turned and ran back to the nursery, pulling back the bed curtains to reveal the two children still slumbering peacefully, despite the rumpus outside their room.

Agnes gave Leah a sharp, reproachful glance. 'That stupid girl is in no fit state to stay with the children,' she said. 'I will ... '

'Return to your room, Mistress Fletcher. I will see the children are not left alone,' Leah responded.

Agnes bent and kissed Henry's curls. Better to be seen to be acquiescent.

'Very well,' she said. 'They should be properly guarded, not left in the hands of that incompetent wench.' She pointed at Hannah. 'You might like to ask her what that man was doing in this part of the house at this time of the night.'

Leah straightened. 'His duty,' she replied, but her tone wavered with uncertainty and she cast the still-dopey Hannah a malevolent glare.

Brown still slumbered outside Agnes's door, and she gave him no more than a cursory glance before slipping back into her room and climbing into the cold bed. She pulled the covers up to her chin, forcing her breathing to steady as she shook from head to toe with cold and nerves.

What now?

She had no choice but to carry on the pretence. Turner would have every one of his men on the hunt for the intruders. Had Daniel gone with them? How would she explain that to Ashby?

Sleep was impossible and as she tossed in the uncomfortable bed, she told herself that all she had to do was show Ashby the empty room tomorrow morning and then she could leave. She repeated the instructions to herself.

In a few hours, she would be back on the road to Seven Ways, but she just had to accept that it would be without the children. Her head had prevailed and she acknowledged Jonathan had been right – better to wait until the King's return and see what could be done. If the King had his gold then he should feel well disposed toward her petition. The thought heartened her.

She closed her eyes to hold back the tears, recalling the warm little body pressed against her, the silken feel of Henry's soft hair beneath her fingers.

A gulping sob racked her body and she rolled over onto her side, drawing her knees up, trying to warm her frozen feet.

CHAPTER 38

*T*he maid's screams still rang in Daniel's ears as he bolted after his brother and Jonathan. The alarm had not reached the kitchens and they paused long enough to pull on their boots. From the main courtyard, they could hear orders being shouted.

Balancing caution with haste they crept through the kitchen gardens to the wooded area where they had left their horses.

Kit handed the two satchels he carried to Jonathan. 'You take them.'

'Why? Wouldn't it be better ... '

Kit shook his head. 'If we encounter trouble I can divert them – you keep going.'

Jonathan hesitated before he gave a curt nod. 'Very well,' he said. 'Daniel, are you coming with us?'

Daniel shook his head. 'I'll go back before I am missed. I have to be certain that Agnes is safe. If I'm missing, suspicion will fall on her immediately. God speed, gentlemen.'

Kit turned to him and gathered him in a brotherly embrace, clapping him on the back. 'Keep safe, Dan, and the girl too.'

'We'll be with you at Seven Ways in a few days,' Daniel said. *God willing.*

'Lovell!' Thornton sounded exasperated. 'We've got to get going.'

Daniel waited long enough to see the two horses spurred into a canter heading toward the track, described by Agnes, which skirted the village.

As he turned and hurried back, lights appeared all over the house and he could see through the window of the kitchen that the servants had gathered in various stages of night attire. Cursing, he found another entry unlocked and slipped into the darkened buttery. He paused to divest himself of his boots and the cloth he had wound around his face, stowing them with his jacket in a dark corner. He pulled his shirt from his breeches and padded in stockinged feet into the kitchen, running his hand through his hair as if he had just been awoken.

'What's the commotion?' he asked the steward.

'Intruders,' the man replied. 'One of the Colonel's men has been badly wounded.'

'Did they get away?'

The man shrugged. 'Turner's sent all his men out into the night. They'll hunt 'em down soon enough.'

'What did they want?' one of the maids asked in a tremulous voice.

'Who knows? They were in the nursery wing when Simpson came across 'em,' another replied.

One woman subsided onto a chair, her hand on her chest. 'Evil men, come to take the children. Are they safe?'

Another woman placed a comforting hand on her friend's shoulder. 'Sleepin' peacefully,' she said. 'Never even stirred.'

'What was this Simpson doing in the nursery wing?' Daniel asked.

They all turned to look at him.

'Well may you ask,' one of the women said. 'After that little tramp Hannah Bell, I'd wager.'

'Where were you?' The steward narrowed his eyes suspiciously at Daniel.

'Me?'

'Aye – your bed is there.' The steward pointed to the bedroll in the corner of the kitchen that had been allocated to Daniel. 'That's not been slept in.'

Daniel looked down at his stockinged toes. His feet felt like two blocks of ice. 'I was with a girl.' He jerked his head at the bedroll. 'Not much privacy there.'

'A girl?' The man bristled. 'I'll not have that sort of behaviour in this house. Who was she?'

'It'd not be seemly if I told you that,' Daniel replied.

'It was me.'

Daniel caught his breath as Sarah Truscott stepped up beside him, slipping her hand around his arm in a proprietary fashion.

'We weren't doing nothin' except a little cuddling and sweet talk. He's got a fine tongue, this one.' She gave him the benefit of a coquettish smile.

The steward straightened, indignation bristling from every pore. 'That's it, my girl. Ye're out on your ear.'

'Oh, I don't think so. Ye need me and ye know it. Handsome here will be gone and there's none here that takes my fancy.' She looked around the household staff.

The steward's mouth opened and closed like the frog he so closely resembled.

Daniel slipped an arm around Sarah's shoulders. 'My mistress'll be gone today and me with her. Rail at me all you like but don't punish the girl for her pretty face. Now, I've a mind for a bit of sleep before her ladyship upstairs starts issuing orders.'

The steward glared at him 'All of you, back to bed. It still lacks an hour or so until we have to be abroad. God knows we get little enough time in our beds.' He clapped his hands to emphasise his order and the servants dispersed. 'And you,' he said to Sarah, who cast a wink in Daniel's direction before following the rest of the servants out of the kitchen.

'As for you, my lad,' the steward wagged a finger at Daniel. 'I'll thank you to keep your hands to yourself in future. Or ... else ... '

With that impotent threat, he turned on his heel and stalked out of the kitchen. Daniel settled into his rough bed and lay awake waiting for the snores of the kitchen boy. When he was satisfied the lad was asleep, he rose and retrieved his boots and jacket, consigning the mask to the fire.

What a damnable mess, he thought as he crouched by the fire, watching the fabric take light. Jonathan and Kit were out in the cold night being pursued through the dark by Turner's men and Agnes … what had happened to Agnes?

He hated himself for abandoning her. He imagined her trapped in the nursery as Turner and his men burst in. He had blithely suggested the worst that could befall her would be eviction, but he knew Ashby and Turner were capable of much worse.

He ran a hand through his hair and glanced across at the servants' stairs. He had to know that she was all right.

The moon had started to set as he found his way through the maze of corridors and stairs to Agnes's chamber. Someone – Agnes? – had provided Brown with a blanket, and as he passed the soldier stirred and swallowed a few times before settling back into a doze. The man would be stiff and cold when he woke.

Daniel tried the door and found it unlocked. It creaked as he opened it. He glanced at Brown but the man didn't move.

'Who's there?' Agnes's voice came from the gloom of the bed.

'Daniel,' he responded.

She was in his arms as soon as he closed the door behind him.

'I was so scared they had caught you,' she mumbled into his jacket. He thought he heard her add, 'I'd die if anything happened to you.'

He tightened his arms around her. 'We all got away. They don't know I am involved.'

She relaxed in his grip for a moment and he brushed the top of her head with his lips, breathing in the subtle scent of rosemary.

If she noticed the gesture, she gave no sign. Straightening and pushing herself away from him, she looked up into his face.

'Are we leaving? Have you come to fetch me? I can be ready in no time.'

He let his hands fall and shook his head. 'We can't go anywhere. Every one of Turner's men, except the man I wounded and that lazy sod out there, are out there on the lookout for the intruders. We would get no further than the stables and we may as well sign our confessions. We have no choice but to complete the charade we set ourselves.'

Her eyes widened and she wrapped her arms around herself. 'I'm not sure I have the strength,' she said.

This time he drew her into him, holding her head to his chest and stroking her hair as she probably would do with Henry, hoping she did not sense his fear.

'Just a few more hours, Agnes.'

He wanted to stay, take this woman to bed, hold her in his arms and tell her everything would be all right in the morning, but he would be lying. For now, it was enough to know she was unharmed and relatively safe. He just had to return to the kitchen and keep up the pretence for a little longer.

Reluctantly, he disengaged her.

'It would do neither of us any good for me to be found here. Try and get some rest, Agnes. You will need all your wits for the morrow.'

She shivered, and he lifted her in his arms and carried her back to the bed, pulling the covers around her. He bent and kissed her forehead, her skin warm and soft beneath his lips. She made no protest, no attempt to detain him longer, and he left her, stepping over Brown's long legs and making his way back to his cheerless billet in the kitchen.

CHAPTER 39

*A*t the sight of four heavily armed troopers on the road ahead of them, Kit issued a string of colourful French expletives under his breath.

Jonathan gave him a sideways glance. 'They've not seen us. What do you want to do?'

'Let them see me. I can lead them off. You keep going,' Kit said.

Jonathan nodded and turned his horse's head back the way he had come. Kit waited until he was safely out of sight before spurring his horse forward. He wheeled the horse as one of the troopers caught sight of him, alerting the others, and took off across the fields, leading them away from the village and away from Jonathan.

The blood pounded in his ears and the wind blew the hat from his head. He let out a whoop. Not since Worcester had he felt the thrill of the chase. He remembered now what it meant to be alive and how very much he had missed it.

The soldiers were hard on his heels and he heard the crack of a cavalry pistol and swore as something thumped into his right arm. The reins fell from nerveless fingers and for a fleeting moment he swayed in the saddle and almost fell, but there was no time for pain. He gathered himself together, securing the reins with his good hand.

Another pistol cracked behind him and he hunkered low over the horse's neck, bracing himself for its impact, but this time his horse took the ball, squealing and going down on its haunches before breaking into a frantic, panicked dash to escape their pursuers. Kit meshed his fingers in the animal's mane, trying to calm it and praying to God that he kept his senses.

A massive hedge loomed ahead and he closed his eyes as the animal ran straight at it, taking it with ease. On the other side, the poor beast went down on its knees and Kit kicked himself free of the stirrups, rolling away as the horse rose unsteadily to its feet and stood with its head drooping, blowing steam in the cold air, its sides rising and falling with the exertion.

On the other side of the hedge, the troopers reined in, cursing. They couldn't see him through the thicket and he heard swearing as they turned their horses, looking for some way around the obstacle.

Finding his own uncertain feet, Kit took a precious moment to inspect the wound the horse had sustained. It looked as if the pistol ball had scored a gash in its flank but not lodged. Nothing that a good groom couldn't deal with. He looped the reins over the saddle and sent it on its way, with a hefty whack on its uninjured flank. It jumped forward, breaking into a canter and he hoped that the troopers would follow the horse.

The warm stickiness of blood ran down Kit's arm and he peered ineffectually at the wound. He didn't think it was too bad, but now the chase was over it had begun to hurt like the devil and if it kept bleeding, he would freeze to death before morning. The wound needed better attention than he could provide. He pulled the cloth he had worn as a mask from around his neck and, cursing, did the best he could to bandage his arm.

He considered surrendering, but there was no guarantee of assistance. He dared not risk imposing on a stranger, even at the point of a gun. Peg Truscott's isolated cottage seemed like the ideal refuge – if he could remember where it was.

Keeping to the shadows, he wound his way around the village, picking up a familiar road. The slightest lightening of the sky presaged dawn as Kit found the path leading to the little cottage. The world had begun to roar in his ears and it took all his effort to stay upright.

To his surprise, a thin light showed around the edge of the door of the cottage. The old lady was evidently an early riser, or else the soldiers had got there first. If Peg had a whole regiment of Parliament horse in her cottage, he was beyond caring. He needed shelter and he needed help. He lurched up the path and banged on the door.

'Who's there?' A quavering voice came from within.

'Mistress Truscott, I seek your aid.' Kit leaned his forehead against the weathered wood of the door.

It swung open and Kit fell forward. Strong arms caught him as his knees buckled.

'Need some help, there?'

At the sound of Jonathan Thornton's calm, measured voice, Kit looked up.

'*Merde*! What are you doing here? You and the gold should be halfway to Worcestershire by now.'

'My horse caught a hoof in a pothole and went down. I managed to get it away from the road but I had to put the poor beast out of its misery.' His lips tightened. 'I can't afford to lose horses and I was quite fond of that one. Don't tell me you lost your horse too?'

'So, I got myself shot for nothing?' Kit grumbled as his legs finally gave way and Jonathan hefted him over to a chair by the fireplace, where he collapsed gratefully into one of the cushioned chairs.

'This is a pretty pickle,' Jonathan remarked as he hunkered down beside Kit and began to unwind the roughly tied cloth from around his arm. 'We've got the gold but no horses. Daniel and Agnes are trapped in the castle and you're wounded.'

'Ouch! Thornton, let the goodwife deal with the wound. I have more faith in her than you.'

Jonathan ceded his place to Peg Truscott, who tutted and clucked as she poked and prodded. 'No ball lodged. Just needs cleanin'. Ye'll live but ye've lost a deal of blood. You need to rest.'

Kit nodded, and addressing Jonathan, asked, 'What did you do with the gold?'

A slow smile twitched at his friend's lips. 'I found a hiding place near where I shot the horse. Didn't want to get caught with the gold on me and I couldn't carry it, even I had wanted to.'

'I hope you can find it again,' Kit remarked drily.

'Just have to look for a dead horse,' Jonathan said.

CHAPTER 40

*A*gnes woke from a fitful sleep to a world still in darkness as Sarah Truscott entered the room carrying a tray from which the scent of fresh-baked bread rose.

'You're early,' Agnes said.

'Place is in an uproar,' Sarah replied. 'Let's get you dressed, Mistress Fletcher. The way the Colonel is rampaging around, I've no doubt he'll be here soon enough.'

'How's the soldier who was hurt?'

'Simpson?' Sarah yanked on the laces of Agnes's bodice. 'Sore and sorry but he'll live. Teach him to go crawling after the skirts of that hoyden.'

'And the intruders ...? They got away?'

Sarah hesitated. 'Aye, except for the one, but you know that.' She lowered her voice. 'You can trust me, Mistress Fletcher. Whatever it is you are planning, I'm your friend. I've no love for Ashby or those Turners. You're the rightful mistress here.'

Agnes grasped the girl's hands. 'Thank you, Sarah. God knows I ... we need friends.'

The sound of heavy, purposeful footsteps in the corridor outside caused Agnes to stiffen. A man's voice raised in furious admonition almost shook the door. From the tongue-lashing Tobias Ashby was giving Brown, he was not in a good mood.

The door flung open and Ashby stood framed in the doorway.

'You – out,' he said to Sarah, who bobbed a curtsey and fled.

'It's very early, Tobias.' Agnes said with a respectful bob of her head. 'Have you not slept, cousin?'

He glared at her with red-rimmed eyes. 'No, I have not. You heard about the intruders?'

'It was hard not to, with that stupid maid's screams and the comings and goings all night. How is the man who was hurt?'

Tobias dismissed Simpson with a wave of his hand. 'He'll live.' He advanced on her. 'I want to know what the intruders knew that I don't. Time you were honest with me, Mistress Fletcher.'

She met his hot, angry gaze. Beneath her ribs, her heart pounded, but she forced a calm smile.

'I have been reflecting on our conversation of yesterday, and I believe that there is a secret chamber concealed in the children's nursery.'

Ashby tossed his head. 'Why didn't you tell me this yesterday?'

Agnes licked her lips, their careful story was unravelling around her and the more lies she told, the harder it became. 'Because I only remembered something James told me as I was going to bed.'

'And what was that?'

Tobias narrowed his eyes and she swallowed. He didn't believe her and, indeed, why should he? From his perspective, the reappearance of Agnes Fletcher and the theft of the gold could not be a mere coincidence.

'When he was a child, he found the entrance to a cavity in the wall between the nursery and the chamber adjoining it. I intended to look for it this morning and come to you with the information.'

'What sort of fool do you think I am, Agnes Fletcher? It seems somewhat coincidental that the men who came last night knew the exact location of this secret cupboard that you have only just remembered.'

Agnes swallowed. 'Choose to believe it or not, for it is a coincidence. It is entirely possible that James got a message out to them before he died,' Agnes ventured but even to her ears, her voice lacked conviction.

She had never been a good liar. 'You yourself said there was an agent sent by the King – by Charles Stuart.'

Tobias took a few steps forward until he was almost on top of her. His fingers closed around her right forearm.

'Come with me, Mistress Fletcher, and let us find this secret cupboard together.'

Tripping over her skirts in her haste to keep stride with the man, Agnes was breathless by the time they reached the children's nursery. Septimus Turner opened the door to them. The maid, Hannah, sat huddled by the fire, sobbing into her apron with Leah Turner looming over her and a birch cane in her hand. Henry and Lizzie, still in their night clothes, huddled together in a corner of the bed, their eyes huge and their frightened gazes fixed on Leah Turner.

Turner closed the door and stood in front of it, barring any exit.

Agnes veered in the children's direction but Tobias dragged her away.

'You are a lying little bitch,' he said and struck her across the face with an open-handed blow that sent her reeling to the floor. Lizzie screamed and Henry started to wail. Clutching her jaw, the world ringing in her ears, Agnes looked up into the man's face. Two spots coloured his cheeks and his eyes glittered in the pale light of the early morning.

She rose slowly to her feet, backing away from him so she stood out of arm's reach.

'You,' Ashby indicated Hannah. 'Tell her what you told me.'

Hannah sniffed, but the look she cast Agnes was heavy with malevolence. 'When Simpson was 'urt, Mistress Fletcher … she said she'd heard me screaming, but I saw her, Colonel, coming out of this room, not from the direction of her chamber. Anyway, she'd not have heard me, not all the way over there, and then Master Henry,' Hannah pointed an accusatory finger at Henry. 'He told me he'd seen her in the night.'

Lies beget lies, Agnes thought, her dazed mind casting around wildly for a plausible explanation. Was it too much to hope that Daniel would come bursting through the door with sword and pistol to sweep her away?

She took a deep, steadying breath. No one would be coming to her aid. Just as it had been all her life, she was on her own.

She looked from one to the other and said in a clear, steady voice. 'It's true. I did come here last night. Very late, after everyone was asleep, including that useless man you left outside my room. I knew I only had a few more hours with the children and I wanted to just sit with them.' Her voice wavered, the emotion coming naturally. 'I pulled the curtains around the bed and I was just sitting there ... '

'Just sitting there?' Tobias expostulated.

'Yes, just sitting with the children. I heard the door open and I was afraid it might be –' she stopped herself before she said "you". 'I ... I didn't want to be discovered so I hid under the bed.'

Tobias frowned and she sensed him wavering. Her story had seemed plausible enough to anyone who knew her as he did. 'So what did you see?'

'Two men – or at least the feet of two men. I dared not move to get a better view. They knew exactly where to go and what they were looking for. They were in and out in bare minutes and then there was an altercation in the corridor. Someone was hurt and that girl,' she looked at Hannah, 'screaming like a fishwife. I waited until I thought it was safe and came out. I had hoped no one had seen me. Sitting with the children seemed a foolish, sentimental thing to do ... '

Genuine tears welled in her eyes.

Tobias cleared his throat and his shoulders relaxed. Was it possible he had begun to believe her? All she had to do was stick to her story and hope he would let her leave.

He gestured at the room. 'So if you know where the entrance to this hidden cavity is, you had better show me now.'

'Behind the tapestry,' Agnes said.

Tobias turned to face the tapestry, hauling it off its rings. The ancient material ripped as it fell to the ground in a cloud of dust. He stood with his hands on his hips, studying the old wainscoting.

'So how do you get in?'

Agnes shook her head. 'I didn't see.'

Tobias felt along the panelling, pressing corners and indentations, but it was Leah who found the entrance, indicating the scuffed foot-prints on the dusty floor.

Tobias grunted, running his fingers along the panelling until he located the catch. The entrance swung open and, stooping, he looked inside. A man of his size would never have fitted through the small opening.

He swore volubly.

'Nothing,' he said. 'Something was here but it's gone.'

He brushed the dust from his coat sleeve and sighed heavily. 'So they got away with the gold, but they won't have gone far.' He smiled without humour. 'My men report that they managed to put a pistol ball into one of 'em. As for you ... '

Agnes's heart skipped a beat, and she schooled her face to remain unconcerned.

Who had they shot? Daniel was still within the castle so it must have been either Kit or Jonathan.

Please, dear God, let them get away. Don't let them die, she thought.

Gathering herself, she looked up at Tobias. 'You have no evidence that I had any involvement. I have admitted to being present in the room but that was as far as it went. My time here is over. I will be leaving as soon as the horses are saddled.'

Lizzie whimpered. Tobias glared at the child with narrowed eyes and she gave a strangled sob and fell silent.

He strode over to the window and stood looking down into the courtyard.

'I think it may be safer for you to stay a little while longer, Agnes,' he said, his voice now a soft purr. He glanced back at her. 'It would be irre-sponsible of me to allow you to travel while such ruffians are still at large.'

'I will be quite safe. My servant –'

'Ah, yes. Your servant, Lucas, is it? What can you tell me about him?'

She licked her dry lips. 'I found him after you left me in London. His last employer had left England and he needed work. I could hardly ride through England as an unescorted woman. He was a good worker and he saw to my needs. I will be quite safe with him. Now, if you will excuse me, Tobias.'

She turned for the door but Turner stepped in front of her, barring her way.

'You'll not leave until the men who stole my gold are apprehended,' Tobias said.

Agnes turned back to face him. 'Your gold? It is not your gold.'

He narrowed his eyes, an avaricious gleam in their depths. 'It was on my property, therefore it is my gold.'

Agnes stared at him. 'If you extend that logic then it is Henry's, not yours. This is not your property and it never will be, Tobias Ashby. Everything on this land is yours only by dint of Henry's guardianship.'

Tobias's gaze flicked to the little boy with a look in his eyes that made her blood run cold.

'Turner. Escort Mistress Fletcher to her bedchamber and ensure she is locked in.'

Agnes stiffened as Turner took her arm. 'You found what you were looking for, Tobias. My obligation to you is relieved. Let me go.'

Ashby shook his head. 'Oh no. There is far more to this tale than I am hearing and I am not convinced by your pretty little tale. Take her away, Turner, and ensure that servant of hers is suitably detained as well.'

CHAPTER 41

*C*hafing with impatience, Daniel paced the kitchen, provoking uncharitable comments from the cook. Sarah had taken Agnes's breakfast up to her but had not returned.

Something was wrong.

When the girl finally appeared at the door, breathless and her cap askew, he knew his instinct was right. She ran to him and grasped his arm, pulling him outside into the yard.

'You've got to go,' she said. 'Turner will be here any minute to lock you up just as they've done Mistress Agnes. Ye're more use to her out there than ye are here. I'll tell her.'

Everything in Daniel's being protested at abandoning Agnes again, but his head won over his heart and he barely had time to collect his few belongings before he heard the sound of heavy feet on the kitchen stairs.

Sarah waited for him in the courtyard.

'Go to my aunt's,' she said. 'I'll come as soon as I can.'

'My horses –'

She shook her head. 'No time. Go, Daniel.'

He took to his heels, making his escape out through the kitchen garden and the woods to Peg Truscott's cottage. At every footstep, he cursed himself for not carrying Agnes away last night when they had the chance. How did they ever think they could carry through the charade? Now she was truly a prisoner, and he had abandoned her not once but twice.

He found the cottage more by luck than good judgment and forced himself to pause, watching the little building for what seemed an age. In the grey half-light, smoke curled from the chimney but he saw nothing and nobody that gave him cause for alarm.

He circled to the back of the house, knocking on the low door. Peg answered it, her eyes widening when she saw him. She stood aside and he all but fell into the gloomy space.

Strong fingers circled his arm and the muzzle of a pistol pressed into the back of his neck.

Daniel swore and whoever had seized him relaxed his grip, the pistol dropping away.

Turning on his heel Daniel found himself face to face with a tall, all-too-familiar man – and he groaned aloud.

Jonathan Thornton should have been well on the road to Worcestershire.

'What in God's name are you still doing here?' he demanded.

Jonathan shook his head. 'Lost my horse. I could ask the same of you. Where's Agnes?'

'Ashby's locked her up and would have done the same to me, but I got away.'

Jonathan ran a hand through his hair. 'So if he had his suspicions before you have just confirmed them. Well done, Lovell. How did you get here?'

'Foot. No time to saddle a horse. The roads and woods are crawling with Ashby's men and I've no doubt they will be here at first light.'

Jonathan jerked his head in the direction of the pallet.

'Your brother's hurt.'

'Is that Daniel?' Kit's voice sounded weak.

Daniel hunched down beside the bed.

'Are you badly hurt?'

Kit shrugged, pushing himself upright with his uninjured arm. 'Nothing serious. Just feel a bit lightheaded.'

Daniel looked around the cottage. 'What a damnable mess. We're never going to get away and what are we going to do about Agnes? We can't leave her to Ashby's mercy. He has none.'

Jonathan looked at Kit. 'Is he always this impatient?'

Kit nodded. 'Always. Sit down, Dan. We're in a bind. I'm hurt ... '

'... and we've no horses,' Jonathan put in. 'Only way out of here is going to be on foot.'

Jonathan held up a hand. 'First, we have to make sure Ashby doesn't find us. Peg was telling me she has a hiding place.'

Peg gestured at the chest that stood against the wall. 'Under there is a cellar. It'll hold you safe and snug.'

Jonathan moved the chest aside, revealing a flagstone with a ring in it. He hauled it up and swore softly.

'It's going to be a tight fit.'

The dog raised its head from its paws and growled. The men froze and Daniel could just make out the thud of hoof beats. Horses being ridden hard in the lane.

'He's coming,' Daniel said.

'I'll help Mistress Truscott with the chest. Get down there, now,' Kit said. 'Take my sword.'

With his good hand, Kit tossed the weapon to Daniel.

At the entrance to the cellar, Daniel hesitated. Memories of the pit into which Outhwaite had consigned him came flooding back. Nausea rose in his throat and he backed away.

'Are you all right?' Jonathan asked.

But Daniel was lost in the recollection of that dark, noisome hole that had so nearly claimed his life. A band tightened around his chest.

'I can't,' he said.

Jonathan touched his arm. 'You must.'

'You don't understand –'

Jonathan's clear gaze met his in perfect understanding. 'I do,' he said. 'Kit told me about your experience in Barbados. You go first. I'll follow.' The shove he gave Daniel was far from gentle, and enough to shake him from his reverie. He caught himself before he pitched into the cellar. Although descending the rickety ladder into the small space made his skin crawl with memories of rats and insects. He sat down heavily on the cold earthen floor, drawing up his knees.

Above him, his brother said. 'No time. You go, Thornton.'

'But –'

'Don't argue. They're here.'

Jonathan all but fell into the cellar in his haste as above them the flag fell back into place and the legs of the chest scraped on the floor.

'Kit?' Daniel whispered.

'Too late,' Thornton replied.

The dark closed in around Daniel and he buried his head in his arms like a small child, trying to shut out the memories of Outhwaite and the dark, dark days he had spent in the Pit.

Jonathan hunched down beside Daniel, the warmth of his body and the touch of his shoulder reassuring in the darkness.

"Ye've faced yer demons, boy," the old woman had said. *"And ye beat 'em down, but they'll keep trying. All your life they'll come a-knocking at the door."*

"You can tell me my future?"

"Aye, but not now, not today. There are still words to be written on that page."

How many words? Were they to be written in ink today?

The door crashed open. Scuffling footsteps and a woman's scream indicated that Mistress Truscott had been detained.

'Where are they?' Ashby's voice filtered down to them, muffled by the flagstone.

'You're hurting me.' Mistress Truscott sounded close to tears.

Daniel tensed, his fingers clenching and unclenching.

Then they heard Kit's voice, clear and untroubled. 'Unhand the woman, Ashby.'

A pause and Ashby said, 'I know you.'

'Eveleigh Priory, 1648.'

Daniel held his breath as Ashby replied. 'Lovell?'

'Christopher Lovell, the same. It was my father, Thomas, you murdered in cold blood.'

'Murdered? It was war, Lovell,' Ashby sounded almost nonchalant.

A long pause followed.

'Ah, yes, war excuses every little misdeed, does it not,' Kit replied. 'So is this still war?'

'Put down that weapon, Lovell,' Turner's voice now.

Kit swore in French. 'Very well. I can see when I am outnumbered. Forgive me if I sit, Ashby. Some fool discharged a weapon in my direction last night, but I suspect you know that."

'Where are your companions?' Ashby's voice rose in crescendo.

'They've gone. Abandoned me to your tender mercies.'

'Gone. How?' Turner's voice now. 'Two men, one horse, by my reckoning. We'll catch them soon enough. In the meantime, secure this man and search this cottage.'

Daniel winced as his brother cried out in pain, no doubt as his injured arm was twisted behind his back.

'Her too,' Ashby said.

'Let the woman go, Ashby,' Kit said. 'She's innocent.'

'Innocent? She is guilty of harbouring villains.'

'I assure you,' Kit's voice had taken on a breathy edge, 'Mistress Truscott only ministered to me under coercion. She is innocent of any wrongdoing –' he broke off as the woman whimpered. 'Leave her!'

'You're in no position to bargain, Lovell,' Ashby said. 'Search every building.'

Daniel held his breath at the sound of scraping furniture and heavy boots above them. The chest was moved aside and Daniel held his breath, expecting any moment that the flagstone would be hauled back, but Turner's men were less than thorough and must have missed the recessed ring in the gloom of the cottage.

'Nothing.' The voice of Septimus Turner.

Ashby grunted. 'Where is my gold, Lovell?'

'Gold?'

Ashby swore. 'So it's going to be like that. Turner, tie these two to a stirrup. A stroll into town may make them more inclined to be cooperative.'

Peg whimpered. 'Please, sir. I've done naught and I know nothing.'

'You can do what you like to me,' Kit's voice rose, 'but not an old woman. If you drag her along behind a horse, you'll kill her.'

The old dog, galvanized by what must have been the obvious threat to its mistress, began to bark.

Ashby swore. 'Get that dog off me.'

'Don't 'urt her. She's old and blind,' Peg pleaded, but the old dog continued to snarl and bark, her fierce defence of her mistress ending in a sharp whine and then silence.

'You are an unspeakable bastard, Ashby,' Kit said.

'Enough from you, Lovell,' Ashby's words were followed by the sound of a fist on bone and a body hitting the floor. Daniel half rose, his fists balled impotently.

'Tie him up,' Ashby said. 'As for you, old woman, I always suspected you of witchcraft, woman. Now your familiar is dead and I've evidence enough in that cupboard to convince me that I am indeed dealing with a witch. Get her out of here.'

'Please, sir-' Peg's plea was cut short and she gave a sharp cry.

Ashby laughed and Daniel's blood ran cold. He had heard that laugh before, on a clear autumn day in 1648. He lowered his head again, trying to shut out the memory of his father standing on the steps of Eveleigh.

"You have my surrender, Ashby," Thomas Lovell had said. "Let my garrison pass unmolested."

Ashby had laughed, that same braying laugh. *"Why would I do that, Lovell? An example must be set. Secure those men and bring them forward. I want them to see what happens to traitors. Turner, your four best marksmen. Tie this man to that column."*

And so they had dragged Thomas Lovell to the slender column that held up the entrance porch to Eveleigh Priory and tied him to it. The four marksmen had arrayed themselves and on Ashby's command the volley had rung out. For a long, long moment there had been absolute silence. Kit had broken away from the men who held him. It had been Kit who cut down his father's bleeding body, cradling him in his arms as he breathed his last.

'They've gone.' Thornton touched Daniel's arm, bringing him back to the present.

Daniel raised his head. Only the faintest light around the edges marked the flagstone that secured them in the cellar.

'We have a problem, Thornton,' he said. 'Ashby's taken the woman too. There is no one to move the chest.'

Even as he said the words, the blood pounded in his ears and his breath stopped in his throat.

Thornton grabbed the back of his neck, forcing his head down between his knees. 'Breathe,' he commanded. 'I need you with all your wits.'

The demons tore at Daniel's chest, sending the world in giddying spirals, and through it all, a voice, calm and controlled, said, 'Breathe … in … out … That's it. The quicker you fight this, the quicker we are out of here.'

Daniel took a shuddering breath and shook off Jonathan's hand. 'We're going to have to work the flag away,' he said. 'That chest is solid but it should move with enough force.'

A long pause before his companion said, 'Is this the moment to tell you that I have a bad shoulder?'

CHAPTER 42

urner came for Agnes in the early afternoon. Ignoring her questions, he took her by the arm, propelling her through the house toward the Great Hall.

An ominous silence hung over the castle, servants scuttling away at the sight of Turner and the guard escorting Agnes. Only at the door to the Great Hall did he pause, looking down at her with his cold, hard eyes. From behind the door, she heard a woman weeping and feared the worst.

Turner's men were gathered in an orderly half circle in front of the dais where the Earls of Elmhurst had presided for centuries and now Tobias Ashby, in the red coat of his military status, complete with the metal gorget around his neck, stood with his hands on his hips.

Ashby gave Turner a nod and the man released Agnes's arm. She rubbed at the place where his fingers had grasped her.

'Stand aside,' Turner ordered his men, and they parted like the Red Sea as Agnes walked forward, coming up short at the sight of the two bedraggled figures arrayed before Tobias Ashby.

Peg Truscott was on her knees, her head buried in her hands, weeping softly; the sound Agnes had heard when she entered. She lunged forward to go to Peg but Turner brought her up sharply, grabbing her arm again and pushing her into line beside the second figure, a man, who stood swaying slightly, his hands bound in front of him, staring resolutely at a point above Ashby's head.

Agnes cast a fearful glance in his direction, fearing it may be Daniel. Her initial relief when she recognized Kit was followed by a growing sense of dread. Kit ignored her but it was too late – her face had betrayed her.

Tobias gave a crow of delight.

'I see you are acquainted with this man, Agnes.'

She glanced at Kit, and for the first time, he turned to look down at her, his unshaven face haggard and streaked with dirt. She had not realized before how closely the brothers resembled each other, and her heart skipped a beat as she took in his condition. Like Peg, Kit's clothes were torn and muddy, as if he had been dragged through the mire. The sleeve of his right arm was stiff with another dark substance – blood.

Agnes looked up at Tobias. 'What do you want of me, Ashby?'

His eyes narrowed. 'It's quite simple, I want my gold – the gold that you and this man conspired to take.'

'You have no proof –' Agnes began.

Tobias dismissed her protests with the wave of a hand. 'What sort of fool do you think I am, Agnes?' he said. 'You are in league with this man, and the other two who are still at large. I am still searching for them.'

Kit's eyes hardened, warning her to keep a still tongue in her head.

Ashby turned and paced the platform. 'I don't think they have left the area. To begin with, they only have, as far as I can tell, one horse between them.'

'Horses are easily acquired,' Agnes said.

'Possibly, but not around here. The nearest place they could find a horse dealer would be Preston. That is some miles away and I have men watching every road.'

Agnes turned to Kit, who met her gaze with clear, steady eyes. Whatever his injury, at least he was not feverish … not yet.

'This man is injured,' she said. 'How was he brought here, and Mistress Truscott, what has she done to deserve such treatment?'

Peg snuffled and raised her face from her hands. 'Oh, Mistress

Fletcher, they tied us to the stirrups and dragged us here like common criminals.'

'Which is what you are,' Ashby barked. 'Thieves, the lot of you, and like thieves, you will hang in the morning.'

A cold band encircled Agnes' chest and she stared up at the man. 'You would hang us? Without trial?'

He shrugged. 'You've had your trial, here and now, and I pronounce you all guilty. You ... ' he pointed at Peg ' ... will hang for giving shelter to the miscreants, and aiding and abetting them, and being a witch, and you two,' he turned back to Kit and Agnes, 'for carrying out the deed in the dark of night.'

Kit narrowed his eyes. 'You have no evidence that this gold you speak of was even here, let alone yours for the taking. If what you say is true and I do not admit it, then show us the evidence it was yours in the first place.'

Ashby smiled. 'Possession, Lovell, possession.' He turned to Turner. 'I want it widely known that these three will hang at daybreak unless the gold is returned to me. I need to flush out the other two. I don't believe they are far away, and they'll come looking for their comrades. I know their type, sentimentalists, like all who still profess loyalty to Charles Stuart. Dreamers and romantics.'

Kit snorted. 'Really? Is that what we are?' He straightened and took a step forward. 'Ashby, your days are numbered. The King will return and there will be a reckoning. Hang three innocent people out of hand and you will pay.'

'The King,' Ashby spat. 'There is no king here yet. I am the law and I say you are thieves and she is a witch,' he indicated to Peg. Raising his voice, he said loudly enough to encompass the whole hall and anyone beyond the door who may have been listening, 'My gold for their lives.'

Peg whimpered and Agnes stooped down and put her arm around the woman, raising her to her feet. Peg shivered as she leaned in toward Agnes.

'Thank you, dear,' she said through blue-tinged lips.

'Tobias, for God's mercy, if no one else's. This woman is old and sick. She needs warmth and care,' Agnes said.

'Tempted as I am to find my cousin's coldest and darkest dungeon, I do not wish to be accused of being unfeeling. Lock them in a cellar, Turner, and provide Mistress Fletcher with whatever she needs to see to Lovell's wound and keep the old woman alive until tomorrow. I would hate for them to become ill or die before I can see justice done. No need to leave a guard.'

'But–' Turner began. Ashby flashed him a thin-lipped smile and Turner nodded. 'I see.'

'Setting a trap, Ashby?' Kit said between clenched teeth.

Ashby took a few steps toward him. 'You know, the interesting thing about you, Lovell, is that I would swear you were hanged a few years back. Some plot to assassinate the Lord General?' When Kit did not reply, Tobias jabbed a finger at his chest. 'You may have escaped the noose once, but not this time. Even if your comrades have a rush of sentimentality and try to save you, I will see you hang.'

CHAPTER 43

*D*aniel perched precariously on the inadequate ladder, his shoulder to the flagstone. With a grunt he heaved again, to be rewarded with the scrape of furniture as the chest shifted slightly. Jonathan, holding his legs, huffed an appreciative grunt, cut short as the rung on which Daniel's feet were braced gave a sickening crack and gave way.

Daniel fell back against his companion and they both tumbled to the floor. Sitting up, he ran his hand through his hair, accompanied by a colourful French curse acquired in his privateering days.

Jonathan blew out a breath and considered the flagstone. They were both tall men but it was two feet above their heads, making it an awkward height to get any leverage without the ladder.

'I won't get enough purchase to shift it more than a few inches,' Daniel replied. 'They must have left the leg of the chest right on top of it, and I swear the woman is storing rocks in it. We'll have to try your suggestion.'

'I'll have to hold you,' Jonathan said.

The tiny space left them little room for manoeuvring and Jonathan's bad shoulder, the legacy of a pistol ball, he told Daniel, hampered his ability to lift Daniel, but Daniel found if he braced his feet against the wall, he could get sufficient purchase to exert his strength against the heavy flagstone.

Taking a deep breath, he grunted as he pushed upwards. This time the chest moved an agonizing couple of inches. Daniel gathered his strength to try again.

'Stop,' Jonathan said in a low voice, releasing Daniel, who let his feet drop back to the ground.

Every nerve in his body strained to hear what Jonathan had heard. They had waited a long time to see if Ashby had left a guard but had heard nothing. Now he could hear the unmistakable tap of light foot-steps on the flagstones.

Daniel drew his knife from his boot.

'Are ye here? Can you hear me?' A woman's voice came from above.

For a moment Daniel thought it might be Agnes and his heart leapt in hope.

'It's me, Sarah Truscott,' the woman said. 'I've come alone. Daniel, if ye're in the cellar,' the girl's voice seemed closer as if she were lying on the floor, talking to the concealing flagstone, 'They've got Peg and Mistress Agnes and a man locked up in the castle and the Colonel says he'll 'ang the three of 'em in the morning if he don't get what you stole from him back.'

Jonathan's fingers tightened on Daniel's arm, telling him to keep silent.

How were they to know that Peg's niece had come alone? Daniel ground his teeth in impotent silence and tightened his grip on the knife. They had no choice but to trust Sarah had come alone, otherwise they could spend days in this cellar before they managed to move the chest sufficiently to get the flagstone up.

'Sarah, we're down here,' he said aloud. 'We can't move the flag.'

'Thank the Lord,' Sarah replied and above them, the chest scraped on the floor. The girl grunted as she tugged at the flagstone. Daniel lent what assistance he could and with a harsh grating of stone on stone it shifted. The men flattened themselves against the wall of the cellar as the square of light was blocked out by the outline of a woman's head covered in a white coif.

'Ye've my word there's no one here but I,' she said. 'I saw 'em bring in my aunt and the other man and heard what the Colonel said about there being two others. I knew one of 'em would be you.'

Jonathan glanced at Daniel.

'She can be trusted,' Daniel answered the unspoken question and looked up at the woman. 'Thank you for coming to the rescue, Sarah. We feared we were trapped down here. Your aunt's hiding place only works if there is someone left on the outside.'

Daniel turned to Jonathan. 'You go first. I'll push you up from below. If you can hook your right arm over, we should be able to get you up.'

It took an undignified amount of effort, but with Sarah pulling and Daniel pushing, Jonathan landed on the floor gasping like a fish out of water. With his years of climbing in rigging, Daniel swung himself up and over the lip of the cellar with relative ease, landing on his feet.

'There was a time … ' Jonathan grumbled, sitting up and dusting off his jacket.

Daniel restored the flagstone and the chest. By the hearth, the old dog lay, its sightless dead eyes turned to the door and a bloody wound on its neck. Sarah crouched down and gently stroked the dog's ears.

'Poor Bonny' she said.

'She was only defending her mistress,' Daniel said.

Sarah rose to her feet, tears pooling in her eyes. 'They dragged my aunt and that other man tied to the stirrups. They were in a terrible state by the time they got to the castle. I didn't have to listen at the door. Ye could hear the Colonel yelling. He said clear as day that if his gold isn't returned to him, then my aunt, Mistress Fletcher, and the man will hang at dawn. Thieves, he called 'em, and my poor aunt, a witch.'

Daniel ran his hand through his hair.

'The man's my brother,' he said in a low voice. He turned to face Jonathan. 'We've got to give him the gold.'

Jonathan regarded him with calm, grey eyes. 'And who is to say if we give him the gold he won't hang them anyway?'

'You're right, he would,' Daniel turned away and paced the floor a few times. He wanted to hit something, just from sheer frustration. 'He has no scruples, but what other choice have we got?'

Jonathan's eyes flickered. 'If we give up the gold it will be on our terms, not his. We have to choose the ground on which we fight.'

'Fight?' Daniel threw up his hands in frustration. 'Thornton, there's two of us and he has a private army of at least two dozen soldiers.'

Jonathan's even gaze met his, a smile lifting the corners of his mouth. 'Oh come, you've not shirked from a challenge before, Daniel. I've overcome worse odds.'

Daniel stared at him. 'Challenge? That is sheer lunacy.'

He stumped out of the cottage and paced the ground outside for some minutes before coming to rest on a fallen tree trunk, his elbows on his knees and his head in his hands.

Jonathan joined him.

'I will offer myself in exchange for the other prisoners,' Daniel said without looking up.

'Why?'

'This was always my mission, not yours and Kit's. You both have wives and families. I have … no one.'

'Hmm,' Jonathan mused. 'And what of Agnes?'

Daniel looked away. 'Agnes's priority has always been the children,' he said. 'I was just the means to get to Charvaley.'

'But you and she … '

Daniel cut his friend short with a bitter laugh. 'Agnes came to me because she felt sorry for me.'

'She told you that?'

Daniel nodded. 'She is under no obligation to me, or … ' his voice strained as he added, 'or me to her.'

Jonathan sighed. 'If I may give you the benefit of my meagre knowledge of women, it seems to me that Agnes is not as indifferent to you as you might think.'

Daniel thought back to the previous night. Agnes had come to him then, throwing herself into his arms. Were those the actions of an indifferent friend? Had that just been the exigency of the moment? He remembered the scent of rosemary in her hair, and her body pressed against him and realized whatever Agnes's feelings for him, his for her were not those of an indifferent friend. He loved her with a physical ache.

'What does it matter what either of us feels if Ashby hangs her tomorrow? It should be me. This was nothing to do with her. Come to that, what does my death matter? As far as the world is concerned I am already dead. That's why I will offer myself in exchange for her and the others.'

'You Lovells have a death wish,' Jonathan said. 'And I don't think your selfless offer will tempt Ashby. Tell me, you know the man marginally better than I. What matters most to Ashby, the gold or the title?'

Daniel huffed out a humourless snort of laughter. 'Can I answer, both?'

Jonathan frowned. 'Both … ' he murmured. 'I think at this point he may settle for the gold.'

Sarah wandered out of the cottage, her arms wrapped around herself against the cold.

'I've been thinking,' she said. 'There's a way into the old part of the castle that the Colonel won't know. It's an old route, used by the soldiers from long ago.'

'A sally port?' Jonathan suggested.

Sarah shrugged. 'Don't know what that is, but it leads directly into the cellars. You may be able to get 'em out without too much trouble.'

Daniel stood up and clasped the girl's face between his hands, planting a kiss on her forehead.

'You are a godsend, lass. Thornton, I'll go in with Sarah once it is dark.'

Jonathan rose to his feet and looked around at the woods and the little cottage. 'There's nothing we can do until dark anyway. If you can get them out, I will wait outside, but I warn you I won't wait beyond two hours.'

'But –' Daniel's protest was cut short by Jonathan.

'Alone and on foot I should be able to reach Preston, and I will raise help from the local authorities. They won't countenance Ashby's high-handed behaviour, not at this point.'

Daniel nodded. 'You just have to make sure you get that help before Ashby hangs them out of hand.'

A humourless smile twitched the corners of Jonathan's mouth. 'That's all we have to do.' He clapped Daniel on the shoulder. 'Let us just hope you can get them out first.'

CHAPTER 44

*A*gnes shivered, wrapping her arms around herself in a vain attempt to keep warm as she paced the floor. The room into which they had been thrown must have been a buttery or something similar in a past life. A long, low, heavy stone bench ran along one wall, below two small windows so grimed with dirt and cobwebs as to admit only the faintest light.

Kit sat on the cold, filthy, flag-tiled floor, with his back to the wall and his eyes closed. Peg huddled in a corner, drawn in on herself. The shock of her capture and the brutal means that had been used to drag her to the castle had broken the old woman.

'Sit down,' Kit grumbled. 'You're making me tired.'

Agnes turned to face him. 'How can you be so calm?'

'I have already been hanged once in my life,' Kit said, all humour gone from his voice. 'Death holds no fears for me anymore.'

Agnes turned away so he could not see her face. 'I don't want to die, Kit.' She choked back the sob that rose unbidden and turned back to face him. 'Why can't we just let him have the gold?'

Kit blew out his breath, making a cloud in the cold air. 'I don't know where it is. Thornton's hidden it somewhere. Anyway, lass, we're not going to die. Ashby's all bluster and Dan and Thornton will find a way to get us out.'

Agnes, who had already envisaged Jonathan and Daniel halfway to Seven Ways, narrowed her eyes. 'You believe that?'

'I know,' Kit said and smiled without humour. 'They don't have a horse between them and they will hardly be setting off on foot with Ashby's men on the rampage.'

In her corner, Peg cried out, and Agnes hunched down beside the old woman, wrapping her arms around her, trying to instil some warmth into the frail old body, but she got no response. Peg threw off her arms and looked at her with unseeing eyes.

The hours passed and the light faded from the window, plunging the room into darkness. Agnes drew the woman tighter into her arms.

The click of the key in the lock made her start to her feet and she braced, every muscle tensed, as the door opened to admit Leah Turner, carrying a basket and a lantern. Agnes rose to her feet, standing like a lioness over her two charges. The two women faced each other across the length of the room.

Leah met Agnes's fierce gaze and gestured at Kit. 'I've brought bandages for him,' she said, 'and some food and drink.'

'Really?' The magnanimity of the gesture caused Agnes's anger with the woman to falter. 'Thank you.'

Leah sniffed. 'I only do what my Christian duty commands.'

'Did you come alone?' Agnes enquired.

Leah set the basket down on the floor beside Kit and held the lantern up to scan his face.

'What's your name?' she asked.

'Kit Lovell, and you, Madame?'

'Leah Turner. How badly are you hurt?'

'It wasn't too bad until your friend upstairs decided to drag me through the slush by my wrists,' Kit grumbled.

Leah's thin lips tightened. 'The Colonel is enraged,' she said. 'I have never seen him like this.'

'I have,' Kit said, holding her gaze with his own.

Leah sighed. 'I try to be a good Christian and not think ill of people.' Her gaze flicked to Agnes. 'Despite what you might think.'

Kit studied her face. 'We can't always help our hearts, can we?' he said softly.

Leah started as if he had pricked her with a knife.

Kit looked up at Agnes. 'Mistress Turner is, I suspect, more than a little in love with the good Colonel,' he said.

'You are talking nonsense,' Leah replied, her acerbic tone restored. 'I need your help here, Mistress Fletcher. There is water in that flask and clean cloths.'

Agnes wiped most of the mud from Kit's haggard, unshaven face and turned her attention to his arm. 'Nasty,' Agnes remarked, looking at the angry, seeping gash that Leah was attempting to clean with another cloth.

Kit glanced at his arm and flinched. 'At least you don't faint at the sight of blood,' he said.

'No. Why? Who does?' Agnes asked.

'My wife. She's utterly useless when it comes to tending to my hurts.'

Kit closed his eyes and endured Leah's efficient ministrations in silence, his lips compressed into a tight line.

'You've done that before,' Agnes said.

Leah looked up. 'In the last years of the war,' she said, 'the King's men took refuge in our town. The fighting was fierce and many were wounded. I was only a girl but we all had to lend what aid we could. I saw things no girl of my age should see.'

Kit's eyes flickered open and he laid his right hand on Leah's arm. 'Thank you, Mistress Turner.'

The woman glanced down, her eyes widening at the sight of his crooked fingers, but she said nothing.

'As I said, I only do what I consider my Christian duty.'

'Perhaps you may find it in your Christian duty to provide us with some blankets. This woman,' Agnes rose and crossed to Peg, 'is blameless and yet she is treated like a common criminal.'

Leah turned her attention to Peg, crouching down beside her. 'Mistress Truscott, can you hear me?'

When Peg didn't respond, Leah looked up at Agnes. 'Her senses are addled?'

'As yours would be, had you been treated as she has.'

Leah sighed. 'I thought I knew Tobias ... ' she began but broke off.

She rose to her feet and turned to face Agnes, once again the Leah Turner Agnes knew, stiff and unbending and convinced of the rightness of her cause.

'I will find some blankets,' she said. 'But I would entreat you to spend your time in prayer and contemplation, Mistress Fletcher. You do not wish to face your God without repentance in your heart.'

'Repentance for what?' Agnes's voice rose. 'I have nothing in this life I repent or regret.'

Leah's brows drew together. 'You are a whore, Mistress Fletcher. You shared your bed and your body with a man, not your husband.'

Two men, not my husband.

Agnes thought of Daniel and a physical ache clutched at her heart. God, keep him safe, she prayed as Leah bent over Peg, trying to wash the worst of the mud from the woman's face and hands.

CHAPTER 45

*D*aniel, Jonathan, and Sarah waited until dark before leaving the relative safety of the cottage. As they skirted through fields and coppices, Daniel wrestled with the nagging fear that Sarah may have been leading him into a trap. Instinctively, his hand tightened on the hilt of Kit's sword, the reassuring weight of a loaded pistol tucked into his belt and the press of his knife secreted in his boot.

The security the weapons gave him was illusory. The fact remained he would still be only one man against a troop of soldiers.

Sarah led them around the rear of the castle, where the last of the old castle walls met the ground. They had left Jonathan in a ruined building about 500 yards from the castle, with the agreement they would rendezvous thereafter Daniel had freed Kit and Agnes.

Daniel needed his knife to cut through the tangled brambles that grew in what would have once been the moat. Sarah chafed in impatience behind him. The rasping of the knife sounded like a saw through wood in the silent night, but no movement came from the walls above. Pushing the sharp, straggling fronds aside, they reached the wall.

Even in the gloom, Sarah led him straight to a small wooden door set low in the wall. It gave with only the slightest push from Daniel's shoulder, the rotten wood making barely a noise. Daniel had to almost bend double to duck under the door and into a low-ceilinged passage.

The dark of the old, noisome space closed in on him and he had to stop for a moment, fighting the constricting band that closed around his chest.

'Are you all right?' Sarah whispered in the dark.

She had collected candles and a tinderbox from the cottage before she had left, and he heard the soft scrape of tinder being struck. Focusing on the tiny light of the candle, the band slowly released its grip and he could breathe again.

Sarah glanced at him and pointed into the velvet darkness beyond.

'This way,' she said.

He grunted an assent, and feeling their way along the slimy walls with their fingers, they edged upwards into the bowels of the old castle.

The corridor brought them out into a large space, crowded with broken furniture and old boxes.

'The cellars,' Sarah whispered. 'My brothers and I used to play down here as children – that's how I know about the old entrance. I'm going to have to snuff the light or they'll see it. Give me your hand.'

Daniel had no choice but to do as she said, and her work-hardened fingers closed around his, leading him on through the maze.

'You're cold as ice,' she said in the dark.

She couldn't see the sweat that gathered on his brow and ran down his face as once again the vice closed on his chest.

When she stopped he almost ran into her. She placed a finger on his mouth.

'Shh … they're just beyond there.'

A faint light illuminated a dogleg in the corridor and Daniel inched forward, peering around the corner. He could see a wide corridor lit by a solitary lantern twenty yards or so ahead of him. One of several doors stood ajar, a soldier standing beside it, his back to Daniel.

Daniel pulled back into the shadows and gripped the girl's arm.

'Wait for me,' he whispered. 'If this goes wrong, get back to Thornton and tell him.'

Pulling the pistol from his belt, he checked the priming.

The guard would have known nothing. The years on the French privateer had taught Daniel some useful skills, including the ability to immobilise a man quickly and silently with the right pressure on a certain point in the neck.

As he lowered the unconscious man to the floor, the unease that had dogged him since entering the castle doubled.

Ashby may as well have left the front door open.

I am walking into a trap, he thought.

Trap or not, what choice did he have?

He flattened himself against the wall beside the door, peering through the gap into the room beyond. A lantern on the floor beside Kit did little to dispel the gloom, and it took a moment or two before he could make out the shadowy forms of two women crouched down beside a crumpled form that could only be Peg Truscott.

He swore under his breath as he recognized Leah Turner, but there was nothing for it. He gently pushed the door open wide enough to admit him.

The squeal of unoiled hinges betrayed him and the two women spun around, rising swiftly to their feet.

'Daniel!'

The light fell on Agnes's face, streaked with dirt and ghostly in the lantern light. He thought he had never wanted to kiss a woman so much as he did at that moment.

'You!' Leah Turner stepped into the circle of light thrown by the lantern. Daniel gave her a cursory bow.

'Mistress Turner, how fortunate to find you here. This pistol is primed and I would advise you to keep your peace. Agnes, is there anything in here we can use to keep Mistress Turner quiet?'

Agnes nodded. 'Some bandages,' she said.

Leah lunged for the door, only to be brought up short by Daniel's arm around her waist.

'I don't think so,' he whispered in her ear. 'Agnes, can you deal with this good lady?'

With Daniel's pistol pointed at her head, Leah made no protest as Agnes gagged and bound her. From the woman's grunts, her bindings may have been a little tighter than was needed. Daniel pushed her down to the floor beside Kit and tied her ankles. Behind the gag, she mumbled something that did not sound particularly flattering.

He turned to his brother. In the dim light of the lantern, Kit looked terrible, his face drawn and his eyes sunk in dark recesses, but his voice sounded strong enough as he said, 'No time for pleasantries – I fear they have set a trap for you, little brother.'

Daniel held out his hand. 'Can you get up?'

Kit's fingers tightened on Daniel's and he hauled himself to his feet. Daniel slid an arm around his brother's waist, securing his good arm across his shoulders. Kit slumped against him. They were not going to get far with him in this condition, Daniel thought grimly.

He turned to Agnes. 'Hurry.'

'I can't leave Peg,' she said.

Daniel glanced at the old woman, who lay huddled on the floor, curled in a ball, gibbering to herself.

'We can't take her,' he said.

'But ... ' Agnes protested.

'No time.'

They turned for the door, only to be brought up short by a large, bulky figure.

'You see I was right, Turner. They are sentimental fools.'

Tobias Ashby stood aside to admit Septimus Turner and two armed soldiers, both with horse pistols drawn and ready.

'Only one of you?' Ashby enquired and he scowled. 'That's annoying.'

Daniel released his grip on Kit, hoping he would keep his feet. He hauled Leah up and pushed her forward, the pistol to her head. She tottered and would have fallen if he had not had a good grip on her arm.

Behind Ashby, Septimus Turner lunged forward, only to be prevented from further movement by his commander's hand.

Ashby let out a deep sigh. 'What are you doing here, Leah? I gave express instructions ... What is your name young man? Not Lucas, I assume.'

'Lovell,' Daniel said.

'Ah ... you must be that annoying youth I recall from Eveleigh.' He

271

gestured at Kit. 'His brother, I presume. Where was I ... oh yes ... if you should happen to harm my dear Leah, my two men here will have no hesitation in cutting down the lovely Agnes.'

The pistols of both soldiers moved obediently to point at Agnes. In the space, they could hardly miss.

'Now I suggest you throw your weapons onto the table there, Lovell.'

When Daniel hesitated, Agnes clutched his arm. 'Daniel, please. He will do as he threatens. You, above all, know it.'

Daniel tossed his pistol and sword onto the table.

'God rot you, Ashby,' he said with feeling, pushing Leah forward into the arms of her brother, who removed the gag from her mouth.

'Kill them!' Leah screamed.

'My dear, it's not quite that easy to just kill people these days,' Ashby said. 'There is also the little question of my property that I want returned. Search him.'

The two soldiers did a quick and efficient job of liberating Daniel of his knife.

'It was a good plan of mine to use your friends as bait, Lovell. Now I shall leave you to consider your position. I think we could all do with a good night's sleep. This time you will find the door locked and two of my best men on the other side of it.'

The door slammed shut, leaving Daniel, Agnes, and Kit standing in the middle of the room.

CHAPTER 46

*A*s the darkness closed in around them. Daniel swore volubly and Agnes heard the crack of wood, followed by a grunt of pain.

'Hitting the table will only give you a sore hand,' Kit remarked. 'Mind if I sit down?'

Agnes blinked a few times, allowing her eyes to become accustomed to the darkness once more. Daniel's shadowy figure stood only a few paces from her and she caught at his arm.

'Daniel? This was not your doing.'

He tensed beneath her fingers. 'Tell me why it's not my fault. I brought you all here in the pursuit of what – a few gold coins?'

'It was not just the gold,' she said. 'I underestimated Tobias Ashby. I thought he had more humanity.'

Daniel huffed out his breath. 'If you had seen him calmly order my father's death you would not think that.' He fumbled with the cords of his cloak. 'I think someone has a greater need of this than me. Where's Peg?'

Groping in the darkness, they found the old woman, curled in a ball. Agnes took the woman's head onto her lap as Kit wrapped her in the cloak.

'I'm sorry to be a trouble,' the woman muttered.

'It's all right, Peg. It's our fault. We should never have involved you. Are you warm now?'

'Better,' Peg replied. 'Still so cold.'

Agnes felt for the woman's life beat.

She took a quick breath. 'She is very weak,' she whispered to Daniel.

'We have to try and keep her warm,' he replied in a low voice. 'Give her to me.'

He took the frail woman in his arms, holding her close against him.

'It's been ... a long time ... since an 'andsome young man held me in arms,' Peg murmured.

Agnes smiled into the dark.

'So, Mistress Truscott, what do the pages of my future say now?' Daniel said.

Peg chuckled. 'They're set now. Your future's here.'

'What does that mean?' Agnes said.

'Peg read my fortune in the palm of my hand,' Daniel said, 'but she said my future had not been written yet.'

Agnes leaned her head against Daniel's shoulder and gently stroked the woman's face and hair, wiping tears away from the cold cheeks. The long, slow, cold minutes passed and Agnes closed her eyes, allowing herself to doze only to be jerked awake as Daniel shifted his position.

'Agnes, I think she's gone.'

'What do you mean?'

'She's dead.'

'No ... no ... no! She can't be dead.'

Agnes searched for a pulse but found none. She lowered her head, letting the hot tears fall on her hands. 'This is all my fault.'

Daniel rose to his feet, still holding the body of the woman, and carried her over to the stone bench. He laid her on it, folding her hands across her chest. Agnes stood beside him, the impotent tears rolling down her cheeks.

In the dark, Daniel found her hand, his fingers curling around hers.

'Do you know any prayers, Agnes?'

She swallowed and recited the only prayer that came to her mind, the familiar words of the Lord's Prayer providing a simple solace.

Daniel released her fingers and crossed to the door. He banged on it.

'A woman has died,' he said. 'If you have a Christian heart, you will see her dealt with the respect she deserves.'

A hard voice came back. 'Orders are no one is to open this door until morning. She ain't goin' nowhere and neither are you.'

'Soulless bastards,' Daniel shouted back.

'Come and sit down,' Kit said. 'It's perishing cold over here by myself.'

Agnes sat down beside Kit and took his hand, chafing the crooked fingers between her palms.

Kit drew his breath in with a hiss. 'Gently!'

'How did you break your fingers?' she asked.

'Someone trod on them,' Kit said, 'a little harder than he needed to.'

Daniel's boots echoed on the cold, stone floor and she moved over, letting him slide down between her and Kit. He spread his cloak across the three of them but it made little difference in the coldest part of the night.

Agnes nestled in closer to Daniel and he slipped his arm around her, drawing her into the warmth of his body.

'You should try and sleep,' he said.

'I'm too cold,' she said, snuggling closer against his solid, reassuring chest. 'It's all gone wrong, hasn't it?'

He heaved a sigh. 'It certainly hasn't gone according to plan. But Agnes, believe me when I say none of it's your fault – just an unfortunate trail of events.'

'Do you think he really will hang us?'

'Ashby is dangerous and unpredictable,' Kit said.

'And greedy,' Agnes said. 'I thought if I came here it would all be resolved but I just made it worse. Henry ... ' She choked on the mere mention of his name. 'He needs me.'

Daniel raised his hand and brushed the hair away from her face as if she were a fretful child in need of reassurance.

'Of course, he needs you,' he said, resting his head on hers. 'You're his mother. I don't know how you have pretended otherwise for so long.'

'His mother?' Kit put in.

No point in denying it.

'Yes. It's a complicated story.'

Kit groaned. 'Agnes … never mind. I am damnably tired. If I am to die in a few hours, I might try and get some sleep.'

When Kit's stentorian breathing assured Agnes he was asleep, she said, 'Daniel, I'm frightened.'

'I have survived worse than this tangle,' Daniel said, stroking her disordered curls. 'There was a time on the *Archangel* when we were after a Spanish galleon and had just about closed with her when three warships loomed up out of the mist.'

'What did you do?'

'We decided on discretion and quietly melted away,' Daniel said.

'You haven't talked about your time as a privateer.' Talking about anything other than their current predicament seemed a welcome distraction.

'Most of the time it was just hard work and boredom,' Daniel said. 'I would never be a sailor by choice. Give me the solid earth beneath my feet.'

'So why stay with them?'

'I had nowhere else to go. Besides, I rather enjoyed being *Le Loup Anglais.*'

'The English Wolf, Was that your nickname?' When he grunted assent, she said, 'How on earth did you earn that?'

'A wolf stalks its prey, doesn't it? There was this one occasion when Broussard was laid up with a fever and gave me command of the *Archangel.* I had word of a Spanish treasure ship out of the New World. We caught sight of it just out of St. Lucia and we stalked it for five days, just to make sure there was no risk of its escort spotting us. They were separated in a storm, leaving the *Christabel* by itself. That's when we took it. The sword I carry was a gift of the captain of the *Christabel.*'

'Why did you decide it was time to come home?'

'We took an English ship and I found a broadsheet in the captain's cabin with the news of Cromwell's death. I talked it over with Broussard, who said it was time to return to France for repairs, and so ... here I am.'

'Here we are.'

Agnes shivered and Daniel slid his arm around her, holding her closer.

'Daniel, what is it like to face death?' she murmured.

His lips brushed her hair. 'It's a strange thing,' he said. 'Hope is the very last thing to go.'

'Did you ever give up hope?'

He shifted slightly and his chest rose and fell in a deep, silent sigh. 'Never once,' he said, 'and I'm certainly not going to abandon it now.'

The sound of voices outside and the turn of the key in the lock brought them both to their feet. Kit muttered something but did not move.

The door opened and the light from a lantern temporarily dazzled them. Turner's voice came from out of the dark.

'Some friends to keep you company.'

The door slammed shut once more, plunging them into the dark.

'This is unfortunate,' Jonathan's voice sounded disembodied in the blackness. 'Mistress Truscott, I do hope you are not hurt.'

Sarah's voice. 'No, sir. I'm fine.'

Daniel groaned. 'What happened?'

'Ah, you are in here,' Jonathan said. 'Let me take your arm, Mistress Truscott.'

The sound of boots on the flagstones marked Jonathan's progress across the floor.

'I can see you now,' he said, his shadowy form looming out of the dark.

'Where's Auntie?' Sarah asked.

Agnes reached out for the girl and drew her into an embrace. 'She's dead, Sarah. Her heart gave out.'

'No!' Sarah's strangled sob was muffled by Agnes's shoulder.

'Why did they let them catch you?' Daniel demanded.

'I'm not sure it was my choice,' Jonathan responded. 'You were right about it being a trap.'

Daniel glanced at the servant girl. 'Sarah, did you betray us?'

Sarah raised her head. 'Me? No! They were waiting for me when I left the tunnel. Turner's men 'ave been holdin' me these past few hours in the guard house. Turner himself brought Sir Jonathan in.'

'They caught up with me about two miles out of the village,' Jonathan said.

'Dear God,' Kit spoke at last. 'I'm not sure I can see how we are going to get out of this, Thornton.'

Jonathan hunkered down beside him. 'Trust in God, Lovell. God and the weakness of man.'

Kit gave a hoarse laugh. 'God? I'm not sure the Almighty himself would have an easy answer to our current predicament.'

Agnes released Sarah. 'There has to be something we can do.'

Jonathan slid down to the floor beside Kit and leaned his head against the cold, damp wall. 'I have every confidence that we will prevail. In the meantime, I think we should try and get some rest,' he said. 'We will need all our wits about us when the sun rises.'

Despite the cold and discomfort, Agnes curled up again in Daniel's arms and allowed her eyes to close, heavy with sleep that could no longer be held at bay. Daniel stroked her hair and she heard his voice in her ear.

'Don't give up hope, Agnes. We will get through this.'

How? Three unarmed men, one hurt, and two women did not seem to stand much chance against a troop of soldiers led by a determined and murderous commander.

Hope ... she understood now. The moment you abandoned hope you gave up on the world.

Daniel was right, they had to have hope.

CHAPTER 47

Under a heavily armed guard, Ashby's raggle-taggle prisoners entered the Great Hall, Jonathan, Daniel, and Kit in front and behind them, Sarah and Agnes. Sarah clung to Agnes's arm, still weepy with grief for her aunt. Ashby had arranged his men down each side of the Great Hall, the two lines closing behind the prisoners as they walked the length of the room.

Tobias Ashby himself waited on the dais, with Turner behind him. Next to her brother, Leah Turner held the two children by the hands.

'Henry!' Agnes lunged forward.

'Aunty Agnes!' Henry wailed and struggled to release himself from Leah's grip.

Daniel caught her by the waist.

'Not now,' he whispered in her ear. 'Your time will come. Sarah, see to her.'

Sarah took Agnes in charge, with an arm around her shoulders.

Henry yelped and fell silent as the fingers of Leah's hand tightened on his shoulder.

Daniel stepped forward before Ashby could speak. He was damned if he would stand there meekly allowing this man to play God with their lives.

'I stand here in the presence of these witnesses and accuse you of the murder of Margaret Truscott,' he said.

Not a muscle twitched in Ashby's face.

'Forgive me if I misunderstand, Lovell, but the only reason Mistress Truscott was taken into my custody is because you and your fellow conspirators made her complicit in your plans,' Ashby said, his gaze travelling along the line of prisoners. 'Guilt by association. As for her death, that is unfortunate but my physician tells me that Mistress Truscott's health was poor.'

'She would not be dead had you not dragged her through the mud and left her to die in a cold cellar,' Daniel responded. 'But then your crimes go back a very long way, don't they, Ashby?'

Ashby waved a hand. 'We are here to talk about your crimes, not mine, Lovell. Turner, shut this man up.'

With a nod from Turner, two burly soldiers stepped forward, taking Daniel by the arms. A third man delivered a punch to his abdomen that drove the breath from his body. Daniel went down on his knees, gasping like a landed fish as he struggled to suck air into his lungs.

Through the roaring in his ears, he heard Kit's laconic drawl, tinged with the edge of his French accent. '*Mon Dieu*, Ashby, you have not mellowed with age. You may as well tell us what you plan to do with us. I have no great desire to prolong this interview longer than necessary.'

'I command you in the name of the King to release us,' Jonathan Thornton said, his voice carrying up into the blackened rafters above them.

'The King?' Ashby replied. 'There is no king here. I see only five miscreants who will be dead before the sun crosses midday.'

Jonathan's gaze flicked to Turner. 'The days of this regime are numbered,' he said. 'The King will return and at such time everything claimed by the Committee of Safety or whoever it is who claims jurisdiction in London will return to its lawful and rightful owner. This is not the time or the place to dispute the authority of the rightful King of England or his servants and agents.'

'Who are you?' Ashby demanded. 'I know the others but you are a stranger to me.'

Jonathan straightened. 'Sir Jonathan Thornton, one time Colonel of the King's Lifeguard,' he said. 'I can assure you that when the King sits once more upon his throne, the fate of those standing before you today will be of some interest to him. You have crimes enough to answer for without adding the murders of innocent people to your list.'

'What crimes?' Ashby sneered.

Daniel struggled to his feet, holding his ribs as he struggled for breath.

'The death of Margaret Truscott and the cold-blooded murder of my father, Thomas Lovell, to name but two,' he said. 'I would wager there are others.'

He looked up at Ashby, seeing the twitch of a muscle in Ashby's jaw that betrayed the man's uncertainty. 'I have waited for ten years to look you in the eye and make that accusation, Ashby.'

'Is this true?' Jonathan asked.

'Thomas Lovell took up arms against the forces of Parliament. He refused to surrender when called upon to do so. An example had to be set. It was war, Thornton. You know how things were.' Ashby licked his lips.

Glancing at Jonathan, Daniel saw no emotion in the man's lean face. Jonathan Thornton was not a man to cross.

'Yes,' Jonathan said at last. 'I know how things were. I saw innocent men die for nothing more than wearing the wrong uniform. That does not make it right.'

Ashby dismissed Jonathan's words with a wave of his hand. 'Enough talk, Thornton. Do you have my gold?'

Jonathan shook his head. 'No.'

Ashby frowned. 'No? I saw the hiding place. Something had been there until very recently.'

'And you have no proof that it was there when we went looking for it,' Jonathan said. 'You can hardly accuse us of stealing something that was not there in the first place.'

Ashby frowned. 'This is wordplay,' he said. 'You are thieves, all of you.'

'And hanging us will not give you what you want,' Jonathan said.

'But it will give me the satisfaction of seeing you all dead,' Ashby responded. 'I've had enough of this. Turner, see the prisoners escorted to the courtyard. We will hang them from the walls.'

Turner stepped forward. He caught the eye of his burly sergeant. 'All you men are dismissed. Return to your quarters and await further orders.'

Ashby stared at his captain. 'What? That's not what I ordered. Back here, all of you.'

But Turner's men continued to tramp toward the door of the Great Hall without a backward glance.

'Turner. Enough of this nonsense. Summon your men back, now.'

Turner did not move. His shoulders rose and fell in a heavy sigh and he looked up past Ashby's shoulder to the high windows with their panes of coloured glass.

'No,' he said.

Ashby's eyes widened. 'No? What do you mean, no?'

Turner returned his gaze to Ashby. 'I meant no.'

'I will have you tried for mutiny,' Ashby raged at Turner.

Turner shook his head. 'I don't think you will. Thornton is right – it is time for a king to rule once more in England. I am taking my men and riding north to join General Monck. I received word from a friend who is with him that he is moving on London. The end is coming.'

'Monck? A traitor?' Ashby stared at his captain.

Turner swallowed. 'In a few months Charles Stuart will once again sit on the throne of this country and there will be a price to pay for those who resisted him, particularly those who participated in the killing of his father. A wise man knows where his allegiances need to lie in times like these and Ashby, your days are numbered.'

The colour drained from Ashby's face. 'You were there too.'

Turner's eyes narrowed. 'But I did not command the guard at the King's execution. You did.'

Turner waved a hand at the prisoners. 'I suggest, if you have any sense left, Ashby, you let these people depart with the children and whatever it was they came here to retrieve.' He glanced at Jonathan and his lips twitched. 'If indeed they did find it. I for one see no evidence that they did.'

'Septimus, what are you doing?' Leah Turner dragged the two children forward to confront her brother.

Turner shook his head. 'It is time to return home, Leah. You are not needed here anymore.'

She glanced at Ashby, 'But Tobias and I … we had an understanding …'

Ashby glanced at her as if noticing her for the first time. His lip curled. 'An understanding? I think not, Mistress Turner. Why would I want a dried-up old maid such as you?'

Leah looked from one man to the other. 'No,' she said. 'It was not supposed to be like this. Tobias should be the Earl of Elmhurst, with me by his side.'

She flung Lizzie to one side, tightening her grip on Henry. From her skirts, she drew a knife.

'Sweet Jesu,' Kit muttered.

Agnes screamed and lunged forward again, to be caught by Jonathan. 'She will hurt the child, Agnes. Keep your peace,' he said.

A shot rang out in the room, reverberating off the ancient walls and setting a pigeon high in the rafters fluttering in alarm. Septimus Turner fell to his knees, looking up at Tobias Ashby with surprise in his eyes before falling forward.

From where she huddled on the floor, Lizzie screamed.

Ashby threw aside his useless pistol and Daniel saw his moment. He took the dais in a couple of leaps, wrestling to free Turner's sword from its scabbard. Ashby, seeing what he intended, grabbed Henry off Leah. The child struggled in his grip, reaching out for Agnes and screaming her name.

Ashby slapped the child hard across the face and Henry's protests died to a quiet whimpering and he stopped struggling.

Daniel gave Agnes a quick sideways glance. She hung in Jonathan's arms, her eyes wide with fear.

'Daniel … Henry …' she sobbed.

Daniel weighed Turner's sword in his hand. It was an Army issue back sword, an inelegant weapon compared to his Spanish rapier, but it would do the task.

'Put the child down and face me like a man, Ashby,' he said. 'Only a coward would use a child as a shield.'

Ashby's gaze flicked around the room. He let Henry fall to the ground and took a step back, drawing his sword. Daniel could do nothing for either Henry or Elizabeth as Leah once more swooped on both children, even as Kit began to move. She moved away from the two men and the body of her brother, the light from the windows glinting on the honed steel of the knife she held.

Daniel considered his opponent. Ashby was older and heavier, but he had a better sword and experience on his side. Daniel knew he was not the swordsman his brother had been before his right hand had been crippled, but close-quarter fighting on the decks of ships had taught him some interesting manoeuvres.

Ashby clearly expected him to move first, and when he didn't the silence hung in the room with an almost palpable presence. Agnes's choked sob echoed around them and Ashby, wearying of waiting, lunged.

As he had thought, Ashby had some classical training in swordplay, but it became clear from their initial conversations, the back and forth of swordplay, that Ashby's technique had been refined on a battlefield with little need for the elegance of the fencing master.

Sparks flew as the weapons came together, Ashby trying to use his superior size to advantage over his lighter opponent, but Daniel had no trouble disengaging. He just needed to keep Ashby moving until the older man tired.

He backed Ashby off the dais, his opponent staggering but regaining his feet with surprising agility for a man of his size. Out of the corner of his eye, he noticed Jonathan, still holding Agnes, move her away, clearing the space on the floor of the Great Hall. He now had the entire room to play with and here his youth came to the fore, forcing Ashby backwards down the hall in a series of thrusts, parries, and ripostes.

Ashby's breath started to come in laboured grunts, sweat sheening his forehead. When Ashby tried to counter, Daniel just skipped aside, leaving Ashby thrusting into thin air. Only a few feet now between Ashby's back and the door to the room. Daniel lunged forward, catching the sleeve of Ashby's left arm. The man yelped and stumbled backwards, his back coming to rest against the solid wood panelling. A feint to the right and Daniel sent Ashby's weapon spinning from his hand, the point of his sword hard up against his neck.

Everything he had imagined in the long, long years since that day at Eveleigh had come to pass. The death of his father, the fateful events at Worcester, his captivity and torture and even the years aboard a privateer – he had laid them all at the feet of this man.

Now, as he looked into Ashby's eyes, he realized how wrong he had been. Yes, Ashby bore the sole responsibility for Thomas Lovell's death, but everything else? The blame for those events rested on his shoulders alone.

'Get it over with,' Ashby panted.

Daniel lowered his sword.

'No,' he said. 'If I were to kill you, I would be no better than you. You will answer for your crimes in a court of law, not by the spilling of more blood.'

Ashby straightened, his fingers going to the cut on his neck where Daniel had pressed a little too hard. A trickle of blood stained his pristine white collar.

He smiled a nasty, humourless smile. 'A court of law? I will answer to no one but my God, Lovell.'

Daniel wrenched the man's arm around behind his back and, stooping to retrieve Ashby's sword, turned to face the room. There remained the problem of Leah Turner.

'Let the children go, Mistress Turner,' Daniel said.

Leah shook her head. 'No. You release the Colonel.'

'I'm not going to do that,' Daniel said.

Out of the corner of his eye, he saw Agnes twist in Jonathan's arms. Jonathan went down on his knees as if he had been felled with a pistol ball. Daniel recognized the manoeuvre and grimaced in sympathy for his friend, but he could do nothing but watch as Agnes flew out of

Jonathan's grip and, with a bloodcurdling scream akin to the war cry of an ancient Celtic warrior, hurled herself bodily at Leah Turner.

Leah had no time to react. As her grip on Lizzie relaxed, the child sank her teeth into Leah's hand and the knife fell from her grip. It took both Jonathan and Kit to separate Agnes and Leah. Kit held Agnes by one arm as Agnes continued to glare at Leah Turner. Jonathan had the other woman but all the fight had gone from Leah. She drooped against his arm, her cap gone from her head and her lank ginger hair falling around her face.

As Agnes's breathing returned to normal, Kit released her, and she sank to the floor, gathering the two children into her embrace.

The men visibly relaxed, and Daniel marched his prisoner down to the far end of the hall, depositing him in a chair. Jonathan, still wheezing from his encounter with Agnes's knee, secured Leah in a similar manner. Daniel tossed Jonathan the Colonel's sword and Kit retrieved Leah Turner's knife.

'What now?' Daniel enquired of no one in particular.

'To be honest,' Jonathan said, 'I think our best course of action is for us to be quit of this place as soon as possible. Much as I would like to see this bastard hang for his crimes, which now include the murder of his own officer, the paperwork ... '

'Agreed,' Kit said.

'You'll let me go?' Ashby put in.

'Not exactly. If you have any sense you will quit England. Everything Turner said is true. Monck is considering marching on London and if he does, the King's return is only a matter of time. If you make the mistake of still being in England, Ashby, I will have the greatest pleasure in seeing that charges are brought against you and that you hang.'

Ashby swallowed. 'Let me go and I will be on the next boat I can find,' he said.

'As for you, Mistress Turner?' Jonathan asked, his tone unnervingly gentle.

Leah raised her head. 'I will take Septimus's body back to our home in Staffordshire,' she said, turning her head away from Ashby.

'Now, how do we explain to two dozen heavily armed soldiers that their commander is dead?' Kit enquired.

Jonathan sighed. 'I suppose that falls to me.'

'The privileges of rank, Colonel,' Kit said.

Henry wriggled out of Agnes's embrace and ran to Daniel, throwing his arms around his booted leg. Daniel hefted the boy into his arms.

'You were very brave, young man,' he said.

Henry touched the scar on Daniel's cheek. 'Now I know you really are a pirate,' he said.

Daniel tightened his grip on the child. 'Yes, I really am a pirate.'

He glanced down at Agnes, who smiled up at him. Nothing and nobody would ever separate her from the children again, not if they valued their lives.

'Thank you,' she whispered.

CHAPTER 48

PRESTON, 30 NOVEMBER 1659

*D*aniel leaned against the doorjamb, watching Agnes as she bent over the bed to kiss the two small heads that rested on the bolster. The only light in the room came from a single candle and the warm, reassuring glow of the fire.

'Are they asleep?' he asked in a low voice.

She looked up and started as she saw him. 'How long have you been there?'

'Long enough,' he said.

He crossed to the narrow cot shared by the two children and looked at them, all care and trouble now banished from their soft, round faces. Something stirred within him. They were not his children, but as he had held Henry's small, trembling body in his arms, he knew he would have killed Tobias Ashby and even Leah Turner without a second thought if it meant keeping the children safe.

Sarah Truscott came into the room, carrying a tray. She set it down on the table. 'Some broth, mistress. You've not eaten all day.'

Agnes nodded and carried the bowl across to the fire. She sat on the stool as Sarah busied herself tidying up scattered clothing before excusing herself and leaving them alone together.

Daniel crouched down beside Agnes, poking the fire into life. It gave him something to do, something to keep his hands busy.

'Kit and Jonathan?' Agnes asked.

'Kit's asleep. The doctor gave him some sort of draught that knocked him out in minutes. Jonathan's reading a book.'

'I keep thinking, if Turner hadn't turned on Ashby we would all be dead,' Agnes said. 'Why did he do it?'

'For completely base reasons. Jonathan bribed him.'

'When?'

'Jonathan let himself be captured and demanded an interview with Turner. He put a business proposition to Turner and the man agreed. From what Jonathan tells me, I think Turner could see that there was no future tied to a man like Ashby, or he would not have acquiesced quite so readily.'

'I'm almost sorry he's dead,' Agnes said.

Daniel shrugged. 'We're here and we're safe. We have the gold, and you have the children. Turner's death was the price we had to pay.'

She set the wooden bowl down. 'You're right, Daniel. We're here. What now?'

Daniel straightened and leaned his hands on the mantle.

Aboard the *Archangel,* his plans had been quite simple. Return to England, find his brother, seek out Tobias Ashby, kill him, return to Eveleigh, and pick up the threads of his life. The reality had proved more complex. Yes, he had found Kit, but the price Kit had paid for his freedom was more than he could ever repay. Yes, he had found Tobias Ashby, but killing the man in cold blood would have reduced him to Ashby's level.

He shook his head. 'I don't know, Agnes.'

He turned to look at her. The firelight bathed her in gold and shadows. She had not slept in over twenty-four hours and her eyes seemed lost in dark circles of absolute exhaustion. A meeting of mutual convenience had become so much more. He couldn't imagine his life without her, but the children had always come first with Agnes, and, rightly, always would.

He wondered if there was still a small part of Agnes that had room for someone else.

'What are you thinking?' she asked.

'I am thinking that is a foolish question that women always ask. A man's thoughts are very simple.'

Her mouth quirked into a smile. 'Food, and ... ' she lowered her eyes, 'How to get the next woman they meet into bed?'

He shook his head. 'No, that's not what I was thinking. There is only one woman I want to share my bed with.'

She looked up sharply. 'What do you mean?'

He had fought a battle, survived imprisonment, torture, and death, and sailed the seas as a French privateer. And yet a fear such as he had never experienced before clutched his heart. He did not want to lose this woman. He just had to find the courage to say a few simple words.

He cleared his throat. 'That night at Seven Ways when you came to me ... was it because you just felt sorry for me?'

Agnes shook her head. 'No. I said that because ... ' she bit her lip, 'maybe I wanted to push you away. You had found Kit and I thought you wouldn't need me anymore. It was easier to hurt than be hurt.' She took a breath. 'I love you, Daniel. I probably have from the moment you rescued me on that street in London, however base your motives were.'

Daniel sucked in his breath and looked away. 'I have to admit, my motives were less than pure, but there has been precious little time for love or tenderness or even affection in my life in the last years. I don't deserve your love.'

She rose to her feet to face him. 'I do understand ... I come with two children and a tarnished reputation, and ... '

She didn't finish. He seized her and wrapped her in his arms, silencing her with a kiss. She responded in kind, joined in a desperate passion that took his breath away. As they broke apart they leaned into each other, forehead to forehead, nose to nose, her very breath his breath. He found her hands, twining his fingers with hers.

'Marry me, Agnes,' he said.

Her fingers tightened on his. 'Daniel ... I ... "

'I understand that the children are a part of you and, God willing, there will be more children.' A thought welled inside him and he allowed it to spill over in a deep-throated laugh of pure joy. 'I want to grow old with you by my side, surrounded by our children and our children's children, Agnes. We can rebuild Eveleigh ... ' He stopped and straightened. 'You haven't given me an answer.'

'You haven't told me why you want to marry me, Daniel.'

He had to think about that one for a long moment. When it dawned on him, he smiled and gathered her hands in his own, pressing them to his heart. 'I love you, Agnes Fletcher.'

'And I love you and I very much want to marry you, Daniel Lovell.'

He wrapped his arms around her and held her close.

'As soon as this matter is settled,' he said. 'For now, you are dead on your feet, Agnes.'

He swept her up in his arms and carried her over to the bed, laying her between the covers.

'Will you stay?' she murmured.

He shook his head as he bent to kiss her. 'Not tonight. Like you, I need my bed and a good night's rest.'

CHAPTER 49

*A*gnes woke to a large, slobbery kiss from Henry. She rolled him over and tickled him until he begged for mercy, with Lizzie joining in until they were one giggly knot. Sarah Truscott entered the bedchamber bearing a tray with fresh bread, jam, and frumenty for the children's breakfast. She set the tray down on the table and extricated the children from the tangle of bed linen.

'Sir Jonathan asks that you join them,' she said as Agnes tumbled from the bed. 'I'll help you dress.'

'You're cheerful this morning,' Sarah went on to remark, as Agnes hummed to herself while she drew a comb through her tangled hair.

Agnes laid the comb down and looked at her reflection in the mildewed mirror provided by the inn. 'I have good reason to be,' she said.

Coiling Agnes's wayward hair into a knot, Sarah smiled. 'Many good reasons,' she said, adding with a cheeky grin, 'but mostly to do with an 'andsome man with a scar on his face?'

'Maybe,' Agnes replied.

She all but bounced into the private parlour with a cheery 'Good morning.'

The three men seated around the table looked up, but Agnes had eyes for only one man. Daniel's smile warmed her as he held out his hand. She placed her hand in his and he raised it to his lips, never once looking away. His grey eyes, soft and smoky and no longer the icy grey of a winter stream, drew her in, and she leaned toward him, kissing him as if they were the only two people in the room.

Jonathan coughed. 'I see. That is how the land lies, does it?'

'About time,' Kit commented. 'We've been watching you two pretending indifference for weeks now. It was getting very tiresome.'

Daniel laughed, drawing Agnes down onto his knee. 'In that case, you will be relieved to know Mistress Fletcher has consented to be my wife,' he said. 'We'll be married as soon as it can be arranged.'

After the acclamations of goodwill died down, Daniel turned to Jonathan. 'How does one get married these days?'

'There is a registrar in the parish,' Jonathan said. 'If you wish to be married at Seven Ways, I know the man. A wedding,' he nodded approval. 'A good excuse for some merriment, if any of us can remember how.'

Daniel glanced at Agnes. 'Seven Ways will suit us. We have nowhere else. My own home is a ruin and I – we – couldn't impose on Kit.'

Agnes glanced at Kit. Although he carried his right arm in an untidy sling, the night's sleep appeared to have restored him and he had some colour back on his face.

Kit's left eyebrow quirked. 'Why ever not? We have a palace of a house that is only half used. But it is in Hampshire, and if you are anxious to settle the matter, and the Thorntons are willing to put up with you, then Seven Ways it will be.'

Jonathan straightened, and Agnes rose from Daniel's knee and took the fourth chair.

'There is still business to be concluded,' Jonathan's long fingers tapped the table. 'What are we to do with the gold now we have it?'

Daniel shook his head. 'My orders were vague. I was to send word to a man called Mordaunt in London and await further instructions.'

'Mordaunt?' Jonathan frowned. 'Do I know him?'

Kit shrugged. 'I had some dealings with him back in the uprising of

'48. He is a conspirator of the first order. I'm not surprised he is in on this.'

Jonathan's mouth tightened. 'Typical. I'll send the message this morning and in the meantime, I suggest we return to Seven Ways. We probably have more priest holes than Charvaley and the gold can be secured there until we hear from this Mordaunt. By the time the message has been sent and instructions received there should be ample time to organize a wedding.'

Kit stretched his good arm above his head. 'An excellent plan, Colonel. I have a yen for your soft beds and good food. I am too old for this rackety life.'

CHAPTER 50

SEVEN WAYS, WORCESTERSHIRE 4 DECEMBER 1659

*A*t the Black Cross in Bromsgrove, Jonathan arranged for a message to go on to Seven Ways ahead of them, so Daniel should not have been surprised at the crowd that gathered in the fore-court for the arrival of the black Elmhurst coach, with Jonathan and himself following on horseback.

As they turned the corner and the house came in view, he drew rein to consider the size of the waiting crowd. He could identify the Thornton clan, but there seemed to be another three women waiting with them.

'Who are all these people?' he asked Jonathan.

Kit peered out of the window of the coach.

He groaned. 'It's Thamsine,' he said, 'and she's brought the whole household with her.'

As the women came forward, he recognised his mother and his sister and a band tightened around his chest. He, in his turn, had been recog-nized. Frances, a young woman now, not the girl he had left behind, broke ranks and ran toward him. He all but threw himself out of the saddle and into the arms of his sister, burying his face in her hair to stop the tears.

'Daniel Lovell, do you have any idea of what I have been through?'

Daniel looked up. The years had not been kind to Margaret Lovell, her hair now steel grey, but as soon as she spoke, Daniel could see that they had not mellowed her and her tongue was as sharp as ever.

Daniel broke from his sister's embrace and covered the distance between them, sweeping her up into his arms. 'Mother, I am so sorry.'

'Put me down, you foolish boy,' Margaret protested without anger. He set her on her feet and she looked up at him, her finger tracing the scar across his cheekbone.

'I had given up hope—' she began and burst into tears.

Frances flung her arms around both of them, also crying.

'When you have quite finished,' Kit's voice broke through the circle. 'I have someone else for Daniel to meet.'

Daniel straightened, hoping that the tears that had been wrung from him did not show.

A tall, elegant woman, with her chestnut hair dressed in fashionable ringlets, stood beside Kit, surveying him with her head tilted to one side.

'Daniel, may I present my beloved wife, Thamsine.'

Daniel swept a low bow, a gesture that lost its impact as Thamsine stepped forward and gathered him into a close embrace.

'You have no idea of how long I have waited to do that,' she said, stepping back with tears in her eyes.

Kit turned to his wife.

'Thamsine, my darling, are you going to explain what you are all doing here? ' Kit began and his eyes widened. 'Don't tell me you brought the children as well?'

'No. They are at home.' His wife's lips tightened. 'I get a few lines scrawled in a message to say you have found Daniel and the two of you are going on a secret mission?' She tapped his injured arm, causing him to wince. 'And look, you managed to get yourself hurt again! Don't expect me to pat your fevered brow.'

Kit threw his head back and laughed. 'That is the last thing I expect of you, Tham.'

In the uproar of reunion, Daniel had lost someone, and he looked around searching for Agnes among the crowd of Lovells and Thorntons.

She stood in the shadow of the coach, holding the two children by the hand, a small, lonely island amid the joyful reunions. He ran across to her, sweeping Henry into his arms and taking Agnes by the hand, all but dragging her across to where his family waited.

'Please allow me to present Mistress Agnes Fletcher,' he said.

Agnes sank into a curtsey.

His mother's eyes flicked from Agnes to the children. 'And whose children are these?'

A spot of colour appeared on Agnes's cheeks. 'My sister's children, Lady Elizabeth Ashby and Henry, the Earl of Elmhurst.'

'Earl or not,' Kate hurried across, 'these look like two children who have had enough of being confined to a coach. Come inside, all of you. There are refreshments in the parlour.'

'Wait!' Daniel said and gathered Agnes to him. 'Before we go any further, I want you all to know that Agnes and I will be wed as soon as it can be arranged.'

He had the satisfaction of seeing his mother's mouth open in an O of surprise, but she had the grace to close it again.

'A wedding? Here?' Nell Longley clapped her hands together. 'How wonderful!'

Kate turned to her husband and held out a folded paper. 'There is a message for you, Jonathan. It arrived this morning. The man said it was urgent.'

Jonathan took the paper and broke the seal, scanned the contents, took a deep breath, and looked up.

'I am sorry, but wedding plans will have to wait. We are ordered to London.'

CHAPTER 51

'*Y*ou can't hide from me forever.'

Agnes looked up from the book she had been reading and jumped to her feet as Thamsine Granville swept into the room. Henry and Elizabeth were happy in the nursery with the young Thorntons and with the men gone on to London, she found herself adrift in the large and noisy household and had retreated to the library. 'I wasn't hiding. I ... '

Thamsine smiled. 'It must be completely overwhelming to find yourself in the company of so many people. I quite understand. Now, let us get down to the important matter at hand. We have a wedding to plan.' She clapped her hands. 'Ladies?'

The door opened to admit Frances Lovell. Frances was much Agnes's age, not as tall as Thamsine, but slender, with her brother's dark hair and grey eyes.

She took Agnes's hands in her own. 'We have endured so many long, bleak years. We yearn for some fun and something to celebrate so I, for one, am delighted. Now, what are you doing for a dress?'

'I haven't thought ... ' Agnes began.

'I have that in hand.' Nell now entered the room, carrying a gown of gold satin bundled in her arms. 'I am afraid it is my wedding gown, so somewhat out of the current fashion, but as Agnes lacks my height there is plenty of material to allow for some remodelling.'

Agnes felt the heat rushing to her cheeks as Nell set the petticoats and bodice out on the table. It was a simple cut with soft lace at the elbows, and to Agnes's eyes quite the most beautiful gown she had ever seen.

'I wasn't expecting any fuss or bother.'

'Nonsense,' Thamsine said. 'We have much to celebrate. A lost brother returned, a new sister found … a King returned, or about to be returned. Stand up, Agnes, and let us try this dress on and see what needs to be done.'

'It is too good for me … ' Agnes began.

Thamsine laughed. 'You should have seen what I wore to my wedding. Pretty enough but I am sure it had belonged to a courtesan of the first order. Now, up on that footstool.'

'But … ' Agnes began to protest, but with three other women all talking at the same time as they pinched, pleated, and pinned the gold fabric around her, she could do nothing but stand meekly and let them have their way.

Margaret Lovell swept into the room accompanied by Kate Thornton.

'Quite lovely, my dear,' Margaret said. 'I forgive my son for springing yet another surprise on me. I'm not sure at my age I should be subject to such torture, but I have interrogated my stepson thoroughly, and as he is incapable of hiding anything from me he has appraised me of your circumstances and character, young lady. Come here.'

Tripping over the excess fabric in the petticoats of the gown, Agnes tottered toward her future mother-in-law. The older woman clasped her forearms, forcing her to meet her eyes. 'Agnes Fletcher, if half of what Kit tells me is true, you are a remarkable young woman who risked her life for two defenceless children. I will be proud to have you as my daughter.'

Agnes glanced around the circle of women, seeing only love and acceptance, and found her eyes beginning to fill. She had been without the love of a mother, sister, or family for so long and yet here were these women, strangers to her but determined to accept her unconditionally for herself and not for what she could do for them. She dashed at the tears.

'Stupid,' she said. 'Stupid ... '

'Not at all,' Kate Thornton said. 'Entirely human.'

Margaret folded Agnes in her arms, and the tears Agnes wept into the woman's bony shoulder were tears of happiness and belonging.

CHAPTER 52

The two men stood in the street, looking up at the faded and chipped sign of The Ship Inn.

Kit sighed deeply. 'I never thought I would see it again.'

Daniel glanced at his brother. In the last few days, Kit had related much of the story of the ill-fated plots of 1654 and the terrifying events that had brought Thamsine into his life. It was clear that the inhabitants of The Ship Inn held a very special place in Kit's heart, and on arrival at the Blue Boar both men had set out on foot to the Old Bayly.

Kit pushed open the door, which creaked on its hinges. At this hour of the day there were few patrons, and a boy engaged in scrubbing one of the battered tables straightened. 'What can I do for you, sirs –' He broke off. 'Cap'n! You came back. I thought you'd forgotten me.'

Daniel smiled at young Matt. 'I promised I would, but look at you. I hardly recognize you.'

In truth, the boy seemed to have grown a foot in the time since Daniel had left him, and no longer had the lean, hungry look of a street urchin. He looked clean, well fed and quite presentable.

'I'll get Nan.' The boy scampered into the rooms beyond the taproom, returning with not only Nan but her brother, Jem Marsh.

Nan shrieked at the sight of Kit and threw herself into his arms, a reaction that seemed so completely out of character that Daniel gave his brother a quizzical glance.

'Kit Lovell.' Jem Marsh, grinning broadly, pumped his hand. 'Ye look well, and you, young Daniel. What brings you back to London?'

'I had made the boy a promise and I came to keep it. If you still want to come with me, you can, Matt.'

Matt moved to stand between Nan and Jem. 'If it's all the same to you, Cap'n,' he said, 'I'd rather stay here. Nan and Jem need me.'

Jem placed a fatherly hand on the boy's shoulder. 'He's a good lad, this one,' he said. 'Hard worker but willin' to learn.'

'I've been goin' to the dame school and learnin' to read and write,' Matt said and lowered his eyes. 'And I have a name now.'

'Matthew Marsh,' Nan said. 'Didn't seem proper, the boy not belongin' somewhere. Had him baptized and everything. Now, how's about a drink for old times?'

Kit and Daniel rolled back to the Blue Boar several hours later to find a sober and mildly annoyed Jonathan waiting for them in the private parlour. Two other men rose from their seats and Daniel sobered immediately, recognizing one as Giles Longley.

Kit launched himself at Giles, flinging his arms around him. 'Longley,' he slurred. 'We are together again. The guardians of the Crown.'

'Quite,' Giles remarked, disengaging himself. 'Good to see you, Lovell … Lovells, both. May I present John Mordaunt?'

Kit straightened. 'Ah yes, I remember you now. Spotty youth.'

Mordaunt flushed. 'That was a long time ago.' He frowned. 'Aren't you supposed to be dead?'

Kit thought for a moment. 'Indeed,' he agreed. 'Quite dead.'

'Our orders are to consign the packages to Lord Mordaunt,' Jonathan said.

'*Lord* Mordaunt?' Kit said. 'My, you have done well.'

'His Majesty bestowed the honour on me back in July,' Mordaunt preened.

'And look how well that turned out,' Kit said drily. 'How many men turned up for your little uprising, Mordaunt?'

Mordaunt mumbled something under his breath.

'Thirty,' Kit said. 'The broadsheets had fun with that one. Very well, Mordaunt, the gold is yours. Use it wisely.'

Mordaunt scowled. 'I am to pass it on to Jack Grenville,' he said.

'Good old Jack,' Kit said. 'Do give him ... on second thoughts, don't. I'm dead, and he may think you are receiving messages from beyond the grave.'

Mordaunt glanced at Jonathan, who shrugged. 'Take the gold, Mordaunt,' he said. 'We are pleased to be rid of it.'

They waited until Mordaunt carrying the heavy satchels had left the room before sitting down. Daniel poured them all wine.

'I hear congratulations are in order, Lovell,' Giles said, raising his cup to Daniel.

Daniel thanked him. 'Are you returning with us?'

Giles nodded. 'Yes. Time for the exiles to return, I think, but before I do, the King promised you his favour if you retrieved the gold. What are you after?'

Daniel stared into the ruby depths of his cup and considered for a long moment. 'I no longer need a pardon for myself,' he said, 'and I do not believe my lands were sequestered.' He glanced at Kit. 'I seek a pardon for my brother.'

Giles raised an eyebrow. 'From which particular crime? There will be a general pardon for all those who died in service to the King, but as for the other... damn it, Lovell, you were an agent of Cromwell's. Good men died.'

Kit, suddenly sober, sighed heavily. 'I had my reasons.'

Giles waved a hand. 'You can tell them to the King. Is there anything else?'

'Yes. I am to marry Agnes Fletcher. I want both of us to be granted the custody and guardianship of the young Earl of Elmhurst and his sister until he is of age, along with his property.'

'That can be done,' Giles said. 'Jonathan has appraised me of the situation there. I believe Ashby is now on the Continent and is hardly a fit person to be the child's custodian. Is that all?'

Daniel nodded. 'That is enough.'

'Good,' Giles grinned and raised a glass. 'To the return of the exiles.'

CHAPTER 53

SEVEN WAYS, WORCESTERSHIRE 24 DECEMBER 1659

*I*n the long years of war and struggle, it had been many years since there had been such a happy gathering at Seven Ways. The Thorntons proved generous hosts, and with Kit and Giles in charge, the lively wedding celebrations had gone on until well after midnight. Thamsine Lovell proved to be a talented singer with a fund of inappropriate tavern songs that even had Tabitha Thornton missing notes on the virginals with laughing too hard.

In the proper tradition, the women spirited Agnes away and saw her properly arranged, in a nightdress borrowed from Nell, the Thornton's guest bed strewn with dried rose petals. A boisterous crowd of men had accompanied Daniel and it had taken Kate Thornton's firm hand to clear the room. As she left, she handed Daniel the key.

'You'll need that,' she said. 'I wouldn't trust your brother.'

Agnes sat up in the bed and drew her knees up under her chin and considered her husband, who stood in the middle of the floor, still clutching a wine glass, his jacket undone and his shirt unlaced.

He set the cup he was holding down on the table and sat down heavily on the side of the bed, running his hand through his already disordered hair. He turned his head and grinned at Agnes.

'Family,' he said. 'Miss them when you're away from them, and can't wait to get away from them when you're with them.'

Agnes smiled. 'I love them all. They are to be treasured, Daniel.'

He reached out and ran a finger down her cheek. 'I am glad you like them.' His eyes softened and she read desire in their smoky depths. 'You are lovely, Agnes.'

'And you are drunk,' she retorted.

He shook his head. 'No, I am completely sober. I wanted all my wits about me tonight. This is our night.'

Agnes shivered. 'And it's a cold one, too. Come to bed, Daniel.'

Daniel picked up one of the dried rose petals, sniffed it, and sneezed. 'What are these for?'

'They're not for anything.'

He rose to his feet, brushing the offending petals from the cover. 'We don't need me sneezing all night,' he said, unbuckling his belt.

Jacket, breeches, and stockings fell into a pile at his feet, and he threw back the covers.

'And your shirt,' Agnes said.

All humour drained from his face.

'Agnes ... last time ... I know you can't ... my back ... ' He coloured and sat down on the edge of the bed again.

Agnes knelt up beside him, tugging the shirt over his head, revealing his back to her. He lowered his head, his hair falling about his face, hiding it from her.

'Agnes, you don't –' he began.

'I do,' she said, tracing each fall of Outhwaite's whip with her fingers. 'They are a part of you,' she said. 'Part of what made you who you are. I'm not sure I would have liked the Daniel Lovell who existed before these were laid upon you. When he tried to break you that man Outhwaite may have killed the boy but he forged the man I love. It could have turned you into a monster like him, but it didn't, because you are essentially a good man, Daniel. I saw it at Charvaley. You could have killed Ashby but you chose not to. That is the man with whom I want to spend the rest of my days.'

She bent her head and kissed each scar.

When he raised his head and turned to look at her, she saw tears in his eyes.

'Agnes ... ' he began but his voice cracked.

Winding her arms around his neck, she drew him down, her eager kisses matching his own as he slid the chemise from her shoulders. She shivered and he wrapped her in his embrace, pulling the bedclothes over them, burying them in a cocoon of their own that excluded the outside world.

The turmoil of emotion and events that had overtaken them over the past weeks were forgotten in their need for each other. No pity this time – Agnes gave herself to him as an equal.

When the first passion was spent they lay together wrapped in a tangle of blankets and sheets, too languid to move, but too alive in the moment to sleep.

Daniel rolled onto his back, carrying her with him. His hands circled her waist and he studied her face in the soft, shadowed light of the dying fire and the single candle that burned on the table.

'You are perfect,' he said in wonder, running his fingers along the soft curve of her hips and the curve of her breasts.

A slow smile lifted the corners of her mouth and she straightened beneath his hands. 'Far from perfect.'

She stooped to kiss him again, her hair tumbling around her face, and he circled her waist with his hands.

'I do love you, Daniel Lovell.'

He released her, answering her smile with his own. 'And I you, Agnes Fletcher.'

He gathered her into his arms, where she fitted as if they had been crafted by a skilled cabinetmaker.

'I am content, Agnes,' he whispered. 'What has been no longer has the power to hurt us, either of us.'

CHAPTER 54

SEVEN WAYS, WORCESTERSHIRE DECEMBER 24, 1660

*I*n the wintry rose garden at Seven Ways, a battle was in progress. The children, well rugged up, darted between the snow-covered garden beds, in a running battle of snowballs, led by Thomas Ashley on one side and Ann Longley on the other. The younger children, the twins Clare and Richard and little Henry, were towed along by older and larger children. Even shy Tabitha joined in the battle. The older women stood on the terrace shouting encouragement. Kit stood with his arm around his wife's shoulder, giving instructions to Tom on the finer art of artillery fire.

Daniel paused at the door that led out onto the terrace and smiled as Agnes hurled a snowball with deadly accuracy, taking Tom's hat from his head. Beside her, Frances appeared to have a ready supply of snowballs, and she showered these on the young man unmercifully.

'Father! You're home!' Tabitha had seen Jonathan and she dropped her missile, running up the path toward the three men.

Kate Thornton whirled around, a smile lifting her face at the sight of her husband.

'Welcome home,' she said.

In two strides Jonathan had his wife in his arms, kissing her with the passion of two young lovers long separated.

Kit cleared his throat, and they appeared to remember the company they were in, separating with an embarrassed cough on the part of Jonathan and a becoming blush on Kate's part.

With his arm around his wife's shoulders, Jonathan surveyed the crowd. 'Exactly how many people do we have staying here? Who are all these children?'

'Mostly mine,' Kit responded. 'Those two,' he indicated two young women, the younger of whom stood beside Tom Ashley, looking up at him with doe eyes, 'are my wards ... and those three,' he pointed at three small girls, 'are ours.'

'I tell him it is God's judgment,' Thamsine said. She looked at Daniel. 'How went your audience with the King? Did you explain about Kit?'

Daniel nodded. 'Yes. You have the King's pardon, Kit, but he counsels against any return to court. Others may not be so forgiving.'

Kit shuddered. 'I can't think of any place I would like to go to less.' He nodded at his brother. 'But thank you. It eases my mind somewhat.'

Daniel clapped a hand on his brother's shoulder. He alone knew the burden Kit carried and would carry all his life. The ghosts of those men who died for his word would haunt him forever.

Nell kissed her husband. 'Welcome home, husband ... How was the King?'

'The King is well, very well,' Giles said. 'He did his utmost to persuade us to stay for the Christmas festivities but,' he glanced at Jonathan and Daniel, 'these two were most insistent we return home.'

Nell tucked her hand into the crook of her husband's elbow. 'Never has anything felt more right,' she said. 'The King is back on the throne of England, and we have our lovely home back and our family around us. This is the perfect Christmas.'

Daniel glanced at Kate. 'My dear Lady Thornton,' he said. 'Your house and your hospitality must be sorely stretched.'

Kate Thornton shook her head with a smile. 'There is nothing that pleases me more than to have people around us again. I would not have invited you all for Christmas otherwise. Now come inside, all of you. There is spiced wine warming in the Great Hall, and you must tell us all the news from London.'

Daniel walked to the edge of the terrace. Agnes stood in the middle of the snowy garden, looking up at him, a snowball still clutched in her hand, wet snow clinging to her hair and clothes.

'Well, are you going to just stare at her, boy?' his mother said. 'Go and kiss the poor girl.'

'And do it properly,' Frances put in.

Daniel took the stairs down into the garden in one bound, sweeping Agnes up into his arms and spinning her around. The children cheered.

Daniel smiled as he set his wife down. 'Should you be playing such roughhouse games in your condition?'

Agnes's hand went to the swell of her belly, still well concealed by her heavy woollen skirts.

'I don't think the baby has any complaints,' she said.

'Good.'

He kissed her again, his hand sliding beneath her cloak to rest on her stomach. From the moment she had told him that there would be a child born in spring, he had been in a state of wonder and awe.

Oblivious to the cheers and catcalls from the crowd around them, she melted into his arms, only to be jerked out of their embrace by a fusillade of cold, wet snowballs.

Wiping snow from her eyes, Agnes looked up at Daniel and grinned. 'Very well,' she said, whirling on the children. 'This is war. Who is with me?'

With whoops of delight, the children joined in, pelting Daniel with hastily constructed missiles. Flakes of snow clung to his hair as he hastened to retaliate. Tom Ashley joined his force and with their small armies in tow, Daniel and Agnes pursued each other around the garden until they subsided, cold, damp, and exhausted, on the stone bench under the bower.

Daniel waved his hand at the youngsters. 'You win,' he said.

Tom Ashley grinned and winked. 'Let's build a snow king,' he said to the children, and they turned to follow him to a patch of snow untouched by human hand.

Daniel slid his arm behind Agnes, drawing her closer. She rested her head on his shoulder.

'You're wet,' he complained.

'So are you,' she retaliated.

He drew in a deep breath, letting it out and watching it fog in the cold air. 'Christmas Day. Do you remember the Christmas of our childhood, Agnes?'

'I can't answer for your childhood, Daniel, but mine was a huge log in the Great Hall, spiced wine, wassailing, and carols.'

'Fifteen years of no Christmas,' Daniel said. 'When we rebuild Eveleigh, we will have Christmas with all the tenants invited to a feast. A roast ox, I think.'

'And plum pudding,' Agnes mused. 'And gifts.'

Daniel straightened. 'Which reminds me, I bring a Christmas present from the King,' he said, producing a paper from deep inside his jacket. He handed it to her and she scanned the contents. He smiled as her face lit up.

'It is official then?' she asked.

'It is. I am now the legal guardian of Henry and Elizabeth,' he said. 'I asked for it to be both of us, but Hyde was insistent a woman could not be made a legal guardian.'

Agnes sighed. 'It is enough,' she said. 'It means we can make Charvaley our home until Henry is of age, and we can rebuild Eveleigh, and … ' She clutched the paper to her chest. 'I can think of no better Christmas present.'

Daniel glanced up at the terrace, at Jonathan and Kate, Kit and Thamsine, and Giles and Nell. To see them all together, content in each other's company, one could almost forget what each one had endured over the past twenty years. The deaths they had seen, the imprisonment, the loneliness, and the fear were now all lost in the past. He let his hand rest on the bump of his unborn child. God willing, this child would never see civil war or its like.

Shrieks of laughter diverted his attention to the gaggle of youngsters clustered around Tom Ashley's snow king, who wore a crown of ivy twirled around his head.

The King sat once more upon the throne of England. Time would tell if he would be a good king, but for now, it was enough that he had returned to a country tired of war and anxious for peace.

The exiles had truly returned to England, and a new age was coming.

AUTHOR'S NOTES

Charles I was executed in January 1649, and for the next ten years, England flirted with a form of republicanism, presided over by the 'Lord Protector', Oliver Cromwell. The young King Charles II made a bid to regain the throne in 1651 but after being resoundingly defeated at the Battle of Worcester (see Jonathan Thornton's story: *By The Sword*), he remained in exile for the next nine years, joined by many of his supporters. Those loyal to the King who remained in England saw their estates seized or had to endure heavy fines.

During this Interregnum (literally 'between Kings'), disenfranchised Royalists plotted to restore the King but without success (see Kit Lovell's story: *The King's Man*). It was only after the death of Oliver Cromwell in September 1658 that the Royalists saw the first glimmer of hope of a return of the monarch. Cromwell's son, Richard ('Tumbledown Dick'), succeeded his father, but he was not the man his father had been and by May 1659 had been deposed and exiled. England was governed effectively by the Army and a 'Rump' Parliament to provide some sort of legislative validity for its decisions.

The Royalists, seeing their opportunity, began to negotiate with different factions within the Government and the Army, leading to a failed uprising in July 1659. In the end the restoration of the King came down to one man, General George Monck, the commander of the Cold-stream Guards in Edinburgh. In January 1660 Monck marched south, carrying with him the support of the Army, and on reaching London deposed the remnants of the Rump Parliament. Negotiations carried out between Sir John Grenville and Monck led to the return of the King to England in May 1660 without a drop of blood being spilled.

These complex events being played out on the wider political stage provide only the backstage noise to this story, which brings together the threads of the preceding two stories, *By The Sword* and *The King's Man*. We are blessed with the knowledge of hindsight but for those living at the time, they had no certainty of knowing how, when or in what circumstances the King would return or even if he would return.

I confess to taking a small liberty with the dates of the King's presence in Belgium and had him returning to Brussels from his negotiations with the Spanish in December 1659, some days earlier than occurred.

With the exception of historical figures such as the King himself and Sir Edward Hyde and John Mordaunt, the people and events depicted in the book are entirely fictional.

Exile's Return marks the end of a long journey that began in my childhood on that fateful visit to Harvington Hall that inspired *By the Sword*. There have been so many people who have helped me along the way and supported my passion to write.

I could not do what I do without the long-suffering support of my husband, David, who makes all things possible and seems to have no objection to being dragged around castles and battlefields. He also takes a sadistic delight in correcting my rough drafts and providing all sorts of advice, whether I have asked for it or not.

I would like to acknowledge one particular friend, Carol H. (to whom this book is dedicated), who fell in love with Jonathan and Kit (Kit in particular!) in their earlier incarnation and has nagged me for years to write the conclusion to their stories. She was right — although both *By The Sword* and *The King's Man* stand alone, without the restoration of the King, there could be no happily ever after for the characters in those books.

And then there is my writer's group, the Saturday Ladies, without whom *Exile's Return* would still be in draft form. They put their collective shoulders behind me and nudged me over the line with cajoling, advice, and downright nagging when needed.

Alison Stuart

THANK YOU

Thank you for reading EXILE'S RETURN.
If you enjoyed this story, I would love you to leave a review or a rating
on your favourite review site or bookstore.

AND YOU ARE INVITED TO SIGN UP TO ALISON'S
NEWSLETTER
for FREE READS and VIP Exclusives, including contests, giveaways and
advance notice of pre-orders.
www.alisonstuart.com

THANK YOU

www.alisonstuart.com

AND THEN MINE ENEMY

If you enjoyed THE GUARDIANS OF THE CROWN series and would like to read more of Alison Stuart's English Civil War novels, the following is an excerpt from AND THEN MINE ENEMY that begins at the start of the civil war in 1642. You may find some characters you recognise from BY THE SWORD have crept into this story...

~

AND THEN MINE ENEMY
CHAPTER 1
England, July 1642

A shudder of rain slewed across the sodden countryside, sending its cold fingers cutting through Adam's already saturated cloak. He huffed out a misty breath and straightened his aching shoulders. Not for the first time, he cursed his brother for summoning him to a meeting Adam knew would inevitably end in grief and recrimination.

The remote inn loomed out of the gloaming and led on by the cheerful light spilling through the front windows, Adam urged his weary horse forward. The miserable beast, the mud dragging at its every step, plodded on.

A young boy ran from the stable, a sack over his head and shoulders. Adam threw him the reins and taking a deep breath, strode into the inn. He tossed his hat and gloves to the innkeeper, his numbed fingers fumbled at the ties of his cloak.

'His Lordship's in the private parlour.' The innkeeper scowled as he held the dripping garb at arm's length.

Adam pushed open the door the man indicated. The two men seated beside a cheerful fire burning in the wide hearth rose to their feet. His half-brothers schooled their faces to a neutrality that Adam knew would not last. As they faced him across the room, a growing sense of despondency gripped him. Once more the cuckoo in the nest, always the acknowledged baseborn son but not even given the protection of his father's name.

Denzil Marchant, just as Adam remembered him, tall and powerful, with a mane of tawny hair like his father, and his younger brother Robin, as tall but of a slighter, elegant build, his hair more auburn and sleekly curling.

'Denzil, Robin,' Adam acknowledged them as he stepped into the room. 'I wish I could say, well met, but I would be lying.'

'Adam Coulter.' The deliberate use of his full name jarred, as Denzil no doubt intended. 'I would scarcely have recognised you. Hardly the darling of the court now, are you?'

'I found lovelocks and pearl earrings something of a hindrance to the life of a soldier.' Without waiting to be invited, Adam poured himself a full measure from the bottle of wine that stood on the table, hoping that they would not mark that his hand shook.

'Foul weather,' he remarked, raising his cup. 'Is there space beside the fire for me?'

Denzil stood aside and Adam took his place beside the fire. Water dripped onto the hearthstone and steam rose from his damp clothing.

Adam took a mouthful of wine. It was surprisingly good for such an isolated inn.

'How is your beautiful wife, Denzil?' Even after all these years, he could not hide the note of derision in his voice.

Denzil's already high colour deepened and his brows drew together at the mention of Louise. 'Louise is with the queen in France.'

So, that particular wound still bled, Adam thought.

'So much has happened in the last years, Denzil. I believe I should now call you Lord Marchant. When did Father die?'

'Some eighteen months past. Even on his deathbed, he refused to call you his son,' Denzil responded with narrowed eyes as he watched the barb go home.

As intended, the cruel words cut like a sword thrust to Adam's heart.

'Why did you come back to England?' Robin spoke for the first time, his tone light and conciliatory.

Adam turned his attention to his youngest brother. How old would Robin be now, twenty-one, twenty-two?

'Because I'm tired of fighting other people's wars and thought I should come home and find a peaceful occupation. Instead, I have returned to a country that talks of war as if it is an inevitability.' Adam turned back to look at Denzil from over the top of his wine cup. 'Is this why you sent for me?'

'I had heard you'd returned and we need men like you, Coulter,' Denzil said.

'What do you mean, men like me?' Adam set the empty wine cup down on a nearby table and turned to face the fire, casually rearranging the smouldering logs with a poker.

'Hardened soldiers. Men who know what they're doing. England is about to go to war led by a bunch of country squires whose only idea of warfare is what they have read in a book.'

Adam glanced at him. 'Men like you, Denzil?'

His brother's moustache twitched and his eyes narrowed.

'Tell me what has happened to England in the six years I have been away? What have I come back to? Because it is not the country I left.'

Denzil's brow furrowed. 'It is indeed a sad country where a King cannot govern without being hindered at every turn by the machinations of his so-called Parliament.'

'It seems to me,' Adam straightened. and kept his voice low and even, 'that we have a King who believes he can rule contrary to the will of the people.'

'The king's greatest enemy is his own parliament,' Robin said.

'The king's greatest enemy is himself.' Adam turned his gaze on Robin.

'What do you mean?' Robin came around to stand beside Denzil.

'I served the king, Robin. I know the character of the man. He has a firm and unshakable belief in what he sees as his divine right to rule. Parliament may have forced him to hand over his powers of taxation and his courts but I cannot see him ever agreeing to surrender his right to choose his own counsellors or to control his army. Nor will he agree to abolish the bishops and the Prayer Book. Isn't that what parliament has asked of him?'

The colour rose higher in Denzil's florid cheeks. 'All that and more, Coulter. They are saying that the king can no longer be trusted to make his own judgments about the men best able to advise him or to control his army. They have driven him from London.'

Adam thrust away from the fireplace and paced the room, running his hand through his hair. 'God's death, do these people who talk of war have any idea what damage a civil war can wreak? I've seen civil war at first hand and I've no wish to see the likes of it in this country.' He turned to face Denzil. 'Whatever you want of me, Denzil, I'll have no part of it. I've come home with enough in my purse for a small estate and I intend to turn my hand to the till not the sword.'

Denzil snorted. 'You'll be bored of that within a month, or you're not the man I remember. Coulter.' His tone softened, almost wheedling. 'Let's put the past behind us. You were young. I can forgive you your indiscretion.'

Indiscretion? Was that the price of a man's life?

Adam's shoulders tensed in the old, familiar way. 'What do you want of me, Denzil?'

'I'm offering you a commission in my regiment of horse.'

Adam raised an eyebrow. 'You have a regiment of horse?'

Denzil raised his chin. 'I've raised the militia.'

'Before the king has even raised his standard? No thank you. I want no part of this accursed affair.'

'Is that your final answer, Coulter?'

'It is. I would be pleased to do as you ask and put the past behind us, but I cannot in all conscience join this venture at your side.'

Denzil's jaw tightened and Adam braced himself for an explosion. Instead, his brother threw up his hands and sighed. 'What will you do?'

'I will do as I said. Continue my journey to Shropshire where I intend to inspect a property and God willing, that is where I shall stay.'

Denzil glanced at Robin. 'You think Shropshire is far enough away to escape our troubles?'

'No. I have lived through civil war, Denzil. It is insidious. It will seek out even the most remote corners of this poor, benighted country.'

Robin cleared his throat. 'We have been wondering about Aunt Joan.'

This shift in the conversation took Adam by surprise. 'Aunt Joan?'

'Yes. She was recently widowed,' Robin looked up at Denzil. 'Denzil?'

'I am now head of this family and I am naturally concerned for her welfare in the coming conflict.'

'That's very touching, but like myself, Joan has hardly been your concern since her marriage.' Adam could hear the sarcasm in his voice.

Denzil's jaw tightened again and he blew out a breath. 'What Robin is trying to say is I am prepared to put her enmity with father aside and offer her the protection of her former home at Marchants, should she wish it.'

Adam laughed. 'Why in God's sweet name would she want to go to Marchants? She hated the place as much as I did.'

'Damn it, Coulter.' Denzil brought a powerful fist down on the table. 'You are trying my patience. As head of the family, I believe it is my place to try and heal the wounds that have divided us for too long. If you are passing Preswood, can you at least take her my message?'

Adam paused. 'Preswood is near Stratford from memory and it would be good to see her again. Very well, I will take her your message.' At the door, Adam turned to face his brothers. 'I suppose I should thank you for the olive branch Denzil, but it's too late. We were a family divided long before this became a country divided.' He inclined his head and walked out of the room, resisting the temptation to slam the door behind him.

~

CHAPTER 2
Preswood Hall, Warwickshire 2 July 1642

Perdita pushed the food around her plate with the knife, conscious that through the interminable meal, Simon's gaze had not moved from her. Across from her, Elizabeth nattered about some matter of local gossip that required no more than the occasional grunt or tsk in response. As Joan's gaze flickered from Perdita to Simon and back again, her brow creased.

'Forgive me,' Joan said. 'Perdita? Simon? Have you quarrelled?'

Simon's eyes widened. 'Quarrelled?' He glanced at Perdita. 'Far from it.' He rose to his feet, his glass in hand, and looked around the table. His gaze returned to Perdita and he smiled, a smile of such sweetness and love that her heart skipped a beat. Was it too late to renege? To turn back the clock to the sweet friendship she had treasured with this man?

'Joan, Elizabeth.' Simon addressed his stepmother and sister. 'It may come as something of a surprise, but Perdita, our dearest kinswoman, has consented to be my wife.'

A squeal of delight ensued from Elizabeth. Joan, not given to overt displays of emotion, cast a quick scrutinising glance in Perdita's direction and she looked away.

'I'm delighted,' Joan said and raised her glass. 'I wish you both much happiness in the years ahead. Were your father still alive, Simon, I know he would approve.'

Elizabeth beamed at Perdita from across the table. 'How I have always longed for a sister.'

Perdita knew she should say something. Her fingers twisted in the chain of her mother's locket as she struggled to find adequate words to cover the tumult of emotions raging in her mind. Simon had resumed his seat but he still gazed at her, a huge grin on his cheerful, freckled face. He leaned across the table, grasping her left hand in his square dependable fingers, pressing it to his lips. He did not need to speak - Simon was incapable of dissembling in either word or gesture.

Perdita pushed back her pangs of guilt. She did not deserve such adoration, not when she felt incapable of returning those feelings. When Simon had first asked, she had hesitated a long while, but he had been patient and his very patience had worn down her resistance. Finally, she had given him the answer he sought, telling herself that Simon was a dear person, comfortable and dependable, and compared with the endless years of lonely widowhood that stretched ahead of her or the prospect of another forced marriage to the likes of Samuel Gray, she could certainly do much worse. Besides their kinship was distant, Her grandmother and Simon's grandmother had been distantly related but no closer relationship existed.

She may not have loved Simon in the romantic sense of the word, but she liked him, loved him as a friend, and perhaps friendship would be enough. Love could come later.

She smiled and squeezed his hand.

'Have you thought about when the wedding is to take place?' Elizabeth asked.

Simon released Perdita's hand and straightened in his chair. 'I confess, I've not given that much thought. With the present state of affairs, it may be prudent to wait until closer to Christmas.'

'What do you mean?' Elizabeth asked.

'You know what I mean, Bess.' Simon said impatiently. 'War is coming.'

'Oh, not that again.' Bess dismissed the troubles between the king and his parliament with a wave of her hand. 'I'm so bored with that.'

'Bess,' Simon began but the crash of a door and the sound of raised voices stopped him mid remonstrance, 'confound it. What is that racket?'

Ludovic, the Clifford's steward, a large, laconic man of foreign background who had been attached to Geoffrey Clifford from long before his marriage to Joan, appeared at the door.

'There is a gentleman here, who insists on an audience with Mistress

Clifford,' he said but got no further as a tall man with rough-cut dark brown hair strode into the room.

He swept the startled company a bow. 'Forgive my intrusion,' he said, rising to address them.

Joan set her glass down and rose slowly to her feet. 'Surely not? Adam?'

'Aunt Joan.' A broad grin split his tanned face and in two strides he had crossed to her, sweeping her off her feet into an embrace.

Bess cast her brother a quizzical glance.

'Good Lord.' Simon blasphemed, rising from his chair. 'Adam Coulter?'

'Simon Clifford.' Adam set his aunt back on the ground and seized Simon's hand. 'It's been a long time.' He looked at Joan and frowned. 'Your wedding, Aunt, if my memory serves me correctly?'

'Yes indeed. Ten years at least.' Joan, her face unusually flushed, recollected herself. 'Ludovic,' she ordered the steward. 'Set another place at the table. This is my nephew, Adam Coulter, who has been abroad these many years. A very welcome guest in this house.'

As Ludovic bowed and withdrew, Joan looked up at her nephew and tapped him on his chest. 'Why did you not send word for me to expect you?'

He flashed her a smile. 'I thought I might surprise you.'

Joan's hand flew to her throat. Perdita had never seen Joan so discomposed. 'Surprise me? Good heavens, Adam, you have just about killed me.' She looked around the table. 'Now, you are acquainted with Simon but I doubt you remember his sister, my stepdaughter, Elizabeth? She would have been barely twelve at our wedding.'

Bess had been staring open-mouthed at the stranger. She managed a wobbly curtsey and a gracious inclination of her head.

'Mistress Clifford, your servant,' Adam Coulter acknowledged.

His gaze moved to Perdita. 'And the last but not the least member of my household is our kinswoman, Perdita Gray.'

Coulter inclined his head. 'Mistress Gray.'

Perdita met the startling intensity of his light grey eyes with equanimity. 'Master Coulter, you are welcome to Preswood.'

Joan had never spoken of her family with Perdita, although Bess had told her the estrangement with the Marchants went back long before Joan's marriage to Geoffrey Clifford. Joan called this man her nephew but why was he introduced as Adam Coulter, not Marchant?

Joan asked the question that burned on Perdita's lips. 'What brings you here, Adam?'

As he took his seat, Adam Coulter turned to his aunt. 'Denzil told me you have been recently widowed.'

The joy drained from Joan's face, the pain of her recent loss stark in her eyes. She raised a trembling hand to her mouth.

Perdita answered for her. 'Last winter,' she said. 'Lung fever.'

Perdita cast a glance around the table. The mention of Geoffrey Clifford brought back unhappy memories from them all. Bess bit her lip and pleated the material of her sleeve while Simon looked up at the ceiling.

Adam laid his hand over Joan's. 'I'm sorry, Joan. He was a good man.' His gaze swept the table. 'My condolences to all of you.'

Joan hefted a heavy sigh and squared her shoulders. 'We miss him, but Adam, did you say Denzil told you? When did you see him?'

Adam's mouth tightened in a grim, humourless smile. 'Somehow Denzil had word I had returned to London, probably through that irritating lawyer. He sent for me and like a good brother I went. The reunion was not a great success.'

Joan's lips parted but Simon interrupted. 'Last I heard you were abroad, Coulter, fighting the German wars. What brings you back to England?'

Perdita detected a momentary hesitation before Adam Coulter replied. 'Tired of the wandering life, Clifford. I've an eye for a small estate in the border country. I'm on my way there and promised Denzil I would deliver a message to Joan.'

Joan's lips twisted in a wry smile. 'A message for me? Is Denzil trying to mend the bridges his dear father burned? First you, and now me? Whatever next? What is his message?'

'In view of your recent widowhood, he is offering you a home at Marchants.'

Joan frowned. 'But I have a home here. Why would I want to return to Marchants?'

'He believes this country is coming to war and is concerned for your safety. Is that what you think, Clifford?'

War. That seemed to be all men could talk of these days. Perdita and Bess exchanged resigned glances. There had been too many dinners recently that had descended into talk of war with the women banished to the parlour.

Simon shifted in his chair and he cleared his throat with a quick sideways glance at Perdita. He knew her views on the subject. She tightened her lips as Simon said, 'I believe so. I already have orders from Lord Northampton to raise my militia in the king's name.'

Adam sighed. 'Then let us pray that wiser heads take counsel and stop this thing before it becomes too late.'

The look of resignation on his face belied his word and Perdita challenged him. 'You don't believe that, do you?'

He looked at her and shook his head. 'No. I think it's already too late. I've just passed through Stratford. Lord Brooke...?' He glanced at Simon for confirmation of the name, who nodded affirmation. 'Lord Brooke had called a muster of the Warwickshire Militia.'

'I know,' Simon said. 'A muster of those militia willing to take up the parliament's cause.'

Adam regarded Simon thoughtfully for a moment. 'I listened to what he had to say. He's an impressive man, Brooke. He talks sense.'

'He's a puritan with his own reasons for wanting parliament to prevail.' Simon paused. 'How many do you think he has gathered to his cause?'

Adam shrugged. 'Not as many as I'm sure he would have liked. A couple of hundred, no more, for all that he was offering the comers five shillings and plying them with food and drink.'

Simon nodded and smiled. 'That'll please Northampton. He's planning a muster at Stratford within the month for the king's cause. Naturally, I will be attending.'

Perdita looked from one to the other. 'Are you saying that this must come to a choice? King or Parliament? Neighbour against neighbour?'

Neither man replied but their silence gave her the answer. 'You men are making this thing a reality. The more you talk of it, the more it becomes a certainty,' she said.

Adam Coulter regarded her for a long moment. 'You are right, Mistress Gray. England has talked itself into war and I fear it is too late to turn back.'

Simon coughed. 'Coulter, you're most welcome at Preswood. Indeed, if you have some days to spare, I need help with my men.' He smiled ruefully. 'I'm not much of a military hand. I've books of course, but it is not the same as practical experience.'

Adam turned to look at Simon. 'Don't ask me to take your side, Clifford. I've already told my brother that I've no wish to fight a civil war in my own country.'

'I'm not asking you to join me, Coulter, but I've a reluctant tenantry armed with antique weapons or whatever they can lay their hands on, and an order from Lord Northampton to present them properly trained at the muster. To be honest, I could use the help of an experienced soldier such as yourself.'

Adam glanced at his aunt. She leaned over and laid her hand on his. 'Stay a little while, Adam.'

He nodded. 'Very well, I'll give you a week, Clifford. What little help I can render is yours.'

A week? Perdita glanced at Simon, knowing his struggles to bring the tenants into some sort of order. From farmers to soldiers. Little wonder they were reluctant.

'Enough of politics,' Joan said. 'I am determined not to let this meal be spoiled by talk of things that, God willing, may never come to pass. This meal is a celebration, Adam. Let us raise our glasses to Simon and Perdita whose betrothal we are celebrating.'

Perdita glanced away as Adam Coulter's direct gaze fell on her again.

'Betrothed? And I have come like a beggar at the feast,' he said. 'I apologise for interrupting what should have been a happy meal with such dark talk.'

Perdita raised her eyes to meet his. 'I think, Master Coulter,' she said, 'that these things should be talked of openly, for all our futures hang on these machinations.'

Joan clapped her hands. 'Enough, Perdita. My nephew has returned from the dead. Adam, I can't believe the change in you. Is this what soldiering abroad does for you? Do you remember Adam at my wedding, Simon? Lovelocks and a pearl earring, quite the courtier.'

Adam touched his left ear, where the faint indentation still marked a young man's fancy.

'That was a long time ago,' he said with a rueful smile, running a hand through his dark, rough-cut locks, bleached at the ends by long days in the sun.

'Over six years, Adam. Not a word,' his aunt chided.

'I never was a letter writer, aunt, and unfortunately for me, I spent a couple of those years immured in Leipzig Castle for my part at the battle of Vlotho.'

Joan gasped. 'I had no idea you were a prisoner. Was there a ransom set for your release? Isn't that how these things are arranged? If I had known...'

'My dear brother declined the ransom,' Adam said with a bitter smile twisting the corners of his mouth. He let out a breath and glancing around the table, he said, 'As you say, enough talk of dark memories.' He raised his glass. 'To Simon Clifford and his betrothed, and, God willing, to common sense and an end of this talk of war.'

For more information and to purchase AND THEN MINE ENEMY visit www.alisonstuart.com